"Well played!" Admiration danced in Cole's blue eyes. **"You helped convince Becca I'm off the market—I could kiss you."**

Kate inhaled sharply, but it didn't seem to put any air in her lungs. "It's, ah, probably best if you don't." She started to take a step backward.

"Oh, I don't know." His voice dropped lower. "Becca's got spies everywhere."

"Cole, I..." Her voice was husky, unfamiliar. Though he was no longer touching her, he stood so close her thoughts were short-circuiting. Could she allow herself to kiss him in the name of convincing Becca he was taken? A flimsy excuse, at best, but so tempting. She swallowed. "I have to go."

"Can I call you later? We didn't finish our conversation."

She lifted up on her toes, pressing a quick kiss against his cheek. It was a peck, nothing more, but effervescent giddiness fizzed through her. She'd surprised herself—and she could tell from his sudden, absolute stillness that she'd shocked him.

"Just in case .... tching," sh

FALLING FOR THE SHERIFF

BY
TANYA MICHAELS

Published in Great Britain 2015
by Mills & Boon, an imprint of Harlequin (UK) Limited,
Eton House, 18-24 Paradise Road, Richmond, Surrey, TW9 1SR

© 2015 Tanya Michna

ISBN: 978-0-263-25282-8

51-1015

Harlequin (UK) Limited's policy is to use papers that are natural, renewable and recyclable products and made from wood grown in sustainable forests. The logging and manufacturing processes conform to the legal environmental regulations of the country of origin.

Printed and bound in Spain
by CPI, Barcelona

Tanya Michaels, a *New York Times* bestselling author and five-time RITA® Award nominee, has been writing love stories since middle school algebra class (which probably explains her maths grades). Her books, praised for their poignancy and humor, have received awards from readers and reviewers alike. Tanya is an active member of Romance Writers of America and a frequent public speaker. She lives outside Atlanta with her very supportive husband, two highly imaginative kids and a bichon frisé who thinks she's the center of the universe.

This book is dedicated to all my fellow parents out there also raising one of those wondrous and terrifying creatures known as a "teenager."

Prologue

Kate Sullivan had barely spoken on the ride from the middle school to the house. She'd worried that if she opened her mouth to say something, she would start yelling. Or crying. Neither seemed like a good idea while driving.

As they walked in through the garage door that led to the kitchen, her thirteen-year-old son, Luke, broke the tense silence. "I know you're pis—"

"Language!" She spared him a maternal glare over her shoulder.

"I know you're *mad*," he amended. The patronizing emphasis he put on the word was the verbal equivalent of rolling his eyes. "But it really wasn't my fault this time."

Lord, how she wanted to believe him. But the fact that he had to qualify his declaration of innocence with "this time" underscored the severity of his recent behavior problems. As an elementary school music teacher, Kate worked with kids every day. How was it that she could control a roomful of forty students but not her own son? Over the past few months, she'd received phone calls about Luke fighting, lying and cutting classes. And now he'd been suspended!

If Damon were alive…

Her husband, a Houston police officer killed in the line of duty, had been dead for two years. Sometimes, standing here in the familiar red-tiled kitchen, she could still smell the coffee he started every day with, still hear the comforting rumble of his voice. But no amount of wishing him back would change her situation.

She didn't need the imaginary assistance of a ghost. What she needed was a concrete plan. Maybe something radical, because God knew, nothing she'd tried so far had worked, not even the aid of professional therapists.

"It wasn't my knife," Luke continued. "It was Bobby's."

Fourteen-year-old Bobby Rowe and his hard-edged, disrespectful peers were part of the problem.

"Which I *tried* to tell the jackass principal."

Kate slammed her hand down on the counter. "You will not talk about people like that! And you aren't going back to that school." It was a spur of the moment declaration, fraught with logistical complications—she could hardly homeschool and keep her job at the same time—but the minute she heard the words out loud, she knew deep down that a new environment was the right call. She had to get him away from kids like Bobby and away from teachers who were predisposed to believe the worst of Luke because of his recent history.

"Not going back?" His golden-brown eyes widened. He'd inherited what Damon used to call her "lioness coloring," tawny blond hair and amber eyes. "I only got suspended for two days. I can't miss the last three weeks of school."

"Maybe not," she conceded, "but I don't have to send you back there next fall."

"But it's my last year before high school. All my friends are there!"

"You'll make new ones. Non-knife-wielding friends."

"You're really going to send me somewhere different for eighth grade just because you don't like Bobby?"

No, kid, this is because I don't like you—at least, not the person he was on the path to becoming. She loved her son, but on the worst days, she wanted to shake this angry stranger's shoulders and demand to know what he'd done with her generous-natured, artistic Luke.

"I won't get in trouble for the rest of the school year," he vowed desperately.

"Good. But that won't change my mind." She glanced around the kitchen with new eyes. Maybe they could both use a fresh start, more than just a school transfer. She'd stayed in this house after Damon was shot because Luke had suffered such a jarring loss; she hadn't wanted to yank him away from his home and friends. Yet, within six months, he'd found an entirely different group of friends anyway. He no longer associated with the kids who'd known the Sullivans as a whole and intact family. "We're moving."

"*What?* Houston is our home. This was Dad's home! He wouldn't want us to leave."

"He'd want me to do whatever is best for you." And Damon would have wanted her to have help. She wasn't too proud to admit she needed some.

Her father, a professor at the University of Houston's anthropology department, was sweet in a detached, absent way, but he was better with ancient civilizations than living people. Damon's parents adored her, but they'd retired to an active senior community in Florida a year before their son was killed. Since she and Damon had both been only children, that left her with just one other close relative. *Gram*. Affection and a sense of peace she hadn't felt in a long time warmed her.

She closed her eyes, breathing in the memory of summers past. When her father had gone on digs between semesters, she'd stayed with Gram and Grandpa on their small farm. Those idyllic months in the town of Cupid's Bow, Texas, had soothed her soul. Chasing fireflies, tending tomatoes in the garden, fishing in the pond, helping make homemade ice cream to put on Gram's award-winning apple pie...

Although Grandpa had died last year, Gram was still in Cupid's Bow and as feisty as ever. She'd mentioned, though, that it was becoming more difficult to take care of the place by herself and frequently complained that she didn't get to see enough of Kate and Luke. What if they moved in with her? It could benefit all three of them.

Or maybe it would be a horrible idea.

Kate had to try, though. If things didn't change, she could too easily imagine Luke growing into the same kind of thug who'd killed his father. It was time for drastic action.

Cupid's Bow, here we come.

Chapter One

When Sheriff Cole Trent walked into his house the second Saturday of June, he was met in the living room by three irate females. It was only six in the evening, but from the looks he was getting, one would think he'd been out all night. Mirroring their grandmother, his five-year-old twins had their hands on their slim hips and their lips pursed. The family resemblance was unmistakable, although the girls were blonde like the mother who'd run out on them instead of dark-haired like Gayle and Cole.

He sighed. "I know I'm a little later than anticipated, but—"

"A *lot* late," Mandy corrected.

Alyssa's blue eyes were watery. "You promised to take us swimming."

"I didn't promise. I said I'd try." Lately, not even trying his hardest seemed like enough. Once the girls had started kindergarten, they'd become hyperaware that they didn't have a mommy like most of their classmates. Last month's Mother Day had been particularly rough. "Maybe we can go to the pool tomorrow. For now, how about I take you out for barbecue?" He made the offer not just to appease the girls but because he was too worn out to cook.

After a morning testifying in county court and an afternoon of mind-numbing paperwork, Cole's plans to get home early were derailed by the Breelan brothers, three hotheads who never should have gone into business together. The shopkeeper who worked next to their garage had called Cole with a complaint that the Breelans were trying to kill each other. After throwing a few punches—and an impact wrench—Larry Breelan was spending the night in a cell. Deputy Thomas was on duty to make sure neither of Larry's younger brothers tried to bust him out. Or tried to sneak in and murder him, depending on their mood.

Gayle Trent shook her head. "Out to eat again? When was the last time these poor girls had a home-cooked meal?"

Lifelong respect for his mother kept him from rolling his eyes at her dramatic tone, but just barely. "I made them fruit-face pancakes for breakfast. And two nights ago we had dinner at your house. With Jace and William," he reminded her. She'd spent so much conversational energy trying to fix up Cole with various single women that she might not have noticed his brothers were even there.

She continued as if he hadn't spoken. "Speaking of home-cooked meals… Do you remember my friend Joan who owns the little farm down by Whippoorwill Creek? We're in quilting club together and she's signed up to help me inventory donations for the festival auction." The four-day Watermelon Festival every July was one of the town's biggest annual events.

Cole had an uneasy feeling in the pit of his stomach. From the gleam in his mother's eye, she clearly wanted something, and he doubted it was for him to donate an item to auction.

He cleared his throat. "Girls, why don't you go brush your hair and find your shoes so we can leave?" As they scampered off to the far-flung corners of the house to search for the shoes that were always mysteriously disappearing, he returned his attention to his mother, as wary as if he were investigating suspicious noises in a dark alley. "So, what's this about your friend Joan?"

"Her granddaughter, who used to summer here as a kid, is moving to Cupid's Bow with her son. We thought it would be neighborly if you and the girls joined us at the farm for a nice Sunday dinner tomorrow. Joan's inviting other people, too. It's a welcome party," she added, "not a romantic setup."

"Would you swear to that during a polygraph test?"

"Are you calling your own mother a liar?" she asked, looking highly wounded while evading his question. "Not everything is about your love life, you know. Joan's great-grandson won't have many chances to meet kids until school starts again in the fall. I'm sure he'd love to meet the girls. And they'd have fun, too. They were bored silly cooped up in the house with me all afternoon. Joan's farm is like a petting zoo."

"Mom, I—"

The cordless phone on the end table rang, temporarily cutting off his words. Gayle glanced at the display, then smirked in his direction. "Becca Johnston."

His stomach sank at mention of the PTA president who'd been relentlessly pursuing him since her divorce was finalized. "Tell her I'm not here."

"And I can also tell Joan you'll be there for the dinner party tomorrow?" Without waiting for his response, she picked up the phone. "Hello? Oh, hi, Becca." She paused pointedly, one eyebrow raised.

Later, he and his mom were going to discuss the laws prohibiting extortion. For now, he gave a sharp nod, exiting the room to change into civilian clothes and get his girls out of there before his mother talked him into anything else.

Behind him, he heard Gayle say, "Sorry, dear. You just missed him."

"WE'RE GOING TO live *out here*?" Luke's voice reverberated with horror as he stared through the passenger window.

The movie he'd been watching on his tablet had ended a few minutes ago and he seemed to be truly registering their surroundings for the first time. During the peaceful stretch when he'd had his earbuds in, Kate had taken the opportunity to remind herself of all the reasons this relocation was going to be wonderful for them. Sure, Kate didn't have a job yet—and Cupid's Bow Elementary wasn't exactly a rapidly growing school—but she still had paychecks coming through the summer. She could give voice lessons or piano lessons if she got Gram's old upright tuned.

"Yep." She smiled at the picturesque pastures and blue skies. It was after six o'clock, but the June sun was shining brightly. "No traffic, no constant city construction—"

"No internet connection, no cell phone reception," Luke predicted.

"That's not true. Last time I visited Gram, I used my cell phone." She didn't volunteer the information that she'd had to stand with one foot in the laundry room and the other on the attached porch, leaning forty-five degrees to the left while holding on to the dryer. Maybe service had improved since then.

"This is the middle of nowhere! Nobody could possibly live here."

She jerked a thumb toward the side of the road. "The mailboxes suggest otherwise." She appreciated that the mailboxes they'd passed were spread out at roomy intervals. They'd had a nice enough home in the suburbs, but the yards were so small that when Damon used to throw a football with Luke, they spent half their time knocking on the neighbor's door to retrieve the ball from the fenced backyard.

"You're going to love it here," she told Luke. "Lots of community spirit and camaraderie, plenty of home-cooking and fresh air."

He rolled down his window, inhaled deeply, then grimaced. "The fresh air smells like cow poop."

She ground her teeth, refusing to let him spoil her mood. *He'll come around with time.* Her first victory might even be as soon as tonight. Gram could cook like nobody's business, and Luke was a growing boy. A couple of helpings of chicken-fried steak or slow-cooked brisket should improve his outlook on life.

They'd be at the farm in twenty minutes. As eager as Kate was to get there, when she spotted the gas station down the road—the last one before Gram's place—she knew she should stop. The fuel gauge was dropping perilously close to E. Plus, it might be good for her and Luke to get out of the car and stretch their legs for a few minutes.

While she pumped gas, Luke disappeared inside to use the restroom. Although she'd lived her entire life in Texas, sometimes the heat still caught Kate by surprise. Even in the shade, she broke a sweat. She tugged at the lightweight material of her sleeveless blouse to keep it from sticking to her damp skin, then lifted her hair away from her neck, making a mental note to look for an elastic band when she got back in the car.

While waiting for Luke, she went into the station and bought a couple of cold beverages. She'd barely pocketed her change before twisting the lid off her chilled bottle of water and taking a long drink. If Luke didn't hurry, she might finish her water and start in on the fountain soda she held in her other hand.

He was taking a long time, and she wouldn't put it past him to stall in a mulish display of rebellion. She turned with the intention of knocking on the door and hurrying him along, but then stopped herself. Half of parenting was picking one's battles. They'd be at Gram's soon, and her grandmother hadn't seen Luke in months. Was this really the right time to antagonize him? She didn't want him arriving at the farm surly and hostile. A smooth first night might prove to all of them that this could work.

Quit hovering, go to the car. She pivoted with renewed purpose. And crashed into a wall that hadn't been there a moment ago. Okay, technically, the wall was a broad-shouldered man at least six inches taller than she. He wore jeans and a white polo shirt—which was a lot less white with Luke's soda running down the front of it.

Kate opened her mouth to apologize but, "dammit!"

was the first word that escaped. A high-pitched giggle snagged her attention, drawing her gaze downward.

Behind the startled-looking man were two blue-eyed little girls. They were dressed so dissimilarly that it took Kate a moment to realize they were identical. One wore a soccer jersey over camo shorts; tangles of white-blond hair hung in her face, and her sneakers looked as if they were about to disintegrate, held together only by an accumulation of dirt. The other girl was wearing a pink dress that tied at the shoulders and a pair of sparkly sandals. Someone had carefully braided her hair, and she carried a small sequined purse.

Great, she'd doused the guy with a sticky soft drink *and* cursed in front of his young, impressionable children. She'd been in town less than an hour and already needed a fresh start for her fresh start.

"I am *so* sorry." She grabbed a handful of napkins off the counter next to the hot dog rotisserie and began frantically dabbing at his chest.

He covered her hand with his. "Let me."

She glanced up, taking a good look at his face for the first time. *Wow.* Like the girls, he had eyes that were as blue as the Texas sky outside, a dramatic contrast to his jet-black hair. And his—

"Mom? What are you doing?"

Perfect. Her son picked now to return, just in time to catch her ogling a total stranger.

Without waiting for an answer, Luke scowled at the man. "Who are you?"

"Cole." The guy had been handsome already. When he smiled, those eyes crinkling at the corners, the barest hint of a dimple softening that granite jaw, he was breathtaking. "Cole Trent."

DESPITE THE EASY, practiced smile that came with being a public official, Cole's mind was racing as he processed the events of the last few minutes. The jarring chill of icy soda, the rarity of finding himself face-to-face with a stranger when he knew almost everyone in Cupid's Bow and, the biggest surprise of all, the jolt of attraction he experienced when he looked into the woman's amber eyes. He couldn't remember the last time he'd had such an instant reaction to someone.

Was his interest visible in his expression? That could explain the waves of hostility rolling off her son as Cole introduced himself.

From behind him, Alyssa's voice broke into his thoughts. "Daddy, can I have a candy bar?"

He turned, shaking his head. "A candy bar will ruin your appetite."

"But I'm hungggrrry." She drew out the word in a nasal whine.

"Which is why I'm taking you to dinner." They'd only stopped because Mandy had insisted she needed to go to the bathroom and couldn't wait another ten minutes to reach the restaurant; apparently, seeing him doused with soda had temporarily distracted her. "If Mandy will—"

"It's not fair!" Alyssa's lower lip trembled. "I didn't get to go swimming like you said. They ran out of the color I needed to finish my picture at art camp. I don't—"

"That's enough," he said firmly.

But Mandy, who could barely agree with her sister on the color of the sky, picked now of all times to demonstrate twin solidarity. She took a step closer to Alyssa. "It's mean you won't let her have a candy bar."

He fought the urge to glance back at the woman with sun-streaked hair and beautiful eyes. Did she think he was inept at handling his own children? "You're supposed to be in the bathroom," he reminded Mandy. "If you'd hurry, we could be on our way to the Smoky Pig by now. But if the two of you don't stop talking back, we're headed straight home. Understand?"

The threat of having to return home and wait for Cole to cook something motivated Mandy. She navigated the tight aisles of chips and road maps in a rush. He returned his gaze to the woman. The gangly boy who'd called her mom had wandered away to refill his soda cup.

"Kids," Cole said sheepishly. "You have days like this?"

"With a teenager?" She laughed, her dark gold eyes warm and understanding. "Try *every* day."

"I keep waiting for single parenting to get easier, but sometimes I question whether I'm making any progress."

She nodded. "Same here."

So, she was single, too? That thought cheered him more than it should. He didn't even know her name. Nonetheless, he grinned broadly.

She returned the smile, but then ducked her gaze to the sodden napkins in her hand. "I, uh, should throw these away." As she walked toward the trash can, he couldn't help but appreciate the fit of her denim shorts.

Quit leering—there are children present. Well, one of his children, anyway. He turned to see if Alyssa had forgiven him yet. In his peripheral vision, he caught the blonde's son pressing a quick finger to his lips as if sharing a secret with Alyssa. The boy quickly dropped his hand and moved away. Alyssa frowned at her purse.

"Sorry again about the soda." The blonde was back, her tone brisk, as if she wanted to put their encounter behind her. "And good luck with the parenting."

Cole hated to let her go. He wanted to know who she was and why she was here. Was she visiting someone in Cupid's Bow or simply passing through on her way elsewhere? Maybe he would have asked if she hadn't seemed so anxious to go. Or if he weren't busy puzzling over Alyssa's strange expression.

"Good luck to you, too," he said.

With a nod, the blonde walked away, holding the door open for her son.

"Can we go now?" Mandy rejoined them, bouncing on the balls of her feet. "I'm starving!"

"Same here." He ruffled her hair, but kept his gaze on his other daughter. "What about you, Alyssa?"

She jerked her gaze up from her purse, a flush staining her cheeks. Even someone without Cole's training in suspicious behavior would have spotted the guilt in her eyes.

"What have you got in your purse?" he asked.

"N-nothing." She clutched the small sequined bag to her body.

He held out his hand, making it clear he wanted to see for himself.

Tears welled in her eyes as she pulled a candy bar from her purse. "B-but I didn't take it! That boy gave me it."

Cole's blood pressure skyrocketed. Alyssa was, by nature, a sweet, quiet girl, but throughout her kindergarten year—after every field trip or class party where other students had mothers present—she'd grown increasingly unpredictable. The teacher who had once praised his daughter's reading skill and eager-to-please disposition had started calling Cole about behavior problems, including a memorable graffiti incident. Now some punk was trying to turn Alyssa into a shoplifter, too? Hell, no.

"HEY!"

Kate jumped at the angry boom, nearly dropping her car keys. She turned to see Cole Trent, the single dad who'd melted her insides with his smile. He wasn't smiling now.

He strode across the parking lot like a man on a mission. One of his daughters was sobbing. The other looked grimly fascinated, as if she'd never expected a simple pit stop to be so eventful.

"Aw, crap." Luke's barely audible words—and the resignation in them—caused Kate's heart to sink.

Not again. Not here! In her mind, she'd built up Cupid's Bow as a safe haven. But how could you escape trouble when it was riding shotgun?

"What did you do?" she demanded in a low voice.

He slouched, not meeting her eyes. "It was only an eighty-nine cent candy bar. Jeez."

Cole reached them in time to hear her son's careless dismissal, his blue eyes bright with righteous fury. "It's more than a candy bar, young man. It's stealing."

Kate's stomach churned. "You *stole*?"

Cole's gaze momentarily softened as he glanced at her, registering her stress. When he spoke again, his tone was calmer. "Perhaps I should reintroduce myself. I'm *Sheriff* Cole Trent. What's your name, son?"

"Luke," he muttered.

"And did you put that candy bar in Alyssa's purse?" the sheriff asked in an unyielding, don't-even-think-about-lying tone.

The boy hunched his shoulders. "I felt bad for her."

Was that even true, Kate wondered, or had her son simply seized an opportunity for petty defiance?

Cole gave his sniffling daughter a stern look. "Luke may have been the one to take the candy bar, but you should have put it back. Or told me what happened. Other people's bad behavior is no excuse for acting badly yourself."

Terrific. Now her son was a cautionary tale for younger children.

"The two of you are going back inside to admit what you did and apologize to Mr. Jacobs," Cole said.

His daughter gulped. The man behind the counter had smiled pleasantly at Kate, but she could see where his towering height, all black clothing and tattooed arms might intimidate a little girl.

"While you're there," Kate told Luke, "ask what you can do to make up for it." He was too young for an official part-time job, but it was clear Kate needed to find ways to keep him busy and out of trouble. "Maybe they could use a volunteer to come by a few times a week and pick up litter in the parking lot."

Cole's gaze swung to her. "A few times a week? So you aren't just passing through or visiting? You're sticking around?"

Was that surprise she heard in his voice, or dread? Given his duty to maintain law and order in the county, he probably didn't relish the idea of a juvenile delinquent moving to town. And Gram deserved better than a great-grandson who caused her problems in the community. Was this experiment doomed to fail?

"We're staying with family in the area. Indefinitely." She forced a smile and tried to sound reassuring. "But I plan to stay out of public until I learn how to properly carry sodas, and Luke may be grounded for the rest of the summer. So you don't have to worry about us menacing the populace, I promise."

The size of Cupid's Bow might make it difficult to avoid someone, but she was willing to try. Between the terrible impression her son had made and Kate's aversion to being around cops since Damon's death, she rather desperately hoped never to see Sheriff Trent again.

Chapter Two

After Luke and his unwitting accomplice apologized to the gruff but fair Mr. Jacobs, Kate and her son resumed their journey. He had the good sense not to resume his complaining.

It wasn't until they were jostling along the private dirt road that led up to Gram's house that Luke spoke again. "Are you going to tell her about the gas station? And the sheriff?"

She sighed. "Well, it wasn't going to be my opening. I thought we'd say hi first and thank her profusely for taking us under her roof before we hit her with news of your exciting new criminal activities."

"I apologized," Luke grumbled. "I even paid the guy, although no one ended up with the candy bar."

"'The guy' is Mr. Jacobs, and you're going to treat him with respect when you see him next weekend." It turned out that the inked man with the gravelly voice visited the pediatric ward of the hospital once a month and gave a magic show. Luke's penance was that he would sacrifice a Saturday morning to work as the man's assistant. "And paying for what you took after the fact doesn't justify what you did. You know better than to steal! Your own father was a policeman, who—"

"My father is gone," he said flatly.

She parked the car, and turned to look at her son. "I miss him, too. And I get angry—at him, at the man who shot him, at the unfairness of life. But lashing out and doing dumb things won't bring your dad back. It only drives a wedge between you and me. I'm still here for you, kiddo. Try to remember that?"

Without responding, he climbed out of the car.

She blinked against the sting of tears, preferring to meet her grandmother with a smile. Joan Denby had lost her husband even more recently than Kate. The two women were supposed to bolster each other, not drag each other further down.

Either Gram had been watching for them, or Patch, the eight-year-old German shepherd, had barked notice of their arrival. Kate had barely removed her seatbelt before Gram hurried out onto the wraparound porch to greet them. In a pair of purple capris and a polo shirt striped with hot pink, Joan Denby was a splash of vivid color against the white wood railing. She looked much the same as she had all those summers when Kate visited as a girl, except that the cloud of once-dark hair framing Gram's face was silver and her lively hazel eyes now peered at the world through a pair of bifocals. Still, few would guess that she was the great-grandmother of a teenager.

"Luke! Katie!" The exuberant welcome in her voice carried on the breeze, and the knot in Kate's stomach unraveled.

Home. Whatever happened during the next few weeks of transition, Kate was suddenly 100 percent certain this was where she was supposed to be. Her vision blurred again, but this time with happy tears. She jumped out of the car, not even bothering to shut the door before rushing to hug her grandmother.

"I've missed you," she whispered fiercely. Even though she now stood taller than the woman who'd been equal parts mom and grandmother to her, Gram's embrace still made Kate feel safer, just as it had when she'd woken from nightmares as a girl or been rattled by a Texas thunderstorm.

"Missed you, too, Katie. So much." Gram patted her on the back, then pulled away to reach for Luke. "And you! I can't believe how tall you're getting. Strong enough to help with farm chores, I reckon. But don't worry," she added with a smile, "I promise to make sure you're well-compensated with your favorite desserts."

"Anything but candy bars," he mumbled.

Kate suppressed a groan at the reminder of their inauspicious entry to town. "We should start bringing in bags," she told her son. "The car's not going to unpack itself."

Gram followed them. "I expected to see you hauling a trailer of stuff."

"We brought most of our personal items, but the furniture's in storage back in Houston." She didn't add that she hadn't wanted to move it all twice in case this relocation didn't work out.

Gram insisted on helping, and Kate gave her the lightest things she could find in the backseat. Kate faltered at the box of Luke's art supplies. It had been sheer optimism on her part to bring them; he'd told her she could leave them in storage—or throw them away.

There'd been a time when he'd never been without a sketch pad of some kind. A few months before Damon was killed, Luke had started working on a comic book series about a superhero on another planet. The interstellar crime-fighter didn't have a family and he'd possessed larger than life mystical powers, but the physical resemblance between Luke's fictional champion and his dad had been unmistakable.

His earlier statement echoed in her mind. *My father is gone.* But he hadn't only lost Damon. In the last two years, he seemed to have also lost his inspiration and his direction. Although there was no need to get the heavy box inside before dinner, she vowed to put the supplies in his room later. Maybe, with time and patience, he'd find his direction again.

Shifting a large satchel against her hip, she pulled a rolling suitcase from the trunk. "Am I in my usual room, Gram?" Even during her trips to the farm as an adult, Kate had stayed in the bedroom where she had so many happy childhood memories.

Her grandmother nodded. "Of course. And for Luke, I cleared out the room where Jim used to work on his model planes. It's not huge, but it's the least girly space in the house."

"I'm sure it will be fine," Kate said gently, hating the thought of Gram boxing up all of her late husband's beloved planes alone. She wished her father was more reliable, that he lived close enough to regularly visit his widowed mother. Not that geography was any guarantee he'd pull his head out of his textbooks long enough to remember his family. The cliché "absent-minded professor" aptly described James Sullivan Jr. The last time he'd had dinner with Kate and Luke, he'd seemed sincerely shocked that his grandson wasn't still nine years old.

Patch met them at the front door with baritone yowls and a tail wagging wildly enough to generate a windstorm. It took a few minutes to get past the excited shepherd and into the living room. Kate took in the familiar surroundings, recalling her grandfather's good-natured complaints about the pink curtains and throw pillows on the sofa. Gram had told him that, if it made him feel better, the color was technically "country rose." He'd also pretended to be annoyed by her collection of carousel-horse figurines, but he'd built her the gorgeous display cabinet that housed them.

The room had barely changed in the last decade. Even the warm, inviting scent was the same. Gram's house always smelled like a combination of the lemony cleaner she used on the hardwood floors and pecan pie.

Luke raised his head, sniffing appreciatively, but it wasn't floor cleaner and nostalgia that captured his interest. "Food!"

Gram laughed. "I have beef stew in the slow-cooker and made a batch of corn bread muffins."

He immediately dropped the large duffel bags, as if preparing to bolt for the kitchen.

"We're not just leaving our stuff all over Gram's house," Kate chided, familiar with his habits. Their home in Houston had often been an obstacle course of discarded tennis shoes, an unzipped backpack with class binders spilling out of it and dirty glasses that should have been carried to the sink. "Once you've got the bags in your room and washed your hands, we'll see about dinner." He must have been genuinely hungry because, rather than flashing one of his mutinous scowls, he dashed down the hallway.

"It's gratifying to cook for someone other than just myself," Gram said, a trace of sadness beneath her smile.

Kate's heart squeezed, but she kept her tone light. "As much food as Luke puts away, you may get tired of it pretty quickly. I insist you let me help with meals. And everything else—cleaning, gardening, whatever needs to be done. I know how seriously you take hospitality, but Luke and I are roommates, not guests who have to be waited on hand and foot."

Gram's eyes twinkled. "Well…now that you mention it, I suppose I could use your help with a welcome party I'm hosting. Tomorrow."

"You planned a party tomorrow?" *So much for settling in slowly.* Kate had hoped to sleep late, then spend the day unpacking.

"*Party* is probably too grandiose a term. It's just a neighborhood cookout. I invited some friends, like the Rosses, who live down the road. You remember they used to let you ride their horses? And I figured you'd want to see Crystal Tucker. Wait—she's Crystal Walsh now, isn't she?" Gram shook her head. "Seems like just yesterday the two of you were sharing cotton candy at the Watermelon Festival, a couple of kids with pigtails and sticky hands. Now you're all grown up with kids of your own!"

Kate and Crystal had bonded quickly after meeting at the community pool and renewed their friendship every summer. An only child, Kate had loved having a playmate in town. Crystal, the middle kid between two sisters, relished the comparative peace and quiet at the Denby farm. The last time they'd seen each other was Jim Denby's funeral, but Crystal, heavily pregnant with twin boys, hadn't been able to stay long. It would be nice to catch up with her. Kate tried to recall the age of Crystal's oldest son, hoping the boy could be a potential friend for Luke. He needed a wholesome peer group—the sooner, the better.

With that goal in mind, she gave her grandmother a grateful smile. "I hate for you to go to trouble on our account, but I'm really glad you're throwing the welcome party. I'm sure it will be exactly what we need."

KATE WAS GLAD her son had the good sense not to show up at the dinner table wearing earbuds—a mandate she'd had to repeat at least once a week back in Houston— but he wasn't the most effusive dinner companion. He wolfed down two servings of stew while barely looking up from his plate, then asked to be excused.

She sighed, wishing he showed more curiosity about their new surroundings and learning about Cupid's Bow. *Let him go.* It had been a long day, and no doubt tomorrow would bring fresh battles. "You're excused, but make sure you rinse your dishes."

He did as asked, then paused in the doorway that led to the hall. "Dinner was awesome," he mumbled in Gram's general direction, the words all strung together. Then he disappeared around the corner.

Kate shook her head. "Well, that was a start, I guess. We'll work on eye contact later."

Gram smiled. "He's had a tough time of it. You both have."

"I know." Lord, did she know. "But that doesn't give him a permanent get-out-of-jail-free card. Losing his dad can't become a habitual excuse for bad choices." She ran a hand through her hair, recalling the incident at the gas station. She'd meant get-out-of-jail in a figurative sense, but if her son didn't get off his current path...

"Katie?" Gram's tone was thick with concern.

Glancing toward the empty doorway, Kate lowered her voice. "We had a mishap on the way to the farm... and by *mishap*, I mean petty larceny. He stole from Rick Jacobs, got caught shoplifting a candy bar at the gas station. Luke didn't even want it. We'd been arguing in the car and I can't help feeling like this was another act of rebellion because he's mad at me. He took the candy bar for a little girl."

Kate covered her eyes, her face heating at the mortifying memory. "He got busted stealing candy for one of Cole Trent's daughters."

"He stole something for the *sheriff's* kid?" Gram made an odd noise that Kate belatedly identified as a snort of amusement.

"Gram! It's not funny."

"It sort of is. Cupid's Bow is small, granted, but there are a couple thousand residents. Of all the people..." She tried unsuccessfully to smother another laugh. "The sheriff! Seriously?"

"Trust me, I wouldn't joke about this. When we met him inside, we didn't know he was a cop. Then he chased us out in the parking lot, understandably furious. I was so embarrassed." And that was after she'd already enjoyed the super-fun humiliation of dumping her drink on him. "Frankly, I'm hoping to avoid Sheriff Trent for the next three or four...ever."

Gram's eyes widened. "Oh, but—surely your paths

will cross again. Like I said, this is a small town. So, perhaps it would be best to get it over with sooner rather than later. Right?"

Definitely not. But since it seemed rude to argue, Kate smiled weakly. "I suppose that's one way of looking at it." Another way to view it was that Kate had enough on her plate already without worrying about alienating a blue-eyed pillar of the community.

CRAP. LUKE SULLIVAN scowled at the prolonged quiet on the other side of the bedroom door. *They're talking about me.* He couldn't make out any of his mom's or great-grandmother's words, but he knew the tense, muffled tone. His mother had used it with his therapist whenever she sent Luke out of the room so the two adults could confer privately. She'd used it a lot on the phone with her friends when she was complaining about Luke's screw-ups.

Suddenly needing noise and lots of it, Luke shoved in his earbuds and cranked up the volume on a hip-hop song. It was enough to drown out the low drone of conversation in the kitchen, but it didn't mute the thoughts bouncing around his brain. He didn't want to be here, in this shoebox of a room that smelled faintly of paint fumes. He liked his great-grandmother, but this was *her* house, not his. He missed home.

And he missed his friends.

He knew his mom didn't like them, had specifically heard her describe Bobby as a "hoodlum," but she didn't get it. When he hung out with Bobby and the other eighth graders, kids looked at him with respect. Bobby was a known badass. He wasn't universally liked, but even being regarded with contempt was better than pity. Luke hated students and teachers and neighbors eyeing him like he was a pathetic baby bird who'd fallen out of its nest and effed up its wing.

He was sick of people asking if he was "okay," like his father's murder was something to get over, equal to bombing a math quiz. He was tired of his mom's stubborn attempts to get him to hang out with his old friends. And her attempts to get him to draw again. What did she care? Comic books were dumb stories that had nothing to do with real life.

In the stories Luke used to doodle, his cyborg-enhanced alien helped people by stopping natural disasters and chasing off enemies. In real life, Luke couldn't even help cheer up a little girl. Stealing the candy had been stupid, and he certainly hadn't meant to get her in trouble. He hated seeing girls cry.

He knew his mom cried. After his dad got shot, she'd cried a lot. They both had. But then she'd pretended to stop. He wasn't stupid, though. He noticed when her face was blotchy. Some nights when he couldn't sleep, he could hear the muffled noise. He hated those nights. He hated that his dad had picked such a dangerous job. He hated that he'd had to leave the only place he'd ever lived. But there wasn't anything Luke could *do* about those problems.

Frustration flooded him, and he clenched his fists.

Yeah, stealing the candy bar had been a dumbass thing to do but it had seemed like such a simple solution, an easy way to make that little girl stop crying. Finally, there'd been a problem that seemed fixable! But he hadn't been able even to fix that. So how was he going to fix the rest of his life?

AFTER THE ACHES and pains caused by loading the car and hours of driving, Kate expected to toss and turn all night. Instead, only a few minutes after her head hit the pillow, she fell into a dreamless sleep. In the morning, she woke to a wave of déjà vu triggered by the scent of coffee. She herself had never developed a taste for it, but Damon hadn't been able to form the words *good morning* without a mug in his hand.

To combat the Texas summer, Gram kept the air-conditioning chugging at a temperature low enough to cool the hardwood floors. Kate slid her feet into music-note slippers given to her by a student at Christmas and padded to the kitchen to help with breakfast. She wasn't surprised that the door to Luke's room was still closed; he rarely got out of bed without parental prompting.

Gram, a natural morning person, beamed at her. "Sleep well, dear?"

"Like a rock, actually." It was the best night's rest she'd had in recent memory.

"I was just about to scramble myself some eggs. Want some?"

"You made dinner last night. It only seems fair that I make breakfast," Kate counteroffered.

"All right. Then I can work on my shopping list. I'm running into town to pick up a few last minute items for the cookout this afternoon."

The two women ate breakfast in companionable silence. Afterward, Gram gathered her purse and keys, saying she wouldn't be gone long. She was just missing a few ingredients for the desserts she planned to bake.

Alone in the quiet house, Kate began unpacking some of her belongings into the closet and bureau. She'd been too drained last night. After making a substantial dent—and finding a casual green-striped sundress that seemed appropriate for today—she headed for the bathroom and showered. She used the blow-dryer with the door open, hoping the noise would jump-start the process of waking Luke. When she knocked on his door, however, there was no answer, not even a mumbled "go away."

She toyed with letting him sleep longer, wondering if that would improve his disposition today, but decided she wanted this opportunity while they were alone in the house to break the news about the welcome party. He might not react with enthusiasm, and she didn't want him hurting Gram's feelings.

"Knock, knock," she said as she pushed the door open.

He was out cold, his breathing slow and even, his shaggy hair going in all different directions, an uneven halo against the pale blue pillowcase. Without the scowl that was rapidly becoming his trademark, he looked a lot like he had as a little boy. Her heart constricted, a tight ball in her chest. She loved her son so much and wanted nothing more than to make his life better, easier. If only he could see that!

She sat on the edge of the bed, saying his name softly, then with more volume, jostling his shoulder.

One eyelid cracked open just enough for him to peer at her in displeasure. "Whaddayawant?"

"To make you breakfast. And to talk. We saved you some bacon," she said coaxingly.

He hesitated, torn between two of his favorite activities—sleeping and eating. Playing video games was also in his top five, but she hadn't hooked up his gaming system last night. Maybe that could be his reward for being well-behaved today.

"Why don't you put on some clothes and brush your teeth," she suggested, "and I'll cook you some eggs. Scrambled with cheese?"

He shook his head. "Fried with the squishy yolk, so that the yellow runs everywhere when you cut it."

"Okay." She rose, leaving the room and giving him some privacy. But she hesitated in the hallway, listening to make sure he actually got out of the bed instead of rolling over and falling back to sleep.

Just as she was setting his plate on the table, he appeared in the kitchen, wearing a pair of maroon shorts with an elastic waist and a charcoal-colored shirt that had once featured the name of a sports team. The letters had faded to obscurity after about a million washings, and tiny holes in the fabric were beginning to appear at the neckline and around the seams. He claimed the shirt was the softest piece of clothing he owned and wore it about three times a week. She really needed to find him a replacement before this one ultimately disintegrated. Although he'd changed, he hadn't taken the time to brush his hair. It stuck out around his face in fluffy spikes.

She handed him a glass of orange juice. "You sleep okay?" Considering the coma-like condition she'd found him in, it seemed like a safe opener.

"No. The bed's lumpy, and the outside noise is weird."

How did he not consider the gentle hum of crickets and tree frogs an improvement over planes landing and periodic car alarms blaring? "There's hardly any noise at all!"

"That's what makes it weird." He stabbed into an egg, watching the yellow ooze across the plate as requested. "Where's Gram?"

"She went out for some groceries." And would probably be home any minute now, so Kate better get to the point. "She invited some people over this afternoon for a cookout."

Luke scowled around a mouthful of bacon. "You want me to spend my afternoon with a bunch of people I don't know?"

"That's the whole point of the gathering, so we can get to know some of our new neighbors. Maybe start making friends."

"I *have* friends. In Houston."

"Well, we aren't in Houston anymore. Gram was nice enough to take us in, and we owe her. Our actions here reflect on her, too."

"So you're saying if we don't fit in, she might kick us out?"

"Of course not!" Her grandmother would never resort to reverse extortion. Was he asking because he feared not being accepted, after the way most of his teachers had labeled him last year, or was he secretly hopeful, wondering if antics at Gram's cookout could be his ticket back to Houston?

"I expect you to be on your *best* behavior," she stressed. "Do not screw this up."

Hurt flared in his eyes, but his tone was his default-mode sarcastic when he said, "So you're saying I *shouldn't* hotwire the guests' cars and do doughnuts in the back pasture?"

"After your stunt yesterday, you don't get to make jokes like that."

"How long are you going to stay mad about that? It was just a stupid candy bar!"

No, it was a destructive pattern of behavior. Then again, if she always acted as though she expected the worst of him, was she creating a self-fulfilling prophecy? "Luke, I—"

Outside, a car door closed, and he shot out of his chair. "I'll see if she needs help bringing in groceries." His gallantry was clearly motivated by an excuse to end the conversation, but Kate would take what she could get.

The screen door clattered as he hurried out of the house, and Kate heard Gram call good morning to him. Decades ago, Joan Denby had been able to coax Kate out of her shell when she was feeling abandoned by her father. Maybe now Gram could work her magic on a sullen teenage boy.

There were so few bags that Luke got them all in one trip. Kate offered to help put away the groceries, but Gram said to just leave them out for baking. She then made Luke's day by giving him permission to hook up his game console to the living room TV while the two women worked in the kitchen.

Once he'd happily scampered off to lose himself in a digital quest, Gram raised an eyebrow in Kate's direction. "Am I wrong, or was there some tension between the two of you?"

"Always."

Gram patted her arm. "Hang in there. The teen years are difficult. I seem to recall a certain summer where you and Crystal fell for the same lifeguard at the local pool and life as you knew it was *over*!" She pressed the back of her hand to her forehead in melodramatic parody.

Kate chuckled in spite of herself. "Okay, I suppose even I had my tantrums."

"And you grew into a wonderful woman. Luke has a good heart."

"I know. I just wish he'd share it with people more often."

Gram disappeared into the walk-in pantry and returned with a sack of flour and an armful of spices. "Do you want an apron to protect your dress? It's pretty. Brings out the green in your eyes." She beamed proudly. "You're sure to make a good impression in it."

Alarm bells sounded in Kate's head, as jarring as a classroom of seven-year-olds all playing xylophones for the first time. Suddenly she recalled a phone conversation with Gram a few months ago. Her grandmother had gently hinted that Luke might do better with a male role model in his life and asked if Kate ever dated. When Kate had said no, Gram had dropped the subject. Now, Kate wondered if her grandmother had simply been biding her time.

"Gram, this welcome party... It's not going to be a lineup of the county's eligible bachelors, is it? I told you, I'm not ready for romance."

Her grandmother smiled sadly. "I lost my husband, too. I understand. But you're in the prime of your life, with a lot of years left ahead of you. Damon wouldn't want you to be alone."

That answer did nothing to settle Kate's apprehension about the party. "Today isn't going to be you, me, and a dozen single guys between the ages of twenty and fifty, right?"

"You have your grandfather's active imagination. As I told you last night, I invited some families. Now, can we get started? I've got several desserts I want to bake, and my oven will only hold so many things at a time."

Telling herself to quit being paranoid, Kate lost herself in the comforting rhythm of working alongside the woman who had taught her how to cook. The first dinner she'd ever fixed for Damon had included her grandmother's chicken and dumplings recipe. The hours passed quickly. In seemingly no time, afternoon sun streamed through the windows and the kitchen smelled like a decadent bakery. Unfortunately, the kitchen was nearly as hot as the inside of a bakery oven.

At least outside there was a breeze. Kate covered long folding tables with vinyl tablecloths, glad she hadn't bothered with makeup. It would have melted away. They drafted Luke to dump ice into the drink coolers and pretended not to notice all the food he stole off the veggie tray. Beans simmered on the stove, and a vat of potato salad waited in the fridge. The smell of brisket cooking made Kate's stomach rumble. While she waited for the grill to heat up so she could throw on some sausages, she opened a bag of tortilla chips and taste-tested Gram's homemade salsa.

Gram handed her a cold water bottle, her eyes glinting with mischief. "You might want this."

Kate nodded. "It's a little hotter than I remembered."

"Well. Everyone needs a little spice in their lives."

As Kate sipped her water, two vehicles came down the dirt road that led from the street to the farm. The second was a battered pickup; the one in the lead was a sedan that was probably older than she was but gleamed as if it were washed and waxed daily. As soon as it pulled to a stop, the back door opened. While the driver and front passenger were still dealing with their seatbelts, two blonde blurs of energy spilled out. Followed by a tall man with ink-black hair.

Cold water splashed over her fingers, making her realize she was squeezing the bottle in her hand. "Gram!" She couldn't keep the note of shrill accusation from her voice. "That is Cole Trent."

Her grandmother ducked her gaze. "Oh. Did I, um, forget to mention he was invited?"

Chapter Three

A single glance across the shaded front yard confirmed the suspicion that had been growing inside Cole as his father drove. Joan Denby's granddaughter was indeed the beautiful blonde he'd met yesterday. Two single moms with sons moving to Cupid's Bow at the same time wasn't impossible, but it would be an unlikely coincidence. When the possibility had first occurred to him that the woman they were welcoming to town was the same one he'd met at the gas station, he'd discounted it because his mother had made it sound as if the newcomer's son was closer to the twins' age.

Then again, his mom had proven that her ethics were flexible when it came to introducing him to single women.

He had to admit, on some level, he was excited to see the blonde again. Judging from her tense body language as she talked to her grandmother, the feeling was not mutual.

"Hey, it's that lady!" Mandy announced as the adults unloaded folding chairs and covered dishes from the car.

Gayle Trent glanced at her granddaughter. "The older one, or the younger one?"

Mandy frowned, momentarily perplexed that someone over thirty might qualify as young. "The one with the ponytail. We met her yesterday. Her son's a big kid. He and Alyssa took a—"

"I *didn't* take it!" Alyssa interrupted, her face splotched with red.

"Why don't we leave what happened in the past?" Cole said, steering his girls away from his mother's blatant curiosity. He had not yet shared the Great Candy Bar Heist with her. "Come on, let's go meet our hostess."

He tried to recall whether his mom had mentioned Joan's granddaughter by name but drew a blank.

"Sheriff Trent!" Joan Denby waved him over with a smile. "So nice to see you—and your girls. They're getting so big. This is my granddaughter, Kate Sullivan. I hear the two of you have met?"

"Briefly, but I didn't catch a name." He set down the chairs he carried and extended his hand. "Nice to officially meet you, Kate."

Her gold-green eyes narrowed and, for a second, he didn't think she would shake his hand. She did, but the contact was as fleeting as social protocol allowed.

"Sheriff," she said stiffly.

He smiled. "Please, call me Cole. I'm off duty at the moment."

His parents had caught up to them and Mr. and Mrs. Ross, who owned The Twisted R ranch at the end of the road, were climbing down from their truck and calling their own hellos. Cole stepped out of the way, giving Joan a chance to proudly introduce her granddaughter. As Kate greeted everyone, her gaze kept darting nervously back to him. The lingering interest would be flattering if not for her apprehensive expression.

He was used to being well-regarded in the community and frankly unsure how to respond to her thinned lips and rigid posture. Did she somehow blame him for her son's actions yesterday? After all, if his daughter hadn't asked for the candy bar in the first place, Luke might never have swiped it. She certainly hadn't made excuses for her son, though. She'd responded to the situation with a directness Cole admired, marching her son back inside to apologize to Rick Jacobs and offer restitution.

"Mom!" The front door banged open, releasing an exuberant German shepherd into the yard. Luke Sullivan emerged on the wraparound porch. "There's some lady on the phone for you."

At the sight of Luke, Alyssa gasped. Apparently, it hadn't yet clicked with her that if Kate was present, her son would be, too. "I do not like him," Alyssa said to no one in particular before stomping off to sit beneath a pear tree.

Mandy watched her sister's retreat with wide eyes, then tugged Cole's hand. "Now what?"

Good question.

"OF COURSE I UNDERSTAND," Kate said into the phone, trying to concentrate on Crystal's words instead of staring at the sheriff through the front window. "We'll get together for lunch or something as soon as everyone's feeling better."

Her childhood friend had called with the news that two of her kids had the stomach flu. When the first one had thrown up, Crystal had hoped it was an isolated incident and had planned to leave her husband at home with the kid. But now that there were fevers involved, Crystal worried that even the members of the household not showing symptoms might be contagious.

"I can't wait to see you," Crystal said, her tone apologetic. "I hate that I won't make the barbecue."

"Me, too." Catching up with her old friend would have been a nice distraction from Sheriff Trent. *Call me Cole.* His rich voice was more tempting than Gram's desserts. "Hey, Crys, do you know much about the sheriff? Gram invited him and his parents."

"Then she has good taste," Crystal said approvingly. "He's a cutie."

Cute did not begin to describe him. The casual cotton T-shirt he wore delineated his muscular arms and chest far more than the crisp polo shirt she'd last seen on him. And she felt foolish for noticing that in the full sunlight, his thick hair wasn't simply black. Half a dozen subtler hues threaded through it.

She was not interested in the sheriff's hair. Or his muscles. Mostly, she just wanted to make sure Luke behaved today and didn't further damage his reputation with the sheriff—or any of the other guests, for that matter.

"One of my boys played soccer in the spring with Mandy Trent," Crystal said. "The sheriff's got his hands full, but he seems like a good dad. And he's considered quite the catch among the women in town. Or would be, if anyone could catch him."

"So he's not seeing anyone?" Kate wished she could take back the impulsive question. The sheriff's dating life was none of her concern.

"I don't think he's gone on more than three dates

with the same woman since his divorce, which was years ago. Popular opinion is that Becca Johnston will wear him down eventually—unless he gets a restraining order. Becca's relentless, never takes no for an answer. Every time she calls, I get sandbagged into chairing some PTA committee or local food drive. If you want to volunteer for something like the Watermelon Festival in order to meet people, you should talk to her. If not, avoid her like the plague. And speaking of plague, I'd better go check my sick kids."

As Kate was replacing the cordless phone on its charger, the front door opened.

"Katie?" Gram's tone was rueful. No doubt she felt guilty for the way she'd ambushed Kate with Cole's presence. "Are you rejoining us?"

Like I have a choice? "You raised me better than to hide in the house just because there's someone I'd rather avoid. I was talking to Crystal. She had to cancel because they're dealing with a stomach bug."

"I'm sorry to hear that. She was excited about seeing you again."

Kate shrugged, trying not to look as disappointed as she felt. "Sick kids come with the parenting territory. I'll see her soon."

"You know, I thought there was a chance Cole might have to cancel," Gram said. "As sheriff, he's got a lot of responsibilities. Just keeping the Breelan brothers under control is practically a full-time job. As fretful as you were about seeing him again, it seemed unkind to worry you needlessly in the event he couldn't make it."

"As opposed to giving me time to mentally prepare myself?"

"Well…we did both agree that it would be best for

you to encounter him sooner rather than later," Gram said, taking some creative license with the conversation they'd actually had. "Please don't be angry. His mother is a close friend. Your paths were bound to cross. Give him a chance."

A chance to what? "I'm not angry, Gram. You invited his family before you knew Cole and I had shared an awkward run-in. I'm sure he's a nice man. But, at the risk of being repetitive, I really don't—"

"Oh, I just remembered! I need to stir the beans so they don't burn on the bottom. Excuse me, dear." Gram moved with impressive speed for a woman over seventy. "Will you let our guests know I'll be back in a moment?"

"For the record," Kate grumbled with wry amusement, "I know perfectly well I'm being manipulated."

Gram flashed a cheeky smile over her shoulder. One thing was for sure, living with a crafty grandmother and an unpredictable teen would keep Kate on her toes.

LUKE JAMMED HIS hands in the pockets of his cargo shorts, wishing he could disappear. With his mom and Gram both inside the house, he didn't know any of the other adults. Except the sheriff—and Luke would rather not face him.

One of the sheriff's daughters was pleading with her dad to kick a soccer ball back and forth; the other girl had gone off by herself. In Luke's opinion, she had the right idea. He suddenly found himself walking in that direction.

Although the twins were technically identical, they were pretty easy to tell apart. The one beneath the tree had a pink backpack and her hair was braided the same way it had been yesterday; she was the one who'd wanted the candy bar. Alyssa, her dad had called her.

She glared when she saw him coming. "I don't like you."

A common opinion. Luke wasn't sure his mom liked him, either. Sometimes, he wasn't even sure he liked himself. "Whatcha got there?"

"Nothing." She hunched forward, protectively. He couldn't see what she was drawing, but he could tell she had a sketch pad in her lap. Crayons spilled from her open backpack across the grass.

"What are you drawing?"

"Go away."

The side of his mouth lifted in a grin. For a little kid, she certainly wasn't intimidated by a teenager twice her height. "I didn't mean to get you in trouble yesterday." Despite the way his stomach had hurt when he'd seen the Trents in the yard, now he was kind of glad they were here. The chance to apologize was an unexpected relief. "I'm sorry. Really."

Her head lifted, and she studied him for a long moment.

"I was just trying to do something nice," he added. "I thought he should have bought you the candy bar."

"You made a poor decision." The way she said it sounded like she was imitating an adult. Her dad, probably.

Jealousy pinched Luke's insides. It caught him off guard whenever he felt this—envy for all the regular kids who still had fathers. It wasn't as if he wanted anyone else's dad to die. He just wished his own was still around. Sometimes Luke could hear his dad's voice so clearly he could almost pretend they were on the phone.

Other days, his dad's voice was faded and distorted, like bad audio on a corrupt game file.

His throat burning, he backed away from Alyssa. "I'll leave you alone."

"Wait! It's a horse." She held up the pad. "But it's not very good."

It was terrible. The legs weren't the right scale to the rest of the body, the neck was weirdly lumpy, and the nose looked like a crocodile snout. Plus, horses shouldn't be purple. But he didn't want to hurt her feelings. What if she cried again?

"Keep trying. With enough practice, you could get so good you surprise yourself." He'd heard his mom say that to music students. He hoped it would be enough to make Alyssa feel better about her mutant horse. He stared at the picture, trying to find a positive. "The tail looks right."

"Thank you." She brightened a little. "My nana said this is a farm. Do you have horses?"

"No. There are goats, though." Taking her toward the barn to look for the goats would kill some time until the food was ready *and* keep Luke away from the sheriff. "Wanna go see them?"

"Okay." She picked up her backpack, frowning as she zipped it. "But don't you dare stick candy in my bag."

He recalled his mom's stern warning. *Do not screw this up.* Everyone thought he was too stupid to learn from his mistakes. "I said I was sorry."

"Then I guess you can be my friend."

"Gee, thanks." His first friend in a new town, and it was a five-year-old girl. Still, as they headed to the barn, he had to admit it was kind of nice not to be walking alone.

COLE HAD JUST retrieved the soccer ball from some rose bushes at the side of the house when his dad clapped him on the back.

"You look like you could use a break, son." Harvey Trent said. "Mandy, I'm not sure your dad can keep up with you! How about Paw-paw takes a turn while your dad grabs a cold drink?" Lowering his voice to a whisper, he added, "And talks to the pretty girl."

Cole groaned. "Did Mom put you up to this?"

Harvey took the soccer ball from his son's hands. "No one has to 'put me up to' enjoying time with my granddaughter."

If Cole's parents thought Kate Sullivan wanted him to talk to her, they must be blind. The woman's "stay back" vibe was so strong, he expected to see gnats and butterflies bouncing off the invisible force field that surrounded her. After the casseroles other women in town had baked him over the years and Becca Johnston's less than subtle pursuit, Kate's disinterest should be refreshing. Except…he wouldn't mind seeing those hazel eyes fixed on him with a feminine interest. There'd been a moment at the gas station yesterday, a brief flicker of connection.

Or was that wishful thinking on his part?

Not that it mattered, he thought as he pulled a can of soda from the cooler and popped the tab. Whatever spark might have been there seemed to have been extinguished when he busted her son. Still, this welcome party *was* in her honor. Not talking to her would be rude. He approached the table where the women were chatting. Mr. Ross stood a few feet off to the side, working the grill.

As Cole neared the group, he overheard Mrs. Ross

bragging about her son, Jarrett. "…so good with young people. He spends a few weeks every summer working at a horse-riding camp. It's a shame he couldn't be here today."

Kate's expression was a discordant cross between placating smile and deer-in-the-headlights stare. Cole experienced a twinge of sympathy. Were they already trying to fix her up with someone? Jarrett Ross was a good guy, but he was gone a lot on the rodeo circuit. Although Mrs. Ross might be eager for her son to settle into a steady relationship, as far as Cole knew, Jarrett was thoroughly enjoying the admiration of his female fans.

"It's also a shame Crystal couldn't be here," Kate interjected, surprising Cole by glancing his way. She was obviously desperate for a change of subject. "If her family had made it, your girls would have had more kids to play with."

"Luckily for me, the girls are pretty good at entertaining themselves. Mandy's happy as long as she has a soccer ball, and Alyssa…" He looked toward the tree where his daughter had been sitting. She was often content with quieter hobbies, like coloring or reading her favorite picture books. But she was no longer there.

Following his gaze, Joan Denby said, "She's with Luke. I watched them walk over that hill a few minutes ago."

"You're kidding." Last Cole had heard, his daughter was still ticked off at the teen. What had enticed her to wander off with him?

Joan nodded. "They headed in the general direction of the barn."

"Maybe I should round them up." Kate shot hastily to her feet.

Was she worried the two kids were into mischief? Cole didn't know Luke Sullivan. Had the kid's shoplifting been an aberration, or was he a habitual troublemaker?

"I'll go with you," Cole volunteered.

Kate bit her lip. Whether she wanted his company or not, it wasn't as though she could forbid him to check on his own child.

They fell into step with each other, making their way down the small green slope that curved behind the farmhouse. The barn was visible, the distance of a couple of football fields away, but he didn't see the kids yet. They might have been inside or around the corner, where the overhang provided shade. Kate was quiet as they walked, her gait stiff. He attempted to defuse the situation with humor.

"Could be worse," he deadpanned. "You could be stuck at the table, sitting through countless pictures of Jarrett Ross's rodeo buckles on Mrs. Ross's phone."

"Did I look as trapped as I felt?"

"So much that I was questioning whether I'd need my hostage negotiation training to rescue you."

Her lips curved in an impish grin. "Think Mrs. Ross would have let me go in exchange for a fully fueled helicopter and a briefcase of unmarked bills? Not that she was the only guilty party. Before she started regaling me with Jarrett's many fine qualities, Gram— *Oh*." She sucked in a breath as her foot slid sideways, catching a root that jutted out from the hillside.

Cole reached for her automatically, his hands going to her waist so she wouldn't tumble. As soon as his fingers settled above her hips, a potent sense of awareness jolted through him. The only thing separating her skin from his was the soft thin cotton of her dress. It was an absurdly tantalizing thought, given the hands-on nature of his job. From shaking hands with voters to demonstrating first-aid techniques in community classes, his days were full of physical contact. Yet he couldn't recall the last time he'd been so deeply affected.

Kate, however, didn't seem to share his enjoyment of the moment. Her eyes were wide, as if she found his touch disconcerting. As soon as he noticed, he let go of her so fast she almost lost her balance again.

He winced. When had he become such a bumbling ass? "Sorry." This time he steadied her with a strictly platonic grip on her elbow.

"No reason to be," she said, her voice shaky. "You were, um, just trying to be helpful."

Exactly. Helpful. Not lustful.

Well, maybe a bit of both. "I didn't mean to startle you, grabbing you like that." The expression on her face had been damned near panicky.

"It's been a really long—" Her cheeks reddened. "I guess I shouldn't be tromping around the farm in wedge sandals. They're not exactly all-terrain. What was I saying? Before?"

The better question was, what had she been about to say now, before she'd interrupted herself to denounce her shoes?

She snapped her fingers. "Oh, I remember! Just that Jarrett Ross wasn't the only man Gram and her friends mentioned. There was also prolonged discussion of one of Crystal's cousins, an accountant named Greg

Tucker? Your mother can't imagine why someone who would be 'such a good provider' is still single."

"Possibly because Greg hates kids," Cole guessed. "Well, *hate* may be too strong a word. But not by much." From what Cole had seen when the Tuckers were together en masse, Greg barely tolerated his legion of nieces and nephews. He was a completely illogical match for a single mom.

"I definitely can't get involved with anyone who dislikes kids. Luke's challenging enough to people who *are* crazy about them." She pressed a hand to her forehead. "Lord, that sounded awful. I didn't mean... I know he didn't make a stellar first impression on you, but deep down he's a good boy."

"All kids make mistakes," he reassured her, remembering his own scalding embarrassment when he was called into the principal's office to discuss Alyssa's marker-on-the-bathroom-wall misadventure. "Even a cop's kids."

Kate's laugh was hollow. "That's exactly what Luke is."

He swung his gaze to her in surprise. "Your ex-husband is a policeman?"

"Was," she corrected softly. "My late husband was a policeman."

He was too shocked to respond. Why hadn't his mother mentioned Kate was a widow? "I—"

"There they are." She gestured toward the left of the barn. The two kids sat with their heads close together as they looked down, too focused to notice the approaching adults. As Cole and Kate got closer, the breeze carried Alyssa's exclamations of delight.

"It's perfect!" she cried. "Except it needs wings."

Luke chuckled. "First you said you wanted a horse, then you said unicorn. Now a Pegasus? What's next, a whole herd?"

"No. I just want one winged unicorn. But she'd look better if she was glittery. Do you have any sparkly crayons?" she asked hopefully.

"Hell, no."

Cole's eyes narrowed at the kid's language, but Kate's fingers on his forearms stopped his intended reprimand. He glanced up, his annoyance fading in the wake of her beseeching expression.

Besides, his little girl was already taking the teenager to task. "You aren't supposed to say the *H* word. Unless you're at church and they're talking about the Bad Place."

"Sorry. I'll try not to say it again," Luke promised.

"That's okay. Sometimes my daddy says it, too."

Kate snickered, and Cole gave her a sheepish smile. "Busted," she said softly.

Luke's head shot up. "Mom?"

"Hey." She stepped away from Cole, putting an almost comical amount of distance between them.

Cole remembered the boy's hostility yesterday when he'd seen the two adults smiling at each other. How long had it been since Luke's father died? As someone who was still close to both of his parents, even as an adult, Cole couldn't imagine what that loss was like for the kid.

"We were just coming to get you guys for lunch," Kate said. "Who's hungry?"

"Me!" Alyssa shot up as though she was spring-loaded. Although Luke showed more restraint, his eyes gleamed at the mention of food.

Both kids hurried back toward the house.

"Be careful," Cole called after his daughter. Her flip-flops weren't any better suited for hiking across rolling pastureland than Kate's sandals were. He glanced down to check for swelling or a limp. "How's your foot? You didn't twist your ankle, did you?"

"I'm fine. Just a little embarrassed. I reacted badly when you tried to keep me from falling. I didn't mean to be ungrateful. But it's been so long since…"

A man had touched her? At all? Cole hadn't exactly swept her into his arms for a passionate embrace. "Did you lose him recently?" he asked in a murmur, as if his regular speaking voice would make the question disrespectful.

She shook her head. "Couple of years. But I've been so busy trying to keep Luke out of trouble that time gets distorted, if that makes any sense."

"It does. My ex-wife left when the girls were babies— she decided she wasn't cut out for small-town life *or* trying to take care of two infants. There are odd moments when our being a whole family feels like yesterday, but other times, it seems like a different existence, altogether. Like remembering a past life."

Kate nodded, looking relieved by his understanding.

Neither of them spoke again until they were close enough to breathe in the spicy aroma of grilled sausages.

"Cole?"

Her soft voice brushed over his skin like a warm breeze. "Hmm?"

"If Gram starts another recitation of the town's Most Eligible Men, will you help me change the subject?

Please. I know her intentions are good—she worries about me being lonely—but I'm not ready to date."

After dozens of frustrating conversations with his mom about his own love life, or lack thereof, he empathized all too well. In fact… He stopped abruptly. "Maybe the two of us can help each other. I have a radical idea."

Chapter Four

Kate blinked at Cole's unexpected—and vaguely unsettling—declaration. "How radical are we talking?"

"I'll explain when we have more time." He flashed her the same endearingly boyish smile she'd glimpsed when his daughter had ratted him out for occasional use of the *H* word. "For now, do you trust me enough to follow my lead?"

He was using *trust* in a casual, conversational sense. Still, trust was a special bond, earned over time. An intimate connection. Errant longing rippled through her.

What is wrong with me today? Her emotional responses were all over the map. From the way she'd nearly bolted when he'd touched her earlier to—

"Katie? Everything all right?" Joan called with a frown. Everyone was seated, and it was obvious they were waiting on the two stragglers.

"Sorry, Gram. We'll be right there." Giving Cole a barely perceptible nod to signal that she'd take her cues from him—and hoping she wouldn't regret it— she strode toward the table.

"Now that we're all here," Joan said, "we can bless the food. Harvey, would you do the honors?"

The kids already had plates piled high. Once grace

was finished, they dug in as the adults served themselves.

Mrs. Trent smiled in Kate's direction. "Alyssa tells me your son is quite the artist."

Alyssa nodded happily. "They don't have horses here, but he knows how to draw one real good."

"Do you like horses?" Mrs. Ross asked Luke. She wasn't deterred by his noncommittal shrug. "Maybe you and your mom can come over sometime and go riding at our ranch. Then you can meet my daughter Vicki, who's home from college for the summer, and of course, Jarrett." This last was aimed at Kate.

Kate grimaced. Couldn't she at least have a moment to savor her grandmother's award-winning potato salad before the matchmaking brigade started in on her again? Some things were sacred.

Gram must have seen her reaction because she was quick to offer an alternative to Jarrett Ross. "You know who else has a nice stable of horses?"

Kate bit the inside of her cheek, desperately hoping that wasn't some kind of euphemism.

"Brody Davenport. He—"

"Ah, but Brody's so busy these days," Cole interrupted. "With Jasmine Tucker."

"Crystal's younger sister?" Kate asked.

"That's right. I forgot Jasmine moved back to town," Gram said, looking disgruntled.

"She was in New York for a while," Mrs. Ross said. "Modeling. Doesn't that sound glamorous? But she's back now and owns the most fashionable boutique in Cupid's Bow. Well…technically the only boutique."

"I should take you by there this week," Gram told Kate. "I'm going to town Tuesday afternoon for a festival meeting. You can come with me, maybe get involved with one of the committees. It's a great way to meet folks."

"Actually," Cole said, "Kate and the kids and I are going to the pool Tuesday afternoon."

"We are?" The words came from Luke but echoed Kate's surprised thoughts.

Cole nodded. "Since I couldn't take the girls swimming yesterday, I already texted Deputy Thomas about my taking off Tuesday afternoon. And when Kate asked if the community pool was as impressive as she remembered, I invited her and Luke to join us."

For a lawman, he was a surprisingly comfortable liar. They'd never discussed the pool. What if she had a terrible phobia of water or something? But the community pool *was* a huge recreational attraction. Decades ago, a family with more oil money than they knew what to do with had donated the funds to build the pool. It was far bigger than any of the public pools in neighboring towns and included a toddler play area, a spiral slide and two diving boards. Given that it was hot enough in Cupid's Bow to swim nearly half the year, the town council deemed the pool worth the extensive upkeep. Kate had been planning to take Luke soon, to help make up for the laser tag arenas and twenty-four screen movie theaters they'd left behind.

And now she was going on Tuesday, with a hot single dad whose merest touch made her nerve endings sizzle. *Maybe "I'm not ready to date" means something different in Cupid's Bow.* She knew Cole was sincere about the outing, or he wouldn't have mentioned it in front of their collective children. Was this where she was supposed to follow his lead?

"Thanks again for the invitation," she told Cole.

It wasn't until everyone finished and people began cleaning up that she had a chance to talk to him alone. Gram sent Kate to get a box of lawn games from the shed, and Cole followed along.

"I hope you didn't have pressing plans for Tuesday," he said sheepishly.

And if she had? She couldn't find it in herself to be annoyed, though. His unexpected fib had saved her from a meeting where she suspected she would have heard about many single male cousins, neighbors, sons and brothers.

"You said your grandmother worries about you being lonely," he continued as they neared the shed. "I'm in the same boat. Mom's been on my case about the girls needing a mother. While I don't disagree in theory, I'm not going to run out and propose to someone just to appease her. I already know most of the women in town, even dated a few after the divorce. But there was never any..."

She turned toward him expectantly, and their gazes collided. His eyes made her nervous; they saw too much. He must be hell on suspects with something to hide. Although, perhaps potential criminals being questioned weren't hung up on how blue his eyes were.

"...spark," Cole finished, his words an ironic counterpoint to the charged air between them.

Heat flooded her face, a mixture of physical awareness and embarrassment. Since Damon's death, no man had grabbed her interest. She hadn't kissed anyone, certainly hadn't thought about doing more with anyone. But when Cole had his hands on her after she'd stumbled, there'd been a definite *zing*. It felt like desire—or the way she remembered desire feeling, when it had still been part of her emotional spectrum. Experiencing it so unexpectedly had caused her to falter worse than the root she'd tripped over.

She attempted a casual, teasing tone. "No spark with anyone? Not even…Becca Johnston?"

He scrubbed a hand over his face. "Only been here a day, and you've already heard about her, huh? See, this is why I've been reduced to shamelessly using you as a human shield."

"I'm not comfortable pretending to date you, if that's what you're suggesting." She opened the door and stepped inside the shed, pausing as she waited for her eyes to adjust to the dim light. "I won't lie to Gram, and it would be extremely confusing for Luke."

"No, I would never feign a relationship, either. But I thought that if the two of us spend a little time together, maybe our families will take that as a sign of progress, be encouraged enough to get off our backs."

So he didn't want to pretend a romance, necessarily. Romance and Cole in the same thought left her momentarily dizzy, although maybe she was just reacting to his nearness. It was close quarters in here. She shook it off, trying to focus.

If the two of them spent a little time in the company of the opposite gender—namely, with each other—would their meddling loved ones relent? Starting a new life here in Cupid's Bow would be easier if she weren't worried about Gram constantly ambushing her with men. Plus, Alyssa Trent seemed to be a good influence on Luke, candy bar incident notwithstanding. The Pegasus he'd drawn might be only his humoring a five-year-old, but it was still the first illustration he'd done in months.

Maybe spending a little time with Cole and his girls would benefit them all. She and the sheriff were on the same page as far as intentions—this wasn't dating. It was a mutually advantageous arrangement.

"I'm in," she agreed. "But next time you announce our plans to a group, you should check with me first."

"Done. You just let me know what you need. We can spend time out and about, introducing you and Luke to as many townspeople as possible, or we can stick to activities like going to the movies, where we don't have to interact much at all but will still be seen together. You may not know it, but the Cupid's Bow Cineplex now shows up to three different movies at the same time."

"Wow. Three whole movies, huh?" Her tone was light, but inside, she experienced a flutter of anticipation at the idea of sitting in the dark next to Sheriff Trent, their thighs pressed together in adjoining seats.

You don't have to sit next to him, she reminded herself. They had children to behave as de facto chaperones. Although she and Luke had never really talked about her dating again—there'd never been a need— she doubted he would be excited about her cozying up to the town sheriff. Best to keep this platonic and businesslike.

And the sooner she got out of the small shed where she was close enough to brush against him with the slightest motion, breathing in the combination of his aftershave and sun-warmed skin, the easier it would be to remember that.

TUESDAY MORNING, Kate worked in the garden alongside Gram while Luke pulled some weeds that were crowding the front steps of the house. Kate was proud of him—though he hadn't exactly volunteered to help outside instead of playing video games, he hadn't protested when she enlisted him, either. The pool was going to feel heavenly after working out in the sun.

Gram adjusted her straw hat for a better look at her wristwatch. "We should go in soon if we want enough time to eat lunch and clean up. I've got that festival meeting today, and you've got your big date."

"It's *not*—" Oops. She probably shouldn't sound so defensive if she and Cole were going to make his plan work. Though she wouldn't lie to make it sound as if they were swept up in the romance of the century, she could at least give the impression she was open to possibilities. "I mean, we'll have the kids with us. It's hardly a candlelit dinner."

"And would you say yes if he asked you out for one of those?" Gram pressed.

No way. The thought of staring across a table into Cole's blue eyes made her palms sweat and her stomach knot. "I… He's an attractive man." Too damned attractive. "And charming." If a woman didn't have an aversion to dating a law officer. "But I'm just dipping my toes back in the water. I'm not ready to think about cannonballing into the deep end."

"All right." Gram studied the tomato plants, choosing a few that were ready to be picked before adding slyly, "But am I forgiven for not telling you he'd be at the cookout?"

"Just this once. No sneak attacks with other men."

"Well, of course not." Gram looked baffled. "Why

would I try to introduce you to anyone else when you and Sheriff Trent are getting to know each other?"

Cole's assessment of the situation had been spot on—without the protection of a few outings with him, Kate might find herself under siege. And once they stopped those outings to make sure none of their children misread the situation? Gram could invite whomever she wanted to the farm, whenever she wanted.

"I'm going to head inside," Kate said. "The heat and the empty stomach are starting to make me queasy." As was the prospect of a dozen gentleman callers, invited for Sunday dinner or to repair the barbwire fence or to check out an imagined sound Gram thought her car engine was making. Frankly, Kate was feeling a little nervous about the message she'd left this morning for the piano tuner. Was *he* single?

She went into the house and showered off the gardening grime, then started preparing lunch. When the phone in the kitchen rang, she reached for it, wondering if it was the piano tuner returning her call. "Hello?"

The last voice she'd expected to hear was her father's.

"Katherine?" He sounded similarly puzzled. "Is that you?"

"Yeah." It was funny—now that Kate was an adult, Gram still called her by the childhood nickname Katie; meanwhile, her father had always used her full name, even when she was a toddler. He'd been young when he became a dad, a college TA who hadn't shirked his responsibility when a former girlfriend left their baby on his doorstep, but he'd always seemed older than his age, treating Kate with formality. There had been hugs and bedtime stories, usually about indigenous peoples, but she couldn't recall him ever tickling her the way she'd seen Cole Trent do with his girls at the cookout. "Is everything okay?" she asked, startled to hear from her dad out of the blue.

"Right as rain. I call one Sunday each month, to check on Mother."

"It's Tuesday."

"Ah. Time gets away from me some between semesters. Now that I've got you on the phone, I can check on you, as well," he said, sounding pleased with his own efficiency. "How long will you be visiting Cupid's Bow?"

"Luke and I moved here, remember?"

"Yes, of course. And are the two of you all settled in?"

"Getting there. Gram threw a welcome party for us, and we made some friends. We're going to meet them at the community pool after lunch."

"Good, good. Your grandmother always did know what was best for you."

Once Gram had taken the phone from her and Kate resumed dicing up boiled eggs for salads, her thoughts returned to Cole Trent. He'd commented that people kept telling him the twins needed a mother, but he obviously adored his girls. She couldn't envision him dumping his children on Mr. and Mrs. Trent, relieved to wash his hands of parenting for a few months. Plenty of fathers out there weren't trying nearly as hard as he seemed to be. She was confident Cole could raise his daughters successfully as a single parent.

It was important she believe that. Because maybe, if *he* could do it, she could, too.

THE PARKING LOT at the pool was pretty packed for a weekday afternoon. Kate climbed out of her car, glad she and Cole had agreed to meet there. His picking her up would have made no sense geography-wise, since Gram's farm was in the opposite direction, and it would have made the outing feel too much like a date. Tugging the hem of the V-necked bathing suit cover that had bunched up while she drove, she turned to Luke.

"You're okay with joining Cole and his daughters for a couple of hours, right? He was just being neighborly when he invited us. That's the kind of town Cupid's Bow is."

Her son stared at her, one eyebrow raised. "It's fine. But you've asked me three times. Why are you being weird?"

Excellent question.

"Sorry." She reached into the back seat for the massive beach bag that held their towels, Luke's goggles and enough sunscreen to protect a small village.

"Luke!" The high-pitched greeting preceded the slap of footsteps on the pavement.

Kate glanced up to see Alyssa barreling toward them in the same flip-flops she'd worn Sunday. Cole and Mandy followed at a more leisurely pace. Alyssa stopped in front of Luke, holding up her hand for a high five. Kate worried that, at some point, her jaded thirteen-year-old might decide it was uncool to have a five-year-old girl as a friend. Thankfully, now was not that point.

He smacked his palm against Alyssa's. "Ready to go swimming?"

"Yep. Daddy has my goggles and my floaties and

I'm wearing my favorite bathing suit." It was a rainbow-colored bikini top with a matching swim skirt.

Her sister was in a sportier one-piece. Kate tried not to think about her own bathing suit. She and Luke had been swimming half a dozen times in the past year, and she'd never once considered the teal tankini immodest. Now, however, she couldn't stop obsessing over the sliver of abdomen that would be exposed once she removed her hooded cover-up. She was a woman who'd given birth; her midsection was no longer the taut skin of a twentysomething. But so what? She wouldn't exactly stand out at the pool.

Yet the idea of being in front of Cole in so little clothing was irrationally alarming. She couldn't even say whether her apprehension was because he wouldn't like what he saw…or because he might like it just fine.

There'd been a couple of times at Gram's farm when his gaze had locked with hers, and she'd felt tingly, as if parts of her that had been long numb were slowly buzzing back to life beneath his notice. It stung, like trying to stand on a foot that had fallen asleep. She wanted no part of the accompanying pins and needles.

So she didn't quite meet his eyes when she said, "Afternoon."

"Kate." His voice was warm and rich. "Good to see you, again."

As the five of them crossed the parking lot, he explained that he and the girls had season passes to the pool. They waited off to the side while Kate purchased admission for her and Luke. On the other side of the ticket hut came the sounds of splashing and laughter and a classic rock standard being played through speakers above the concession area.

No sooner were they through the turnstiles than Mandy kicked off her shoes. "High dive, Daddy?"

He chuckled. "Let's work our way up to that. And let's find some chairs so we can put all our stuff down."

"What about my floaties?" Alyssa asked, sounding anxious.

"They're here." Cole patted the side of his duffel bag. "But are you *sure* you don't want to try going in the water without them first? You were getting really good at swimming." To Kate, he explained, "We went with some friends to the river a few weeks ago. The current was stronger than she bargained for."

"She swallowed so much water she puked!" Mandy said. "It was gross. She—"

"That's enough, Amanda."

"But I didn't even get to tell how…" She wilted beneath the blistering force of her father's glare. "Okay, okay."

"Kate? Is that you?"

Kate turned to see Crystal Walsh. "Hey!" She hugged her friend. It was the only time she'd seen the brunette as an adult when she wasn't pregnant. "I take it everyone's feeling better?"

Crystal nodded. "It was just one of those twenty-four hour bugs, thank goodness. The weekend was pretty miserable, but we're all okay now. The kids were getting stir-crazy so I asked Mom to stay at the house with the little ones during naptime so I could run the older two to the pool." She gestured toward a group of kids shouting in the shallow end. "'Marco' belongs to me. One of the 'Polos,' too. I wasn't expecting to see…you."

The mischievous lilt in her tone and sparkle in her green eyes made it clear she wasn't necessarily surprised to run into Kate; after all, the two women had spent so much of their adolescent summers here Gram had teased them about growing gills. The surprise was that Kate was here with Cole.

Crystal peered past Kate, waggling her fingers in a small wave. "Afternoon, Sheriff."

"Nice to see you, Mrs. Walsh. We missed you on Sunday."

It wasn't until Kate turned to include Cole in the conversation that she realized he'd removed his T-shirt. He'd balled it up and was in the act of tossing it atop their other belongings. *Holy abs.* She'd noticed at the cookout that he had a well-muscled chest and forearms, but her imagination hadn't done him justice. Now that he was standing there, shirtless and tanned, she found herself relieved he already knew her friend. Because there was no way Kate could find her voice to make introductions. Her tongue was glued to the roof of her mouth. Her eyes felt frozen. She couldn't look away.

Blink, woman.

"Mom?" It took her son's voice to break through the trance. "Can we get in the water now?"

"That's probably a good idea," Cole said, as he checked to make sure Alyssa's water wings were secure. "In another ninety seconds, Mandy's going to start climbing me like a deranged chimpanzee." The little girl was already impatiently shifting her weight from leg to leg, her face screwed up in consternation.

"What's 'deranged'?" she asked.

Luke laughed. Although Kate couldn't hear his response as they headed toward the pool, Mandy's subsequent shriek of outrage carried. With the four of them out of earshot, Crystal slugged Kate in the arm, smirking her congratulations.

"Girl, you work fast! Two days ago you're asking for information about him, and now you're on a date? There are women in this town who've tried for years. Becca Johnston's gonna *hate* you," she said gleefully.

Oh, good. Because one of Kate's goals for her first week in Cupid's Bow was to antagonize the town's cross between Watermelon Queen and the Godfather. "It's not like…" She chewed the inside of her lip, trying to decide what to say. If she assured her friend that Becca Johnston was welcome to him, then she wasn't living up to her end of the bargain. Kate was supposed to be Cole's shield against soccer moms and predatory divorcees.

Finally, she shrugged. "He mentioned that he was taking his girls swimming. I'd wanted to bring Luke here to prove there was something he'd like about Cupid's Bow, and Cole was nice enough to invite us along."

Crystal's expression faded from impish to sympathetic. "Luke's not too excited about the move, huh? I've never lived anywhere but here and neither have my kids, but I imagine starting over must be tough." She reached out to squeeze Kate's hand. "I'm here if you ever need to talk. I actually called your Gram's house this morning to invite you to lunch this week, but there was no answer. Then one of the twins starting crying before I could leave a message."

"How about lunch this Saturday?" Kate asked. Luke would be busy with his version of community service, giving Kate a couple of hours to herself once she dropped him off at the hospital.

"Perfect. My husband will be home with the kids. If you want, I can check with my sisters and see if they're available? Reconnecting with old friends is bound to make the move easier."

"Sounds great, thanks. And there might be one other thing you can help me with," Kate said. "Could you mention to other moms you know that I'll be offering piano lessons soon? If anyone's looking for a teacher…"

"Will do." Her smile turned sly. "You know, it might help you drum up students if word gets out that you and the sheriff are an item. All the women in the area will be super curious about you."

"Oh, I don't think it's accurate to call us an 'item.' This is our first…date." The word was simultaneously awkward and exotic on her tongue, as if she were attempting to speak a foreign language.

"Yes, but it took you only two days to get this far! He didn't waste any time. And who can blame him? You look fantastic," she said, her reassurance easing the misgivings Kate had experienced since shrugging out of her bathing suit cover.

"So do you," Kate said.

"*Pfft*. What I look like is a woman who's had five kids." But she said it with the easy contentment of a woman who loved her life and was comfortable in her own skin. "Come to think of it, I should probably double-check that my kids aren't trying to drown each other. I'll call you about Saturday. Meanwhile, enjoy your…" Her words faded into nothingness as they both watched Cole hoist Mandy onto his shoulders. His biceps and chest flexed and rippled.

"Well." Crystal sighed. "Just enjoy."

Actually, Kate didn't *want* to spend the afternoon

enjoying her view. She and Cole had agreed it would be bad for their kids to get the idea that there was a real romance brewing. Staring adoringly at him would confuse the issue. If she talked long enough about the risks of sunburn, would he put his shirt on? Plenty of guys in the pool, including her son, wore swim shirts. Of course, if she hinted that she wanted Cole to wear a shirt, he might realize how much of a distraction she found his bare torso. That was a humiliating thought.

You are a mature woman. Get it together. She trudged into the water, annoyed with herself for acting as if she were the same teenage girl who used to hang out here with Crystal twenty years ago. *You'll be fine as long as you don't look directly at his arms.* Or shoulders. Or abs. Nothing below the neck. Except that still left his killer blue eyes.

Luke had been absorbed into the group game of Marco Polo. Encouraged to see him interacting with some kids in his approximate age range, she gave him his space, gravitating instead toward Cole and his girls. Cole was trying to convince Alyssa to give up her water-wings long enough to practice floating on her back.

"I'll be right there with you," he promised. "I won't let you sink."

"But…" Fear crowded her expression.

"Oh, stop being such a chicken!" Mandy scolded. "You've done it before."

"Amanda, why don't you sit out for a minute," Cole said, "and think about how *you'd* feel if someone taunted you for being afraid of something?"

Kate half expected the little spitfire to retort she wasn't scared of anything, but instead she paddled her way to the side of the pool. Cole turned to lift her onto the edge. At the top of his rib cage was a puckered circle, white against the rest of his sun-kissed skin, about the size of a half dollar. Kate sucked in her breath at the evidence of injury. Her pulse quickened. Had he been shot, too? Stabbed? Had—

"Kate, are you okay?" He came toward her, his usual stride hampered by the waist-deep water. "You're pale."

"You were hurt," she said, her voice raspy as unpleasant memories and emotions churned inside her. "On the job?"

To her surprise, he laughed. "Nothing like that. This scar dates back to childhood. Horrible toy box accident caused by my brother William." Understanding filled his eyes. "Was your husband… Hey, Luke? Can you come keep Alyssa company for a minute?"

Moments later, her son was cracking seahorse jokes with the little girl as Cole led Kate to some steps in the only shaded corner of the pool. The water was cooler here, and they had the illusion of privacy. Everyone else was frolicking in the sunlight.

"Why don't you sit down?" Cole suggested.

"I'm fine," she lied, feeling like a first-class moron. She'd nearly had an anxiety attack. And over what, a freaking *toy box injury*? She grated out a harsh laugh. "Thank God this is not a real date. Can you imagine what a date would be thinking about me right now?"

"That you were married to a man you loved deeply and that you're still understandably sensitive about his death. That is who you were thinking about, right? Your husband?"

She nodded, covering her face with her hands. "Damon. He was shot."

Cole sat on the step next to her, radiating compassion. Pity would have made her even more uncomfortable than she already was, but this felt different. He was just a solid, reassuring presence, ready to listen. Even though she hadn't planned to say more, words spilled out of her anyway.

"I was always so proud of his job," she said. "He took protecting and serving very seriously. Luke saw him as a hero. But ever since Damon died, I get jumpy around people in that line of work. I can't stop thinking about how dangerous the job can be. I know you're all carefully trained, but…"

"If it makes you feel any better, Cupid's Bow is pretty low-key. Most of the crimes I deal with are drunk trespassers cow-tipping or the occasional loon trying to spray-paint a proclamation of love on the town water tower."

Yeah, but who was to say those drunks weren't armed? And being sheriff was a complex, county position. Cupid's Bow was his home base, but his job took him into other communities. Still, she appreciated that Cole was trying to make her feel better.

She smiled weakly. "You forgot candy bar theft."

"Yeah, we're definitely cracking down on that. There's talk of putting together a task force," he teased.

She laughed, starting to feel like herself again. "The community pool is a weird place for emotional confessions. But you're…easy to talk to."

"It's not me, it's the badge. Most people are trained from a young age that they can trust law enforcement, depend on us in a crisis."

"I don't know about that. Besides, you aren't wearing your badge." She was suddenly reminded of how little either of them wore. The concrete step put them in close proximity; his bare arm rested ever so slightly against hers. Their legs were stretched out together, hers looking uncharacteristically delicate next to his darker skin and taut calves. If she tilted her head just a few inches to her left, it would be on his shoulder.

Her heartbeat accelerated again, but this time, it wasn't the irrational panic that had pounded through her when she saw his scar. Her body was reacting in a number of tiny ways, all of which felt confusing and wrong after discussing Damon's death.

She shot to her feet. "I'm keeping you from your girls."

"Kate, it's okay."

"I know Mandy's itching to try the high dive with you. Why don't you take her, and I'll keep working with Alyssa on her swimming?" she offered. "I was a pretty timid kid myself. Maybe I can get through to her."

At the moment, Kate felt a strong kinship with the little girl. Because if there was anything Kate understood with perfect clarity, it was the terror of suddenly finding yourself in over your head.

Chapter Five

In the end, Kate didn't think she could take the credit for drawing Alyssa out of her shell and helping her enjoy the water. Luke was a natural with the little girl, alternately goading her like a resolute personal trainer and making her giggle. After she'd had sufficient practice floating on her back, Luke coaxed her to jump in from the side of the pool. At first, he'd stayed in the water to catch her. As she gained confidence, the two of them began jumping in together. Alyssa, merrily oblivious to the physics of water displacement, seemed determined to eventually make the bigger splash.

She jumped into the air, tucked her knees against her chest and yelled, "Cannibal!"

Kate did a double take, then looked to her son for confirmation. "Did she say—"

"You just now noticed? It was so funny the first time I didn't correct her." Then he launched himself into the air. "Cannibal!"

If Kate hadn't noticed the mispronunciation sooner, it was because she'd been lost in melancholy what-ifs. Since she and Damon had both been only children, it had seemed natural for them to raise just one kid. Being a policeman was a noble calling, but it sure wasn't a fast track to riches. Ditto teaching at a public school. They'd thought that by having a single child, they'd be better able to afford luxuries like memorable family vacations. They'd talked about seeing Europe one day. Her eyes burned with unshed tears. There had been so many things they'd planned to do "someday."

Now, watching Luke with Alyssa, she realized her son might have made an excellent big brother. Though he'd never specifically voiced a wish for a younger sibling, had he subconsciously wanted one? Kate had spent a lot of time during the past year thinking about his need for a role model. Maybe it would be equally beneficial for keeping him out of trouble to *be* a role model.

He bobbed to the surface of the water. "Know what we haven't tried yet, Aly?"

"Aly?" the girl echoed.

"Yeah. Short for Alyssa," he explained. "Like how everyone calls Amanda 'Mandy.' Aly can be your nickname."

"Oh." Her eyes widened. "Miss Kate, I have a nickname!"

"Anyway," Luke said, not sharing her fascination with the topic, "we haven't done the slide yet. Wanna go?"

Actually, Kate thought the little girl was starting to look tuckered out from trying to keep up with a thirteen-year-old boy. "I have an idea," she countered, "why don't we go to the concession stand first and get some slushies? Then you can reapply sunscreen and hit the slide."

Once they'd agreed on that plan, Luke jogged down toward the deep end to see if Cole and Mandy wanted to join them for a snack break. Alyssa scowled as she watched him go.

"Daddy and Mandy are probably having a lot of fun," she said, wrapping a giant pink princess towel around herself.

"I thought you were having fun, too."

"Yeah. But…" She stared at the ground. "Mandy always calls me a chicken. Like when Daddy makes us go camping. I get scared of the bugs. And camping is dirty. And when we camp at the lake, we hafta fish, too. Do you *know* how gross fish guts are? It's like the high dive."

Kate tried to puzzle through that comparison. "The high dive is gross?"

Alyssa shrugged. "How would I know? I'm too scared to go up there. Maybe Mandy's right. I am a ch—"

"Aren't you in ballet?" Kate took her hand, leading her toward the winding line in front of the concession stand. "Your nana mentioned your recital last month."

Alyssa nodded happily. "I wish ballet class was in the summer, too. I like to dance."

"And your recital was in front of an audience, right?"

"On a real stage at the big kid high school! There were really bright lights and costumes."

"Have you ever heard the term *stage fright*?" Kate asked. When Alyssa looked at her blankly, Kate explained, "Plenty of people are terrified to perform in front of an audience. The idea of doing a play or dancing or singing in a choir makes them feel like they might throw up. You don't sound like you were scared."

"Why would I be? Dancing is *fun*. Not like mosqui-tos or getting water up my nose."

"Good points. But the fact that you can get up in front of people without being nervous makes you a very special kind of brave," Kate told her. "You are not a chicken. Besides, it's normal to be afraid of some things. No matter how tough a person acts, everyone has fears. Including your sister."

"What about grown-ups?" Alyssa asked. "Do you ever get scared?"

Oh, kid, if you only knew. "Lots of things frighten me."

"You think even my dad gets scared?"

Probably every time he crossed paths with the in-famous Becca Johnston. "I'm sure he does. Ask him about it sometime. Just remember, even though you're afraid of some things, you have courage, too."

"Thank you, Miss Kate." She repositioned her towel so that it was more like a cape and twirled in a circle, whooping, "Make way for Aly the Brave!"

"Wow." COLE WAS genuinely impressed as he joined Kate in line. "What kind of magic did you work on my daughter, and can you teach me your mystical ways?"

When he'd left Alyssa, her lower lip had been trem-bling over the possibility of floundering in the water. Now, she was spinning and shouting declarations of bravery. Mandy had joined her in the grass off to the side of the concession stand, arms outstretched as they whirled in giggly circles. Cole felt dizzy just watching his blonde mini-tornadoes.

Kate smiled. "Alyssa and I had a chat about the

different ways to be brave. I think she's feeling better now."

"Thank you. Mandy and I chatted, too. About calling people chicken and the consequences she can expect next time it happens." After setting his daughter straight about teasing, he'd planned to follow her off the high dive a few times, then come back to check on Alyssa's progress. But he'd let Mandy cajole him into "just five more minutes." Repeatedly.

She'd been having so much fun, and it was good exercise. *Plus, you were avoiding Kate.* Truthfully, he wasn't sure Kate had wanted his company after telling him about Damon's shooting. On the rare occasions he got choked up over something, he preferred to be left alone.

That wasn't the only reason he'd given her space, though. After she'd confided in him, he'd had an overpowering urge to take her in his arms. It was a completely inappropriate impulse, and he'd stayed away until it passed.

He'd expected going through the motions of a date to be more cut and dry. Mastering a degree of detachment was necessary for anyone in law enforcement. On the few real dates he'd been on in recent years, he'd never responded so strongly to anyone—emotionally or physically.

Of course, very few of his dates had included being half naked, either. At the moment, Kate had her arms folded across her chest, and he deserved a freaking medal for not staring at her cleavage.

It took every ounce of his discipline to keep his gaze trained on her face. Did she know how mesmerizing her eyes were? They were kaleidoscopes of color, with flecks of gold that reminded him of history class and the brief Texas Gold Rush. It had never amounted to much, but looking into her eyes made him empathize with the miners who'd temporarily lost their heads, beguiled by temptation.

"Where's Luke?" she asked, rescuing him from his fanciful thoughts.

"Oh, he said he'd catch up." Cole pointed to where the boy stood a few yards away, talking to a girl with a towel around her shoulders. "Um…did he happen to mention any drug references to Alyssa? Maybe jokingly? One of the locals informed me that my daughter was yelling 'cannabis.'"

"What? No, he misheard," Kate assured him. "She was yelling 'cannibals.'"

He blinked, not sure how to process that.

"So Luke's talking to someone around his own age?" She craned her neck, doing a credible job of trying to peek without looking as if she were watching.

Cole nodded. "Apparently the girl's beach towel bears the logo of some 'sick' video game. That's good, right? Luke commented on it, and suddenly the conversation became boss battles and cheat codes and a bunch of acronyms I couldn't decipher. I thought that, since he's still in our line of sight, it would be okay to leave him there. Do you mind?"

"Not at all. I'm relieved. School in August will be a lot easier if he meets other kids first. She looks about his age. Know who she is?"

"Arnold Pemberton's daughter. He's a trucker, and his wife's a nurse at the county hospital. I'm pretty sure the girl's name is… Sarah?" He glanced over his shoulder, hoping it would jog his memory. She was leaning toward Luke, who was a head shorter than she was, and laughing delightedly at whatever he'd said. "I'm also pretty sure she's flirting with your son."

"You think?" Judging by Kate's startled expression, girls had not been a big part of Luke's life thus far.

"Well, you're a woman—you tell me. What are the signs when a girl likes a guy?"

"I, uh…" Twin spots of color bloomed in her cheeks. "Oh, hey, it's our turn to order!"

Huh. Cole couldn't help thinking that, in his experience, stammering and blushing were *also* signs of liking someone. Or had his perspective—and ego—become skewed after months of Becca Johnston and other local women pursuing him? Kate was difficult to read. She was still deeply affected by her husband's death and had said more than once that she wasn't interested in dating.

Yet, at times he could swear the magnetic draw he felt was mutual. *Or maybe her flustered response was because you embarrassed her by putting her on the spot.* Maybe.

Regardless, as he placed his order, he found himself grinning with a lot more enthusiasm than an orange slushie warranted.

STARING THROUGH THE windshield on Saturday morning, Luke was no more impressed with the scenery than he had been when they arrived a week ago. It was so *flat* here. And rural. Still, despite the uninspiring landscape, he had to admit the last few days hadn't been all bad.

His mom had taken him to the pool twice, and he and Sarah Pemberton had exchanged usernames.

They'd spent a couple of hours Thursday in PVP mode, then gone on a campaign yesterday before the lag time got too problematic. Gram did not have the fastest internet connection in the universe.

His mom seemed to have a decent week, too. After the piano tuner had come on Wednesday, she'd spent a lot of time practicing. He'd heard her in the room they were now calling the "music study" singing along with the piano notes. It wasn't until he'd listened to her that he realized how rarely she did that anymore. She used to sing all the time, sometimes just under her breath while she cooked, other times really belting out songs, especially in the car. Half the stuff she liked was from before he was born, and he mocked her about being old. Secretly, he liked some of it. Bon Jovi wasn't bad.

Right now, they were listening to one of his Mom's playlists, but she wasn't singing or humming. Even with the music, it was too quiet in the car. He felt like she wanted him to say something. Would it make her happy if he admitted Cupid's Bow didn't suck as much as he'd expected?

"Are you nervous about today?" she asked.

He shrugged. "I dunno." He hadn't thought about it much. Helping Mr. Jacobs entertain sick kids was his punishment for giving Aly that candy bar. Luke supposed he deserved it, but the situation was weird. Adults said all the time not to talk to strangers, now his mom was dropping him off to spend half the day with one.

"Cole... Sheriff Trent," she corrected, "assured me that Mr. Jacobs is a good guy who's done lots of things in the community. Sponsors youth sports, played Santa Claus one year at the Christmas tree lighting."

Luke snickered at that, remembering the man's tattoos. An inked Santa?

"Anyway, if you have questions about what he needs you to do, don't be afraid to ask him."

He rolled his eyes. "I'm not scared of him, Mom."

"Good. And you'll have your phone on you at all times. Call me or text me if—"

"I know how to use the phone, Mom."

Her sigh made him feel ashamed, but seriously, did she have to talk to him like he was Aly and Mandy's age?

"How much farther?" he asked.

"About ten minutes."

"Can I get online when we go back to the farm? Sarah said she might be around." Even though she was a grade behind him, it would be cool to know someone at the middle school. She also had a brother in the high school who played football for the Cupid's Bow Archers. Stupidest mascot ever.

"Whether you get to play depends on how you behave for Mr. Jacobs and what Gram's doing this afternoon. It is her TV, you know." She paused, slanting him a glance. "Sarah seems nice."

"Yeah. She's okay."

"Just okay?"

He squirmed in his seat. He knew what his mom was asking, but he doubted Sarah would look at him like *that*. For one thing, he was too short. And his hair was starting to look ridiculous, long enough to hang in his eyes. "Can I get a haircut soon?"

"Sure. We can look for a place in town tomorrow, or you can go with me on Monday to Turtle."

He'd heard Gram and his mom talk about how there

wasn't really a music store in Cupid's Bow. But else-where in the county, where they had an award-winning high school band, there was a decent-size store where Mom could get sheet music and a metronome and other stuff she wanted for teaching. He didn't know what dumbass had named the towns around here, but he couldn't imagine going to a football game between the Cupid's Bow Archers and the Fighting Turtles. Sheesh.

Hoping to discourage his mom from asking more about Sarah, he turned up the speaker volume. "Isn't this one of your favorites?" he asked.

She snorted. "Subtle, kid." But she stopped bad-gering him.

At the hospital, they followed signs to volunteer parking. Luke couldn't remember ever being in a hos-pital. He knew his mom had gone to one after his dad's shooting, but it had been too late by then to say good-bye.

His father hadn't survived the ambulance ride. Luke had asked his mom once if she thought Dad had been scared. She'd said he probably wasn't conscious for much of it; she tried to make it sound peaceful, like he'd simply drifted off, without pain or panic, and never awakened. But that image had terrified Luke. For months after his father's death, he'd been scared to sleep, irrationally afraid he might not wake up in the morning.

The trouble at school began when he started fall-ing asleep in classes, then irritably swore at one of his teachers. He'd met Bobby in detention hall. Talking to Sarah was a little like talking to Bobby because neither of them asked about his father. Bobby hadn't cared, and Sarah didn't know. Maybe Luke could make new friends here who didn't treat him like he was freaking delicate, didn't make him feel weak.

For the first time, he thought this move might work out okay. Even if the school mascots were ragingly lame.

He and his mom took an elevator from the parking garage to a main lobby, then followed a mazelike series of corridors to the pediatric ward. He found the murals of bright blue birdies and pastel pink bunnies a little insulting. No matter what you drew on the walls, it didn't change the fact that people were sick.

He started to worry that Mr. Jacobs might be going for some kind of cartoony image, too. What if he dressed like a clown to cheer kids up, or wore a top hat and glittery cape for his magic show? Worse, would he expect Luke to wear some silly costume? But Mr. Jacobs, who stood chatting with a nurse in the hallway, was dressed pretty much the same way he had been last time Luke saw him—black shirt, black jeans, boots. He looked like a man you'd see smashing a beer bottle over someone's head in a bar brawl; instead he was accepting a lollipop from a woman in Sesame Street scrubs.

Mr. Jacobs walked toward them with a grin. "Well, if it isn't my assistant for the day, Sticky Fingers."

Luke felt a blush climb his face, but at least the man didn't sound angry.

"Nice to see you again, Mrs. Sullivan. Are you still comfortable leaving Luke here with us, or do you want to stay for the shows? We have different performances for the younger kids and the older crowd. Splitting them up makes it easier to fit everyone in the room, too."

His mom hesitated as she considered the offer, and

Luke worried she might decide to stick around. With school being out for the summer, he saw her all day long, every day. He needed breathing room.

Luckily, she shook her head. "Thanks, but I have plans to meet a couple of friends for lunch. I'll be back at two. Luke knows how to reach me if you need me sooner. Be good, okay?" She reached out and ruffled his hair.

That settled it, he was *definitely* getting a haircut.

"Thank you for giving him this opportunity, Mr. Jacobs," she said. "It might be good for him."

"Both of you call me Rick, please. I have to admit, as far as assistants, I'm partial to Nurse Amy, the cutie who's helped me before. But she has more important duties. Maybe if this works out, Luke can come back next month, too."

Give up another Saturday when he hadn't even done anything wrong? Then again, at least the hospital was air-conditioned. Luke had decided while doing chores this week that it must be a thousand degrees at the farm. His mom gave him a quick hug goodbye, and Luke couldn't help grimacing at the display of affection.

"The thing about mothers," Rick said as she walked away, "is that they may cramp our style, but they love us more than anyone else ever will. I left home at seventeen, thinking I was too badass to need my mama, but I cried like a little bitty baby when she died two years later. Appreciate yours while you have her."

The thought that anything could ever happen to her caused an icy hand to clutch Luke's heart. He couldn't lose another parent. "Yes, sir."

"Come on, my stuff's in the big room at the end of

the hall and I need help setting up. I might even have time to teach you a couple of card tricks before we get started. At the very least," he drawled, "I can teach you enough sleight of hand that you'll be too suave to get caught boosting candy bars."

"That is never going to happen again," Luke said. "The stealing, I mean."

"Good. Maybe there's hope for you yet, Sticky Fingers."

"I SHOULD NEVER have let her join us for lunch." Crystal leaned across the table, complaining good-naturedly to Kate. "My little sister's life is so exciting that the rest of us seem dull in comparison."

Looking at Jasmine Tucker, known to friends and family as Jazz, Kate had no trouble believing the woman had been a model. All the Tucker girls were pretty, but Jazz was downright arresting. Her auburn hair was cut in an asymmetrical bob, highlighting elegant cheekbones and bright green eyes.

Jazz laughed dismissively. "Dull? With five kids? Please. They're always doing something to keep you on your toes."

"True," Crystal agreed. "How I'd love to get through the rest of the summer without a single trip to the ER."

"Besides," Jazz added, "life in New York wasn't nearly as glamorous as it sounds. There was a lot of getting up at four a.m. and waiting around. And rejection. And living in cramped quarters with roommates so we could afford rent. I'm happy to be home." She reached for the last piece of corn bread in the basket at the center of the table. "And, damn, I missed the food."

"Food's not the only thing you like about being back

in Cupid's Bow," Crystal said knowingly. "And I don't think reuniting with your sisters is why you're always grinning these days, either." Their other sister, Susan, worked for the county school district; Crystal had told Kate the two women should discuss teaching jobs, but Susan hadn't been able to join them today.

Kate couldn't help smiling at Jazz's obvious bliss. "I hear you and Brody Davenport are pretty much inseparable."

"It's bizarre because, on the surface, we have nothing in common." Jazz stirred her straw around in her sweet tea. "I'm obsessed with fashion and getting the boutique off its feet, and he's busy with his family's ranch. We have totally different interests and temperaments, but…" Considering how her eyes glowed when she talked about him, finishing her sentence wasn't necessary. "You know, I asked him out once, when we were in high school, and he shot me down."

"Which he has spent plenty of time trying to make up to you since," Crystal said.

Jazz smile was pure satisfaction. "Oh, yes he has. What about you, Kate? I hear you're seeing someone new. A certain local sheriff?"

Actually, she hadn't seen him since their afternoon at the pool, although they'd spoken on the phone. He'd called about piano lessons. Alyssa was hinting that she was interested, but Cole wasn't sure whether the sudden desire stemmed from an earnest appreciation for music or growing affection for Kate.

"You made quite an impression," he'd said. "She'll be heartbroken if you and Luke don't come to the girls' birthday party."

"I'll put it on our calendar," Kate had promised.

That had earned a chuckle and the explanation that he still hadn't figured out when or where the party would be, although their birthday was rapidly approaching.

"Ladies," Crystal sat back in her chair, beaming. "We have done very well for ourselves! Me, happily married to the guy I've loved since high school, Jazz practically living at the ranch with her hot cowboy, and now Kate is with dreamy Sheriff Trent!"

Kate was amused by her friend's enthusiasm, but quick to add, "We've only been on one date." The unfamiliar word was getting easier to say. "That's not exactly in the same league as—"

"Well, hey there, Crystal." A strawberry blonde who towered at near-Amazonian height stopped by their table. She nodded to each woman in turn. "Jasmine. And… I don't believe we've met?" She extended a hand to Kate, her nails painted the same frosted pink as her lipstick. "Becca Johnston."

Gulp. Kate shook her hand. "Kate Sullivan. Just moved to town. My son and I live with my grandmother out by Whippoorwill Creek."

"Would that be Joan Denby? Lovely woman. She's on my committee for the Watermelon Festival. I wish she'd brought you to the meeting this week. I can always use an extra pair of hands."

It was difficult to tell from her toothy smile whether this was an overture of friendship or an obscure threat to chop off Kate's hands.

"Kate's been pretty busy," Crystal said loyally. "Unpacking, getting reacquainted with the town, preparing to offer piano lessons."

"Are you? My Marc-Paul has a natural aptitude for music," Becca said. "Do you have a card?"

"Uh…no." Maybe she should put that on her to-do list. "Like Crystal said, I'm still in the early preparation stages." Becca didn't need to know that Cole was bringing Alyssa over Monday evening for a trial lesson.

"Best of luck," Becca told her. "I'll just have to keep tabs on Joan so I know when you're ready to take students. I have to dash, but it was nice to see you ladies. Crystal, you'll be at the parade meeting tomorrow?"

"With bells on."

No one at the table said anything as Becca exited the restaurant, catching up to the rest of her party.

"Is it just me," Jazz finally said, "or when she said she'd 'keep tabs on Joan', did anyone else picture her hiding out in the bushes, watching the house through pink binoculars?"

"She does seem a little…intense," Kate said. "But hospitable." After all, she'd encouraged Kate to get involved and had all but signed up her son for lessons. Kate needed students, and she needed word of mouth in the community. She suspected Becca Johnston could provide plenty of that.

"Not just intense, think the word you're looking for is *eerie*," Crystal said. "Downright eerie. We no sooner mentioned the sheriff and, *whoosh*, she materialized out of nowhere."

Jazz laughed. "She and her friends were seated in the other room and on their way out when she heard you mention Cole. You *were* being kind of loud."

"Comes from living in a house with five kids," Crystal said. "A person learns to speak up if she wants to be heard over the chaos."

The two sisters were still good-naturedly heckling each other when the waitress brought the bill. Crystal insisted on paying, to celebrate two of her favorite people being back in town.

"Do you have time to come by the boutique?" Jazz asked Kate as they rose from their seats. "I'd love for you to see it. And, you know, buy stuff."

Kate grinned. "Sounds fun, but by the time I got there, I'd only have a few minutes before I had to head back to the hospital to pick up Luke." She hoped his afternoon had gone well. She'd wanted to text him and ask for an update but after how prickly he'd become in the car, she'd received the message. No hovering.

It was difficult to know how much space to give a kid, especially one with a checkered past. It would be irresponsible parenting not to monitor him some, but she also had to give him room to be independent, to build trust.

There wasn't parking in front of the shops and restaurants lining Main Street. Instead, there were two lots at either end. The Tucker sisters had parked down by the pharmacy, while Kate's car was in the other direction, past the only bookstore in town.

She waved goodbye to them on the sidewalk. "Jazz, I swear I'll come by the store soon. And Crystal, I'll call you about getting the boys together." Her friend's oldest child was a girl, but she also had an eleven-year-old son. They'd talked about taking him and Luke bowling or horseback riding at Brody's ranch. Jazz had chimed in that Brody was an only child and, like Kate, he occasionally found it lonely. He'd bonded quickly with Jazz's nieces and nephews and claimed to love having kids around to liven up the ranch.

"As long," Jazz had qualified impishly, "as we can return them to their proper owners afterward."

After parting ways with her friends, Kate tried to stay under the shade of store awnings as she made her way down the equivalent of a few blocks. The town's movie theater dominated the center of the street, across from the bank. She was looking around, taking note of minor changes and marveling at how much had remained the same when she realized there was a man standing on the sidewalk in front of her. A uniformed man who'd yet to notice her because he was scowling at a window display.

"Cole?" It was the first time she'd seen him dressed in his khaki sheriff's uniform, and it made his profession that much more real. He was no longer just the doting father who'd kicked a soccer ball in Gram's front yard or the dad who'd given his daughters piggyback rides in the pool. This man oversaw everything from traffic violations to local manhunts to security at the county courthouse. He exuded power and authority.

"Hey." His lips curved in a smile so welcoming it sent a shiver dancing up her spine. When was the last time anyone had looked that happy to see her?

Well, Gram was always thrilled when Kate showed up, but there was a decidedly wolfish quality to Cole's grin that Gram didn't have.

"You're a sight for sore eyes," he told her.

"Thank you. And you look…very official." His badge glinted in the sun, and the dark green tie he wore was a classy touch. Aware that her physical perusal was lasting a beat too long to be casual, she turned to see what he'd been looking at with such exasperation.

They were in front of the toy store. On the other

side of the glass, rows and rows of dolls stared back at them, from baby dolls whose boxes were captioned with promises to "spit up, just like a real infant!" to fashion dolls whose separately sold wardrobes and accessories probably added up to one of Kate's car payments.

"Is it just me," Cole said out the side of his mouth, "or do their eyes follow you wherever you move?" He rocked from one side to the other, keeping a wary gaze on the dolls. "Why would a girl ever want one of those things?"

"Ah. Birthday shopping?" she guessed.

"More like preshopping investigation. I'm on my lunch break. I grabbed a sandwich at the deli and decided to stroll through town, do a little window-shopping for inspiration." He sighed. "Mandy's easy to buy for. I got her a pair of rainbow-striped shin guards, a fishing rod that's a miniature version of mine and the next two books in a series she likes about a crime-fighting panda. Alyssa…I don't know. At first, a doll seemed like a good idea, but I'm not sure if I could sleep with one of those things in my house."

Kate smirked. "I promised your daughter that even her big, strong dad was afraid of something. I just didn't realize it would be baby dolls. But I have to admit, they freaked me out a bit when I was a kid." Something about the plastic faces that were so human and inhuman at the same time. "How about a stuffed animal instead? More cuddly, less creepy."

"That's smart. I mean, she already has a bunch, but she seems to love them all. I can find her a cute teddy bear. And the sporting goods store had a pink fishing pole that—"

"You do know she hates fishing?" she interrupted, imagining the disappointed expression on Alyssa's face when she opened that gift.

"Alyssa? No, she doesn't. We fish every time we go camping, and—"

"Oh, boy." Apparently, the girl who'd had no trouble opening up to Kate hadn't confided her true feelings about either activity to her dad. Had he really not noticed her lack of enthusiasm? "Cole, I don't think she likes to camp, either."

"What?" He rocked back on his heels, his forehead puckering. "Are you sure you aren't taking some remark out of context? This is the same girl who cries cannibal instead of cannonball, so you have to take what she says with a grain of salt."

"This was pretty clear cut. I hate to break it to you, but she talked about how she doesn't like camping because it's dirty and there are bugs. And because you make her go fishing."

"*Make* her? But the girls... They've always been excited about our trips."

Both of them? Kate didn't think so. She recalled Alyssa's pinched expression when she'd commented that her dad and Mandy were probably having a lot of fun in the deep end. Without her.

Kate took a deep breath. "You and I haven't known each other long, and I don't want to overstep or sound like I'm criticizing..." Especially since her only child was currently working off his candy-bar debt to the business owner he'd robbed. What the hell did she know about perfect parenting?

Cole surprised her with a sunny smile. "Whatever it is, you don't have to worry about hurting my feelings. Years with my mother have given me a thick hide when it comes to surviving unsolicited advice. Besides—" he reached down to squeeze her hand "—I trust your opinion."

He did? She glanced down, watching the slide of his fingers across hers as he dropped his arm back to his side. For a moment, she couldn't recall what she'd intended to say.

"Goodness gracious." A feminine voice trilled from across the street. "We just keep running into each other today!"

Kate glanced over to see Becca Johnston and her two friends emerging from the flower shop. Becca marched across the street, not bothering to check for traffic. Granted, with Main Street being a mostly pedestrian area, there were rarely cars. But there was something about the commanding woman that suggested she could halt oncoming vehicles using only the power of her mind.

At Becca's approach, Cole stiffened. Without thinking, Kate reached for his hand, meaning to repay the brief gesture of encouragement he'd given her a moment ago. But Cole not only laced his fingers through hers, he used their shared grasp to tug her even closer, pulling her against him. He rubbed his thumb over Kate's surprisingly sensitive palm, and her breath caught. That shouldn't feel so good. Or so personal, like an activity unfit for a public street.

"Sheriff Trent." Becca's eyes narrowed as she stared at their joined hands, "I'm so glad to see you. The festival committee hopes to recruit you for a fun volunteer opportunity. We have an idea that will not only be an exciting addition to the last day of the festival, it will help raise money for an important cause."

"Thanks for thinking of me," Cole said, his cordial tone threaded with trepidation. Kate mentally added "festival committee" to his list of fears, right under "dolls who follow you with their glass eyes."

He cleared his throat. "But as I said last year, when I got asked to man the kissing booth, I really need to stay available for crowd control and security."

Kissing booth? Kate bit the inside of her cheek to keep from laughing. She could just imagine the long line for a shot at the sheriff's lips.

"Ugh." Becca wrinkled her nose. "Kissing booths are unsanitary. We will not be doing that on my watch. What I have in mind would only pull you out of the crowd for a few minutes on Saturday, then you could get right back to work."

Becca's friends had joined her on the sidewalk and were both bobbing their heads in supportive agreement. "Becca's thought of everything," one of them chirped.

Undoubtedly.

"You know how on the Saturday of the festival we've traditionally sold grilled hamburgers and hot dogs, with the proceeds going to the fireman's fund?" Becca asked. "I know how to drive that amount even higher."

Gram had mentioned that one of Cole's brothers was a firefighter. Whatever favor Becca planned to ask, she wasn't making it easy for him refuse.

"This year, I'm thinking…" She paused dramatically. "Bachelor auction! We'll call it Heroes and Hamburgers. While people are sitting down to lunch, we'll auction off dates—to be scheduled for a later time—with local heroes like firefighters and policemen. The committee brainstormed almost a dozen candidates. Deputy Thomas is single and your brother William. And of course there's *you*." She smiled expectantly.

"Oh, I, uh…" If Cole pulled Kate any closer, she would be inside his uniform with him. Lord, he smelled good. "There are different degrees of being single," he hedged.

Kate shifted, resting her head on his shoulder—both to lend credence to their implied relationship and because she simply couldn't resist the opportunity. Unlike when she'd felt unnerved by his closeness in Gram's shed, there was no risk here. Under the guise of his "human shield," she was free to indulge any reckless impulses she would otherwise suppress.

Becca's smile had become a tight mask. It looked so inflexible Kate was surprised the woman could still form words. "So you two *are* dating? Kate can bid on you. The more people who participate, the more money we raise."

Oh, yeah, Kate could bid—assuming the First Bank of Cupid's Bow offered bachelor auction loans. If not, she had a feeling she knew exactly who would win a date with Cole.

"Besides," Becca added in a silky tone, "even if some other woman does land you for an evening, I'm sure Kate understands that it's for a good cause. She and I were just talking in the Smoky Pig about how she could help with the festival."

Cole's gaze swung to meet hers. "You were?" His surprise was lined with betrayal, as if he'd caught her fraternizing with the enemy.

"It came up in a roundabout way," Kate admitted, feeling guilty that she hadn't warned him Becca was in the vicinity. She decided to make it up to him by rescuing him from this conversation. Straightening, she flashed a broad smile at the other woman. "Tell you what, give me a few days to warm him up to this auction idea, and we'll get back to you. Now, if you ladies will excuse us, Cole was just walking me to my car. I'm afraid I'm running late."

Cole seized the opportunity for escape. As the three women called their farewells, his long-legged stride took the sidewalk whole squares at a time. He held Kate's hand all the way down the street, not letting go until they'd rounded the corner into the public parking lot. Then he swept her into his arms for an exuberant hug.

"Well played!" Admiration danced in his blue eyes like sunlight on ocean waves. "Advice on Alyssa's birthday gift *and* you helped convince Becca I'm off the market? I could kiss you."

She inhaled sharply, but it didn't seem to put any air in her lungs. "It's, ah, probably best if you don't." She started to take a step backward, but there was a car in her way.

"Oh, I don't know." His voice dropped lower. "Becca's got spies everywhere."

"Cole, I…" Her voice was husky, unfamiliar. Though he was no longer touching her, he stood so damned close her thoughts were short-circuiting. Could she allow herself to kiss him in the name of convincing Becca he was taken? A flimsy excuse, at best, but so tempting. She swallowed. "I have to go."

"Can I call you later? We didn't finish our conversation."

The one where she'd been pointing out potential mistakes he was making as a parent? It was so flattering to know he valued her opinion. Exhilarating, even. To hell with the jittery butterflies in her stomach. Hadn't she recently given a lecture on bravery? Maybe it was time Kate reclaimed some of her own.

She lifted up on her toes, pressing a quick kiss against his lips. It was a peck, nothing more, but effervescent giddiness fizzed through her. She'd surprised herself—and she could tell from his sudden, absolute stillness that she'd shocked him.

"Just in case any of Becca's spies are watching," she murmured.

"Right."

"So… I'll be waiting for that call. You have Gram's number. Now, I really, really have to go. I'm not even sure it's mathematically possible to get to the hospital on time. Not while obeying the speed limit, anyway."

Cole's gaze captured hers, his grin wicked. "On the record, I would never condone a traffic violation. Off the record? If anyone has a shot at talking her way out of a ticket today, it's you."

She grinned in return, twirling her key ring around her fingers. As she climbed into her car, she thought it might be worth speeding if the result was Cole chasing after her. *Yeah, but what then, genius?* Everything she'd told him about needing to focus on Luke, about her hyperawareness of the dangers of a policeman's job, still held true.

Hypothetically, being chased might be fun. But in reality, she wasn't ready to be caught.

Chapter Six

It was like something out of a pod-person science fiction film. Except, Kate mused as she handed the salad dressing across the table to Gram, she was pretty fond of the alien who'd replaced her son. Ever since she'd picked him up at the hospital, Luke had been uncharacteristically animated. Rick Jacobs was getting a thankyou note in the near future, accompanied by a plate of brownies.

Luke had played video games before dinner, and Kate overheard him telling Sarah through his headset all about the kids he'd met today and about the motorcycle Rick was rebuilding and how the two of them were already brainstorming ways to improve on the entertainment for next month. After dinner, Luke eagerly helped load the dishwasher and waved Kate and Gram into the living room so he could perform a few magic tricks he'd learned.

Gram was impressed. She clapped her hands, then turned to Kate next to her on the couch. "Either your son is a natural illusionist, or my eyesight's going a lot faster than I thought."

Kate laughed. "No, he nailed it. Good job, kiddo.

Maybe the middle school here has an annual talent show."

"School talent shows? Lame, Mom." But he grinned as he said it.

The three of them spent a rather enjoyable evening together, watching a competitive reality show and exchanging comments on their favorite singers. The entertaining color commentary from Luke and Gram was almost enough to distract Kate from the phone that wasn't ringing. When Cole had mentioned calling, had he meant tonight or a more generic "later"? Maybe he was too busy. Or he'd forgotten.

During a commercial, Kate realized Gram was nodding off. Kate gently shook her awake. "How about we get you to bed? You'll be a lot more comfortable there."

"True." Gram gave her a sleepy smile. "Guess I can't stay up as late as you young people anymore. Goodnight, Katie." She blew Luke a kiss, then shuffled down the hallway.

Luke rose from the chair he'd been sprawled in, pulling the ever-present earbuds from the pocket of his shorts. "I'm going to watch some YouTube videos in bed, okay?"

"Only the channels and vloggers we've already agreed on," she reminded him.

"I know, Mom."

"I love you," she called after him.

He smiled over his shoulder. "I know that, too."

Alone in the room, she switched off the television and the lamp. There was a full moon tonight. So much light spilled through the windows that she had no trouble seeing where she was going. She went to her room and pulled on a soft purple nightshirt that fell to her knees, then padded barefoot to the kitchen, telling herself she was going for a glass of water. But she was peering into the freezer and weighing ice cream options when the phone rang, making her jump.

"H-hello?"

"Did I wake you?" Cole's tone was contrite.

"Not at all." A silly grin stretched across her face, and she closed the freezer door. "Luke and I just turned off the TV a few minutes ago."

"I meant to call earlier, but it turned out to be a pretty active Saturday night. What is it about a full moon that makes people more rambunctious? I just dropped off a drunken nineteen-year-old with his extremely angry parents, down the road from your Gram's place." He paused. "Any chance you want to talk in person?"

"Yes." Anticipation thudded in her veins. "But Gram's already turned in for the night. I'll meet you on the front porch."

"See you in a minute."

Should she change back into her clothes, or just throw on a robe? She wasn't wearing any makeup, but it was dark out, so she brushed that thought aside. She slid on her music note slippers and belted a black robe around her waist. Then she flipped her head over and brushed her hair, fluffing it into shiny waves that fell against her shoulders.

She was just pulling two cold beers left over from Gram's cookout from the fridge when a pair of headlights illuminated the front half of the house. She tossed a rawhide bone to Patch to keep the dog busy instead of whining at the front door to join them. Then she stepped outside, hoping Luke didn't emerge from his room to catch her flirting with a man in her pajamas.

Watching Cole unfold himself from the driver seat highlighted how tall he was. Tonight, he wore his hat with his uniform. He looked very official. And very masculine.

She waited for him on the top step, holding out one frosty beer. It was a nice counterpoint to the heat that lingered long after sundown. "You're off duty now, right?"

"Yes. And thank you."

Aside from a small wrought-iron table, there were only two pieces of furniture on the porch—the padded bench swing and Gram's rocker in the far corner, where she liked to sip her morning coffee and watch the sun rise. Kate wasn't ready yet to sit in the swing with him; the proximity might cause her to forget the things she'd meant to say. Instead, she took a moment to gather her thoughts, sipping her beer and studying the breathtaking sky. So many twinkling stars were crowded together that it seemed impossible to pick out individual constellations.

"Wow." She leaned her head against the railing, marveling at the sight. She'd have to bring Luke out here some evening. "Living in the city, I forgot how beautiful this was. We didn't have stars like this in Houston."

"Actually," Cole teased, "I think the stars are the same no matter where you are. It's where you are that gives you a different perspective."

That was true of a lot more than stars. If she were someone other than Officer Damon Sullivan's widow, she would feel completely different about standing here in the dark with the all too appealing sheriff. She might not be staring at the sky in an attempt to keep platonic distance between them. If she were Becca or one of the other women from town... A giggle escaped her.

"Something funny?" Cole asked.

"Sorry. I was thinking about Becca. She'd probably kill to be in my fuzzy slippers right now."

"I am very glad it's you here with me."

She was glad, too. She just couldn't bring herself to say it.

"So." He cleared his throat. "Before Becca accosted us today, we were discussing my daughter. There was more you wanted to say?"

"Obviously, I don't know you and your girls very well." It was weird to think she'd only met them a week ago. They already felt like an important part of her life in Cupid's Bow. "So maybe I'm off base, but sometimes outsiders have a clearer view of a situation. When we were at the pool, I got the impression Alyssa feels really left out. I think she hasn't mentioned how much she dislikes camping or fishing because she's trying hard to fit in with you and Mandy."

It had taken Kate a while to translate the girl's statement that fish guts were comparable to the high dive; they were things Cole and Mandy had in common that Alyssa did not.

"Damn," he said under his breath. "I know the girls have different interests, but I had no idea camping made her miserable. I wish she'd felt comfortable talking to me...or that I'd been more observant." He gave a bark of self-deprecating laughter. "I'm supposed to be skilled at catching clues and reading people! I wish I knew how to bond with her. Soccer and fishing are easy, but I don't think they have father-daughter ballet classes in town.

"Besides," he added, "the sight of me in a tutu? She'd be in therapy for years."

Kate laughed. "I don't think you have to go as far as a tutu. You just have to find a way to show her you value *her* interests, too. What have you decided for the girls' birthday party?"

"I haven't." Dropping his hat on the table, he raked his fingers through his hair. He sat in the swing and kicked his long legs out in front of him. "My mother keeps trying to take the whole thing over, and it's tempting to let her. She has a better understanding of the frilly feminine stuff than I do. But she also has an agenda. If I let her make the plans, the event could end up being me, the girls and a dozen single moms with their children."

Kate recalled having a similar suspicion about her grandmother's cookout. But there hadn't been a dozen men, only one very memorable man. Gram was a shrewd woman.

"I haven't hit on an idea that will wow both the girls," he continued, "although I guess we could just reserve a pavilion at the park and have another birthday celebration of cake, piñata and outdoor games. That's what we did last year." He grimaced. "And now I'm realizing all those games were right up Mandy's competitive, sports-driven alley. What if Alyssa didn't have any fun at her own party?"

"Oh, I'm sure she…" The kneejerk reassurance died on her lips. For all she knew, Alyssa hadn't enjoyed the party any more than she enjoyed the father-daughter camping trips. "There was cake and she got presents, right? She had to enjoy it some."

"Maybe. For two people who look exactly alike, they have nothing in common."

Nothing in common. It was the second time she'd heard that phrase today. "Oh! You gave me an idea." She joined him on the swing. "Your girls may have different personalities, but they can't be any more different from each other than, say, a small-town cowboy and a New York City fashion model."

He quirked an eyebrow. "Are you talking about Jasmine Tucker?"

"And her boyfriend Brody. Mandy likes outdoor stuff, right? And Alyssa begged Luke to draw her horses, so is it safe to assume she likes them?"

"As far as I know. But up until this afternoon, I thought she liked camping."

"Jazz excels at 'frilly' and 'feminine.' And she mentioned today that Brody likes having kids around. I wonder if they'd let us use his ranch one afternoon for a special birthday party? You could handle the invitations and all the food. Jazz and I, if she agrees, can make sure to add touches Alyssa will appreciate." Since Kate only had a son, she had to admit, it was fun coming up with ideas that were more girly. What if, in addition to standard face painting or temporary tattoos in the goody bags, she and Jazz organized small makeover stations?

Cole shifted, looking caught between gratitude and guilt. "It sounds like you'll be going to an awful lot of trouble on behalf of my girls. You sure you don't mind?"

"I'm a teacher, remember? I miss working with

kids." The sooner she got piano lessons organized, the better. Although, she had mixed feelings about signing up Marc-Paul Johnston as a student. She wondered if he was easier to manage than his mother. "Besides, your girls are sweet. Alyssa reminds me a tiny bit of myself at that age. We both come from households with single dads."

"Was yours clueless, too?"

"He was…withdrawn. Gram did a lot to compensate." She tilted her face toward him. "You are an excellent father, but we can all use a little help sometimes."

"My girls and I were lucky to meet you." He brushed her hair away from her face and tucked a strand behind her ear. Then he gave her a wry, lopsided smile. "But your generosity is making me feel really selfish."

"Selfish? You worked all night, then drove that kid home instead of calling his parents to come get him. Now that you're off duty, there are any number of ways you could be kicking back, but you're here brainstorming how to be a better dad."

"Maybe. I'm also the guy who sort of used his daughters as an excuse to spend more time with a beautiful woman."

"Oh." She didn't know what to say. The compliment sent little tremors of pleasure through her.

"And I've been thinking about kissing you all night."

Her breathing quickened. They both knew he didn't mean the kind of kiss she'd given him earlier. Was she prepared to offer more? Her sensual side had been dormant for over two years. Was she ready to open the floodgates? "I…don't want that."

"Liar," he said lightly. But he stood, giving her space. She was pretty sure that if his mouth had met hers, he would have overcome her objections in three seconds flat. She was relieved he hadn't tried. Ninety-nine percent relieved. One percent devastated.

"I've taken up enough of your time for one evening." He settled his hat on his head. "Thank you for the beer and the brilliant party suggestion. I'll call Brody Davenport first thing tomorrow and throw myself on his mercy. Will you talk to Jazz?"

"Absolutely."

She rose, deciding she might as well go in if he was leaving. The stars were still beautiful, and she supposed she could stay outside and enjoy the peace and quiet. But it was hot out here, making her feel restless and prickly. *You honestly believe it's the temperature making you uncomfortable and not thwarted desire?* No, but denial was her prerogative.

Cole opened the door for her. "Kate? I have five-year-old twins. If there's one thing I've learned, it's the importance of patience." He brushed the pad of his thumb over her lower lip, the delicate caress making her ache. "See you soon, sweetheart."

HARVEY TRENT RAISED his bushy eyebrows, shifting in his recliner to glance at Cole. "I understand pool parties and costume parties—there may even have been a toga party in my misspent youth—but what is a Runaway Ranch?"

Cole laughed; leave it to Alyssa to make her birthday sound as if it were being held at a home for troubled youth. "Not runaway. Runway."

Alyssa looked up from the sheets of construction paper she was folding in half for homemade invitations. Cole would be sending out evites, too, but why discourage her creativity? Some of the guests would appreciate the personal touch. "Runways are fancy stages, Paw-paw."

Both girls had been asleep by the time Cole got home last night. This morning, he'd called an extremely helpful Brody Davenport, then he'd told the girls about Kate's idea over brunch. They'd seemed excited, especially Alyssa, who hadn't stopped talking about it all day. He was glad they were at his parents' house for Sunday dinner so she had a fresh audience for her fervor.

The front door banged open, and Mandy barged into the house at her usual full-throttle speed. She went straight for the kitchen, either for something to drink or to plead with her grandmother for a predinner snack. Cole's brother William trailed her inside, holding a soccer ball and shaking his head.

"Tag, someone else is it," he said as he plopped down on the floor with Alyssa. The tallest of the Trent brothers, he looked like a giant next to her. "I should have stayed inside with you. This looks a lot less strenuous than trying to keep up with Mandy-pants."

"What's 'strenuous,' Uncle Will?"

"Short answer, your sister is a handful. What are you working on?"

"Birthday party invitations. Nana gave me paper and markers. But she didn't have any sparkly crayons."

"You think that's bad," Will said, his expression grave, "you should have grown up trying to share a pack of six crayons with two brothers. We didn't even have purple—we had to color something red, then go over it again in blue."

Alyssa's eyes were wide. "Is that true, Daddy?"

Cole laughed at his brother's version of the walking-to-school-uphill-both-ways speech. "No."

"Of course not," Harvey said, sounding affronted. "I made sure they had a roof over their heads, food on the table and adequate crayons."

Gayle poked her head around the corner. "I'm about to put the chocolate cake in the oven. Who wants to lick the beaters?"

Alyssa raced toward the kitchen. When properly motivated, she could move just as fast as her sister.

The three men turned their attention to the baseball game on television. Jace's favorite team was playing today, but the youngest Trent sibling wasn't here to see it. He'd bailed on dinner because of a "hot date." Cole assumed that meant it was a first date—at most, the second. With Jace's attention span, the flame often extinguished itself before a third.

During a commercial, Will told his brother, "Becca Johnston came to the station this week. Have you heard about her idea to raise money for the firemen's fund?"

"The bachelor auction?" Cole sighed. He really did need to give her an answer. And, considering the cause, he knew what his reply would be. He just wasn't ready to surrender yet. "Are you participating?"

"Sure. I'll probably drum up a lot of money in pity bids." Will had said more than once that the worst part of being dumped by his fiancée in a small town was that everyone knew. Hell, half the town had been invited to the wedding that hadn't taken place.

"Or," Cole corrected, "women with discerning taste will bid on a date with you because you have a heroic job, a way with kids and the Trent family good looks."

Harvey nodded. "Damn straight. It's in the genes."

"What about you? Going up on the auction block?" Will asked. At Cole's reluctant nod, his brother smirked. "Wonder how long Becca's been saving up, waiting for a chance to put her plan into action. You know, I hear she had a wealthy uncle in Turtle who recently passed. Maybe he left her an inheritance."

Cole chucked a sofa pillow at him. "You're making that up." *I hope.*

"Did you just throw part of my decor?" his mother demanded from the doorway.

William laughed. "Busted."

"Quit roughhousing and come to the table," Gayle said firmly.

While people passed their plates for servings of roasted chicken and three-bean salad, Gayle praised Will's decision to do the bachelor auction. "I think the event is a great idea," she said. "And while I think everyone understands it's just for charity, not necessarily a venue for romance, who knows what could happen? Maybe you'll meet a nice girl."

"Like Miss Kate," Alyssa said around a mouthful of chicken. "She's super nice."

"Miss Kate?" Will asked.

"Daddy's new friend," Mandy said. "She just moved here."

"She helped me swim better. And she says I'm brave."

"And she's coming to our party! It was *her* idea to go to a ranch. I get to have a cowgirl birthday!"

"And she's gonna teach me to play the piano!" The two girls spoke over the top of each other in their eagerness to extol Kate's virtues.

"She sounds really special." Will leaned back in his

chair, regarding his brother with surprise. "I can't be-lieve this is the first I'm hearing about her."

Cole wasn't sure how to respond. He'd promised Kate not to lie outright about their relationship, not to embellish it to a point where his girls became con-fused. He'd already skirted the boundaries of honesty by cuddling with her in front of Becca Johnston and her festival-committee minions.

But holding Kate didn't feel like deception. It felt like heaven. He still wasn't sure how he'd managed to walk away from her last night without kissing her. She probably had no idea how alluring she'd looked, bathed in the moonlight, the breeze toying with her hair the way he'd wanted to do. Even her outfit of robe and fuzzy slippers, which had been more ador-able than sexy, had generated lustful thoughts because she'd looked ready for bed. And thinking about bed in relation to Kate...

"Cole?" Will snapped his fingers. "Damn, you've got it bad, don't you?"

"Uncle Will! We aren't supposed to say the *D* word," Alyssa chided.

"Except when beavers build them," Mandy said.

Gayle berated her son for language at the table and Mandy asked her grandfather how animals like bea-vers and birds learned to build dams and nests in the first place, leaving Cole to his own thoughts. Which were dominated by Kate.

Maybe Will was right. *I do have it bad.* If he was this centered on Kate after only a week, how much worse would it be once he finally did kiss her? Because they were going to kiss eventually.

Weren't they? He understood that she needed to

take things slowly, but there was no mistaking the way she'd looked at him on her front porch. She wanted him. Whatever else she felt—and he imagined it was complicated—desire was somewhere in the mix. That gave him hope.

Knowing that he'd see her again tomorrow, for Alyssa's trial piano lesson was a kind of wonderful agony. He couldn't wait to be around her, appreciated every instance of getting to know her better, but it was difficult not to press for confirmation that she was attracted to him, too. *Do not rush her.*

No matter what his instincts urged him to do in the heat of the moment, he couldn't risk scaring her away. It had been so long since a woman had mattered to him like this, since he'd entertained thoughts of an actual relationship. This romance stuff was trickier than he remembered.

THANK GOD FOR triads and arpeggios. Losing herself in the familiar patterns of the keyboard and demonstrating major chords to Alyssa, Kate was almost able to forget that Cole was sitting in on the class, watching from the chair in the corner.

Okay, *forget* wasn't the right word. He had too much magnetism for that. But she'd stopped glancing in his direction every three seconds, so that was progress.

She'd agreed to his request to monitor the intro class grudgingly, which was unprofessional. With any other parent, she would have encouraged it. Quietly observing the lesson allowed a parent to not only get an idea of what they'd be paying for but to hear Kate's advice on hand positioning and practice times, which they could reinforce at home.

Cole had said they didn't even own a piano, although Alyssa toyed with the one at her grandmother's. He wanted to gauge his daughter's interest and see if the purchase of a midpriced electric keyboard was warranted. The feel wasn't precisely the same and not all keyboards had the touch sensitivity for volume control, but Alyssa could start learning notes and practicing rhythm.

At the moment, the girl's expression was filled with pride over locating middle C and playing it with the E and G.

"And that's a chord," Kate congratulated her. "Now let's try a scale."

When Cole and Alyssa had first arrived, the three of them chatted about music and the girl had expressed skepticism that all songs could possibly come from eight basic notes.

"But they can be put together in endless variations," Kate had said.

"What's 'variation'?"

"It's when you can do an activity one way," Cole had explained, "but there are a bunch of other creative ways to do it, too."

Kate's cheeks had warmed as her thoughts took a decidedly nonmusical direction. It had been a long time since she'd had to consider even basic…activity. Much less *variations*. Thank goodness Cole's attention had been on his daughter. If he'd glanced in Kate's direction, her face really would have gone up in flames. He'd gone on to illustrate his point with a painting example, reminding Alyssa that people could finger-paint or use a brush or, in the case of his repainting his daughters' room, even a roller.

"How was that, Miss Kate?"

Kate blinked, realizing her pupil had attempted a scale and she'd missed it because she'd been too busy thinking about Cole. And variations. "Um…you're off to a fantastic start, but we all get better with practice." Which begged the question, how rusty did a person's skills become after two years with no practice? The mind boggled.

Knock it off! She really needed to stop thinking about sex. Unfortunately, she doubted that would be possible until she got Cole out of the house. She'd had trouble sleeping after he left last night, tossing and turning. When she'd finally fallen into an exhausted slumber, it had been deep. This morning, she'd awakened with no memory of what she'd dreamed. But given the mental flashes she had whenever she looked at him, she could take an educated guess. The sooner he left, the sooner she would stop having those R-rated flashes.

Had half an hour passed yet? She discreetly checked her watch. *Eighteen minutes?* Hell. She was already feeling so high-strung that she feared what she might say or do in the next twelve.

She reached down for the bag next to the piano, wishing she'd left the sheet music she'd purchased in the car. That would have given her an excuse to exit the room and clear her head, or to send Cole away for a few minutes. "So now that you know what the eight basic notes are, I'll show you what they look like on paper. Once you learn to read music—"

"Hey, Mom!" Luke hollered a greeting as he entered the house. "Is Aly still here?"

Gram's voice was lower, but Kate could make out her reproachful words. "Well, *obviously* she is. Sheriff Trent's car is parked right out front. But I thought I told you we weren't going to interrupt their lesson?" It had been Gram's idea to take Luke out for ice cream earlier so Kate could concentrate on her work.

On my work, or on the sheriff? Because once regular lessons started, Kate didn't imagine Gram planned to vacate the house for all of them.

Despite Gram's valid reprimand, Kate was grateful for her son's interruption. Alyssa hopped off the piano bench and ran out to say hello.

"Maybe that's a good stopping point for today," Kate said, looking in Cole's general direction without actually meeting his eyes. "Let her practice chords and scales for a few days, see if her enthusiasm wanes."

"Okay." He stood. "But I wouldn't bet on it. She may be quieter than her sister, but she's equally stubborn. Family trait. When we get invested in something, we don't give up easily."

She recalled what he'd told her last time he'd been here, that he was a patient man. It was a seductive quality. Not only did Kate appreciate his control, it was heady that he considered her worth waiting for. Yet she couldn't in good conscience encourage him. Potentially wicked dreams aside, she couldn't say when, if ever, she might be ready to be more than his friend. Or his daughter's piano teacher.

Holding back a sigh, she exited the music room. The kids stood in the hall, where Alyssa was commenting on Luke's hair being "all different." He ran a hand self-consciously over the new cut. When the stylist had finished yesterday, Kate had been surprised at how much older he looked. He'd had the same shaggy mop, give or take a few inches, for years. *He's growing up.* And

Damon wouldn't be here to see it. To teach him how to drive or to give him advice on dating.

Gone were the days when Kate woke up unsure how she'd make it out of bed in the morning. She'd made it through the worst of grieving her husband. But it still caught her at odd moments. She could go for days on end without thinking about him, then *bam*. And the past week had been worse than usual.

She knew it was because of Cole. Was it the tangled emotional response of finding another man attractive that dredged so many memories of Damon to the surface, or was it the men's shared profession making her dwell on her days as a cop's wife? How could she ever be with a man who did the same job without being constantly reminded of Damon?

"Mom? You okay?" Luke peered at her with concern, then immediately raised his gaze to Cole, who stood behind her. The accusation in Luke's expression was blatant. Kate was on the verge of tears; clearly her son blamed Cole.

Mercifully, Alyssa steered the conversation to her birthday party, asking Luke to help with the face painting.

"What about birthday gifts?" Luke asked. "Know what you want?"

"A pony."

He laughed. "I don't think I'll be able to afford one of those, even if I help Gram weed the garden all week *and* offer to mow the front yard."

Cole reached out, cupping Kate's shoulder and she almost jumped. "Thank you, again, for suggesting the party venue. Both girls are *very* excited."

"You're welcome." Did it make her crazy that she

had simultaneous urges to pull away from him and lean into his touch? "Jazz thinks the whole thing sounds like fun. She's going to provide some funky accessories and stuff from the clearance rack of her boutique, and we're meeting at a big arts and craft store one county over to buy supplies for 'photo shoot' backdrops. I just hope Becca doesn't find out we're working on that instead of floats for the parade. Spending time on nonfestival projects this late in June may actually be against the town bylaws."

He grinned down at her. "Rebel. The good news is, if you get arrested, I happen to know where the keys to the jail are." He hesitated as if he wanted to say more, but then shook his head. "Alyssa, we should get home and make sure Mandy hasn't driven Nana crazy by now."

"Okay. See you this weekend, Luke."

"Bye, Aly." He high-fived her.

Kate expected the little girl to head toward the front of the house. Instead, she whirled around and threw herself against Kate's waist in a hug. "I love you, Miss Kate."

It was hardly the first time a kid had professed that sentiment. Heck, Kate herself had said the words to favorite teachers and piano instructors when she was a girl. *Don't read too much into it.* Kids were more open and spontaneous with their affections. Just because Alyssa had blurted an impulsive "I love you" didn't mean she was mentally auditioning Kate for the role of stepmother.

Trying not to blow the moment out of proportion, Kate responded the same way she did with kids at school. She squeezed the little girl back. "Love you, too."

Once the Trents had gone, Kate slumped on the couch, feeling drained. "Anyone want to watch a DVD?"

"I was about to take a bath," Gram said, "but you two can start without me."

Kate turned to her son. "You interested in a movie, or would you rather play online with Sarah?"

"Isn't that your friend from in town?" Gram asked. "She's pretty."

Luke jammed his hands into his pockets, staring intently at the ground. "I guess."

"You two saw Sarah while you were in town?"

Her son nodded, still addressing the floor. "She was in line with her brother at the ice cream parlor. He's old enough to drive."

It appeared the lively mood Luke had been in since volunteering with Rick had finally worn off. "Did the two of you argue or something?"

"No. Can I go to my room?"

"Sure." Kate was taken aback. He didn't want to watch TV *or* play video games?

She gave him a few minutes to himself, then went to investigate. It didn't matter so much that he told her what was wrong, just that he knew he *could* tell her. She knocked on the door, waiting for the muffled reply before she pushed it ajar. He was stretched across his bed on his stomach; he pulled out one earbud, his expression quizzical.

"Hey," she said. "I realize I've said this before and that I run the risk of crossing into lame territory, but you know you can talk to me right? It may be hard to believe that I was once a teenager, too, now that I'm so old—"

"Ancient," he said with the ghost of a smile.

"Right. But I might be able to identify more than you think." Back in Houston, he probably would have kicked her out of his room by now. But here, he didn't have Bobby and his cronies to confide in, so he might be desperate enough to take her up on her offer.

He sighed. "Sarah and her brother were getting ice cream on their way home from bowling in Turtle, and she said we should go bowling sometime."

"I see." No, she really didn't. How was the casual invitation reason to be upset? "And you're afraid you can't pick up the spare? Or that you'll look 'derpy' in the rented shoes?"

"Mom. Do *not* try to use my words." He sat up. "I like bowling, I guess. The problem is Sarah."

"You don't like Sarah?"

"I like talking to her online. When we're comparing sniper shots or divvying loot, knowing what to say is easy. It's not awkward or personal. But IRL..."

"Translation for the ancient lady, please."

"In real life. When I'm talking to her through the headset, it's fun. At the ice cream parlor, trying to talk to her made my stomach hurt. I didn't even want to eat my ice cream, but I was afraid to hurt Gram's feelings. I may throw up," he said.

So either her son had his first significant crush, or that stomach bug Crystal's family suffered was making its way through town.

"You've got a case of nerves. Like when Alyssa was worried about swimming without her water wings." Tactical error—Luke's glare made it clear he didn't appreciate being compared to a five-year-old girl. Kate held up her hands. "I'm not downplaying how you feel, I swear. In fact, I have the same problem. When I'm in a classroom, I know exactly what I'm supposed to be teaching or saying. But as you said, personal relationships are tough. There are one-on-one situations where I get completely tongue-tied."

Hopefully, he wouldn't ask her to elaborate. She didn't think her son really wanted to hear about the buzz of hormones she felt whenever Cole Trent got close. Or how the more time she spent with Cole, the more she second-guessed and triple-guessed what she wanted.

"My analogy about Alyssa was just to demonstrate that, most of the time, our fear of something is way worse than the actual consequences. She was terrified of swimming without the floaties, but as soon as she took them off, she had a blast. She didn't drown, she didn't get water up her nose. Swimming wasn't the hard part at all. The hard part was taking the risk."

"Yeah, that *sounds* good. I mean, I hear what you're saying. In theory, I'd love to be more badass. But it's hard to do IRL."

She empathized so much so that she overlooked the mild profanity. "You are one hundred percent right." *And I am one hundred percent hypocrite.* Was she really going to nudge her son to take risks when she, a grown woman, was too chicken to let a man kiss her on her grandmother's front porch?

"All right, lecture over," Kate said. "I'm going to pick out a movie, preferably one with cheesy dialogue and terrible CGI, and make popcorn. Join us if you decide you want some company. And Luke? Think about what I said. I won't force you to go bowling, but consider what you might be missing out on."

It was sound advice. Now she just had to figure out how to take it herself. How much was she willing to trade away to stay in her comfort zone?

Chapter Seven

Although Brody had assured Cole they could fit a lot of kids in the barn in the event of rain, Cole was glad the weather was cooperating for the birthday party. There was a soft breeze that kept the summer day from being too punishing, and the sky was dotted with puffy white clouds that looked more cartoon than real. But the best thing about today so far was that his daughters hadn't stopped smiling since they'd arrived.

Jazz and Kate had hung a banner over the cattle guard at the ranch's entrance that wished Amanda and Alyssa a happy sixth birthday. The slogan said Fun is Always in Fashion. Closer to the main house, the women had set up a red carpet where guests could get their pictures made. Or they could have their photo taken in the small corral where Brody stood with a shaggy pony. Kids who wanted to really get in the spirit of things could wear either a white cowboy hat and plastic badge or—for the more devilishly inclined—a skull and crossbones bandana and black hat. On one side of the barn were two booths for face painting and makeup application. Around the other side were games like horseshoes and plenty of folding chairs for parents and guardians to observe the frivolity.

From his current vantage point atop the sloping lawn, Cole could see Mandy winning a stick-pony race and watch Alyssa hamming it up in front of one of the photo stations. Giant posters were tacked on the side of the barn; his daughter posed in front of the Eiffel Tower in a beret, iridescent scarf and rhinestone-rimmed sunglasses.

Everything looked fantastic—especially the woman who had helped organize it all. When he'd gotten his first glimpse of Kate, he'd been speechless. He always thought of her as beautiful, but he was used to seeing her in casual settings. Jazz had applied just enough makeup to highlight her beauty and had done something to her hair, sweeping it to the side with a hint of curl, reminding him of vintage Hollywood.

"If you mock me," Kate had grumbled, "I won't be held responsible for my actions. Jazz said we had to look appropriately 'fashion forward.' I feel like an idiot. Grown women should not be wearing rompers."

He hadn't even noticed what she was wearing until then—and he wasn't entirely sure what *romper* meant but the bottom half of her outfit was shorts. The green color was gorgeous on her and although there was nothing provocative about the neckline or the silhouette of the outfit, when she turned away he'd noticed the skinny slit in the material that started at her neck and went all the way to her waist. It was such a slender gap, not truly revealing anything, but he found himself growing more obsessed with it as the day wore on. She was easily the sexiest woman on the ranch, no offense to the model who'd chipped in to make this day so much fun for his girls.

"Nice party, bro."

Cole turned to see his brothers approaching. Jace was balancing a paper plate on one hand and carrying a soda can in the other. After getting input from both his mom and Kate, Cole had decided the simplest way to handle food for this many people was to have it catered. A large table held aluminum trays of chopped beef and pulled pork. Buns were in plastic bags at the center of the table. There was a vat of coleslaw nearly as big as the birthday cake, and a wicker basket full of individually bagged chips. Earlier, he'd stared at a little girl for a full minute, trying to make sense of the design she'd had painted on her face before realizing it was smeared barbecue sauce.

Will wasn't carrying food, but he had two soft drinks. He handed one to Cole.

"How many people are *at* this shindig?" Jace asked. "Cupid's Bow isn't that big."

"We invited all the kids from Mandy's co-ed soccer team, the eight girls from Alyssa's ballet class and assorted other folks. Like their unreliable uncle who cancels family plans in favor of chasing women," Cole drawled.

"Dude." Jace gave him a look over the rims of his sunglasses. "Don't expect me to apologize for sowing my oats. It's not like the serious-commitment, settling-down thing worked out so well for the two of you, Dumped and Divorced."

Will smacked their younger brother on the back of the head; Cole jabbed him in the shoulder.

"And you bullies wonder why I duck out of family events," Jace grumbled. "Not that there was any chance of my missing this. I adore my nieces."

"They adore you, too," Cole admitted.

"Probably because they consider him a peer," Will said. "Maturity-wise."

"I would never flip the bird at a children's birthday party," Jace said. "But know that I am giving you the finger in spirit."

Will ignored this, addressing Cole instead. "We're headed to sit with Mom and Dad and eat some lunch. My plate's already at the table. Care to join us?"

Cole hesitated. He should probably eat some of the food he was paying for, and in a little while, he'd be too busy supervising present opening and the paint-ball war he still couldn't believe he was allowing. But he was reveling in watching his girls enjoy their big day. "In a few minutes. I like this view too much to give it up just yet."

"I'll *bet*." Jace elbowed him in the ribs.

Cole followed his gaze and saw Kate, bending forward slightly to apply adhesive gemstones to a little girl's cheek. "Hey!" He barely stopped himself from covering his brother's eyes.

"We don't get to ogle our brother's girlfriend," Will said. "Not even when she looks like that."

Girlfriend? That was one hell of a leap, especially given that Cole had never even kissed her. It bothered him that his brothers used the term so casually. What if one of the twins heard? They'd pestered him throughout the school year about their motherless state, drawing comparisons to their classmates' families, and he didn't want to fill their heads with false hope. "Don't call Kate that. We're not... Technically, we aren't dating."

"But everyone in town is talking about the two of you," Will said. "And at Mom and Dad's, you let me believe… If you invented this relationship to get Mom off your case, I may have to kill you. Because now that she thinks *you've* found a wonderful woman, she's started in on me."

Jace, however, was delighted by Cole's admission. "You mean she's single? Then it's high time for her to meet the best looking Trent brother."

"You're not seriously considering hitting on her?" Cole demanded.

"What? You just said there's nothing between you."

"That is not what I said. At all." There was definitely something between him and Kate. He just didn't know how to label it. "Besides, she's older than you."

"Fine by me." Jace waggled his eyebrows. "Older women know things."

An involuntary growl rumbled in Cole's throat. "What I meant was, she is a responsible adult. You are not." The idea of Jace getting involved with a single mother was laughable. "She already has one juvenile delinquent in her life. She doesn't need another." The words were flippant, not truly a criticism of Luke Sullivan.

Despite giving the impression that he was a troublemaker when they'd first met, the kid was proving to be a softie. He was patient and accommodating with the girls, especially Alyssa, and when Cole had stopped at the gas station the other day, Rick Jacobs had added his own favorable opinions.

"I don't have to stand here and take this abuse," Jace said. "I can go sit with Mom and Dad and let *them* abuse my life choices. I think Mom's favorite phrase since I quit college is 'woeful lack of direction.' It's been a few years. You'd think she would let it go."

Though he was registered as one of the town's volunteer firemen, his steady job was bartender. Their parents didn't think it was steady enough—not that Jace was overly perturbed by their disapproval. "I'll catch up with you guys later."

Will waited for a moment, then asked, "So what's the problem?"

"With our brother? I have many theories."

"Come on, what is this hogwash about you and Kate not dating? The last time I saw you, both your daughters were raving about her and you were staring into space with the dopiest expression possible. I believe *smitten* is the word. So what gives?"

"She's a widow," Cole said, hating the word. Aside from the obvious negative connotations of loss, it was an oversimplification. Kate saw herself as someone's widow, but she was so much more than that. "Her husband was a cop. She says being around anyone in that line of work makes her jumpy, that she can't stop thinking about the inherent dangers of the job."

Will sucked in a breath through his teeth. He knew firsthand that careers could create major problems in relationships. His ex-fiancée had cited his job with the fire department as a reason for backing out of their wedding. "That's..." He clapped Cole on the back. "Sorry, man."

The tone of sympathetic finality rankled. "Hey, I was just explaining why it would be premature to call her my girlfriend. I didn't say I was giving up on her. This isn't insurmountable."

"Are you planning to retire from law enforcement?"

"Don't be an idiot."

"And her husband is always going to have been a cop. No altering that. If she considers it a deal breaker—"

"Couples overcome obstacles," Cole snapped. Not that he and his ex-wife had. Neither had Will and Tasha. But some people did. He ground his teeth, missing the sense of peaceful contentment he'd been enjoying before his brothers interrupted. "Why are you here ruining *my* day? Go pop a kid's balloon or trip a little old lady or something."

Will looked sheepish. "You know I'm cynical for my own reasons. I didn't mean to aim it in your direction. But, Cole, if you already know something is likely to be a problem down the road, is it really worth going down that road? I've been through a breakup a hell of a lot more recently than you, so take it from me…"

As if she somehow felt she was being watched, Kate looked up suddenly. She glanced around and when she spotted Cole, a grin spread across her face. The sight of that smile hit him like moonshine, going straight to his head and sending a rush of heat through his body.

"Then again," Will amended as Cole waved to her, "*I* don't have a woman in my life smiling at me like that. Feel free to ignore everything I said."

"Already planning on it."

"THERE YOU GO! All done," Kate pronounced. She stepped back so the little girl in the soccer jersey could jump down from the chair. She'd asked for blue eyeliner and a blue flower on her cheek, made up of little gems, to match her team colors.

"Looks like another satisfied customer," Crystal said from behind her. Her five-year-old son was one of the invited guests, and she'd come to the party early to help Jazz and Kate set up. "Have you had a chance to eat yet? If not, I can take over here for a bit."

"Actually, according to your sister's schedule, all the kids are going to be herded to the tables for presents and cake in about three minutes. You know, I remember Jazz as being flighty when we were kids, but she grew up to be scary organized."

"She's having a lot of fun today," Crystal said. "As the baby of the family, she got bossed around by me and Susan a lot, and now you've put her in charge of something where she gets to tell a ton of people what to do. She's in heaven. Plus, she's handing out business cards and coupons for her boutique left and right."

"I'm glad. She deserves to get something out of today. Cole paid us for all the supplies, but I know she's donated some stuff from the store. He really appreciates it."

Crystal looked over to where Cole stood talking to his brother. Kate had met him when he first arrived; William Trent looked a lot like Cole, except taller and broader with the merest scruff of a beard dotting his jaw. "So how are things with you and the sheriff? I'm guessing pretty darn good since he can't take his eyes off you."

"That's an exaggeration. He's been busy with his family and the party guests." He'd had to break up a fight between two little boys earlier, and there'd been a minor first-aid crisis in the form of a bee sting.

It occurred to her that since she was so aware of everything Cole had been doing, maybe *she* was the one who couldn't take her eyes off *him*. He'd caught her looking more than once, and the glances he'd given her in return made her glad to be a woman.

"I'll say this," she told Crystal, "he does seem to appreciate the hair and makeup job your sister did."

"Yeah, there's a reason Susan and I both begged her to do our makeup at our respective weddings." She paused, giving Kate a sly smile. "Just a little something for you to keep in mind, in case things get serious."

"Crystal!" How had her friend made the leap from *one* date at the community pool to a hypothetical wedding? "I haven't even known the guy a month. And I'm not sure I'll ever remarry." She'd given her heart to Damon. It was difficult to imagine making that level of commitment a second time.

Crystal's teasing expression dissolved. "I'm sorry. Was that insensitive? It's just really nice to see you happy after everything you've been through. You haven't stopped smiling all day. But I was only joking around. I know you and the sheriff are in the early stages of your relationship."

Really, *really* early. If their so-called relationship were a movie, the previews wouldn't even be showing yet. Seating hadn't even started. The two of them were still standing awkwardly in the corridor with their popcorn, waiting for the theater to be cleaned.

She sighed. "In the unlikely event that I do marry again—far, far in the future, when people are driving hovercrafts instead of cars—I don't think it could be with someone like Cole."

"A sexy responsible guy who's great with kids and beloved by an entire community?"

"Someone in law enforcement. There would be so many painful memories. And I'd worry all the time."

Crystal pursed her lips, looking as if she itched to say more.

In spite of the difficult topic, Kate chuckled. "Out with it, Crys."

"Since I can only imagine what it was like for you and haven't faced anything like it myself, I may not be entitled to an opinion."

"Yet I feel confident you have one."

"Well, I understand why you'd worry," Crystal said, her voice gentle. "How could you not? But…don't you ever watch the news? There are a billion reasons to worry about your loved ones, regardless of their occupations. We can't let that stop us from living. Tragedy happens. Someone could die just—"

"I get your point." Kate held up a hand. "But maybe save the gruesome examples of death and catastrophe for when we're *not* at a birthday party for six-year-olds?"

"Right." Crystal ducked her head, her expression abashed.

The six-year-olds in question had obviously been alerted it was time for gifts and cake. Children began swarming from all directions, putting Kate at the base of an uphill stampede. She joined the migration, glad for an excuse to end the conversation with Crys.

But even though she'd escaped her friend for the moment, Crystal's words stuck with her. *We can't let that stop us from living.* That's not what Kate was doing… was it? She'd met with six potential students and their parents this week and was seeing progress in Luke. Life was good.

Yet she couldn't deny those moments when she yearned for more.

With not one but two guests of honor, there were a ton of presents to unwrap. Kate and Luke gave Mandy a board game that had been one of Luke's favorites when he was younger and Alyssa a pink metronome. Kate was surprised when, after the girls opened those two boxes, Luke turned to the gift table and picked up two very tiny packages in unevenly taped construction paper.

"These are from me," he added.

When Kate saw that he'd given them each a chocolate bar, the same brand he'd stolen, she didn't know whether to laugh or groan. On the other side of the table, Cole's eyebrows shot skyward as he stared the boy down.

Luke grinned. "Bought and paid for with my own money. You can ask Rick."

By unspoken agreement, the girls saved their dad's presents for last. Mandy tore through the packaging and was already putting on her new shin guards by the time Alyssa got to her final gift, a soft stuffed horse with a very sweet expression. She let out a squeal of delight but then mock-scolded, "It was supposed to be a real pony, Daddy."

"You're out of luck on the pony front," Cole told her, "but there is something else at the bottom."

"Sparkly crayons!" Alyssa came out of her seat and ran around the table to hug him. Over the top of her head, Cole's gaze met Kate's. *Thank you*, he mouthed. She wasn't sure she deserved the credit—he'd decided for himself not to go with a creepy doll, and all she'd done was nudge him in an appropriate direction—but the gratitude in his eyes left her feeling tingly and appreciated.

After the gifts, it was time to sing "Happy Birthday to You" and blow out the candles. Then Cole and Kate were planning to duck away and get the next activity ready while the kids ate.

The paintball activity had been Kate's suggestion. It was how her art-teacher friend celebrated the last day of elementary school with graduating fifth graders. Kate hadn't been sure if Cole—or Brody—would agree since the mess factor was intense. But the paint was washable, and neither man had been fazed. Brody said ranch work was always a mess; this would have the added benefit of being colorful. While Kate and Cole prepared the ammunition for the battle, Jazz and Cole's mom would distribute old T-shirts to use as protective smocks.

Cole snagged a paper plate with a slice of cake on it and came toward her. "Want a bite?" he offered.

"No, thanks." His being this close put a quivery feeling in her stomach. Needing to focus on something else, she watched happy kids scarf down cake and ice cream. "So far, the party seems like an unbridled success. If you'll excuse the horse pun."

"The girls are having a blast. I owe you big time. Let me buy you dinner sometime this week?"

Dinner, as in a date? "I… Jazz did just as much work as I did. Possibly more."

"Good point. Brody and Jazz should join us. Will you find out what night works best for them?"

She blinked, startled to find that she suddenly had plans for a double date. But she couldn't think of a reason to say no that didn't sound completely ridiculous. *Then say yes.* "All right." Crystal would be thrilled.

Cole looked pretty happy about it, too. "I can't wait." He grinned down at her, his gorgeous blue eyes crinkling at the corners, melting away the last of her reservations. And most of her ability to think straight.

Weren't they supposed to be doing something right now? Jazz had helped put together a very thorough agenda, and Kate didn't recall a time allotment for "moon over the sheriff."

"Balloons," she blurted.

He nodded. "Let's get to work."

Their version of paintball was to put paint in water balloons. According to the emailed instructions from her friend, if they tried to fill the balloons ahead of time, they risked the paint hardening. Brody had given them use of an outdoor sink behind the barn, and all the supplies were waiting for them there. With a couple of water bottles and funnels, they would fill half the balloons with lime green paint, for Mandy's team, and the other half with bright purple, for Alyssa's. When there were no balloons left to throw, a panel of judges would look at the color splotches on each child to decide which team got the most hits.

There were large rubber buckets on either side of the sink where they would gently deposit the filled balloons. While they worked, Jazz would keep the kids busy with a game of musical chairs. Afterward, children would report to the barn to be divided into teams and collect their ammo. Kate put some paint in an empty bottle, then turned the spigot to add water. Then she capped it and shook vigorously.

"You want to be *very* careful filling the balloons," Kate stressed as she handed Cole one of the funnels. "If you don't use enough water, they won't pop on impact. But too much and—"

"This isn't my first time, sweetheart. Trust me to know what I'm doing."

She responded to the mischief in his tone with a wicked smile. "Even an experienced man can benefit from a few pointers."

"Fair enough." His eyes locked on hers. "But give a guy the chance to show you what he can do first."

The air in her lungs was suddenly too thick to breathe...which maybe accounted for how light-headed she felt. Having played piano for most of her life, she'd developed pretty good manual dexterity. Yet now her fingers were clumsy. It took two attempts to knot the balloon in her hand. She willed herself to concentrate. After half a dozen balloons, she established a cadence. Fill, tie, bucket. Fill, tie, bucket. Fill, tie—*sploosh*.

Startled by the sound, she glanced over at the exact moment Cole swore. A splatter of neon green was dripping from the center of his T-shirt toward the hem. Both of his hands were stained; he looked like the lead suspect in a leprechaun murder. Laughter bubbled up inside her, and she bit her lip, trying in vain to contain it.

His own lips twitched. "Don't you dare say I told you so."

"Wouldn't think of it." Stifled giggles fizzed in the back of her throat like carbonation bubbles. "It would be redundant."

He rinsed his hands in the sink and splashed water at the splotch on his shirt, smearing it into a much bigger mess.

"And petty," she added. "And uncharitable. Hey, Cole?"

He swiveled his head toward her, eyes narrowed in warning.

"Told you so."

"That does it." He cupped a double handful of water and advanced on her.

Laughing uncontrollably, she scrambled back, forgetting about the bucket of balloons behind her.

Cole lunged just as she wobbled. He caught her waist with wet fingers, spinning her toward the side of the barn and away from the paint-filled balloons. "That would have been bad. On the other hand," he said as he righted her, "you would have had the most colorful butt on the ranch."

She'd been enjoying their playfulness, but now, pressed between him and the barn behind her, the moment changed. His gaze dropped to her mouth, and her breath hitched. Hunger that felt at once familiar and alien tightened inside her.

Trying to joke away the nerve-racking desire, she said, "A gentleman wouldn't comment on a woman's butt."

There was no humor in his eyes. "I don't suppose a gentleman would kiss you, either?"

Her brain failed. She couldn't find words for a reply. *So who needs words?* What she needed—what she *wanted*—was the man in front of her.

Lacing her hands behind his neck, she tugged him toward her and stretched up to meet him. His muscles were bunched with deliciously masculine tension, as if he were fighting the urge to take control of their kiss. Her lips brushed his, tentatively. It had been years. She was only half certain she remembered how to do this. Yet she knew Cole was the right man to refresh her memory.

She kissed him again, and her confidence amplified. So did the need spiraling through her.

"Kate." His voice was a ragged murmur. He pulled back slightly, studying her face as if looking for the visual confirmation that this was okay.

She could only imagine what he saw in her expression, but it must have been encouraging. His eyes darkened, and his hand cradled the back of her head. His lips claimed hers in a hot, openmouthed kiss that—

"Daddy?"

Cole recoiled so quickly it was pure luck *he* didn't topple the bucket of water balloons.

Oh, no. No, no, no.

Kate turned her head and saw not just one but both twins. Their matching jaw-dropped gapes made them more identical than Kate had ever seen them.

"You were kissing Miss Kate," Mandy said slowly, as if still trying to process what had happened.

You and me both, kid.

Cole glanced from them to Kate. "We, uh—"

"They're in love!" Alyssa let out a whoop of excitement that debunked the myth of her being the quiet twin. "This is *better* than a pony. Can I be the flower girl at the wedding?"

"What?" Kate's voice came out in a horrified squeak. "Honey, no, it—"

"Why do you get to be the flower girl?" Mandy demanded. "What about me?"

"You don't even like dresses! Weddings are fancy!"

"There is not going to be a wedding," Cole boomed, trying to be heard over all three females.

"Er...everything all right here?" Jazz asked, rounding the barn. "The girls were antsy to know when we could get started, so we were coming to check your progress." Her tone was apologetic. "They ran ahead of me. And then there was yelling."

Kate faked a smile, although her stomach was churning. There were a lot of ways her first kiss in years could have gone wrong; this wasn't one of the ways she'd imagined. "The good news is we have a bunch of balloons ready. Maybe you can start organizing the troops while we finish up the last few."

"Sure." Jazz put an arm around each girl. "C'mon, you two, why don't you go select your teams?" She ushered them to the open pastureland where the battle would take place, and Kate squeezed her eyes shut, wishing she could go back in time.

"I'm not sorry I kissed you," Cole said, sounding a touch defensive.

She cracked one eye open. "Me, neither."

"Really?" A smile lit his face.

"Really. Although," she added wryly, "in retrospect, this might not have been the perfect place for it." Regardless of the damage control he'd have to do—no doubt Alyssa would want to start drawing wedding invitations with her sparkly crayons—today had been a revelation. A part of herself Kate thought might have been lost forever had reawakened with gusto. Whatever else happened, knowing that made her feel more like a whole person than she'd been in a long time.

Cole snickered, and she raised an eyebrow. "What's funny?"

"We have matching blobs." He nodded downward, and she realized that his green paint was now smeared across her top, too. Thank goodness the paint was washable.

"Think we can fill the rest of these without mishap?" she asked.

"I'll be extra careful," he promised. "But...all things considered, I'm glad the other one exploded."

Grinning, she got back to work. Brody and Will began lugging buckets of balloons to where the kids were waiting. They stood in two groups, calling good-natured taunts to each other. Well, mostly good-natured.

Kate was surprised to see Luke sitting off by himself instead of lined up with the others. Granted, he was older than most of the other guests, but she couldn't believe he would pass up the chance to hurl paint-filled water balloons. As Cole explained the rules—and consequences for rule breakers—to the teams, she crossed the grass to her son.

"Hey," she said. "You don't want to participate?"

"Does it *look* like I want to participate?"

She drew back, startled by his hostile tone. "What's wrong?"

He stared at the dirt, nonresponsive.

"I thought you were having fun today," she prodded.

"That was before I saw you sucking face with the sheriff."

Chapter Eight

Gram glanced up from the kitchen table, where she was working a jigsaw puzzle. "How was the…?" Her question trailed off when Luke stomped past the kitchen and into his room. A moment later, the door slammed.

Kate winced, wondering if she should go after him. *And say what?* At the party, she'd taken a stern approach, reminding him that she was his mother and that disagreeing with her actions didn't entitle him to speak to her disrespectfully. Recognizing that his mood was volatile, she'd told Cole they were going to duck out early. The girls had lots of other people to keep them entertained, and paintball had been the last activity on the itinerary anyway. She'd hugged Jazz goodbye and offered to come back later to help with clean up. Jazz had told her it wasn't necessary, that Susan and Crystal were going to pitch in and then the three sisters planned to order pizza and have a movie marathon.

In the car, Kate had softened her approach, acknowledging that she and Luke had never discussed the possibility of her dating and telling him she completely understood if it was a difficult adjustment for him. She'd tried to get him to discuss what he was feeling, but he'd said thinking about it was gross enough without rehashing it aloud. So she'd decided to give him time.

"What was that about?" Gram asked. "He was in a good enough mood when the two of you left."

"Oh, Gram." Tears pricked Kate's eyes. "I don't know what I'm doing."

Her grandmother crossed the room to hug her. "You're not the first mom to feel that way, and you certainly won't be the last. Want me to make you some tea?"

Not if it was caffeinated. She was so keyed up already, caffeine would send her through the roof. "Cole and I kissed. Luke saw it."

"Ah." Her grandmother was silent a moment. "Something stronger than tea, then?"

Kate gave her a watery smile. "Yes, please."

Gram went to a cabinet on the other side of the kitchen and pulled out a bottle of what had been Grandpa Jim's favorite whiskey. She filled a couple of glasses with ice, and the two of them went out to the porch where they could speak without being overheard.

"Thank you." Kate tucked her legs under her on the swing and took a cautious sip of the whiskey. The first swallow burned, but the second one was smooth.

"I have a confession to make," Gram said, taking a nip of her own whiskey. "When Cole announced you'd made plans together, on the very first day you were introduced, I was skeptical. It seemed too fast for my restrained granddaughter, and I thought perhaps I was being...what's the word the kids use? Played! I thought you were playing me. Obviously, I was wrong."

Not so much. "Is 'restrained' a good thing or a bad thing?"

"It's just who you are, darling. You've never been one to make snap decisions."

"Except moving to Cupid's Bow." That moment in her kitchen had felt like an epiphany.

"Maybe that decision was made long before you consciously realized it. No offense to my son, but I always thought you belonged here."

It was true. Cupid's Bow felt more like home than the apartment she and her father had lived in for her entire adolescence. She hoped one day Luke would consider the town home, too. He'd been doing so well until today. How could she blame him for taking the sight of her in a man's arms badly when it had taken her weeks to adjust to the idea?

The two women drank in silence, and Kate almost laughed when Gram refilled their tumblers. At this rate, Luke would see her kissing a man and tottering tipsily through the house in the same day. *Mother of the freaking year.*

Gram stared into the distance, her smile sad.

"Thinking about Grandpa Jim?" Kate asked softly.

"Every day. I knew from the age of twelve he would be the love of my life, and he was. When you told Jim and me that you were engaged, I knew Damon must have been The One. I know how carefully you consider things, and I could hear it in your voice, how happy you were, how *certain*."

Emotion clogged Kate's throat, and she nodded.

"You loved him so much." Her grandmother reached over to clasp her hand. "Nothing will ever take that away or diminish it, not even letting yourself fall in love again."

"Oh, Gram, it's too soon to know whether that will ever happen."

"Really?"

Kate bit her lip. As Gram had pointed out, Kate was guarded with her emotions. If she weren't already falling for Cole—if part of her didn't at least acknowledge it as a possibility—would she have been making out with him at his daughters' party? What had seemed like such a clear decision with his hands on her was muddled now.

"You'll fall in love," her grandmother insisted. "You have a generous heart. Maybe it won't be with the sheriff—although he gets my vote—but you have too much to give to be alone."

"I'm not alone! I have you and Luke."

"Don't be obtuse, dear." Gram stared out across the sprawling yard again, but this time her gaze focused on something specific. "Looks like company."

Kate followed her gaze, watching the car turn onto the farm's dirt road, and her heart jumped. "Cole."

"I'll just leave you to entertain your gentleman caller." It took Gram two tries to successfully rise from the swing. She snickered. "Not as steady on my feet as I was expecting. Good whiskey." She had just disappeared back inside when Cole parked in front of the house.

Oh, boy.

Now what? Last time they'd been on this porch together, Kate had desperately wanted to kiss him. Knowing firsthand what his kisses were like only intensified that ache. But if Luke caught them canoodling twice in one afternoon, he might do something insane like try to hitchhike back to Houston.

"H-hey," she greeted Cole, not standing. She was unsteady enough around him even without the whiskey. "Where are the girls?"

"My mother, who is a saint, should be corralling them into the bathtub even as we speak. Two kids on sugar highs, covered in washable paint." He shook his head. "Suffice to say, they've declared this the most awesome birthday in the world history of birthdays."

"I'm glad."

"Nope. I'm not convinced that's your 'glad' face." He sat in the spot Gram had vacated, brushing a hand over Kate's cheek as he peered at her. The gentle touch was enough to send a small quiver of anticipation through her. "Talk to me, Kate."

"Luke didn't find the day quite as awesome as the girls did." She sighed. "He was trailing after them, coming to offer his assistance with water balloons, too."

"He saw us kiss?" At her nod, Cole's expression turned somber. "That explains your hasty exit."

She'd implied Luke wasn't feeling well when she left but hadn't offered any specifics. "His reaction was a little different than Alyssa's."

"You mean he didn't immediately volunteer to be the ring bearer at our wedding?" He winced at her expression. "Sorry. I thought maybe the situation called for levity."

"I'm not sure what the situation calls for. He was furious on the ride home. He's barely speaking to me."

Cole straightened. "Would it help if I tried talking to him? Man to man, as it were?"

"Um...that may be the worst idea I've ever heard."

He blew out his breath in audible relief. "Praise the

Lord. I mean, I felt I should offer, since I'm responsible for the riff between the two of you, but I don't know what I would have done if you'd said yes. I'm used to talking to five-year-olds who adore me and are easily distracted by sparkly objects. An angry teen is outside my wheelhouse."

She chuckled at the admission. "Wait…what do you mean you're responsible? *I* kissed *you*."

"So you did." His smile was smug and very, very male. "You also agreed to have dinner with me this week. The next night I'm scheduled to be off duty is Tuesday. Coincidentally, Jazz and Brody are available then."

She hesitated, unsure what to say. Part of her couldn't imagine anything more enjoyable than an evening out with her friends and Cole. But was it worth further distressing her son?

"This is becoming an alarmingly long pause," Cole said. "An insecure guy might think you were trying to decide how to get out of dinner."

"I don't know." She stood, unable to meet his gaze. "Maybe going out with you would be a mistake. You didn't see how upset he was when we got home."

Cole followed her, looking mildly annoyed. "You really want to skip over 'maybe he needs some time' straight to 'let's call the whole thing off?' Is this about Luke, or about you?"

"You're a parent. You know making sacrifices comes with the territory."

"True. But you can't live your life jumping through hoops for Luke."

"Actually, he's my son, and I can live *my* life however I choose. And I think it's unbelievably arrogant to give dating advice when, by your own admission, you haven't made time for romance in your life, either."

"There was no one worth the trouble before," he said, his tone softening. "Now there is."

Touched by that declaration, she let him pull her into an apologetic embrace.

"I didn't mean to sound high-handed," he said. "Of course it's your life and you have to make the decisions you feel are best. But kids are resilient. Don't you think he'll get used to the idea?"

"I just relocated him from the only home he's ever known. He's already having to adjust to a lot."

Cole released her. His frustration was evident on his face, but his voice was contrite. "I told you I was a patient man, yet here I am pushing. I just… There's something powerful between us, Kate, and I'd like to see where it takes us."

After today, she couldn't deny the escalating attraction they shared. It was where that attraction would lead that gave her pause. If dinner Tuesday were only some people getting together to eat, she'd go in a heartbeat. Children rarely needed therapy because their mothers went out for hickory-smoked ribs. But by Cole's own admission, a date with him would be more than that. It would be another step forward on a perilous road to an unknown destination.

Then again, how could she ever expect her son to grow accustomed to their moving forward if she herself couldn't get comfortable with the idea? She turned away, considering. The memory of kissing Cole was vivid, but not just the physical part. She was struck by that moment when he'd paused, holding in check his own desires to make sure it was really what she wanted.

There'd been so much tender concern in his gaze that it made her ache.

"Okay," she said, quickly before she could change her mind. Again.

"You'll have dinner with me Tuesday?" His voice was nine parts joy, one part disbelief.

She nodded. "It's a date."

WHEN LUKE HAD awakened the first time on Sunday to morning sunlight filling his room, he'd rolled over and gone back to sleep. But now it was past noon. He kept his eyes tightly closed, willing himself back into the refuge of sleep, but it was pointless. He wasn't tired.

He was, however, starving. And he had to go to the bathroom.

Sitting up, he eyed his closed door, the much-needed barrier between him and the rest of the world. *I do not want to go out there.*

But remaining in his sanctuary was no guarantee that he wouldn't have to face his mom. Eventually, she would knock and try to talk to him. As if he had anything to say besides "yuck." What the hell was wrong with her? She'd been at a birthday party for little kids. Nobody needed to see *that*.

Except he couldn't seem to unsee it. The image of her macking on the sheriff had plagued him all night long.

Ever since they'd left the ranch yesterday, Luke had been trying to remember a specific instance of his mom and dad kissing. He couldn't do it. Oh, he knew he'd seen them kiss, but he couldn't pinpoint an actual, individual memory. And it seemed wrong that he couldn't remember his dad kissing her but now he was stuck with a visual of some other guy doing it.

Through the door, he heard the house phone ring and his mom's muffled voice as she answered. Good. Maybe he could run to the bathroom, then snag some food to bring back to his room while she was distracted. Yet he'd no sooner grabbed a sleeve of crackers from the pantry when his mother came toward him with the cordless phone.

She handed it to him. "It's Sarah."

He groaned at the ambush. Last night, he hadn't felt like answering any of his friend's texts, but that hadn't dissuaded her from sending them. So he'd turned off his phone.

"Hello?" he snapped.

There was a pause. "Hi to you, too, Grumpy."

"What do you want?"

"My cousin is coming to visit, and my brother and I are trying to plan a couple of things to do while he's in town so he won't be bored silly. We'll probably go to a matinee tomorrow." She hesitated. "I thought… well, would you like to come with us?"

"No." He didn't want to deal with people. Not his mom, not Sarah, not anyone.

From across the kitchen, where she was making a sandwich, his mother frowned at his tone. Obviously she thought he was being rude. Well, eavesdropping was rude, too.

"Are you gonna be online later?" Sarah asked, a little wobble in her voice. "Because I just got the code for a new DLC and—"

"I don't want to play or go to the movie. And I don't want to talk to you! Take the hint already."

She gasped. "You don't have to be a jerk about it." Then she hung up.

Crap. Sarah was right. He *had* been a jerk. Knowing he'd hurt her feelings made him feel like he'd swallowed live goldfish and they were wriggling through his gut. Why couldn't she have left him alone? Now he'd probably lost his only friend in this stupid town.

He remembered the day he'd drawn that horse picture for Aly. *"I guess you can be my friend."* Aly was a cute kid, but he didn't want to see her again. How could he be around her without thinking about her dad with his mom?

His mother was like Bobby Rowe. That comparison would probably make her head explode, but Bobby had a thing for redheads. Every girl Bobby had ever talked about or asked to a school dance had red hair. Maybe Luke's mom had a thing for policemen. That was one explanation for why she'd be all over some guy she'd only known a few weeks.

"Luke." His mom set the sandwich on the table in front of him. "You were really unkind to her. I'm disappointed in you."

That was nothing new. "She should have got a clue when I didn't respond to her texts," he muttered.

"Don't blame her for your actions." She sat in the chair next to him. "And don't blame her for mine, either. I know you're upset that Cole and I—"

"Can we not talk about that?" He resisted the urge to clap his hands over his ears, but just barely.

"We'll need to eventually, because I'm seeing him again. For dinner on Tuesday. I realize this can't be easy for you, but—"

"I'm not hungry." He shoved the sandwich away.

He noticed her jaw tighten, but she didn't make him eat. "I have two piano students coming today, and I don't need you snarling at them. Maybe it would be best if you spent the afternoon in your room."

Fine by me.

Stalking down the hallway, he thought he heard a sniff behind him, but he ignored it. Just as he ignored his own sniffles as he shut his door once more.

ON MONDAY MORNING, Kate went on a cleaning frenzy fueled by nervous energy. She had only one piano student scheduled for that afternoon—Alyssa Trent—and she was worried about how the lesson would go. Had Cole successfully convinced his daughters that he and Kate weren't planning to head down the aisle?

As Kate stowed the furniture polish and cleaning rag back under the kitchen sink, she comforted herself with the reminder that at least Cole wouldn't be the one bringing his daughter. It seemed too soon for him and Luke to be under the same roof. Cole was working today, and he'd left a message that his mother would drive Alyssa to the farm. Frankly, Kate wasn't sure how her son would act toward Alyssa, either, but since Gram was at quilting club, Kate didn't have an easy way to get Luke out of the house. *If only he'd accepted Sarah's invitation to the movies.*

Kate's heart hurt for the girl, whose overtures of friendship had been so adamantly rebuffed. She hated that Luke was sabotaging himself, but this wasn't the first time he'd fallen into self-destructive behavior when upset. She found herself grateful that no man had attracted her attention back in Houston; she could only imagine the trouble Luke would be in right now if he were still hanging out with Bobby and his cohorts.

Patch barked cheerfully, letting her know they had company, and Kate reached the front door at the same time Mrs. Trent did.

Kate waved the woman and her granddaughter inside. "Nice to see you both again."

Rather than returning Kate's smile, Alyssa hopped from one foot to the other, her face tense. "I hafta use the bathroom, Miss Kate."

"Right down the hall."

As the girl hurried away, Gayle said, "Sorry about that. I shouldn't have let her order the large soda with lunch."

"No problem. She's my only student today, so if we start a few minutes late, I can make up the time. Do you want to sit in on the lesson, or wait in the living room? You're welcome to watch television if you like."

"I believe I'll curl up on the sofa and read if you don't mind." She pulled a book out of her purse. "I'm halfway through a great mystery and can't wait to find out who the killer is."

Kate smiled noncommittally. Personally, she stayed away from mysteries and thrillers. She hated the reminder that bad guys were out there. In the case of her husband's killer, he'd been caught and sentenced, but seeing justice served had done nothing to bring Damon back to her.

"You don't like books?" Gayle asked as she settled on the couch.

"Oh, I love to read. The darker stuff just isn't for me. I prefer laughing my way through a book and knowing there's a happy ending."

"So, you like romances. I shouldn't be surprised." Gayle grinned. "According to my granddaughters, you're *definitely* a fan of romance."

Embarrassment heated Kate's face. "I, uh…"

"No need to feel bashful. I'm thrilled my son is finally falling for a good woman. And both the girls have taken a shine to you."

Kate glanced down the hallway, willing Alyssa to return. Immediately. "Thank you. But…"

Gayle arched an eyebrow. "Uh-oh. Don't tell me you're planning to break his heart."

How invested was Cole's heart? Kate knew his mom had interfered in his love life before, and she wouldn't put it past the well-meaning woman to exaggerate.

"I don't think people ever really plan for that," Kate said. Sometimes it just happened. It was impossible to know the future. "Can I ask you a personal question?"

"Yes, especially if it's about Cole. I have many adorable stories about his childhood."

Kate grinned, charmed by the mental image of Cole as a little boy, with those laser-bright blue eyes. "Maybe another time." She looked down the hall, verifying that the bathroom door was still closed, then lowered her voice. "You're the mother of a sheriff and a fireman, both jobs that include a lot of inherent risk. Don't you worry about them constantly?"

"You're a mom yourself, so you know the answer to that. Of course I worry. We all worry about our children, even those who grow up to be accountants or retail cashiers."

Kate supposed that was true.

"My pride in my boys is stronger than my fear. Jace, the youngest, makes me want to pull my hair out sometimes, but even he is dependable in an emergency and quick to help others. I consider my sons modern-day heroes. They're noble and kind." She sighed. "But not very lucky in love. I'm hoping that will change."

Kate bit her lip. "Cole and his brothers are great guys. I'm sure they'll find women who see that." She just didn't know yet if she would be one of those women.

GRAM LEANED BACK in her armchair, temporarily abandoning the knitting she'd been doing. "When I was a girl, our house had a basement and sometimes Mama or Daddy would send me down the stairs to fetch something. I never told them, but I was *terrified* of that basement, even up 'til I was sixteen. I only mention it now because you're looking down the hall at Luke's door the way I used to eye that basement door. What are you afraid of—that he's going to come busting out of that room, wild-eyed and screaming when Cole picks you up for dinner?"

Maybe. Kate sat on the very edge of the sofa, trying not to wrinkle the sundress she'd chosen. "I don't know what I'm afraid of." Parenting failures, love, loss, the uncertainty of the future. "A little bit of everything, I guess."

Gram peered over the rims of her glasses. "Well, stop it."

Kate couldn't help chuckling at the command. *If only it were that simple.* "I hope Luke doesn't give you any trouble while I'm gone."

"Frankly, I'd be surprised if he even shows his face. Been keeping to himself a lot the last few days."

Kate nodded. She'd overheard him trying to talk

to Sarah through the gaming headphones, but apparently his friend wasn't ready to forgive him. Luke had logged off, dejected. Kate thought it might be a nice gesture for him to do something "in real life" with her, so that Sarah knew he saw her as a real friend and not just someone to campaign with when he needed help defeating a level. Kate had suggested as much, but he'd simply glared. Her son wasn't particularly receptive to her advice right now.

Patch ran to the front door with a bark and a wagging tail, and Kate's stomach felt the exact same way it had the single time she'd allowed Damon and Luke to talk her into riding a roller coaster with an upside down loop. While she took a deep, calming breath, Gram answered the door.

"Sheriff." Gram's tone was rich with humor. "I expect you to have her back at a reasonable hour. It's a weeknight, after all."

Cole grinned. "Yes, ma'am." Then his gaze shifted to Kate. "You look fantastic."

The time she'd taken with her hair and makeup had definitely been worth it. At the girls' party, Jazz had given her an undeniably fashionable appearance, but that look hadn't really been Kate. She was glad Cole was equally impressed with the real her. "Thank you. So do you." But then, he always did.

He held out his hand, and as she walked toward him, her nerves evaporated. There was nowhere she'd rather be tonight than in this man's company. "Don't worry, Mrs. Denby," he told Gram, "I won't keep her out past curfew."

Once they were on the other side of the door, Cole surprised Kate by pulling her closer for a quick kiss hello. "I couldn't wait until the end of the evening to do that," he said.

She was glad he hadn't, but couldn't resist teasing him anyway. "Are you also the kind of person who eats dessert first?"

His gaze dipped from hers, traveling the length of her body and back. "If dessert looked as delectable as you? Hell yes."

Warmth filled her, and the way he gallantly opened her car door for her only amplified it.

There was a police radio in Cole's car, but he turned it off as he slid into the driver's seat. "They can reach me on my cell if there's a real emergency," he said. "Besides…"

Although he didn't finish his sentence, she could guess from his expression what he was thinking. He wanted to protect her—and protect their date—from reminders of his job. She sighed, recalling his mother's words from yesterday. Cole was noble and heroic. Kate would never want to change that about him. Being sheriff was a big part of his life. It must sting to feel as though he had to tiptoe around it, never discussing his job the way normal couples did on normal dates.

If she was going to attempt dating him, she should commit to it, not settle for a half-ass effort. "So what made you decide to go into police work?" she asked. "Family member on the force? The desire to help citizens in a crisis or return stolen purses to damsels in distress?"

At first, she thought his pause was because she'd surprised him with the question. After a moment, it became clear he was stalling on purpose. "I don't think I want to tell you. The answer makes me a lot less cool."

She laughed. "We're single parents. There are plenty of things that make our lives uncool. If it makes you feel any better, it's not like I expected this evening to end with me wearing your leather jacket and riding home on the back of your motorcycle."

"I was inspired to be a cop because of a TV show."

"That's not embarrassing. Police shows are a television legacy."

"Miranda's Rights," he said.

It took her a moment to place the name. "The old soap opera?"

"It was my mom's favorite when I was little. She had it on every afternoon, and I thought Miranda had a really exciting life. One season, she was abducted by aliens! Life around here was pretty dull, in comparison. The entire time I was growing up, I did not meet one person who suffered from amnesia or discovered they have an evil twin."

Kate snorted with laughter. "That's the reason you wanted to become a cop? So you could experience aliens and amnesia?"

"I was young and impressionable. And you are a very cruel woman, prying for personal secrets just so you can make fun of me."

"Sorry," she lied, still laughing. "I just wasn't expecting an answer like that. Now it makes me curious about those stories your mom offered to share yesterday. I'm sincerely hoping that you used to pretend to be your own evil twin. Or that you feigned amnesia to get out of a math test or something."

"You know, I was just thinking last month that I'd love to send my parents on a cruise. A long, *long* cruise, far away from beautiful blondes looking to mock me."

He paused, then added slyly, "Maybe I should ask your grandmother for intriguing stories about your childhood."

That sobered her quickly. "Truce? I never bring up your affinity for cheesy soap operas, and you don't interrogate Gram."

"I don't know." He smirked. "Now you have me curious."

Kate had always loved music and grew up with a tendency to sing no matter where she was. Unfortunately, as a child, she hadn't always understood the lyrics of certain songs she caught on the radio, which had led to more than one inappropriate public concert. She remembered Gram hustling her out of a grocery store one day after a woman in frozen foods stared at Kate in horror.

"Change of subject," she declared. "Where are we going to eat?" Culinary selections in Cupid's Bow were limited. The food was all good, but there weren't many choices.

"Actually, I'm taking us to an Italian place a couple of towns over. I hope Jazz and Brody don't have any trouble finding it. After all the work the three of you did giving my daughters an amazing birthday, I wanted to do something special in return. Plus, the long drive gives you and me more time together." He slanted her an avid look that made her pulse race, then smiled sheepishly. "I may also have been motivated by the fact that Becca Johnston is hosting a volunteer dinner at my favorite in-town restaurant."

Kate grinned. "Well, at least you're man enough to admit you're avoiding her. Did you give her an answer on the bachelor auction yet?"

"Yeah, I caved. I sent an email agreeing to participate but am dodging her suggestions that we get together to discuss specifics in person. Kate, I know it's presumptuous to ask you to bid, but…please, please don't let that woman get me."

"You realize that in order to stop her, I'd probably need to take out a mortgage on the farm?"

"I will pay you back every dime. Who needs savings? For all I know, my girls won't want to go to college anyway. Maybe they'll take after their Uncle Jace."

She would have laughed if she hadn't spent so many sleepless nights fretting over her own kid's future. She'd invested some of the life-insurance money to help pay for college, but more than once, she questioned whether he'd even be accepted anywhere. University enrollment would require improved grades and fewer disciplinary problems. Being suspended from school didn't look good on an application.

"Auction aside," Cole said, "you are planning to visit the festival, right?"

"Isn't it mandatory for all Cupid's Bow citizens?" she teased. "I've been under the impression that one would be run out of town for skipping it."

"Correct. Unless you have a note from the doctor excusing you."

"I used to go every summer with my grandparents. I'm looking forward to it." The festival would kick off next Friday. Kate had already agreed to join Gram for a couple of volunteer events.

"I'll be working in an official capacity for most of festival weekend," Cole said, "but I'm supposed to have a few hours free Sunday afternoon. Do you think maybe we could go together? All of us, the kids, too."

Oh, boy. She could just imagine the sneer on Luke's face when she informed him of that plan. As his mom, she could force him to go. But it was difficult to force someone to have a good time. The last thing she wanted was for his dour attitude to ruin the girls' fun. And the girls presented an entirely different problem. Would seeing Luke and Kate together only encourage their dreams of getting a stepmom?

Part of her yearned to say yes, but she couldn't bring herself to agree without further consideration. Instead she joked, "Let me get this straight—you want me to commit to being your date for the festival *and* to bidding on you for yet another date? That's a lot of investment on my part when we've barely even started our first date. What if tonight's a disaster?"

He laughed. "You don't have to give me your answer yet. I can wait. But, for the record? Tonight's going to be wonderful."

Chapter Nine

Kate was having the time of her life. The mushroom ravioli she'd ordered had been well worth the drive, the dinner conversation was punctuated with frequent laughter and Cole somehow made her feel like the most beautiful woman in the room, despite the fact that she was seated across from a woman who, up until Christmas, had been a professional model. *And to think you almost told him no when he asked you out.* She leaned against the high-backed booth with a happy sigh. *New policy. From now on, always tell Cole yes.*

A blush climbed her cheeks as she considered situations far racier than dinner.

"Kate?" Jazz tilted her head, studying her from the other side of the candlelit table. "You okay? You look flushed."

Turning toward her, Cole tucked her hair back to study her face. Even that slight touch sent tingles up her spine. For the past hour and a half, they'd been in repeated contact. He'd held hands with her, their legs brushed beneath the table, and at one point when the restaurant's air-conditioning had kicked on, he'd seized the opportunity to put his arm around her and pull her close because she "looked cold."

"Everything all right?" he asked softly.

The heat she'd been feeling intensified. "Must be the wine I had." Or the fact that she hadn't been able to stop thinking about kissing him again all night. It was ironic that the more fun she had on their double date, the more she couldn't wait to leave and get him alone. He was an undeniably attractive man, but his attentiveness to her was even more arousing than his physical appearance.

"Want me to catch the waitress's attention and get you another glass of ice water?" He scanned the dining area, pausing to nod hello to a man approaching their table.

"Evenin', Sheriff." The stranger was tall and handsome. He held a black cowboy hat in his hand, and his sun-streaked hair was attractively scruffy, as was the hint of beard that shadowed his jaw. "Brody."

Brody shook the man's hand. "Jarrett. You know Jasmine Tucker and Kate Sullivan?"

The man's smile widened. "Afraid I haven't had the pleasure. Jarrett Ross. Are you ladies from Cupid's Bow, too?"

Jazz nodded. "Cole promised the food would be worth the extra drive. He's obviously not the only one who feels that way." The dining room was packed.

"This place stays busy," Jarrett agreed. He held up one of the buzzers used to signal when a table was ready. "My date and I are hoping we'll have time to eat and still catch a movie after this."

"I knew there had to be a date somewhere," Brody said. "With you, there's always a pretty woman involved."

"Look who's talking," Jarrett said with a wink in Jasmine's direction. "Tiffani's in the ladies' room."

Brody and Jarrett chatted about ranching business for a few minutes. Kate liked horses, but not enough to focus on the conversation with fantasies of Cole crowding her thoughts. He caught her watching him, and grinned. His hand dropped below the table to caress her thigh. Despite the fabric of her dress and the linen napkin she had across her lap, the slow stroke of his thumb felt as intimate as if he were touching bare skin. If she were alone with him right now...

"Oh, that's us." The pager in Jarrett's hand flashed red. "You guys enjoy the rest of your evening. I'm sure I'll run into you at the Watermelon Festival." He scowled. "Somehow Becca Johnston convinced me that because of the equine therapy work I do with disabled children, I have to be part of her 'heroes' auction. That woman is frighteningly persuasive."

As he walked away, Cole added, "Or just frightening, period."

Jazz craned her head to watch Jarrett go. "He'll have no trouble raising bids. You know I love you, Brody, but speaking on a completely objective level as someone whose former career centered around the human form...whoa."

Kate laughed, temporarily distracted enough from lusting after Cole that she finally recognized Jarrett's name. "Wait, *he's* the rodeo cowboy Gram's friend was trying to set me up with?"

Cole poked her in the shoulder with his index finger. "Don't even think about it. You are currently unavailable." Though his tone was playful, there was a note of possessiveness she found thrilling.

"Don't worry, I don't want anyone but you."

His eyes darkened, and she knew that if they weren't sitting in a crowded restaurant right now, he'd be kissing her breathless.

"Aww." Jazz had her chin propped on her fist, grinning at them as if she were watching a favorite romantic movie. "Nothing makes me happier than seeing two terrific people fall in—"

Bracing herself for the impact of the word *love*, Kate's entire body stiffened. Noticing, Cole cut off Jazz's sentence. "Yeah, seems like Cupid's Bow is sure getting a workout lately," he said, putting enough jocular emphasis on the pun to make the other couple groan.

For her part, Kate wanted to hug him in gratitude. She hoped her involuntary reaction hadn't hurt his feelings, but she deeply appreciated his sensitivity. There was no pretending they hadn't entered a relationship, whether she'd been looking for one or not, but to admit she might be falling in love with him? She wasn't ready to jump off that cliff.

"How did Cupid's Bow get its name anyway?" Jazz asked. "Anyone know?"

"Topography," Cole said. "When you look at a map, the town border is roughly bow-shaped."

Brody chuckled. "Guess Cupid's Bow sounded friendlier than Archery or Longbow, Texas. Definitely more tourist appeal than Death by Arrow, Texas."

Kate managed a laugh along with the others, but her heart wasn't in it. Just because an arrow was shot by Cupid didn't make it any less dangerous.

As far as Cole could tell, the evening had lived up to his initial promise of being wonderful. Frankly, it had been a gamble to make that boast. Kate's misgivings about dating were completely understandable. But since she was uncertain, he'd decided he just had to be confident enough for both of them. It had worked pretty well.

The only misstep at dinner had been that moment when she'd almost panicked over Jazz's careless phrasing. As close as he'd been sitting to Kate, he'd imagined he could actually feel the pounding of her pulse. She'd gone momentarily wild-eyed. But after he changed the subject, she'd eventually relaxed again.

Still, she was a lot quieter during the drive back to her grandmother's farm than she had been on the way to the restaurant. Maybe she was sleepy and pleasantly mellow from a rich dinner and two glasses of wine. If she were regretting their date, she would be leaning away from him, not angled in his direction and holding his hand while he drove.

Perhaps the lull in conversation was simply because she was enjoying the music from the radio. Her fingers periodically tapped along with the beat, moving across his knuckles in unconscious rhythm. As he turned onto the dirt road that marked Denby property, Kate reached for the volume button, humming softly as an acoustic ballad began.

"I love this song," she said.

Cole had been wishing he could prolong their time alone—once he pulled up in front of the farmhouse, there was a possibility their goodbyes would be monitored by Joan. Or, worse, Luke. Kate's statement gave him the excuse he'd needed. He put the car in Park and hit the button to lower the windows so that the music floated out into the night. Then he removed his seat-belt and got out of the car. She regarded him curiously.

He came around the other side and opened her door, holding out one hand. "Dance with me?"

She hesitated only a second, then reached over to bump up the volume again. A poignant melody combined with the drowsy pulse of tree frogs and crickets. Kate wrapped her arms around his neck and let him pull her much closer than would have been appropriate at the local dance hall. It felt indescribably good to have her against him. Too good. As they swayed together, his body responded with the full force of desire he'd tried to temper all evening. His senses had been filled with her, the sound of her laugh, the scent of her shampoo, the lushness of her curves as his body brushed hers.

Standing this close, there was no way to hide the effect she had on him, so he owned up to it instead, hoping the feeling was mutual. "You are a very sexy woman. It's been driving me crazy all night, in the best possible way." He held his breath, waiting to follow her lead. If she shied away—

"Cole?" Her fingers skated up the sensitive nape of his neck and threaded through his hair. "Kiss me."

He was eager to oblige, yet savored the moment, first pressing a kiss to the delicate skin beneath her ear, then dotting his way across her cheek. When his mouth reached hers, she melted in his arms, her lips parted in invitation. His tongue slid across hers, and he nearly groaned with pleasure. Their kiss went from explorative to hungry, his hand tangled in the soft cotton of her dress as he crushed her against him.

The billions of stars twinkling in the summer sky

were nothing compared to the stars he saw when Kate kissed him. His need for her made him feverish, reckless. The last time he'd considered trying to seduce a woman in the back seat of a car, he'd been in high school. Perhaps if he had a blanket or a coat to spread on the ground...

With great reluctance, he broke their kiss, needing a moment to catch his breath. And rein in his libido. It wasn't until he released her that he realized not only was a different song playing, it was fading to its last notes.

"That was..." She touched a finger to her bottom lip, her expression awestruck. The look in her eyes was a greater stroke to his ego than every compliment he'd heard his entire life, added together.

His laugh had a rough, strangled quality to it. "Keep looking at me like that, and I might forget that the gentlemanly thing to do is to take you to your front door and call it a night."

She inhaled deeply, and he couldn't help but admire the swell of her breasts at the neckline of her dress. "Part of me doesn't want to call it a night."

Which meant that part of her *did*. Shoring up his self-discipline, he stepped away from her. Too bad it wasn't thirty degrees cooler. Chilly evening air would help him clear his head.

It was a pretty night, though, and he was greedy for more time with her. "Want to walk from here?" he asked.

"Sure."

He turned off the car, locked it and pocketed the keys. Then he twined his fingers through hers and they headed down the informal, winding driveway that cut through the pasture. Ahead, lights shone through the front windows of the farmhouse. Was her grandmother waiting inside to gently interrogate Kate about their evening? If he'd left the twins with his mother, he knew Gayle would pepper him with questions the second he crossed over the threshold. Instead, he'd hired a sitter and hadn't told his mom or his daughters about his date. If Kate agreed to come with him and the girls to the festival next Sunday, Alyssa and Mandy would have proof soon enough that he was seeing her. If she said no, he didn't want them to be disappointed.

And how will you *handle it if she says no?* Disappointment would be too mild a word to cover his feelings if Kate didn't want to see him again.

"I have a confession to make," he said.

"Please tell me it involves another soap opera from the eighties," she teased. "Because that would make my night."

"Brat," he grumbled affectionately. "No, I was going to say that, as much as I enjoyed tonight, I'm eager to see you again when I don't have to share you with anyone else."

She slanted him a look that was difficult to read in the dark. "I'd like that."

"Maybe I could cook you dinner." The offer surprised him. When was the last time he'd cooked for a woman? "I'm sure Mom would be willing to keep the girls at her place for a few hours." It would mean admitting to his mother what his plans were, but he was willing to endure one of his mom's inquisitions in order to get unchaperoned time with Kate.

"Sounds wonderful."

"I'll check my schedule and call you so we can figure out a time." He was relieved that he sounded normal and not like a lovesick fool who was already counting the hours until he could be with her again.

KATE WAS AT the desk in her room, checking email on her laptop when the phone rang late Thursday morning. Since she knew Gram was in the house, she ignored it and started typing her response to the high school drama teacher, who'd written to ask if Kate offered voice lessons. The high school would be putting on a musical in the fall, and the teacher thought it might be wise to call in reinforcements for helping the teens prepare.

"Katie?" Gram knocked on the bedroom door. "Phone for you, dear."

Was Cole calling to cancel their dinner date this evening? It was a completely irrational thought—she had no reason to expect him to bail—but she'd been thinking about tonight so much, it was the first thing that occurred to her. When she'd accepted his invitation, she hadn't expected their next date to be quite so soon. But as he'd explained when he phoned yesterday, between duty at the county courthouse and the upcoming festival, his schedule was pretty packed for the next week and a half.

She opened her door. "Thanks, Gram." She raised the receiver to her ear, torn between fierce hope that Cole's plans hadn't changed and the niggling, cowardly hope that he *did* need to postpone. Based on how he'd kissed her the last time he'd seen her—and how she'd kissed him back—she knew their physical relationship was escalating. Was she ready for that? "Hello?"

"Hi, Kate. I hate to do this to you, but I need to cancel. Monica's got a bad summer cold."

Kate blinked. "Mrs. Abernathy?"

"Yes. Sorry, I shouldn't have assumed your grandmother told you who was calling. I'm afraid Monica won't be able to make it this afternoon."

"Oh." Relief that it wasn't Cole on the phone flooded her, overwhelming her so completely that it took a moment to collect her thoughts. "I'm sorry to hear she isn't feeling well. Just call me back when she's doing better, and we'll schedule a makeup lesson."

"Thanks for understanding. I'll talk to you soon."

As Kate disconnected the call, she was struck by the revelation of how much she wanted Cole. The sheer joy that had filled her when she'd realized it wasn't him, that he wasn't abandoning their plans, was staggering. To some extent, it was even liberating. Yet, now that she'd confirmed how much the night ahead meant to her, the unoccupied hours between then and now yawned in a void, the perfect incubation conditions for self-doubt.

In dire need of moral support, she dialed Crystal's number, expelling a pent up breath when her friend answered. "Hey, it's Kate. You know how we've been saying we should get Luke and Noah together? By any chance, could we do that today? I'm having dinner with Cole tonight, and I desperately need to be distracted so I don't spend the next seven hours fixating."

"Dinner, again?" Crystal whistled. "Jazz said she and Brody just went out with you guys. Two dates in one week—tell me again how this isn't serious?"

I can't. Not when she'd spent the majority of her waking hours obsessing over their last date, replaying his kisses in her mind. She'd even downloaded that ballad they'd danced to, had listened to it so often in the last day and a half that Luke and Gram were beginning to look at her strangely. "So…do you have some time this afternoon?"

"Well. I did have scintillating plans to do laundry— you wouldn't believe the amount of clothes five kids go through— and clean out my refrigerator. Obviously, I'll be brokenhearted to have to reschedule all that, but since it's for you…"

After a few more minutes of discussion, they decided to feed their respective children early lunches, then meet at the community pool. Kate knocked on the door to Luke's room to alert him to the day's agenda. He didn't react with anything as drastic as a smile, but he nodded quickly. He was probably getting cabin fever hanging around the farm.

He was almost cordial during lunch. Though she hated to jeopardize that progress, it was time to tell Luke about her plans to go to the festival with Cole. She broached the subject on the way to the pool, while he was buckled into the passenger seat and couldn't retreat to his room.

"Luke, you know the Watermelon Festival is coming up, right?"

"Duh. Everyone's been talking about it since we got here. These people take watermelon *really* seriously."

That made her laugh. "The festival is a town tradition and, believe it or not, a huge tourism draw. I was planning on taking you."

He shrugged. "'Kay."

"It's a four-day event and we don't have to go every day, although Gram mentioned there are some stations that could use a little extra volunteer help. But on Sunday, the last day…" She cast him a nervous glance, unsure how he'd react. "The sheriff and his daughters asked us to join them. We could all go together."

His expression tightened. "Don't you two get sick of each other? You're going out with him *again* tonight and I haven't complained about how gross that is. But that doesn't mean I want to be with you on one of your dates! That I want to see…"

"Luke—"

"I don't want to talk about it."

"Tough." She'd tried to be patient, but they couldn't resolve anything with him holed up in his room. Gram had coaxed him out to earn some allowance with farm chores, but he'd avoided interacting with Kate. "We have to do plenty of things in life we don't want to do." Like saying goodbye to loved ones. Like figuring out how to move on, no matter how painful or daunting that was.

Of course, her insistence that they discuss the issue was funny given that she still didn't know exactly what to say. She kept it basic. "Cole is a very nice man. I'd like for you to get along with him."

He shot her a look that made it clear he considered this an insane request. "You never liked my friend Bobby. I don't have to like your *friend*, either."

She silently counted to ten. "Maybe that will come in time. You do have to be civil, though. That's non-negotiable. We're joining him and the girls next Sunday, at least for an hour or two. The twins look up to you. Can you try to leave the attitude at home?"

"We don't have a home," he said under his breath.

So much for her hope that he was warming up to

life in Cupid's Bow. She thought wistfully of his buoyant mood after he'd volunteered at the hospital with Rick. Then he'd befriended Sarah. He'd been making strides in the right direction. *Until he saw you and Cole kissing.* Knowing what a setback that had been for her son, how could she justify going through with her date tonight?

Cole's words on Gram's porch came back to her. *You can't live your life jumping through hoops for Luke.* For so long, it had felt as if she weren't living life at all. At best, she'd been coping, merely surviving from one day to the next. She'd shown up at work, taught her students songs and gone home to Luke in the evenings, usually with dread over the latest notes from his teachers. There hadn't been anything she'd looked forward to, nothing she'd anticipated with joy.

Even the nervous fear that gripped her when she pondered her feelings for Cole was preferable to that bleak numbness.

"Just promise me, Luke, that you won't be insufferable at the festival. Don't be rude to Cole or his daughters."

"Fine."

Having extracted that agreement, no matter how surly, she decided to count this conversation as a win. Or at least as a strategic advance in the ongoing battle of motherhood. Deciding to be a gracious victor, she turned on the radio and left him in peace for the rest of the ride.

When they reached the pool and she spotted Crystal unloading five children and all their swim paraphernalia from a minivan, Kate felt a twinge of guilt.

"Thank you so much for meeting me," she said as

she leaned in the van to help unfasten a one-year-old from a car seat. "I didn't think about how challenging it must be for you to make spontaneous plans."

"Don't mention it," Crystal said. "The kids love to come. It's early enough that I could even bring the little ones and they will absolutely *crash* later. Come naptime, I'll be singing your praises while I indulge in some peace and quiet."

"All the same, as far as I'm concerned, you're a superhero." Kate felt as if she had her hands full with *one* child, and Crys managed five? It was odd to think that their oldest kids were roughly the same ages. Crys had a child in middle school, one in elementary school, one in preschool and two toddlers. Starting all over with babies at this point felt incomprehensible.

But what about stepchildren? The thought came totally out of the blue. Kate's kneejerk reaction was instant denial, but didn't she know better than most that there was no way to know what the future held? That was true of the blessings as well as the tragedies.

Between the two adults and the assistance of the older kids, they herded the small children and a metric ton of towels, floatation devices, face masks and dive toys onto the patio area. After making sure everyone was adequately covered in sunscreen, Crystal and Kate agreed that the oldest kids could go to the main pool. Meanwhile, they took the twin toddlers and the five-year-old to a soft-surfaced fountain play area where they could run squealing through cooling jets of water.

"You sure *you* put on enough sunscreen?" Crystal asked Kate with exaggerated concern. "I'd hate for you to get sunburned before your big date. Nothing kills a

moment like a man reaching for you and you responding with 'ow!'"

"Hey!" Kate cupped her hand in a bubbling spray
and splashed her friend. "You're supposed to be dis-
tracting me from the big date, remember? Not torment-
ing me about it."

"Oh, please." Crystal put her hands on her hips.
"Other people are willingly babysitting your respective kids so you can have a child-free evening and the
incredibly hot sheriff is making you a home-cooked
meal. Which part of that is ammunition for torment?"

Kate made a mental note to try to babysit for Crystal sometime soon; surely she and her husband could
use the time to reconnect. "No, it all sounds heavenly.
Except…without the angelic, saintly behavior."

"Ah, now that sounds promising! Got naughty
plans?" Crystal waggled her eyebrows. "The man does
own handcuffs."

Kate blushed so dramatically she probably did look
sunburned to anyone looking her way. "Not helping,
you lunatic!"

Crystal giggled, and her boys wanted to get in on
the fun. Splashing and laughter commenced. Kate was
holding one of the twins, swooping him toward his
mom in threatening pursuit when she caught sight of
her own son standing by the pool. Although it was
difficult to be certain from this distance, it looked as
if he was talking to Sarah Pemberton. Had Luke re-
paired his friendship after hurting the girl's feelings?
Maybe Sarah had just needed a little time to forgive
him—just as Luke needed time to accept his mom's
relationship with Cole.

The anxiety that had been plaguing her all day

suddenly seemed ridiculous. Stress was no match for standing in the sunlight, surrounded by laughing children.

A few minutes later, Luke raced over to the kiddie area. "Mom! Can I go out with Sarah and her brother and her cousin tonight? Her brother and cousin are both old enough to drive. They want to see a movie and get a burger afterward. I have plenty of allowance saved up to pay," he added when she didn't immediately agree.

Money hadn't been her chief concern, although she was glad he'd volunteered to spend his own cash. Ideally, she'd be home to both vet Sarah's brother before he drove with Luke in the car and to make sure Luke arrived back by curfew. But, as far as she knew, Gram would be around. Plus, Kate had been the one who'd encouraged Luke to go out among real people, instead of only interacting with online avatars. Wasn't it better for him to be out with other teens than at home, giving her date with Cole too much thought?

"All right. I'd like a number for her parents, though, so I can confirm with them that this okay. I need a clear itinerary of what movie showing you'll be at, nothing R-rated." The cashier wasn't allowed to sell tickets for R-rated films to minors, but she knew exceptions got made. "You have to be home by ten-thirty. And do I even need to add that I expect you to behave?"

He folded his arms across his chest. "I will if you will."

KATE WOULD HAVE recognized which house was Cole's even if she weren't staring at the street number on the gleaming white mailbox. The sheriff's car in the driveway was a dead giveaway, for starters. But the front yard looked exactly as she would have imagined. The yard was perfectly manicured, hinting at a resident who liked order, but there was nothing fussy or feminine— no flowers or decorative seasonal banners. There were, however, chalk drawings on the sidewalk, a soccer goal set up for practice in the yard, and a glittery purple bike with training wheels leaning up against the house, beneath the shelter of a front porch overhang.

She climbed out of her car, nervously tugging her halter top into place. After her trip to the pool today, she'd toyed with the idea of stopping by Jazz's shop to buy something special to wear. She'd ultimately decided against it, though, having already endured teasing innuendo about her love life from one Tucker sister today. More important, she wanted to feel at ease, comfortable in something she already owned. The green-and-blue halter dress was one of the sexier items she owned, while still being completely appropriate for late June.

The accompanying strapless bra and lacy black panties she wore beneath were slightly less appropriate.

She'd barely knocked when Cole opened the door. He looked incredible in a pair of jeans and an untucked button down shirt. She found his still damp hair and bare feet oddly endearing.

"Right on time," he said, leaning in for a quick kiss as he ushered her inside. "I should have asked earlier, but you're not allergic to seafood are you?"

"Nope. Sounds great—and smells delicious. I brought these for you," she said, stating the obvious as she passed over the pan of walnut fudge brownies she'd baked.

His eyes lit up. "Oh, good. If the pasta doesn't turn out right, we can skip right to this."

She laughed, following him through a living room decorated in warm earth tones to the kitchen. At the sight of the drawings hung on the fridge with magnets and the two pink-edged pony placemats on the table, her heart gave a funny thump. Her thought from earlier in the day haunted her: *What about stepchildren?* She still couldn't imagine ever again exchanging wedding vows. But she had to admit, Cole's daughters tugged her heartstrings. Plus, his being such a good dad was part of his appeal.

"The girls are with your parents?" she asked, leaning against the granite-topped counter.

He nodded. "They're, um, spending the night. Mom thought a sleepover might be fun."

Her cheeks warmed. A sleepover *would* be fun… although there was no way she'd tiptoe into the farmhouse at sunrise, hoping no one had noticed her all-night absence.

"Can I get you a glass of white wine?" he asked.

"Yes, please."

"Just between you and me, I'm usually a beer guy, but white's supposed to go well with shrimp." He grinned as he poured a glass of sauvignon blanc. "I thought I'd shoot for classy tonight. The girls chipped in, too. They haven't cleaned with so much purpose since last December, when they were trying to impress Santa Claus. You should feel honored."

"I definitely do." But there were nerves, too. After all the effort he'd gone to, she hoped she could muster enough appetite to do dinner justice. "Anything I can do to help?" Standing here sipping wine and thinking about how good he looked in jeans felt unbelievably decadent.

He shook his head. "French bread's in the oven, salad's tossed and waiting in the fridge. We should be all ready in a few minutes."

"You thought of everything."

"Including the after-dinner entertainment." With a grin, he pulled open a drawer and pulled out a DVD.

When Kate read the title on the cover, she laughed out loud. "The pilot episode of *Miranda's Rights*?"

"Mom got it for me a couple of birthdays ago, as a joke, and I never even took the cellophane off. If it turns out to be any good, I will feel vindicated. If, on the other hand, it's as terrible as I suspect..." He glanced her way, the heat in his gaze hotter than the blue flames on the stovetop. "Well, then we may have to come up with other ways to entertain ourselves."

NORMALLY, THE SMELL in the diner would have Luke salivating for a double cheeseburger. He wasn't really hungry, though. He'd eaten so much popcorn during the movie that he felt kind of nauseated. Plus, he'd been uncomfortable since they left the theater. Sitting in the backseat of the car with Sarah made his stomach feel funny—even before her cousin Elliot started in on him.

After they'd exited their movie, Elliot had suggested they duck into one of the other theaters for a "bargain double feature."

"The trick is to do it one person at a time, casually," he'd said, "like you're just coming back from the bathroom."

"Nah, we don't have another two hours anyway,"

Sarah's brother had said. "Luke's gotta be home by ten-thirty."

Elliot had rolled his eyes. "What the hell? Doesn't your mom know it's summer? It's not like this is a school night."

Luke hadn't known how to respond. Luckily, Sarah had interrupted to ask if anyone else had recognized an actress in the movie. Conversation shifted to television shows while they waited to be seated at the diner.

When the hostess finally showed them to a table, they passed Rick Jacobs, sharing a platter of buffalo wings with a couple of burly men in baseball caps. Rick nodded hello but didn't intrude. He knew how to give a guy space, unlike Luke's mom. Before she'd allowed him to go out for the night, she'd called Mrs. Pemberton and practically asked for the life history of Sarah's brother. Luke wouldn't have been surprised if she'd had the sheriff run a background check before agreeing that Luke could get in the car with him.

Once they were all seated, Elliot took a renewed interest in Luke. He glanced from Sarah to Luke, an unpleasant grin on his face. "I don't know how I feel about some punk dating my little cousin. How do I know you're good enough for a Pemberton?"

Sarah kicked him under the table. "We're not dating." Her face was bright red as she said it. Was she humiliated by people thinking she and Luke were more than friends?

Elliot ignored her. "She says it was just you and your mom who moved to this Podunk town. What happened to your dad—he take off?"

"Died," Luke snapped. So far, he and Sarah had

avoided having that conversation, and he resented El-liot's asking.

"Oh. That's tough luck, kid." Elliot leaned back, looking genuinely sorry. Maybe he didn't completely suck, although Luke wished Elliot didn't view him as a "kid." There was only a four-year difference between them. "My dad ran off a couple of years ago. Mom's not terrible, but you should meet some of the losers she dates. That's why I visit my aunt and uncle as often as possible."

Luke was surprised to find himself on common ground with the guy. "I don't like *my* mom's boyfriend, either."

"Sheriff Trent?" Sarah turned to him, surprised. "He seems okay to me."

Elliot disagreed. "That a-hole gave me a speeding ticket during spring break. I wasn't going that fast. Any decent dude would've let me off with a warning."

By the time the waitress came to take their orders, Luke and Elliot had bonded over their shared dislike of Cole Trent. As Luke talked trash about the guy, he ex-perienced a brief moment's guilt, picturing Aly's face. She'd be hurt if she overheard his comments.

But she wasn't here now. It wasn't as though Luke was saying anything bad about *her*. When the food came, Luke discovered his appetite had returned. He plowed through his onion rings, embellishing the story of how he'd first met the sheriff and his daughters. He was beginning to think Elliot was a lot like Bobby Rowe—a good guy to have in your corner, you just had to impress him first. And Elliot was guffawing at Luke's shoplifting story.

Luke had another twinge of guilt, recalling that it

was Rick he'd stolen from. *I gave it back. No harm, no foul.*

"So you took stuff right under the sheriff's nose and put it in his own kid's purse?" Elliot cackled. "Priceless. That took guts, Sullivan."

Luke had left out the part about not finding out who Cole was until afterward since the sheriff had been in civilian clothes. "Yeah, but he caught me. Oops, right?" He rolled his eyes, trying to look nonchalant about his brush with the law.

By ten o'clock, Luke was feeling better about the evening. Sarah was quieter than she usually was while barking out locations of loot while they were gaming, but even she had giggled during Luke's story about the gas station heist. He wished he didn't have to go home so soon. Lame curfew. What did his mom care when he got back, anyway? She was probably still out with *him*. Luke's stomach tightened, making him regret the onion rings.

Sarah's brother calculated the bill, and they all dropped cash into the middle of the table. Luke still had a couple of fives left over and tucked them back into his pocket. While they waited for the waitress to bring change, Elliot leaned across the table with a grin. "Hey, Sullivan, know what you should do?"

"What?"

Elliot pointed across the way where an older couple were leaving their booth. As they walked away, the man tossed a bill on the table for a tip. "You should snag that. Bet you could buy a couple of candy bars for that little girl, and the funniest part is, the sheriff would have no idea they were 'stolen.'" He hooted with laughter, amused by his own scheme. "You could even show him the receipt!"

Luke frowned. "I don't know." He'd seen the candy bar as belonging to the station, not a person. Their waitress tonight had done a good job. Swiping tip money was stealing from *her*. What if she needed it?

Elliot raised an eyebrow. "I thought you had guts. Were you even telling us the truth about taking stuff before?"

"Lay off," Sarah's brother said. "Let's just get out of here."

"Why, because little Luke has to get home for beddy-bye time?" Elliot sounded disgusted, their earlier solidarity disappearing. "Come on, man up, Sullivan, it's just a few bucks. No one's talking about breaking into the bank."

Next to Luke, Sarah squared her shoulders, surprising all three of them when she said softly, "I'll do it."

THEY NEVER ACTUALLY got to the soap opera pilot. Over a thoroughly delicious dinner of shrimp pasta, they'd spent so much time discussing music that, by the time they loaded the plates into the kitchen sink, Kate wanted to see his CD collection. They'd laughingly cited bands that would be relationship "deal-breakers" if they discovered either of them owned albums by those artists. Cole pulled a couple of velvety brown throw pillows to the floor and they sat there eating brownies and reminiscing about the first live concerts each of them had attended.

When Kate ran across a CD by a jazz artist she'd never heard of, Cole put in the disc. Piano and saxophone filled the room, and he asked her if she wanted to dance.

She smirked. "Is that your go-to move, Sheriff Trent? Ask a girl to dance, and the next thing you know, the two of you are making out?"

"Damn, you're on to me. Guess it's time to drop the pretense," he said, taking the CD case from her hand as he leaned tantalizingly close, "and just skip to the making out."

His lips closed over hers, tasting like Cole and chocolate, and she went dizzy with bliss. Their kisses were languid and unending, the most perfect seduction she could imagine. He swept her hair to the side, giving him better access to kiss her neck and tease her earlobe with his tongue. She shivered, the lazy pleasure she'd been enjoying yielding to neediness.

He rolled her back against the pillow, nipping at her throat as his hand skimmed her ribcage toward her breast. She ached with the need to be touched there. By the time his palm covered her through her clothes, she couldn't contain a moan. She turned onto her side, hooking one leg over his, trying to bring their bodies closer together, which wasn't easy in a skirt. She wished her dress was gone. She wished he'd untie the halter top knotted at her nape.

But then she'd be undressed in front of him, would make love with him.

Well, *yes*, her hormones agreed ecstatically. That was the point. Yet her mind didn't seem to agree. She'd be making love with a man. Who wasn't her husband. It was like a macabre sort of virginity; there could only be one first time. Eyes burning with conflicting emotions, she rolled back, putting nearly a foot between them and trying to gulp in air. Damn it. This was no time for a panic attack!

"Kate?" To his credit, Cole didn't crowd her. He paused, searching her gaze. "Was I rushing you? We don't—"

"You didn't do anything wrong. I was enjoying everything we did. I wanted more."

He arched a brow, no doubt wondering why she'd suddenly bolted if she were enjoying his kisses so much. Unfortunately, she didn't know if she could explain without sounding nuts. She wanted to have sex with Cole. She *really* did. And the visceral realization of how much she wanted it had broken her heart.

She sat up, tucking her knees to her chest. "After Damon died, I didn't want to take the sheets off our bed. I knew that we'd slept in them together for the last time, and I didn't want to wash them. It was like… When you lose someone, it seems like it would be all at once. They're alive, then bam, they're not. But that's not how it is. You lose them in a thousand little ways, over and over." A hot tear hit her arm, and she wanted to kick herself. They'd been having a wonderful night, and she was completely ruining it with her maudlin nonsense.

"Kate, it's okay."

She sniffed. "I want…you. But once I sleep with you, it's another way I've said goodbye to him. A really big way." She'd survived painful milestones like her first birthday post-Damon, the first Christmas without him, the smaller moments like the first time she'd picked up the phone and started to call his cell before remembering there'd never again be an answer at the other end. She'd worried about the first time she kissed another man, but kissing Cole had been so effortless and natural. It had given her an unrealistic sense of how easy this would be. "I th-thought I was ready…"

He stood, crossing the room, then returning a moment later with a tissue box.

She took it gratefully but couldn't meet his gaze. What was the point in getting dolled up for a date if she was going to end up red-nosed with mascara pooling down her cheeks?

He knelt in front of her. "Sweetheart, look at me, please."

Right now, the idea of letting him look into her eyes made her feel as exposed as if she were naked. She was trying to psych herself up to accomplish the tiny act of bravery when a jarring sound cut through the jazz still softly playing.

"That's my phone." She shot to her feet, grimly thankful for the interruption. Intellectually, she knew she and Cole would have to discuss this if there were any possibility of them moving forward. But emotionally, she wanted time to put this raging embarrassment behind her before facing him again. The number on her cell phone display was Luke's. Was he calling to let her know he'd made it safely home before curfew?

Maybe it was fortuitous she and Cole had stopped when they did. She couldn't imagine trying to pause in the middle of sex to talk to her son. "H-hello?"

But it wasn't Luke's voice that answered her. "Ms. Sullivan? This is Rick Jacobs, calling on Luke's behalf. I'm at the diner on Main Street, where your son is currently talking to the manager. It might be a good idea for you to come down here."

"Is he okay?"

"Yes, ma'am…but maybe in a little trouble. There seems to be some suspicion that he stole cash off a table, although Luke's insisting the witness misunderstood."

It wasn't my fault this time. How often had she heard statements like that back in Houston? She choked back a sob, recalling her optimism earlier in the day. It seemed her confidence in herself and in her son had been misplaced. "I'm on my way."

Chapter Ten

Luke was beginning to think he was going to hurl the onion rings back up. The flinty-eyed manager who'd hauled him into the stuffy back office clearly didn't believe Luke's story—that a breeze had fluttered the five-dollar bill to the floor and Luke had simply picked it up to put back on the table. Telling the truth would land Sarah in trouble. Luke wasn't about to rat her out.

After saying she would take the tip money, she'd shot him a nervous smile as soon as Elliot was busy looking at his phone. Luke had the impression Sarah was trying to do him a favor so that her cousin would stop harping on him. Luke had wanted to tell her not to, but the words had stuck in his throat. After all, *he'd* been the one bragging about stealing in the first place.

Instead, he'd formulated a plan. He'd let Sarah swipe the money, then replace it with the cash in his pocket once the Pembertons were a few feet ahead of him. No harm, no foul. Except, a nosy customer who'd seen him standing at the table with a five in his hand had misunderstood the situation and accused Luke of stealing. The waitress who'd given him his onion rings with a friendly smile had glared daggers at him and called for the manager, asking that Luke be banned from the diner.

Elliot had glared, too, probably putting together what Luke had really been doing. He'd told the manager he and his cousin had to get Sarah home by curfew. That was when Rick had stepped up, saying that he was a friend of Luke's mother and would call her. The Pembertons had bailed, leaving Luke behind.

Now, Luke sat at the front of the restaurant, where people traditionally waited for a table, with staff members eyeing him like he was a criminal while his mom made the drive from the sheriff's house. Rick sat next to him, not abandoning him like the Pembertons, but not saying much, either. Luke wanted to ask if the man believed him, but it was difficult to get the question out since, technically, Luke wasn't telling the whole truth.

Still, the silence was grating his nerves raw. He sighed as he watched his mom's car turn into the parking lot. As much as he wanted to get out of here, he dreaded facing her. He had an image of himself grounded until he was roughly Gram's age. "Mom is gonna lose her sh—her mind," he amended at Rick's reproachful look.

"Stop giving her reasons to," the man said bluntly.

Luke slouched down, wanting to insist this was all Elliot's fault. The creep had been goading him since before they even got to the diner. *So why didn't you ignore him, genius? Why try to impress him with the stupid candy-bar story?* Not only was his mother going to be mad about Luke stealing, which he hadn't even done, she was going to be ticked that her date had been interrupted. From the goofy smile she'd had all afternoon, he knew she'd really been looking forward to it.

She was not smiling when she walked inside. Her cheeks were blotchy, her eyes overly bright.

"Mom!"

Rick put a hand on his shoulder. "I'm going to have a word with your mother."

The two adults stood off to the side, keeping their voices low. Luke couldn't hear what they were saying, but his stomach sank even lower every time his mom darted a glance his way. He wished he knew whether Rick was putting in a good word for him or throwing him under the bus. He squirmed in his seat, wondering if the man would want his help again for the hospital magic show. Luke had enjoyed that. Performing for those kids had made him feel the same rush of pride he used to get when he showed his comics to classmates who thought the drawings were cool. He missed that.

Finally, Rick squeezed his mom's arm and, with a nod in Luke's direction, left. Next, she had to talk with the manager. Luke gathered from the bits he overheard that, since there wasn't hard evidence that he'd been planning to walk out with the money, the manager didn't feel as though he could ban him for life. However, he stressed that any time Luke came to the diner in the future, he would be watched *very closely*.

How was that fair? Elliot would go back home, in no trouble at all, Sarah got to keep the five dollars she'd taken, but Luke would be treated like a criminal any time he had a craving for onion rings. Which, actually, might never happen again. Those might be ruined for life.

"Let's go." His mother's voice was so soft his ears strained to hear her.

Was it a good sign that she wasn't yelling? Maybe

she just wanted to get him inside the car, away from witnesses. The farm was miles away from Main Street. He imagined his mom shoving him out of the vehicle in some darkened ditch. Even as the picture looped over and over in his mind like a GIF, he knew she'd never do anything like that. *She loves me.*

He swallowed, waiting as she unlocked the car. "How, um, was your date?" He wasn't sure why he asked, but he had to say something. And he didn't want to talk about what had happened in the diner. Besides, if there was even a slim possibility that talking about the sheriff might put that goofy smile back on her face, perhaps she'd be in too good a mood to ground Luke for sixty years.

"Don't you *dare.*" Her voice was still low, but it sounded like a growl now, more ominous than it had in the diner. "It's not easy for me, knowing you hate my relationship with Cole, but I respect your right to have feelings on the subject. Have enough respect for me not to stoop to brazen manipulation. It's insulting and dishonest."

"I'm sorry," he mumbled, a little surprised to find that it was true.

They'd been driving for five minutes before he spoke again. The tremor in his voice made him feel like a crybaby, but he couldn't help it. "I didn't take that money, I promise."

Her silence was louder than any of the video games she told him to turn down because she could hear them even through his headset. "Give me one reason why I should believe you."

Because it's the truth. But it was only part of the truth. He'd screwed up. Staring out the window into the darkness, he promised himself that he'd find a way to make it up to her.

KATE HAD BEEN so caught up in the emotional upheaval of her evening that she'd completely forgotten to call Gram. When her cell phone rang and Gram's picture flashed on the screen, shame filled her. It was now fifteen minutes past when Luke was supposed to have been home. Gram was probably worried sick.

"Luke's with me," she said as soon as she answered the phone. "There was…a bit of a problem at the diner where he and his friends stopped, so I'm giving him a ride home."

"Oh, well, I'm glad to hear that! Not the problem part, of course. But that you know where he is and I don't have to break the news to you that he missed curfew."

"We'll be home in ten minutes," Kate said, "maybe less."

"If it's all the same to you, dear, I'm going to turn in. See you in the morning? Oh, and in case I forget, Mrs. Abernathy apparently referred you to some other moms she knows. You had two calls from parents who want to meet with you. I wrote their numbers on the pad by the phone."

"Thanks, Gram." Kate bit her lip, thinking about the latest trouble Luke was in and the trouble they'd collectively caused since arriving. "Before I meet with any other prospective clients, are you *sure* you're okay with this parade of people in and out of the house?" Tomorrow was shaping up to be a busy day.

Gram chuckled. "Are you kidding? I haven't had so many visitors in years! Patch is in heaven." She sighed. "It's been lonely since I lost Jim. You and Luke have done so much to change that. I'll miss you if the two of you ever move."

"We're not planning on going anywhere," Kate said.

"Well...you never know, dear. You're still young. You may build a home elsewhere."

A home, or a family? From the sly, expectant tone in Gram's tone, she was hoping tonight's date with Cole had gone well. Thinking about it still mortified Kate. She'd wanted him so badly, yet...when she could have had him, she'd freaked out. Sophisticated sex goddess, she was not.

Kate wished her grandmother a good night, then disconnected. Ever since Rick Jacobs had called her, she'd been too furious with Luke's bad judgment to question why he'd bothered to steal a few bucks anyway. After all, this was the same kid who'd once inexplicably snatched a candy bar. But now, she couldn't help wondering, had his getting in trouble tonight been an attempt to sabotage her date?

She tried not to think that, on some level, she might have been glad for the excuse to leave.

FRIDAY PASSED WITHOUT Kate talking to Cole. As he'd warned when he said Thursday was their best option for dinner, his Friday was pretty busy. As was hers. So she managed to escape the day without any cringe-worthy rehashing of what had happened between them.

He left her two voice mails, and she sent him a text assuring that she and Luke were both okay and that she and Cole would talk soon. He'd wanted to come with her last night to the diner, but she'd refused. Partly because she'd desperately needed space and also because it was awkward when your boyfriend was the sheriff and your son was exhibiting criminal tendencies.

Now that Friday was over, Kate wanted to slip into

the oblivion of slumber and forget everything for a few hours. Heaven knew she should be exhausted. Last night, she hadn't been able to sleep a wink. But two hours after she'd retired to bed, sleep still eluded her. *Insomnia: 2, Sullivan: 0.*

Aggravated, she flipped over on her stomach. She never slept on her stomach, but she'd already tried both sides and lying on her back. Nothing was working. She had too many thoughts and worries buzzing through her, as well as a growing regret that she'd avoided speaking to Cole. *Coward.*

He'd been so patient and understanding with her, but patience wasn't infinite. How long would his last before he decided to wash his hands of her and find someone with fewer issues?

In addition to her emotional turmoil over the sheriff, she still had to decide what to do with her son. At lunch today, he'd broken down and told a convoluted story about how Sarah's cousin had bullied Sarah into stealing the five dollars. Either Luke was lying or Sarah was a thief or her cousin was a bully—possibly a combination of all three. While the details were fuzzy, she had the sense that he'd acted out of misguided teen nobility to protect Sarah, probably to make amends for the cruel way he'd spoken to her earlier in the week. But, honestly, when was her kid going to start learning from his mistakes and show better judgment? Had she moved him away from one peer group full of bad influences just to get him involved with another that was equally questionable?

Okay, lying on her stomach wasn't doing a damned thing to soothe her. She was half-heartedly entertaining the notion of a shot of whiskey when the phone rang, causing her to sit straight up in bed. It was pretty late for a call, especially in Cupid's Bow. Across the hall, she heard gentle snoring in her grandmother's room, so she hurried to the kitchen to grab the phone before the caller woke the entire household.

"Hello?" she said, keeping her voice low.

"Kate?" The woman on the other end of the phone sounded unsteady. "It's Gayle Trent. I—"

"Oh, God." She clutched the receiver so tightly the plastic creaked in protest. Her heart stopped. "What happened to him?" There was only one reason the sheriff's mother would call her in the dead of the night.

"He's all right, dear. He's in stable condition, and the doctor says he may not even have to stay the night. But I thought you should know."

Kate was suddenly shaking so badly she couldn't stand. She sat straight down on the floor, not bothering with the distance between her and the nearest chair. "Cole's at the hospital?"

"Yes. Deputy Thomas told us they answered a domestic disturbance call tonight. Cole was stabbed. An…an anterior stab wound, the doctor said. He lost a lot of blood, but he's going to be…" Her voice caught, broke.

There was a sob and rustling, then a male voice. "Kate? It's Will. I'm here with Mom and Dad. Cole's going to be all right," he said fiercely. "They're just running tests to make sure there was no perforation or occult trauma. We should be able to see him soon."

"I'll be there in ten minutes," Kate said.

He laughed, a brief rusty sound. "You can't make it to the hospital from Whippoorwill Creek in ten minutes."

The hell she couldn't.

But reality caught up to her as she fished her car keys out of her purse. For starters, she probably shouldn't show up to the hospital in nothing but a nightgown. And it would be irresponsible to leave in the middle of the night without writing a note that said where she'd gone and when she expected to be back. Plus, the last thing she wanted was to cause any accidents in her haste to get to the hospital, so she resolved to stick to the speed limit. More or less.

It was a fight, though, to keep her foot from mashing the accelerator through the floor. Her rush was twofold. Not only did she need to get to the hospital, to see Cole with her own two eyes, she needed to outrun the horrible, ice-cold déjà vu running through her veins. *I can't do this again. I can't.*

She clung to Will's assurance that Cole would be okay. This was completely different than when she'd rushed to the hospital the night Damon was shot—too late to say goodbye. The memories haunted her, overlapping with reality, and by the time she parked in the visitor's deck, scalding tears poured down her face.

Will was waiting for her, his handsome face haggard with worry. But he tried to cover his own concern with a smile. "No tears, darlin'. My brother is ornery, much harder to take down than this. I promise. Mom and Dad are in with him now. He asked me to take you straight back when you arrived."

She mumbled something that might have been thank you, but she wasn't sure. Words had lost meaning. She was only processing half of what Will said. She felt as if she were trying to walk on the ocean floor. Sound and movement were distorted, and she felt cold all over.

The world didn't start to right itself again until she stepped into the partitioned room where Cole sat on a hospital bed with an IV in his arm. His family stepped out to give them a moment of privacy, and Kate went straight to him, running her hand over his bare chest, needing to feel the solid heat of him. Normally, she appreciated any chance to see him shirtless, but the large white bandage covering the side of his torso made her want to vomit. She tried to muffle her cry with her hand and failed miserably.

"Kate, I'm okay." He started to put an arm around her, then cast an impatient glance at the machines monitoring his vitals. He wasn't especially mobile, and he had to be in pain. "Look at me, I'm okay."

"This time!" What about the next time someone was drunk and disorderly? Or if he pulled over the wrong motorist? Or the day some crackpot figured out how to successfully get a gun into the courthouse? "You were lucky."

His lips quirked in a wry half smile. "If getting stabbed is your idea of good luck, I'd hate to—"

"Please don't joke. Not about this. Not about your safety." She was backing away from him as she spoke, as if her being here was somehow dangerous to him. *No, his being close is a danger to you.* What had she been thinking? How could she let herself fall for another man, especially the sheriff? She'd known it was a bad idea, but he'd won her over with his patient coaxing and his devilish blue eyes and how great he was with his girls.

"I can only imagine how hard this is for you," he said, holding out a hand, trying to draw her back to him. "I wish my mom hadn't called you, but—"

"Her not calling wouldn't have changed the fact that you're hurt. Just like my ignoring the risks won't save me from getting hurt. I knew better!" She glanced at him and for a second, in the double vision of her tears, there were two Coles.

Both were shaking their heads at her. "Don't do this," he insisted. "You're overreacting because of your past, because you lost Damon."

"I'm not reacting to my past—it's too late to change that—but I am trying to safeguard my future. Because I finally, vividly, understand how much you could break my heart. I can't…" *I can't do this again.* She swallowed hard, determined to choke out the last words. He at least deserved to hear her say them. "Goodbye, Cole."

WHEN LUKE GOT up Saturday morning, he knew as soon as he left his room that something was wrong. On the way to the bathroom, he heard mom and Gram talking in weirdly hushed voices, the kind he recognized from after his dad's death. His first fear was that they were talking about *him*. What if that stupid five dollars in tip money turned out to be his mom's breaking point and she was considering something drastic, like sending him off to military school or something? Then he heard the words *stab* and *hospital*.

"Gayle called me with an update while you were in the shower," Gram said.

Gayle Trent? Luke suddenly realized that they were discussing the sheriff. Cole Trent had been stabbed? Panic twisted in Luke's gut. Aly and Mandy shouldn't grow up without a dad. No kid should have to grow up without a dad!

When his grandmother added, "He's at home and doing better," Luke sagged in relief, reaching out to support himself against the wall.

"But he's plenty ticked off," Gram added. "I can't believe you dumped a stab victim while he was still in the hospital." She sounded disappointed. There was a lot of that going around in the house lately.

Wait, Mom had broken up with the sheriff? Luke wasn't sure how to feel about that. He hadn't liked Cole—it was impossible to like someone you suspected was trying to get your mother in bed. But she'd looked so happy the other day.

"Gram, I can't. Not again. I made myself way too vulnerable. I suppose I should be glad Luke hated us dating. What if he'd gotten attached? He's already lost so much. How would it have affected him if he and Cole bonded, then we broke up? Or Cole got… If he…"

She was crying. Luke fisted his hands in helpless frustration.

Gram's voice was soothing now, not chiding. "I understand the desire to protect yourself and your son. But how much can you realistically shelter yourself? Just getting into a car can be dangerous, yet people do it every day."

"People need to get places. I don't *need* to date the town sheriff."

It got very quiet in the kitchen, and Luke wondered if they were done discussing the subject. He should go. He was in enough trouble without his mother catching him eavesdropping. Just as he turned to leave, he heard Gram make one last point.

"I love you, dear, and it was a tragedy your husband was taken from you so young, but you're not the only one who's lost the man you love. Don't you think I'd give anything I had for one more day with my Jim? Even if I knew I'd lose him again afterward, I'd cherish that limited time. Because, really, that's all any of us have, even in the best of situations—limited time."

It was a morbid thought for a sunny Saturday morning, but, as Luke crept away, he couldn't get the words out of his head.

ALTHOUGH THE DOCTOR had only technically cleared Cole for desk duty, to reduce the risk of his popping his stitches, by Thursday Cole was desperate for more to do. An abyss of misery yawned at his feet, waiting to swallow him whole whenever he was inactive. Thankfully, his brother took pity on him.

"You can't help set up the booth," Will stressed when he picked up Cole in his truck. "But you can supervise and delegate. The guys will listen to you. Then once we're in good shape for the festival kickoff tomorrow, I'll buy you lunch."

This week was all about festival preparation, but Cole had never cared less about the damned Watermelon Festival. This year, it was simply a reminder that his date for Sunday never wanted to see him again. And to add insult to injury, in about forty-eight hours, he would probably be purchased for a date with Becca Johnston.

Hell, maybe he should just go out with her anyway. He'd say this for her, she was stalwart. Not the type to head for the hills over something as minor as a paltry stabbing.

As soon as he'd seen Kate's pale face in the hospital, he'd known. They were over, practically before they'd begun. He wasn't sure which of them he was angrier at—her, for prioritizing fear over what they could have had together; or himself, because she'd warned him since day one that she was still too fragile for a relationship with him and he hadn't listened.

Trying to push Kate from his mind, he climbed out of Will's truck, calling greetings to other firemen who were helping erect a booth for safety demonstrations and the stage for the auction that would ultimately benefit the fire department. For about half an hour, he actually managed to convince himself he was being useful. It was the closest he'd come to approaching cheerful in days.

But it was damned difficult to push someone from your mind when she was walking toward you with a hesitant expression and a banner painted with pink letters that were outlined in green and flecked with black. Seeing her knocked him so off guard that it took him a second to realize the letters were supposed to represent slices of watermelon.

"Hi." She approached carefully, as if he were a feral animal. Truthfully, there had been moments over the past few days when that seemed like an accurate description of his mood.

"Hi." He let his gaze flick in her direction without lingering on her. Looking at her was too painful. "So, you got pressed into volunteer service, huh?"

"Gram thought I could use the…"

Distraction. Did that mean she'd been moping around the farm? Was it possible Kate was missing him as much as he missed her?

"How's the wound healing?" she asked. "Gram's

been giving me updates from your mom, but I guess I need to hear it for myself. How are you?"

He made himself meet her gaze then, letting her see exactly how he was doing. He was miserable. She might be worried about the stabbing, but her words to him at the hospital had sliced through him with far more pain and destruction than that blade.

"I…" She dropped her gaze, but not before he caught the tears glistening on her lashes. "I'm sorry I interrupted. I saw you here and had to check to see if you were okay."

No. I'm not. "I'll live." Which was more than she allowed herself to do. Cole knew seeing him in the hospital had to have been emotionally wrenching, but in retrospect, he couldn't help wondering if she would have found a reason to end things anyway. She'd obviously been conflicted at his house Thursday night, then she'd avoided him the following day. If his injury hadn't prompted her mad dash to the hospital, would she have continued to avoid him? Would she have gone longer and longer without returning his calls and eventually found an excuse, such as her son's antics, to keep from being Cole's date to the festival?

Although the idea of her with another man caused Cole to grind his teeth in jealous fury, he would rather see her on another guy's arm than watch her hide behind fear and the hostilities of a thirteen-year-old. Kate was a passionate, bighearted woman with a lot of love to give. If only she were brave enough to let herself.

The silence between them had passed awkward about six seconds ago, and Cole sighed, knowing he should cut her loose. "Thanks for checking on me. I hope you and Luke have fun at the festival this weekend. Don't let your grandmother or anyone else work you too hard."

"Thanks. I… I hope you feel better soon."

And then she was gone. He wanted so badly to chase after her, to implore her to change her mind. But he'd been coaxing and cajoling since they'd met. There was a line between patiently wooing, and stalking. Besides, he had his pride—or at least the tattered remains of it.

Cupid's Bow was a small town. She knew where to find him if she changed her mind.

LUKE WAS SURROUNDED by what felt like hundreds of happy people—and he hadn't even thought Cupid's Bow *had* hundreds of people. Maybe some of the people playing midway games, signing up for the watermelon-eating contest and buying giant turkey legs dripping in grease were out-of-towners. He didn't care so much about their origins as he did their collective good mood. He was desperately hoping it would rub off on his mother.

She was starting to scare him. He knew she was crying when no one was around to see; her puffy, red eyes were unmistakable. But she seemed determined to have fun at the festival with him. She'd been smiling all day, but not a real smile. It was like he'd gone to town with a creepy animatronic version of his mother.

Even now, she was staring at him with that fixed smile and blank eyes. "What do you want to do now? There are some arts-and-crafts demonstrations. I know you might be a little old for some of those, but you've always had so much natural talent. Or we could try out some of the rides, although I'm not sure my dinner's had enough time to settle," she warned.

"Or we could just go home," he said. She seemed pretty sad there, but, somehow, out among all these happy-happy festivalgoers, it was even worse.

"This early?" she asked. "Are you sure?"

He shrugged. "You said it was a four-day thing. We should pace ourselves."

"All right." Was it his imagination, or was there a hint of relief behind her plastic expression?

They crossed between a snack shack and a small stage where regional choirs were performing patriotic songs, headed in the direction of the parking lot down the street. It wasn't until they'd left some of the noise behind him that Luke realized someone was calling his name. He and his mom turned at the same time, and he felt a wave of surprise when he saw Sarah running down the sidewalk after him. They hadn't really spoken since the night at the diner. Seeing her now, he felt a flash of joy—he'd missed her—tempered by wariness. He didn't even know if he was allowed to talk to her, or if she'd joined Bobby Rowe on his mom's forbidden list.

"Hey," he said noncommittally, darting a nervous look in his mom's direction.

It took him a second to realize there was an adult trailing Sarah at a much more sedate speed.

"That's my mom," Sarah explained. "We tried to catch up with you earlier in the crowd, but lost you during the parade. Luke, I owe you an apology, and your mother one, too, for the trouble I caused. I've already told my parents about what happened. Mrs. Sullivan, Luke didn't take that money." She hung her head. "I did. It was stupid. My cousin Elliot more or less dared one of us to, and I should have just told him to shut up. Luke was only trying to put the money back."

Next to him, his mother shifted and he was relieved to see the freaky masklike expression disappear. She looked like herself again. "You were telling me the truth. I'm sorry I didn't believe you more wholeheartedly."

"I'm sorry you've had so many reasons to doubt me," he mumbled.

Mrs. Pemberton was introducing herself to his mom and apologizing for Elliot's role in everything. "My nephew hasn't always been a troublemaker, but he's not taking his parents' divorce well. Rest assured, my children won't be going anywhere unsupervised with him for a long while. In fact, they're both currently grounded, although I have to make an exception for the Watermelon Festival."

Luke's mom managed a small laugh. "Absolutely. After all, it's in the town bylaws."

"Well, we won't keep you," Mrs. Pemberton said. "Sarah told me last night what really happened, and when we spotted you today…"

"I wanted to fix things," Sarah said shyly. "I hope we can be friends again."

Luke grinned. "You forgave me for being a jerk on the phone. I guess I can forgive you for being a notorious criminal. But…we should probably avoid the diner next time we go out for burgers."

"I'll text you when I'm not grounded anymore."

"She's a nice girl," his mom said as they resumed their walk to the car. "I'm glad to see you making friends in Cupid's Bow."

His mother had friends, too. She liked hanging out

with Crystal and Jazz. But he wasn't stupid. He knew the person who meant the most to her in this town was the sheriff.

All week, Luke had been cringing at his mom's secret crying jags, which reminded him of when his dad died. But in a way, these were worse. No power on earth could have brought his dad back. There was nothing they could do.

But her relationship with Sheriff Trent? In theory, that was fixable. So maybe he should follow Sarah's example and do something to fix it.

Chapter Eleven

On Saturday, Kate woke to a truly horrendous stench wafting into her room. It smelled as if someone was throwing old tires onto a bonfire nearby. Just as she was swinging her feet to the floor in order to go investigate, there was a knock on her bedroom door.

Before she had a chance to answer, Luke peeked his head inside. "I brought you breakfast in bed," he informed her.

Oh, good Lord. He was the bearer of the stench. He came into her room with a tray that included a glob of purple she assumed was grape jelly with bread somewhere underneath it and charred eggs.

She swallowed hard. "Wow. To what do I owe this… surprise?"

"Mom, we need to talk about your love life."

"Uh…" It generally took her brain about an hour to start functioning properly. She was ill-equipped to take on a subject fraught with that many landmines.

"Look, I know this is a heinous topic for both of us," he said as he shoved the tray into her hands, "but sometimes people have to discuss things even when it's not comfortable."

She blinked, relatively certain he was parroting

back something she'd recently said to him. *He listens!* Who knew?

"About Sheriff Trent—"

"You don't have to worry about that relationship anymore," she assured him. "That's over."

"But you love him. Don't you?"

There it was, the question she'd been trying not to ask herself. Fired at her from her thirteen-year-old with the precision of a sniper. "I…" Was it too late to pull the blankets over her head and pretend she was asleep?

"I think you should go for it, Mom."

"*You do?* Who are you and what have you done with my son?"

Shamefaced, Luke sat on the mattress next to her. "I guess I've been kind of obnoxious about the whole thing. When I miss Dad, I like to think about the three of us together. It's comforting to remember you with him. Seeing you with someone else…well, it made me want to blow chunks."

"So why the change in her heart?" she asked. This week, she'd fielded well-meaning lectures from Gram, Crystal and even Brody Davenport when she'd run into him at the supermarket, although his had been far more subtle. But the very last person she'd expected to encourage a reconciliation with Cole was her son.

"As much as I hate seeing you with the sheriff," Cole said, "it turns out, seeing you *without* him is even worse."

She bit the inside of her cheek, feeling guilty. She'd made an attempt to act normal this week, not inflicting her misery on the rest of the household, but she'd obviously failed.

He fidgeted, not meeting her gaze. "Do you remember when you told me we were moving to Cupid's Bow and I complained all the time?"

"*All* the time," she agreed. "Twenty-four-seven."

"Every time I whined about coming here, you told me to think positive. So why aren't you, Mom? It seems like you're making decisions based on worst-case scenarios."

My God, he's right. Was that really the example she wanted to set for him? Gram had pointed out rather pragmatically that everyone had limited time, and no one could foresee when that time might come to an end. So did Kate want to spend whatever years she had joyously embracing life—and love—and teaching her son to do the same? Or did she want to cower in fear, shying away from risks?

A smile spread across her face, and she felt lighter than she had in days. "You know, kiddo, for a thirteen-year-old, you can be pretty wise."

He grinned, looking pleased with himself. "Does this mean you'll get him back?"

She prayed it wasn't too late after she'd rejected Cole when he was wounded. "First, we need a real breakfast. Then we need a plan."

WHEN THE AUCTIONEER called his name, Cole limped out onstage. He'd been on his feet for what felt like forty-eight hours straight and had spent so much time shifting his weight to compensate for the pain in his side that he'd made his leg sore. Plus, there was always the slim hope that if he looked like damaged goods, women wouldn't bid on him. Let them save their money for guys like Jarrett and Will.

Or not, he thought with an inward sigh as Becca Johnston belted out a bid. Cole scanned the assembled crowd, hoping this would end quickly so he could go grab a hamburger. His gaze snagged on one familiar face.

Kate was here? He'd hoped she would stay away. Their last encounter had been awkward enough. But he supposed she was just doing her civic duty.

He was so stunned to hear her declare, "Forty dollars!" in a voice that rang like a bell, he almost toppled over. Forty? The highest winning bid so far had been eighty-seven bucks. Cole was almost halfway there. Why would she bid on him? She had to know he wouldn't hold her to their previous agreement, not now that she'd walked away from the possibility of a future with him.

Another woman called out forty-five dollars, and Becca immediately countered with sixty. The auctioneer looked at Cole with blatant approval, then attempted to whip the women into a bidding frenzy. By the time they passed the hundred dollar mark, Cole's heart was in his throat. His gaze was locked on Kate's as he tried to decipher her motives, but he couldn't tell anything from here. Except that her smile was the most beautiful sight in all of Cupid's Bow.

When Becca Johnston reached one hundred and twenty-five dollars, Cole wanted to slump in despair. Kate hadn't wanted him when she could have him for free; surely she wouldn't pay triple digits for the privilege.

"One forty."

"One sixty!"

"One sixty-five." Kate's eyes never left his.

"One hundred and ninety dollars," Becca said, studying her manicure as if she could do this all day.

An expectant hush fell across the crowd. "Two hundred," Kate said. But her voice trembled slightly. Piano teachers didn't make tons of money. On either side of her, Jazz and Crystal were digging through their pockets and purses.

"Two hundred and fifteen." Becca sounded aggrieved now. Her hands were on her hips, and she was glaring in Kate's direction.

Kate squared her shoulders and lifted her chin. "All I have to offer is two hundred and twenty-eight dollars...and faith. Faith in love and second chances and the courage to pursue happiness. I'm just sorry I hadn't saved up enough of it before now."

Cole's heart was bursting with pride in her—and joy over her words. If he weren't worried about popping his stitches, he would have jumped down from the stage already to kiss her. A loud sniffle distracted him, and he glanced in surprise at Becca Johnston.

"Oh, just give it to her," Becca said, wiping at her eyes with the side of her hand. "I can't top that."

As the audience broke into applause, Kate ran to the edge of the stage. Will was suddenly there to give her a boost up onto the platform.

Then she was in Cole's arms, and his leg didn't hurt anymore. Neither did his side. Or his heart.

He pulled her close for a kiss, murmuring, "I love you," against her lips.

"I love you, too. I thought it was too soon to say, but what am I waiting for? Life is precious. And I want to spend as much of it with you as I can."

"Even when it gets scary?" he asked.

The specter of fear crossed her face, but she smiled anyway. "When it gets scary, you'll just have to hold me and make it all better."

"Deal."

As Luke joined the rest of them at the shaded picnic table, he saw the sheriff steal another kiss from his mom. Somehow, it didn't seem as gross as it had before. Maybe because Luke was in such a good mood.

"I never thought I'd win a trophy for anything besides video games," he said, setting the gold cup on top of the table.

His mom laughed. "I don't know what they were thinking, letting a teenage boy participate in an eating contest. The rest of the competition didn't stand a chance."

Gram grinned. "Lots of winners this weekend. Luke won the watermelon-eating trophy, you won a date with the sheriff…"

"Ha," Kate scoffed. "I didn't win it. I paid for it."

Cole put his arm around her. "I promise to be worth every penny."

Okay, now they were getting too sappy. To distract himself, Luke turned to Aly on his other side. She was coloring on a sheet of paper. "Whatcha drawing?" he asked.

"Us." She pushed the paper toward him so that he could see the representation of him, the twins, Cole and his mom, all holding hands and smiling underneath a rainbow.

"Hey, you only used the sparkly crayons on the

adults," he commented, noticing how the tallest of the two stick figures shimmered. "What about the rest of us?"

She shrugged, then pointed to where his mom was whispering something to the sheriff. "Don't they seem extra-sparkly?"

"Yeah. Yeah, they do." He grinned from ear to ear. If anyone had told him a month ago that his mom would look this happy—or that Luke would be having fun in Cupid's Bow—Luke would have assumed it was some weird practical joke.

"Daddy, can I go with Nana to get an ice cream?" Mandy asked suddenly, spotting her grandparents at the nearby frozen desserts vendor.

"Sure," Colc answered, barely taking his eyes off Luke's mom.

Aly frowned. "But she had a funnel cake a little while ago. And a popsicle! We're never allowed to have that much junk food."

Luke laughed, lowering his voice to a conspiratorial whisper. "Want to know a secret about adults? Sometimes when they're in a *really* good mood, they give permission for stuff they would normally say no to."

"Really?" Her face brightened, and she scampered off the bench, inserting herself between her dad and "Miss Kate" to show them her drawing. Once she had their full attention, she beamed up at them. "So, about my pony..."

* * * * *

"Is it okay with you if I move a little closer?"

He chuckled. "We're supposed to be in love. I think you're allowed to get as close as you want without asking permission."

She stepped in and leaned her head on his shoulder. It felt good there. Felt right. As if his body remembered their intimacy. He took his hand from her waist and wrapped it around her, securing her against him, and she let out a contented sigh.

He imagined leaning down, finding her lips and losing himself in her kiss. Then taking her by the hand down the hall to her bedroom...

Except they had an audience.

And they were pretending.

This wasn't real. He couldn't let himself be lulled into falling for the very story they were spinning for the press. He released her and stepped back.

"Look, I should head home."

"I'll be in touch first thing in the morning."

He settled on the same greeting he gave his brothers' fiancées, and kissed her cheek.

Then he left the apartment. Quickly. Because the stupid part of his brain had told him to kiss her again. And this time, not on the cheek.

* * *

His 24-Hour Wife
is part of the Hawke Brothers trilogy:
Three tycoon bachelors, three very special mergers...

HIS 24-HOUR WIFE

BY
RACHEL BAILEY

Published in Great Britain 2015
by Mills & Boon, an imprint of Harlequin (UK) Limited,
Eton House, 18-24 Paradise Road, Richmond, Surrey, TW9 1SR

© 2015 Rachel Robinson

ISBN: 978-0-263-25282-8

51-1015

Harlequin (UK) Limited's policy is to use papers that are natural, renewable and recyclable products and made from wood grown in sustainable forests. The logging and manufacturing processes conform to the legal environmental regulations of the country of origin.

Printed and bound in Spain
by CPI, Barcelona

Rachel Bailey developed a serious book addiction at a young age (via Peter Rabbit and Jemima Puddleduck), and has never recovered. Just how she likes it. She went on to earn degrees in psychology and social work but is now living her dream—writing romance for a living.

She lives in a piece of paradise on Australia's Sunshine Coast with her hero and four dogs, where she loves to sit with a dog or two, overlooking the trees and reading books from her evergrowing to-be-read pile.

Rachel would love to hear from you and can be contacted through her website, www.rachelbailey.com.

This book is for Charles Griemsman, who's worked on all my Desire books since 2009. Charles, you are an absolute pleasure to work with, and have such an excellent eye for story. Thank you for making my books better!

Thank you to Barbara DeLeo, Amanda Ashby and Sharon Archer for your brainstorming and suggestions. Also to Amy Andrews for my favourite line in the book. You're all amazing!

One

Callie Mitchell straightened her skirt, took a deep breath to calm the butterflies in her stomach and followed the receptionist to Adam Hawke's office on the top floor of a downtown LA office building. The central operations of his company, Hawke's Blooms, took up the entire floor and, as CEO, Adam had a corner office, which had to have killer views.

In hindsight, it had probably been a bad idea to stop on the way for a little Dutch courage—especially because it had been alcohol that had started this whole crazy mess—but she'd needed some help. It wasn't every day a woman had an appointment to see her secret husband.

In fact, she hadn't seen him once in the three months since their wedding day, so this was quite the momentous occasion. They'd met at an industry conference in

Las Vegas just over two years ago and spent an amazing night together, then had hooked up again at the following year's conference. Third time had been the charm—this year they'd added vows to their rendezvous.

The receptionist opened the door and waved her through and suddenly Callie was standing in front of him. The man she'd spent the most explosive times of her life with. The rest of the world faded away, leaving only him. The oxygen must have faded away, as well, because suddenly she couldn't get her lungs to work.

The receptionist had slipped out and closed the door behind her, leaving them alone, but Callie couldn't find a word to say. Although Adam wasn't saying anything, either.

He was as perfect as she remembered, which was a surprise—she'd been certain her imagination had embellished things, that no man could be that gorgeous. Yet here was over six feet of proof standing before her. His green eyes were as intense, his frame as broad and powerful as the image she had in her mind's eye. But he was wearing a suit with a crisp white shirt and dark blue tie. Most of her memories were of him stretched across the Vegas hotel sheets wearing nothing but a smile.

He cleared his throat. "You look different as a brunette."

She'd gone back to her natural caramel brown about three weeks ago, but instead of telling him that, she heard herself say, "You look different with clothes on."

His eyes widened, and she covered her mouth. That Dutch courage had been a very bad idea.

Then he laughed, a low rumble that seemed to fill the room. "I'm starting to remember why I married you."

"And what drove you away again," she said and

smiled. After a day spent in bed, gradually sobering up, Adam had suggested a divorce. She'd been having so much fun—and was, in all honesty, so dazzled by the Adonis who'd proposed to her—that she would have given their marriage a shot. But she'd had no rational argument for staying together, so she'd agreed.

Still, after three months, neither one of them had started those divorce proceedings. She didn't know Adam's reasons, but there was a small kernel of hope deep in her chest that maybe he wasn't quite ready to cut all ties with her yet.

He indicated two upholstered chairs near the windows, which, sure enough, offered a premium view of Los Angeles below. "Take a seat. Can I get you a drink?"

She knew he probably meant coffee or tea, but still she winced, remembering the gin she'd stupidly had before coming. "No, I'm fine. I won't be here long."

He nodded and took the chair across from her. Then his expression turned serious. "What do you need, Callie?"

For a moment all she could focus on was the sound of her name on his lips. His voice was deep and still sent a warm shiver through her. Three months ago he'd whispered her name in the heat of passion. Had murmured it when she'd kissed the smooth skin of his abdomen. Had shouted it as he'd found his release. More than anything, she wanted to hear him say her name again. Then his question registered, and she straightened her spine.

"Why do you think I need something?"

His forehead creased into a row of frown lines. "I just

assumed…" He let the sentence trail off. "After all this time, I figured if you were contacting me, you must—"

"I don't need anything," she said, holding up her hands, palms out. "I'm here as a courtesy, to let you know something."

His jaw hardened. "You're getting married?"

The way his mind worked was intriguing. She remembered that from their short time together—she'd been constantly fascinated by the things he said.

"No, I'm up for a promotion." Her PR firm had finally given her a chance to make partner—something she'd been working toward for years—and she wasn't going to let the opportunity go.

"Congratulations," he said. "So how does this involve me?"

"They've given me an assignment. If I handle this project well, I'll make partner." At twenty-nine, she'd be the youngest partner in the history of the firm.

He raised one eyebrow. "What's the assignment?"

"The Hawke Brothers' Trust." His company's new charity raised money for homeless children; it had already made a splash with various events, including a bachelor auction, and was now ready to move to the next level. Something Callie was looking forward to being a part of.

"Ah," he said, and rubbed the back of his neck. "I didn't realize Jenna had brought in your company."

Adam's future sister-in-law, Princess Jensine of Larsland, had helped to create the charity and was in charge of day-to-day operations. Callie had suspected Adam wasn't aware that her company had become involved. Which was why she was here, warning him, before she started work on the project.

"There was a good chance we'd run in to each other in a meeting or something, and I wanted to give you a heads-up before that happened."

"I appreciate it. So," he said, offering her half a smile, "how have you been?"

Despite being married, they didn't really know each other well enough to catch up. They had no basic information to catch up on. So she said, "Good, and you?"

"Good," he said, nodding.

It was awkward, so she took a breath and refocused. "I was thinking that maybe we should have our stories straight in case anyone puts two and two together."

He rubbed a hand over his chin. "You mean about us being married?"

"Since I'll be working with members of your family, it's a possibility."

"It won't happen. They don't know I—" He swallowed. "They don't know what happened."

"You didn't tell your family that you got married?" She hadn't expected he would brag about a short-lived Vegas wedding, but equally, she hadn't expected that he'd keep it a secret from his two brothers. In the short time they'd spent together, he'd mentioned he was close to his younger brothers.

He shifted in his seat. "Did you tell your friends and family?"

"I didn't tell everyone, but I told my sister." She moistened her lips. "You seriously didn't tell anyone?"

His face was unreadable. "I don't generally telegraph my mistakes to the world."

Asking her for a divorce had pretty much shown he had thought of their wedding as a mistake, but still, there was something in the way he held himself tall in the chair—and in his tone as he said it—that had made her feel small and insignificant. She'd thought of their time together as something wild and crazy, something out of character, where they just went too far. She hadn't thought of herself as someone's mistake. It hurt more than she would have expected.

But now that he'd made his feelings crystal clear, the stupid part of her needed to let go.

She took a breath. "While I'm here, we really should talk about a divorce."

"Already underway," he said without hesitation. "I've filled in the paperwork and was just waiting for my brother's wedding to be over before filing it."

"Oh, right. Good." Everyone knew Adam's younger brother was marrying Princess Jensine of Larsland, so Callie could see that he wouldn't want to draw attention when the media could be hunting for stories.

"I didn't want my alcohol-fueled decision to have ramifications for him."

Flinching, she stood and hitched her bag over her shoulder. "I should go. Let me know when you're ready to file the divorce papers."

"Callie." He reached out to her as he stood, and then let his hand drop. It was the first time his voice had held a note of tenderness since she'd entered his office. He'd been the only man who'd ever affected her with merely his voice, and she wobbled. "I'm sorry," he said. "That was probably harsh. I don't want us to part on bad terms."

"It's fine," she said, summoning a polite smile. "But I've taken up enough of your time. I just wanted to give you some forewarning and I've done that, so I'd better get back to promoting the Hawke Brothers' Trust."

He held her gaze for a heartbeat or two, searching her eyes. Then he nodded and stepped back. "Okay. Let me know if you need anything."

Callie smiled and slipped out the door. Halfway down the corridor, her cell rang, and she paused in the reception room to answer it. A colleague's name flashed on the screen: Terence Gibson. He'd recently been up for the same promotion as Callie and his competitiveness had bordered on excessive. Since she'd been offered this project with the chance to win the promotion if she did well, she knew this wasn't going to be a congratulatory call.

"Hi, Terence," she said.

"I can see why the partners gave you this assignment," he said, not bothering to hide the malice in his voice.

She punched the elevator button. "And why is that?"

"Being married to one of the clients will certainly give you an edge."

She froze.

"Oh, you mean they don't know about your marriage to Adam Hawke? Oh, dear. I wonder what upper management will say when they find out. It will hardly make them feel as if they can trust you, and I hear they value open and clear communication in their partners."

The elevator arrived but she ignored it, sagging back against the wall. "How did you...?"

"You really need to work on your poker face, Callie. The expression when they told you it was for the Hawke Brothers' Trust would have told anyone watching closely enough that you had some sort of connection. The question was only about which brother. After a bit of searching I found that you married one of them three months ago. Although I couldn't find a record of a divorce anywhere. I assume that's where you are now? With your husband?"

Her stomach clenched tight. "What do you want, Terence?"

Despite asking the question she had a pretty good idea of what the answer would be.

"Stand back from this assignment and let them hand it to me."

It was what she'd expected him to say, but still, the gall of the man, the entitled arrogance, was staggering. "You know I won't do that. It would be handing you the promotion, as well."

"Then I'll sell the story to the tabloids," he said, his voice almost gleeful. "I'm sure you can imagine what a PR disaster that will create. They'll love an exposé about the future prince's brother having a drunken wedding in a tacky Las Vegas chapel."

"No." It would overshadow her assignment and ruin her chances of the promotion.

"Then step away now and give me a clear shot at the partnership."

So either she stepped back and let Terence have the partnership, or she stayed and he caused a scandal, meaning he'd probably get the partnership instead of her anyway. Neither of those choices was appealing, but she especially didn't like giving in to blackmail. She needed time to think. To find a third option. She had to stall him.

"Give me a few days to think about it. Even if I tell the partners I can't take the assignment I'll need some time to come up with a believable reason."

"You have one day. Twenty-four hours."

The line went dead.

Callie blew out a breath, turned on her heel and headed back to Adam Hawke's office.

Adam stood when Rose, his receptionist, buzzed to tell him Callie Mitchell wanted to see him again. It had barely been five minutes since she'd left. He told Rose to let her through, and then had a look around the room for something Callie had forgotten. He couldn't find anything. But then, he was hardly focused enough to be sure.

Since she'd first made the appointment yesterday, he'd been unsettled. He'd dreamed about her last night, about their time together. About making love to her. Though that wasn't uncommon—he regularly dreamed about making love to her.

Which just showed how bad she was for his equilibrium. Control over himself and his life was important to him, and Callie made him feel off-center—a feeling he disliked intensely.

Then from the moment she'd appeared through his door this morning, he'd barely had two functioning brain cells to rub together. Hell, he hadn't even greeted her, just made some inane comment about her hair. Though her reply had been memorable...

He prayed this would be a short visit so he wouldn't make a fool of himself by blurting out something worse than what she'd said.

After a knock on his door, there she was again, as if conjured from his dreams, her rich, caramel-brown hair hanging sleek around her shoulders, her olive skin smooth. He knew from experience the taste of that skin, and his heart skipped a beat as the memory flooded his senses.

"Did you forget something?" he managed to ask.

She shook her head, her silver-blue, almond-shaped eyes serious. Something had changed.

She tipped up her chin and met his gaze squarely. "We have a problem."

He was careful not to touch her and set off more memories as he moved behind her to shut the door and lead her to one of the chairs they'd occupied only minutes before.

Once they were settled, he said, "Okay, tell me."

"A *colleague* of mine," she said, her emphasis on the word *colleague* telling him much, "noticed my surprise when I was given this assignment and started digging. He's found our marriage license and is threatening to tell the tabloids."

Adam swore under his breath. "What does he get out of it?"

"He wants this promotion and he wants me out of the way. He thinks the media coverage of your secret Vegas wedding will overshadow any PR work I do for the trust, and he's probably right. He wants me to refuse the assignment and let him have it."

"Like hell." There wasn't much that Adam hated more than a bully, and he refused to let Callie become the victim of one while he had any power over the situation. "The trust won't work with a man who's blackmailed his way to get the role."

"If I step back and you refuse to work with him, he'll probably still plant the story out of spite. We'd both still lose."

Callie's entire demeanor was professional, but underneath she had to be rattled. Every protective instinct inside him reared up, ready for whatever needed to be done.

"Give me one minute."

He stood, strode over to his desk and pressed the buzzer for his receptionist. "Rose, cancel all my meetings for the rest of the day."

"Certainly. Do you want me to give a reason?"

"Just that something unexpected has come up. Then reschedule them as soon as you can."

"Consider it done."

He grabbed a legal pad and pen and returned to his wife. It wasn't just Callie's job in danger, though that alone would be enough to make him take action. No, he wouldn't let his stupid mistake create trouble for his brother and future sister-in-law. His Vegas wedding had been out of character for him, and since then he'd taken the consequences seriously—he hadn't let himself drink more than a glass or two of alcohol at a time, and rarely let his control slip even an inch. This was just another consequence that needed addressing.

And he could fix this. That was what he'd always done in his family—fix things. The only difference was that this time, Callie was the one with the PR expertise.

"So, how do we handle the PR fallout when the story hits the press?"

A tentative smile crept across her face. "You want me to stand up to him?"

"Well, I certainly don't want you to give in to blackmail." He frowned, searching her features. "What did you expect me to say?"

"I don't know. Thing is, I don't really know you that

well, so it's a pleasant surprise that you're willing to stand behind me."

She might not know him as well as, say, his brothers did, but surely she at least knew this much of his character? "Callie, I know our history is a little unconventional, but don't ever doubt that I'll stand behind you."

"Thank you," she said, and for one brief, shining moment he recognized the passionate woman from Vegas who'd snagged his attention from the moment he'd laid eyes on her in the bar. "That means a lot. And it goes both ways."

"I appreciate it. Now, what's our first move?"

She tapped a bright red fingernail against matching red pursed lips as she thought. "We need to get ahead of the story. Be on top of it and create our own story."

"Sounds good," he said. "How do we do that?"

"We need to come up with our own version of our wedding." She rose to her feet and started pacing, her words coming rapidly. "Create a new truth—it was love at first sight. Make it a sweet story, not the sleazy version that the tabloids will want to print, and get that new truth in the media ASAP to beat the other story. My contacts will help get it out quickly."

Adam made a few notes, and then looked them over. "It doesn't seem like enough—it will be one version versus the other."

"True," she said, holding up an index finger, "but that's only step one."

He smiled. "Good."

"The second part is to give them the current story."

He made another note on the legal pad and asked without looking up, "What sort of current story?"

"Something about us." She stopped pacing.

"About us being together?" he asked warily.

"That would be best." She rested her hands on her hips, her mind obviously going at a million miles per hour. "Perhaps that we're ready to have a real wedding."

He hid the instinctive flinch. If they were to find a workable solution, he needed to be open to all ideas in this first brainstorming phase. "How does that help?"

"Then, the story of our Vegas wedding becomes a very sweet, love-at-first-sight beginning to our current relationship and can't harm my career or your family. I'll let my bosses know before the story appears, and apologize for not disclosing the fact sooner, saying we'd agreed not to tell anyone before the announcement."

"A wedding," he said, this time allowing his skepticism to show.

She shrugged one slim shoulder. "It doesn't have to be forever, just until the story dies down and we can quietly separate and go back to our normal lives."

"How do we explain the intervening months?"

"I'm not sure. Give me a moment."

Again, she tapped her nail against pursed lips and, as he watched, he sat back. She was even more beautiful in real life than she'd been in his dreams last night. They'd been back in the Vegas hotel bed where he'd kissed that same lush mouth and covered her naked body with his. His blood began to heat. He stared at the light fixture in the ceiling as he brought his wayward body back under control.

"Okay," she said, gracefully sliding back into the chair across from him. "What if we say we gave it a go at the start but circumstances tore us apart. However, we never lost touch and recently we've begun to work through our problems and can finally announce that we're ready to begin a life together as husband and wife."

He released a long breath, mentally checking all angles. "That roller-coaster history will feed in to the explanations when we break up again afterward. What will it take to convince them that we didn't just make this story up as a stunt?"

"Besides the story itself, which we'll give to an entertainment journalist I trust, I'll have friends leak details to key journalists. We'll also need to appear in public together, and do some media interviews. Then we'll have the wedding."

The last item on her list caught him off guard. His mouth dried. "You really want to go through with an entire wedding?"

Callie, on the other hand, seemed entirely unfazed by the prospect. Apparently she had nerves of steel. "We're already married, so it won't change anything legally. Either way, we'll still need to get a divorce at some stage."

Adam swallowed hard. She was right. Besides the cost of a wedding, which would barely make a dent in his bank balance thanks to the success of Hawke's Blooms, marrying her again wouldn't make any important difference—they were already married. But being around her, spending significant amounts of time near that lush mouth, just might change everything…

Two

Four and a half hours later, Adam looked around his brother Liam's living room at his collected family. Liam and his fiancée shared the sofa, a baby in each of their laps. On the opposite sofa were his youngest brother, Dylan, and his fiancée, Faith. Dylan and Faith now split their time between New York and LA; Adam was lucky they happened to be in town for this meeting. His parents were in two armchairs near Liam's elbow, and he and Callie rounded out the group.

Everyone was chatting in twos and threes, catching up on each other's news. But it was time to face the music. Adam's gut clenched tight.

He turned to Callie and quietly said, "Ready?"

"As I'll ever be," she answered, her expression not giving away much.

Bracing himself to lay out his mistake in front of

the people whose opinions counted the most, Adam cleared his throat. His family quieted and turned to him, waiting.

"Thanks for adjusting your schedules so you could come out here on short notice. I needed to introduce you to Callie Mitchell. Callie is taking over the PR for the Hawke Brothers' Trust."

Both his brothers raised eyebrows at him, but Jenna jumped right in. "I'm thrilled to meet you, Callie. You probably already know, but I head up the trust, so we'll be working together."

Callie smiled back. "I'm looking forward to it."

"However," Liam said, his head cocked to the side, "this raises the question of why you're introducing her to all of us and not Jenna."

Dylan held up a hand like a stop signal. "Are you about to try and talk us in to some crazy-ass PR stunt like the bachelor auction?"

Adam snorted. "As I recall, that stunt seemed to work out well for you." He looked pointedly at Dylan's hand holding Faith's—she was the person who had bought the package of three dates with Dylan at the auction.

Dylan grinned, acknowledging the point, and then leaned in to kiss Faith's cheek, which had turned pink.

"So why are we all here, then?" his mother asked.

Adam drew in a breath and cast another quick look at Callie, to ensure she was coping with his family's antics. Besides being a little tense—which was to be expected under the circumstances—she seemed fine.

"Callie and I..." he began, wishing he was anywhere but here. "We knew each other before she took this account."

Dylan made a sympathetic sound. "Callie, sweetheart, if you've dated my brother, let me apologize now. He can be a little—"

"Uptight," Liam interrupted.

"Yeah," Dylan said without missing a beat. "Let's go with uptight."

Adam pinched the bridge of his nose. His life was unraveling and they wanted to take the opportunity to rib him?

"She didn't date me," he said when he knew his voice would be even again. "She married me."

After a moment of stunned silence, the room erupted into questions, each being called more loudly than the one before. Even the babies, Jenna's daughter, Meg, and Liam's daughter, Bonnie, joined in on the action, laughing and waving their arms around.

Callie looked over at him, her eyes wide. He didn't know much about his wife, but from her reaction he guessed she didn't come from a boisterous family. This was a baptism of fire into the Hawke clan.

"Sorry," he said, and offered her a tight smile. He loved his family, but they tried his patience at least half the time. He turned back to the horde. "If you'll give me a chance, I'll let you know what happened."

The noise immediately stopped, and Adam could breathe again. "Callie and I met at a conference in Vegas several years ago. We've spent time together at the same conference for three years running and at this last one, we made a spur-of-the-moment decision to get married."

Liam was first to find his voice. "I assume alcohol was involved?"

"Please tell me there was an Elvis impersonator officiating," Dylan said, clearly loving the entire debacle.

Adam kept his voice even. "Alcohol on both sides, and no Elvis impersonator."

His mother leaned forward in her chair. "From the fact that this is the first we're hearing about it, you clearly didn't plan on staying married. So why are you telling us at all? Are you hoping to make a go of it now?"

"Hey!" Dylan said before Adam could reply. "I just realized why you refused to be part of the bachelor auction. You were already married."

Adam winced. The auction had taken place just after he'd arrived home from the fateful weekend in Vegas. He might not have been telling the world about the wedding, but neither would he lie and pretend to be a bachelor. However, he ignored the question and turned back to his mother.

"Callie was given this account by the partners of her firm without them knowing about our connection. Unfortunately, a colleague of hers found out and is hoping to blackmail her into handing the project over to him so that he can get the promotion when it's completed."

"That's awful," Faith said. "I hate petty politics like that. Can't you tell the partners?"

Callie leaned forward. "I could, but the story would probably get out anyway, and I think with Adam's connection to Larsland's royal family through Jenna, combined with his profile here in LA, the tabloids would have fun with the story."

"And," Adam added, "that could be disastrous for the trust. Donations could dry up. Not to mention the impact it could have on the coverage of Liam and Jenna's wedding."

Both Liam and Jenna opened their mouths to speak,

but Callie got in ahead of them. She was a quick study in how to deal with his family, and he appreciated that.

"It's okay," she said. "We have a plan."

Callie looked to Adam, as if for permission to explain. He nodded—it was her idea, so it was only fitting that she explained it.

"We're going to take control of the story and announce our new relationship. We'll speak to some journalist friends of mine and have it run in the media, complete with photos. The story will then be about an unconventional start to a sweet relationship. Hopefully, the interest will die down and we'll be able to go back to normal sooner rather than later."

"New relationship?" his mother asked hopefully.

Adam almost laughed. Of the entire crazy story, *that* was the phrase his mother had focused on.

"Sorry, but the story is fake. Callie and I will wait until any interest has blown over, then quietly get a divorce. The only ones who will know the truth are the people in this room and Callie's family."

His mother looked disappointed, but there was nothing he could do about that. Besides, she'd soon be gaining two new daughters-in-law. She was doing well enough without him having to add to the count.

"I'm worried you're doing this for us," Jenna said with a hand on Liam's thigh. "You don't have to—we'll be fine."

They might be fine, but he'd be damned if he'd let his drunken mistake hurt his brothers or Jenna's family. It was his mess and he'd clean it up.

"Callie and I have discussed the potential ramifications on your family, Jenna, but also on the trust and

Callie's career. We've agreed this is the best course of action."

"What can we do to help?" Liam asked.

"We have the situation in hand," Callie said. "All you need to do is play along and attend the wedding."

Faith sat up straighter, as if she'd had an idea. "I can do a story on the wedding flowers on my TV segment if that will help."

Faith had recently started a job with a nationally syndicated gardening show, doing regular segments on flowers and floristry. The job was based in New York, and now she and Dylan split their time between New York and LA.

Jenna nodded. "Liam has a new flower, a snow-white tulip, almost ready to go. Instead of an event for this one, we could use the wedding as its launch. That will give the media something else to focus on besides digging for the truth."

That could help. Liam's work breeding new strains of flowers had been part of the reason their company had made a mark in the world of flower retailing. Jenna had organized red-carpet launches for the past two new blooms, and Faith's skills as a florist had ensured the most recent, the Blush Iris, had been presented to best effect, garnering them maximum exposure.

"It's gorgeous," Faith said, turning her excited gaze to Jenna. "Since you weren't firm on a name yet, perhaps we could tie it in? Call it the Bridal Tulip."

Jenna and Faith fell into a conversation about the flowers, while his parents took the opportunity to welcome Callie into the family, even if only temporarily. Adam watched, until his brothers approached him, blocking Callie from view.

Liam pulled Adam to his feet and clapped him on the back. "I can't believe you'll be the first of us to get married."

"Will be?" Dylan said. "He already *is* married. We're going to have to watch his drinking from now on."

Despite knowing it was a good-natured joke, Adam bristled at the thought of having to be watched like a child by his younger brothers, of all people. He tried to move away, but his brothers had boxed him in.

"You know," Liam said, pretending to think, "I don't remember the last time I saw him drunk."

Dylan grinned. "Now we know why. It makes him feel matrimonial."

Ignoring them, he shouldered his way past, reached for Callie's hand and then raised his voice to be heard over the din. "Much as I'd love to stay and enjoy Liam and Dylan's brand of support, Callie and I have to leave. We're meeting with her family, as well, tonight."

Within a few minutes, they had extricated themselves and made it to the car. Yet, even as he started the engine, his shoulders wouldn't relax. No one liked to have their screwups made into a joke, but still, it had rankled more than it should have for his family to witness the consequences of the only time in years he'd lost control.

And this farce was only just beginning…

Callie glanced over at her husband's strong profile, and a shiver raced down her spine. She'd spent most of the day with him, but there was something different about being in close quarters together in the dark cabin of the car. More intimate than a large, bright office and much more personal than a room with his entire family.

She felt the pull of him more strongly here, with nothing to claim her attention but his masculine beauty. His scent. Him.

His hands were firmly gripping the steering wheel and he seemed unsettled.

"That went okay?" she ventured.

"Sure, if you like publically admitting to your drunken mistakes and having them turned into wise-cracks by your brothers."

At the words *drunken mistakes*, she cringed. Her re-action was stupid since she already knew Adam regret-ted their marriage, but still, she couldn't help it. It was like a slap in the face.

No point being squeamish now, especially when it was her job that was forcing them to make their situa-tion public. She sat up straighter. "Let's put your broth-ers behind us and move on."

"Fine with me," he said, rolling his broad shoulders. "Fill me in on your family so I'm prepared before we arrive. Are they likely to mock? Chase me with a shot-gun?"

"No, it'll be all safe and calm. My parents are both teachers, happily married and loving parents. They'll want to know the details, but ultimately they'll support whatever I choose to do."

"Siblings?" he asked as he smoothly overtook a car full of teenagers who had their music up loud. She tried not to be mesmerized by the way his hands and arms worked to control the car.

"One sister, Summer. She's also my roommate." And best friend. In fact, Summer was the only person Callie had told about Adam when she'd returned from Vegas. She'd spilled the beans on the spontaneous wedding,

her toe-curlingly handsome new husband and her hope
that it might grow into something more one day. A hope
that had turned out to be in vain.

"Will she be there tonight?" His voice was deep and
rumbling, almost a physical presence in the car.

"She said she'd come for moral support. She already
knew about Vegas, and I filled her in on the phone this
afternoon, so she's up-to-date on the plan."

She and Summer had always been inseparable. Even
since she was ten and Summer was eleven, they'd had
a plan to conquer the world. As they'd grown up, the
plan had changed a few times, but their ambition hadn't
wavered. By the time they'd reached college and found
they both had a flair for PR, they'd decided that they'd
one day open their own firm, Mitchell and Mitchell. In
the meantime, they were working in different firms so
they could gather a broader range of skills and contacts.
Either one of them making partner would give them the
best springboard into their own firm, so it had always
been a priority.

Along the way, they were both supposed to find men
they loved, but who were also movers and shakers. Men
with power and social influence. Men somewhat like
the man sitting within touching distance from her now.
Her husband.

The remnants of a child's idea of a successful life
could still be seen in their life plan, but it was more than
that. It was the American dream. Their parents were
comfortably middle-class, and happy with their lot, but
Callie and Summer had always dreamed of more.

That she had accidentally ended up married to someone who didn't want to stay married only set their life
plan back a little. But she and Summer would get through

this and get back on track after Callie was free to divorce Adam Hawke.

As they neared her parents' house, she gave directions until they finally pulled up in the driveway. Summer's car was already here, so they were all systems go.

"What a nice home," Adam said, his tone polite.

Callie looked at the modest, single-story brick house, conscious of how it must seem to him. The gardens were bursting with flowers, but to Adam's expert eye, they would be nothing special—daisies and other plants that were easy to grow. And, though she knew he'd come from humble beginnings, it must have been a long time since he'd been inside a house that wasn't luxurious and stylish. She wondered what he was thinking, but his expression gave nothing away.

"Come on," she finally said. "Let me introduce you to my family."

By the time the mission was complete and they were on their way back to Adam's car with Summer walking beside them, almost an hour had passed.

"That went quite well," Summer said brightly.

Callie returned the smile but couldn't match the wattage. "I think they're disappointed in me."

Adam whipped his head around to face her, his dark brows drawn together. "They should be proud of you. Any parent would be proud to have a daughter like you."

Callie stilled. It was the first compliment Adam had given her since the night of their wedding. And even then, he'd been light on the complimenting front. It sent a happy buzz through her bloodstream, to her fingers and toes, and she was appalled. She couldn't let a simple compliment from Adam Hawke affect her this much. It would be granting him power over her.

She braced every muscle in her body, bringing her reaction to him under control.

"Thank you," she said through tight lips.

Without looking at her, Adam gave a quick nod, and then thumbed the keyless lock.

Summer watched the exchange with a thoughtful expression before she added, "They're not disappointed. They're just surprised. It will take them a little while to process it all, but they'll be fine. It will take everyone a little time before it feels natural. Including you two."

"We don't have a lot of time," Callie said.

"That's true." Summer folded her arms under her breasts and regarded them both. "I'm just going to come out and say this. You two don't look like a couple in love."

Adam shrugged. "If you're looking for someone who gushes, you've got the wrong man."

Summer shook her head. "It's more about how comfortable you seem around each other. Or, more precisely, how uncomfortable."

"We'll be fine when the curtain goes up," Adam said dismissively.

Callie bit down on her lip. Summer was right. No one would believe the story they were going to try to spin if it wasn't backed up by nonverbal communication between them, and she and Adam weren't in the least at ease in each other's company.

"What do you suggest?" Callie asked.

Summer tapped her index finger against her lips and considered them. "A bit of rehearsal time should do it."

Callie suppressed an involuntary shiver at the

thought of *practicing* touching Adam. Since she'd arrived in his office this morning, they'd barely touched. But memories of touching him freely—of being touched by him—were burned into her brain. No one had ever made her come alive like Adam. She might have been under the influence of alcohol when she said her vows, but she'd been equally influenced by the man himself. By his touch. By his hands. By his mouth.

Even now, in her parents' driveway, she felt her heart pick up pace at the prospect of experiencing his touch again.

Adam, however, seemed unmoved. His decision about their marriage must have been mainly a result of the alcohol. If she wasn't careful, she would make a fool out of herself while they rehearsed. What she needed was a chaperone. Someone to remind her that this was all make-believe.

"Will you help?" she asked her sister.

Summer smiled. "Of course. How about now? We could grab some takeout and go back to the apartment."

"I don't think it's necessary," Adam interjected, everything about him screaming reluctance.

Callie took a step closer, until she was a hand span away, and reached up to cup the side of his face with her palm, ignoring the part of her that demanded she take it further. His jaw was lightly stubbled, and his skin was warm and enticing.

Adam's eyes widened with surprise and his spine went ramrod-straight.

With great effort, Callie took a step back and met his gaze, hoping that nothing in her own betrayed her. "That's what Summer's talking about. We need to be comfortable enough with each other that our reactions to unexpected touch won't give the game away."

Adam blew out a breath and leaned against his car. "And you're suggesting we practice."

Callie nodded. "Don't worry. It will be aboveboard. Summer will be there as our outsider point of view. If we're going to do this, we need to do it properly."

"Okay. How about you go back with Summer. Give me directions to your place and I'll pick up some food on the way."

As Callie told him how to get to her apartment, her stomach fluttered. She was going to spend the evening practicing touching Adam Hawke.

Or, more precisely, she was going to spend the evening pretending to be unaffected while her husband touched her. And she wasn't even sure that was entirely possible.

Three

Adam shifted the bags of food to one hand and pressed the buzzer for Callie's apartment. When he'd woken this morning, he'd grabbed a quick coffee before heading for the gym. His head had been full of thoughts about the day ahead: a meeting with a potential supplier and some paperwork he needed to catch up on. Not once had he even come close to imagining how the day would truly unfold.

Less than twenty-four hours since Callie had crashed back into his life, his schedule, his family and his life were all in a mess.

He was used to being the one who solved problems, not the one in the middle of the trouble. But one day with Callie Mitchell had turned the tables on him.

And worse, he might be getting ready to participate in a sham of a marriage, but he'd learned one thing today—his desire for his wife was anything but imaginary. It threatened to overwhelm him anytime she was near. But he had to keep any reaction to her buttoned down. If he was to survive what was coming with his sanity intact, he'd need to keep a very clear line between what was real and what was part of the PR plan.

The door buzzed and opened, and he headed into the foyer and took the elevator to the sixth floor.

Callie was waiting in the doorway to her apartment, giving him a nervous smile, and his shoulders relaxed a little. He was glad he wasn't the only one uncomfortable about the situation.

He held out the bags in offering. "I wasn't sure what you liked, so I got sushi, Chinese and pizza."

Summer popped her head around the corner. "Great. I call dibs on the sushi." She grabbed the bags and headed back into the apartment, leaving him in the doorway with Callie.

She'd changed into jeans and a sky-blue top, and her long, caramel hair was caught up in a sleek ponytail. She looked understated and utterly desirable.

"Look," she said, digging her hands into her pockets, "I just want to say how sorry I am that you're caught up in this."

He frowned, not quite following her thinking. "I signed the marriage license right beside you."

"But no one would ever have known if it wasn't for my job. And my slimy coworker."

"Still not your fault," he said dismissively. "Besides, you never know what journalists would have found once they started digging for dirt when Liam and Jenna's wedding drew closer."

If anyone was to take the lion's share of the blame, it

should be him. Among his brothers, he'd always been
the one who could be relied upon to be the most responsible, a trend that had started when they were kids
and his parents would leave him in charge of Liam and
Dylan. It was one of the reasons they'd voted him CEO
of the entire Hawke's Blooms company.

Whenever he'd relaxed his guard too much in the
past, bad things had happened. Like when he was thirteen and making out with his first girlfriend behind
the sheds after school, and a ten-year-old Dylan had
wandered off and been missing for two hours. Adam
had been frantic. He'd eventually found Dylan safe, but
with cuts and bruises from a fall. Adam had been more
careful to watch his brothers after that.

Then there was the time he'd let himself get rolling drunk on a trip to Vegas and wound up married...

He followed Callie into the spacious apartment and
across to the kitchen. Summer had pulled out some
plates and cutlery and she handed them to him to take
to the table.

As he watched the sisters work together, a thought
occurred to him. "Have either of you had to do this
with clients before?"

Callie's brows drew together. "Pretend to marry
them?"

"Ah, no," he said as he put down the food. "I meant
coach people to act like they were..."

"In love?" Summer observed, and he gave a curt nod.

Callie pulled out a chair and sat across from where
he was standing. "No, this is a first for us."

He should have been disconcerted by their lack of
specific experience, yet part of him was glad. If she'd
been a professional at being able to fake adoration,

while he was an amateur, the situation would have been too uneven. He hated feeling like he was in someone else's hands.

"Actually," Summer said, "we should be starting now. You two sit beside each other."

His instinct was to keep more distance between Callie and him—to keep out of arm's reach—but the suggestion was reasonable. A couple in love would take every opportunity to be close. He crossed around to the other side and sank into the chair beside Callie's.

This close he could smell her coconut shampoo. It immediately brought back memories of his fingers threaded through her glossy hair. Of it spilling across the pillow while he was above her. His skin heated and suddenly his tie was too tight around his throat. He loosened it and tried his best to appear impervious, which was easier said than done.

He glanced casually at his wife as he spooned fried rice onto his plate. "I assume your plan is that we spend some time near each other so we become accustomed to the other's presence."

"Pretty much," Callie answered. "Though we should do some deliberate things, as well, not just passively sit beside each other."

He stilled. He was only just coping with sitting this close. "Define *deliberate things*."

Callie shrugged as she grabbed a sushi roll from the platter. "Occasional touches. Holding hands. Just so when we do it for the cameras, neither of us flinches. We need to seem used to it."

He relaxed again. That made sense and didn't seem too intimate. As long as he had his reactions to her under control, it wouldn't be a difficult task.

Bracing himself, he reached over and threaded his fingers through hers. "Like this?"

"Just like that," she said, her expression professional. But there was a small catch in her voice. "And we should talk about our jobs, and things that married people would know about each other."

Talking. Far preferable to more touching. Holding hands and talking. He could do that.

He rolled his shoulders back, trying to relieve some of the tension that had taken up residence there. "What do you want to know?"

While they ate their meal, she asked questions about his company and he answered. The entire time, he was pretending to be a man unaffected by the woman he was pretending to be in love with. And it was so far from the truth it was laughable—pretending not to be affected was taking so much of his attention he was lucky he didn't stab himself in the eye with his fork.

"This is going well," Summer said, taking another sushi roll. "Adam, how about you feed her something?"

Erotic images of feeding his new wife strawberries in his Vegas hotel room flooded his mind, and he froze. He'd had so much to drink that day that he shouldn't recall it clearly, but he did. He thumped his chest once with his fist to get his lungs working again.

Suddenly, he realized he hadn't replied, and his face probably had a weird expression. He coughed to try to cover it. Summer and Callie, however, had noticed, and each raised an eyebrow.

"Sorry," he said. "This is just awkward."

While Callie looked down at her plate, Summer regarded him with a quizzical expression. "You've never held hands with a woman or fed her food? That's all this is."

"If I was involved with a woman," he assured her, "these things would definitely happen, but organically."

Callie drew in a shallow breath and met his gaze, and he was certain she was remembering the same moments he was. When she'd laughed and flirted with him at the conference cocktail party. When he'd rested a hand on hers at the bar. When they'd kissed and his world had tilted. When they'd only just made it back to his room before tearing each other's clothes off. When they'd shared more champagne in the bed and accidentally spilled some on their bodies…

The air felt thick with the memories, and Callie's eyes darkened. Most of the blood in his body headed south, but Adam refused to let himself get carried away. He flicked a glance at her sister, who was watching the interplay from across the table, and sighed. This situation wasn't about what he wanted in this moment. It wasn't about fun or entertainment—they were practicing so the world thought they were in love, and he had a responsibility to play his part. He would do that and do it well.

He locked down every physical reaction to the woman beside him, every stray thought or memory. Then he found a fake smile and gave it all the enthusiasm he had, and fed Callie a spoonful of his rice.

She gave him the same overly bright smile back and opened her mouth to receive the fork.

"That's better," Summer said. "Though, Callie, can you put your fingers around his wrist to hold it steady?"

Callie complied and Adam refused to react to the warmth of her hand encircling his wrist. To the scent of her skin as she leaned in. To the effect on his body of seeing her lush mouth opening.

"Great," Summer said. "Now look into each other's eyes."

Holding his expression in place, Adam focused on Callie's silver-blue eyes, and thought about the pile of paperwork waiting for him on his desk. Spreadsheets and graphs. Anything to ensure he didn't let himself get caught up in a moment that wasn't real.

Callie looked back at him as she gripped his wrist a little too tightly and ate the food from his fork.

Summer sighed. "That wasn't believable. How about we clear these plates away and try a few poses in the living room?"

Callie winced. It was a small movement, and if he hadn't been this close and focusing on her face, he might have missed it. He turned his wrist so he could grab her hand and gave it a slight squeeze, offering reassurance. As he realized what he was doing, he felt like laughing. He'd never had trouble attracting women in the past—hell, he'd even attracted this very woman in the past—yet here he was, offering reassurance because she was going to have to spend a few minutes touching him.

After the table was cleared, they moved into the living room and Callie's sister spent ten minutes arranging them in various poses. It was awkward and he'd pretty much rather be having a root canal than be arranged like puppets by someone he'd just met. Worse was that he was still fighting the simmering desire for his fellow puppet.

Finally, Summer said, "Hang on. Let me show you something." She grabbed a digital camera and hooked it to a laptop, then took a few photos of Adam with an arm around Callie's waist. "Have a look at these."

Adam moved to the laptop screen and saw the image. He looked stiff and unnatural, and Callie looked almost pained.

"That's not good enough," he admitted.

Callie bit down on her bottom lip. "We're going to have to try harder." She spun away from the laptop and the evidence of their awkwardness, and took in the room. "What if we put on some music? Maybe we could dance. That would give us something to actually do so we didn't feel self-conscious."

"Good idea," he said. In one sense the closeness of dancing could be dangerous, but if he and Callie took back control of the situation he also might be able to regain control of his body. It was worth a try.

Summer headed for the sound system in the corner, and seconds later, a modern day crooner's voice filled the room. Adam held out a hand to Callie. "Shall we?"

She smiled at the formality of his offer and took his proffered hand. "We shall."

Her palm was smooth and warm; the friction of her skin sliding over his set off a depth charge down deep in his belly.

He guided her to an open space between the living room and the entryway that had polished wood floors and less obtrusive lighting. Then he pulled her into his arms and led them in a simple dance step. With the music filling the air, it felt more natural than the poses they'd been trying.

"You were right," he murmured. "I do feel more comfortable."

"Me, too," she said. "Is it okay with you if I move a little closer?"

He chuckled. "We're supposed to be in love. I think you're allowed to get as close as you want without asking permission."

She stepped in and leaned her head on his shoulder. She felt good there. Felt right. As if his body remembered their intimacy. He took his hand from her waist and wrapped it around her, securing her against him, and she let out a contented sigh.

He imagined leaning down, finding her lips and losing himself in her kiss. Then taking her by the hand down the hall to her bedroom...

Except they had an audience.

And they were pretending.

This wasn't real. He couldn't let himself be lulled into falling for the very story they were spinning for the press. He released Callie and stepped back.

"I, er," he said, and then cleared his throat. "That seemed to go better."

Callie nodded. "I was less self-conscious. What did you think, Summer?"

Summer held up her camera and pointed to the laptop. "Excellent. Once you two started dancing, it was totally believable. Just remember how you did it when photographers ask you to pose."

"Sure," Callie said, her voice a little husky. "We'll pretend we're dancing."

Adam rubbed two fingers across his forehead as he contemplated having to repeat this. "Will do," he said, throwing a glance at the door. He needed some space to clear his head. And to rein in his body. "Look, I should head home. Thanks for your help, Summer." He stuck out his hand, and Summer shook it. Then he turned to Callie. "Callie, let me know when you have an interview set up and I'll clear my schedule."

"I'll get on it first thing in the morning."

He nodded. After the dance they'd shared, it seemed ridiculous to offer her the same handshake as her sister, but then again, they weren't actually dating. He settled on the same greeting he gave his brothers' fiancées and kissed her cheek.

Then he left the apartment. Quickly. Because the stupid part of his brain had told him to kiss her again. And this time, not on the cheek.

Once he was safely inside the elevator with the doors closed, he thumped his head back on the wall and swore. Next time, he'd have better control over his reactions to Callie Mitchell. Next time, it would simply be like two actors in a scene.

Next time...

He groaned and thumped his head against the wall again as he realized this was only the beginning.

Two days later, Callie found herself with a journalist, walking through the Hawke Brothers' flower markets. She was wearing a pale gold dress and kitten heels, her hair and makeup photo-ready.

Adam was striding a few steps ahead with the photographer, who wore ripped jeans and a faded T-shirt. Adam, in contrast, was in a tuxedo, parting the crowd like Moses at the Red Sea. No one walked the way Adam Hawke did—powerfully, and always with a purpose. The jacket fit his shoulders perfectly, highlighting their breadth and strength. It was mesmerizing.

"You sure lucked out in husbands," Anna Wilson

said as she walked in step beside Callie. Anna was the first journalist she'd called when looking for a place to launch the story. She was already a friend, and she had a reputation for writing good, solid stories on famous people that neither simpered over the subject nor made snarky digs.

"Yep, Lady Luck was kind to me that night." Memories of twisted white sheets and Adam's naked physique rolled through her mind, causing her mouth to suddenly go dry.

"Maybe I should try Vegas," Anna said. "If I'm going to try my luck anywhere, then surely luck's hometown will work as well for me as it did for you."

A stab of unease hit Callie squarely in the belly. Luck hadn't smiled on her in Vegas. It had given her a night in heaven, sure, but the price had been high. Spending this time with Adam now might just drive her insane.

"You're not wearing rings," Anna said suddenly.

"Rings?" Callie repeated.

"You know," Anna teased, "those little bands we traditionally exchange when we get engaged and married."

Callie frowned, surprised at herself for missing this detail. When they'd originally exchanged vows, they'd paid for cheap rings that had come from a tray kept under the counter at the chapel. She and Adam had both taken them off the next morning. Hers was in her makeup case where she'd tucked it after sobering up, and she assumed Adam had thrown his away.

"We're getting new rings for the new ceremony," she said, thinking on her feet. "It's symbolic of us starting fresh."

Anna smiled dreamily. "I love that idea."

Adam stopped in front of a large flower stall with

shelves covered in buckets of bright blooms in every color. He said a few words to the photographer, and then turned to Callie. "How about we take some of the photos here?"

She surveyed the scene. The backdrop would provide color and evoke happiness, and the light was good. "This would be great," she said, moving to take Adam's hand.

He leaned in and placed a lingering kiss on her lips, and her pulse went into overdrive. It wasn't difficult to find the blissed-out expression that she was supposed to be faking—in fact, she knew it was on her face, whether she wanted it there or not.

Anna glanced around and conferred with Ralph, the photographer, and then said, "This is good. How about we start with you replaying that kiss for us?"

Callie glanced up at Adam and he looked for all the world as if he could think of nothing better than kissing her again. He clearly had the acting thing down pat. Of course, he probably did still desire her—chemistry as strong as what they'd shared wouldn't likely disappear overnight, but she was well aware he didn't want to give in to it again. And one thing she'd learned about Adam Hawke in the short time she'd known him was that he had iron willpower.

"It would be my pleasure," he said, and wrapped an arm around her waist, pulling her against him as he lowered his head. This time it was no peck on the lips, it was more. So much more. Tempting, sensual and knowing. It was everything. She slid her hands along his wrists, past his elbows to grip his biceps through his shirt, partly to keep him in place and partly to hold herself up.

He trailed his lips to the corner of her mouth and then across to her ear. Whispering her name, he sent a shiver across her skin and bit gently on her earlobe. She turned her face, searching for and finding his kiss, feeling as if she'd found her home, as well.

They eased apart and Callie held on to his arms for an extra beat, her knees too wobbly to hold herself upright, her mind too dazed to think clearly.

"Adam," she whispered, and in response a lazy smile spread across his face.

"That's great," Ralph said. "Just hang on a sec while I adjust some settings."

Surprised out of the little world she'd been in with Adam, Callie took a step back. She hadn't given one thought to acting during that kiss or its aftermath. She'd forgotten the photographer was there. Forgotten the rest of the world. In that moment, she couldn't look at Adam. Didn't want to know if he was looking down on her with pity for getting carried away, or if he was looking at something else, disinterested in her now that they'd performed for the camera. And if he was as off-kilter as she was? Well, some things were better not to know.

To give herself something to do, she turned to take in the picturesque markets around her, the beautiful displays of flowers of all kinds, all colors, and waited for her breathing to return to normal.

As she turned farther, she felt her dress catch on a bucket of lilies near her feet. Not wanting to hurt the flowers, she picked up her knee-length skirt and took a step back.

"Hang on," Adam said, looking at her hemline. "You have pollen on your skirt."

Callie sighed. Pollen was almost impossible to get

out of fabric, and this was a good dress. She went to rub her thumb over it, but Adam held up a hand. "Wait. Rubbing it will only make it worse."

He kneeled down in front of her and took the skirt from her hands, inspecting the stain. Then he retrieved something from his pocket.

"What's that?" She tilted her head to try and see around him to what he held.

Holding it up for her to see, he gave her a quick smile. "Sticky tape. I always carry a roll when I walk through the markets."

"Just normal, everyday tape?" she asked, skeptical about what he was doing, but prepared to give him the benefit of the doubt.

He nodded. "Best thing for it."

She watched as he ripped off a small strip and carefully laid it across the pollen before peeling it off. There was something strangely like a fairy tale about standing amongst the flowers in a pale gold dress with a handsome man on bended knee before her. The fact that he was doing something as practical as helping with her with a pollen mishap, instead of declaring undying love and offering her his kingdom, only made it all the more perfect. Adam Hawke stole her breath no matter what he was doing.

He stood and held the tape out to her. "All gone."

His voice was low and the sound wouldn't have reached the ears of those around them, which made the moment feel intimate despite the topic.

She laughed softly, unable to help herself—it just all seemed surreal. "I can't believe you just did that."

"You learn a lot of tricks when you grow up around flowers." His green gaze was smoldering, out of proportion to a discussion about flowers and pollen, but then again, whenever he was near, she felt her reactions were out of proportion, too.

She moistened her lips, and his gaze tracked the movement. The idea of losing herself in his kiss again pulled at her, drew her with a powerful intensity, but she wouldn't forget the photographer again. She angled her head to where the others stood, watching them, and Adam gave her an almost imperceptible nod.

He straightened his spine, took her hand and turned to Ralph and Anna. "If we go a bit farther down this way, we can get some shots with the Midnight Lily in the background."

Since the Midnight Lily had been developed by Liam and launched less than twelve months ago, it had become one of Hawke's Blooms' signature flowers. And that fact served to remind Callie that this was business to Adam—this session with the photographer and this entire plan. And that included the kiss they'd just shared.

She'd been in danger of being swept away in a moment that wasn't even real.

She couldn't afford for that to happen again. It would be too easy to fall in love with Adam Hawke, especially if she let herself believe he had feelings for her. That way led to heartache a thousand times worse than what she'd experienced when he wanted to call off their short-lived marriage. They were both just playing the roles they'd agreed to when they'd devised the plan.

Now all she had to do was make sure that she didn't fall for her own lies.

Four

Callie was just out of the shower when she heard her sister call out.

"It's gone live," Summer was saying from two rooms over.

"The interview?" Anticipation quickened her movements as she dried off, put on her silk robe and headed for the living room.

"Yep. I didn't expect they'd run it for a few more days yet."

Callie stood behind her sister and peeked over her shoulder at the laptop screen. All the breath left her body as she saw the page. She and Adam had never had a photo taken of themselves together before—their relationship was hardly significant enough to warrant that—and they'd never shared a bathroom to get ready to go out and caught sight of themselves side by side in the mirror, so she hadn't seen an image of them as a couple reflected back at her. She'd failed to realize the startling effect it would have on her.

There were a few shots of her with Adam among the flowers, but the biggest photo, the one taking up about half the page, was Adam kneeling at her feet, the hem of her dress in his hand.

"That photo is great," Summer said, pointing to the same one Callie was looking at. "The composition is genius. Was that arrangement the photographer's idea or yours?"

"Ours," Callie said faintly, still trying to take it all in.

"Good work. And your expression is perfect. You look totally smitten. All that practice paid off."

Callie couldn't reply; she just kept staring at the photo. Because her sister was right—the woman in that photo looked completely smitten by the man in front of her. And the scary part was she hadn't been pretending. Neither of them had known their picture was being taken.

Pulling the robe tighter, she slid into a chair, leaving her sister to scroll down and read the story. Callie had bigger things to worry about just now. Like whether she was in over her head...

"Hey, wow," Summer said.

"What?" Callie braced herself, unsure if her system could handle anything more than her new emotions for Adam Hawke being on display for the entire world to see.

"I just checked the magazine's social media pages and they've shared it with the headline, 'Princess Wishes New Brother Well on Vegas Elopement.'"

Callie winced. "That wouldn't have been Anna's headline."

"But it's working. Look how many shares it's had."

Callie watched in astonishment as Summer flicked through the various pages. "I didn't think it would be this popular. We only wanted something to counter possible bad stories."

"You've got way more than that," her sister said, grinning. "You've gone viral, baby."

She blinked. Viral? She'd lived her entire life under the radar—it seemed surreal that people were reading about her, sharing her story on social media. "But why?"

"Never underestimate the pulling power of a princess. Especially when rumors are circulating that the Queen of Larsland herself might be flying over to attend your wedding."

"I hope Jenna isn't regretting being involved."

"I'm sure she understands how the media works. Besides, it's not all about her. That photo of Adam kneeling and you being all adoring is like something straight out of *Cinderella*. What was he doing, anyway?"

"Getting pollen off my skirt." She looked at the photo again, remembering that she *had* felt as if she was in a scene from a fairy tale when it happened.

Summer sighed happily. "Even more chivalrous. That picture is gold."

Callie's stomach clenched. This was moving so fast. "I have to call Adam and warn him." She stood and grabbed her cell but stilled when Summer gasped. That sound hadn't been like any of her other sounds of glee as she scanned the pages, and it made Callie instantly uneasy.

"There's a photo of our front door." Her sister's voice was wary.

A wave of anxiety washed over her, making her skin cold. "They found where I live?"

"Worse than that. That photo was taken this morning."

Her lungs froze. Phone still in her hand, Callie moved to the window and sure enough, there was a small but focused group of paparazzi camped around the entrance to her apartment building.

"They're here," she said, her voice uneven. "It's ironic. We spend a good portion of our working lives trying to get stories to go viral, and the one that has is…"

"You," Summer said as she joined Callie by the window.

"Yeah, me." She wrapped her arms tightly around herself. "I honestly thought this would only make a little splash."

"Good news for the Hawke Brothers' Trust, though, since it got a mention in the article. And good news for the trust is good news for your partnership prospects."

The cell in her hand chimed and she glanced at the screen. Adam. Her heart lurched, and she wasn't sure if it was because she was going to have to fill him in on the developments, or if she was glad to hear from him.

She swiped the screen. "Hi, Adam."

"Callie," he said, his deep voice seeming to smooth its way across her skin. "Have you seen the story?"

"Yes. I was just about to call you about it, actually. There are photographers outside my apartment."

Adam swore. "I'm leaving the office now. Pack a bag."

"Wait. What for?"

"You and Summer are coming to stay with me. My security is better."

Part of her wanted to protest—the secret feminine part that was still shocked about the expression on her face in those photos. But she couldn't afford to let that part take control of her decision. She took a breath and called on her professional side. He had a point—she wasn't looking forward to walking through that mob on her way out.

"That might be best," she said, watching the paparazzi through the window. "But don't come here. I'll leave as if I've been visiting my sister. If everything in our story was true, we'd most likely be living together. I'll pack and send someone back to get the bags later."

Summer started pointing and gesturing, asking if she was going to move in with Adam. Callie nodded, and mouthed, "Wait a sec."

"Good call," Adam said. "What about Summer?"

"She's flying out in a couple of hours and will be away for a few days. Once they realize I'm at your house, they'll abandon this place, so it should be quiet again by the time she gets home."

"Okay. I'll meet you at my house in one hour—is that enough time to pack and drive over?"

"Perfect," she said, trying not to sound reluctant.

"I'll also send someone over to wait with Summer and drive her to the airport. Just in case the vultures don't leave with you."

Callie flicked a glance at her sister. "Thank you, I'd appreciate that."

One drunken night in Vegas was having more ripple effects than she could have predicted—even Summer was having her life impacted. Now the challenge was to surf those ripples and get good outcomes for everyone. All while avoiding slipping under and drowning.

Perhaps the biggest danger of drowning was going to be moving into her husband's house. Living with Adam Hawke while pretending to be in love with him. Possibly the craziest plan she'd ever made.

Adam waited in front of his beach house as Callie made her way up the driveway. Restless energy filled his body, and it took all his self-control not to fiddle with the coins in his pocket or tap his foot on the ground.

She pulled up in front of him and stepped out of the car, looking around to take in the surroundings. The ocean breeze flirted with her long hair and she put a hand up to hold it off her face.

His heart skipped a beat at the sight of her. Since the very first moment he'd spied her at the conference they'd both attended two years ago, she'd affected him this way. Stolen the breath right out of his lungs and made the world practically tip to the side.

And that reaction was the exact reason he refused to pursue anything with her—the morning after their vows, or now. She made him feel off balance. She crowded his brain. That wasn't a way he wanted to live his life.

When he'd been young, before his family had moved to California, he'd been close to his grandfather. He'd been named for his father's father, and the love he'd had for him had been mutual. The elder Adam Hawke, however, had been crazy about his second wife. *Crazy* being the operative word. She'd been flippant and unfeeling, and barely tolerated his family—especially a small boy who hung around too much.

His grandfather had done the lion's share of babysitting Adam once Liam and Dylan had come along, and Adam had adored that special time with his grandfather. Then his step-grandmother had decided that five years of her life was enough to spend married to a farmer and living on a working farm, and threatened to leave.

Blinded by love, her husband had sold the farm—his children's inheritance—and used the money to take her on trips and spending sprees. *Anything* to keep her. She'd hung around until the money dried up and then left anyway.

Adam's parents had already packed their belongings into their car and headed for the West Coast to try their luck now that they'd lost the farm that had been their home and provided their jobs.

Broken and alone, abandoned by the woman he'd called the love of his life, Adam's grandfather had taken his own life.

His parents had broken the news and tried to shield the boys from the worst of it, but Adam was older and had demanded to know the details.

That awful day, standing out in their flower fields so that Liam and Dylan wouldn't overhear, listening to what his parents would divulge and filling in the blanks himself, Adam had made a decision. He'd been twelve years old, but he'd known exactly what he was promising himself.

He'd always be the captain of his own ship. He would never fall for manipulating behavior, or let someone influence him into a major decision against his better judgment.

Obviously his grandfather hadn't entered into his second marriage thinking he was handing over control of his life, despite how it had ended up. And that was the reason why Adam had always needed to be extra vigilant. Anytime he'd been dating a woman and started feeling his guard slipping, or that his mind wasn't one-hundred-percent clear and focused, he got out quickly.

Callie was a threat to that.

He didn't need any more evidence than the fact that he'd gotten drunk and married her.

Yes, Callie Mitchell was most definitely a woman with whom he needed to keep up his guard.

As she walked the distance to reach him, he locked that guard in place around him and double-reinforced it. He was impervious.

"This place is gorgeous," she said, her silver-blue eyes sparkling in appreciation as she took in the views.

He allowed a smile. "It's my favorite place." The ocean soothed him; often it was the only thing that could calm his soul. "Come on inside and I'll show you around."

She followed him up the three steps to the wide porch, and then paused at the open front door and said, "Thank you for the invitation."

Wanting to get this done as quickly as possible, he nodded without stopping, continuing through the entranceway and indicating with a wave of his hand that she should do likewise. He took her on a tour of the main parts of the house, allowing her a moment when the view of the Pacific Ocean through the floor-to-ceiling windows in the living room snagged her attention. They finally ended up in her bedroom.

"This is yours," he said, holding the door open. The

walls and trim were all pure white and the floor was polished wood. The king-size bed was draped in a comforter that was all blues and greens, mirroring the brilliant hues of the view through the window. A decorator had furnished the room following Adam's request to keep it simple.

"I love it," she said, looking from the bed to the window and around the room. "I might never leave."

Reflexively, he flinched, and unfortunately she caught the small movement.

"I was joking, Adam. Relax. I don't have plans to insert myself into your life." Then she laughed. "Okay, I suppose that's what this entire plan is designed to do. But I meant in reality. I won't be trying to snag you or anything."

"I didn't think you had ulterior motives," he said truthfully and blew out a breath. "I'm just not used to living with anyone, so this will be an adjustment."

She arched an eyebrow. "You've never lived with anyone?"

"Not as an adult, no. I have a full-time housekeeper, but she doesn't live onsite. For most of the time that she's here, I'm at work so I don't see her all that often."

Callie lowered her voice. "Does she know? The truth about us?"

He was sure his housekeeper was trustworthy—she'd been hired by Katherine, their family's housekeeper who still worked for Liam and Jenna, and Katherine's standards were ridiculously high. But trust didn't come easy to Adam at the best of times.

"I've given her a week off on full pay so we don't have to worry about her discovering our arrangement. She normally cooks for me, but it seemed easier to just order takeout while you're here and keep everything private."

"That's probably a good idea. But I can cook, and I don't mind making our meals."

That would be cozy. Sharing a meal at night that she'd cooked for them. And cozy home-cooked dinners sounded like the last thing he should be doing while ensuring his guard stayed in place.

He held up a hand. "Your time is valuable. How about we compromise and I'll ring a catering company and get them to deliver some prepared meals. We'll also need to order some groceries for lunches and snacks."

Her eyebrows shot up. "You'll be home for lunch?"

"I've taken a week off," he said, his casual tone belying the fact that he hadn't had a week off in four years. "I told my office that we're basically newlyweds so we're taking some time together. But we'll both be able to work from home."

Callie glanced around the room and frowned. "I wasn't planning on staying here in some kind of lockdown."

"It helps the believability of our story." And if he could feel other reasons tugging at him? They were best left unexplored. "Besides, if we're not coming and going then those photographers at the gate will get bored and leave. After the week, the story will have lost its urgency and we can resume our normal lives."

"Except for the wedding plans," she said.

"Except for the wedding plans," he agreed. "You'll probably want to stay here after the week, right up until the wedding. But the media's attention will move on enough that you won't be restricted here all that time."

"Okay, sure." She fiddled with the hem of her top—the only crack in her facade of composure. "I'll do the lockdown. My main focus is the Hawke Brothers' Trust account, and if anything that will be easier to work on while staying with a member of the Hawke family anyway. I've brought my laptop, so I can work from this room easily enough."

"I think we can do better than that." He headed for the hallway and opened the door across the hall. "This guest room is also at your disposal. I have some office furniture being sent over from Hawke's Blooms' headquarters. It should be here in the next hour, and we'll rearrange and set it up in here."

She glanced around again and bit down on her bottom lip. "You didn't have to go to that much trouble, honestly."

"It was only a phone call." He shrugged a shoulder. "This is a guest wing, so you won't be disturbed. My home office is off the living room, and my bedroom is at the other end of the house."

Before she could reply, ringing came from her handbag, and she fished out her cell.

"It's my boss," she said, her expression telling Adam that she was bracing herself for the call.

He nodded and stepped toward the door. "You take it and meet me in the living room when you're done."

As he left the room, he closed the door behind him to give her some privacy and headed for the living room. The windows overlooking the ocean called to him, and he drifted over. Being near Callie—having her in his home—and not reacting to her was testing his will. The effort it took to not allow his desire to intoxicate him left room for little else, making it difficult to form coherent thoughts. Watching the rhythmic crashing of the waves calmed him. Restored order to his mind and system.

Her footsteps sounded faintly at first, and then grew louder as she came down the hall and entered the room. But he was reluctant to turn. He'd only just found his equilibrium again and here she was to destroy it.

"Mesmerizing view," she said softly from beside him.

Her floral scent surrounded him. He took a deep breath and let it out slowly before replying. "It is."

She didn't face him, just stood with him, looking out over the expanse of ocean. Eventually, she said, "My boss saw the internet coverage and he's thrilled. He said if it all comes together, the partnership is mine."

"That's great." This situation needed to lead to a whole heap of good outcomes to be worth the tension it was creating inside him, and one of those outcomes was to boost Callie's career.

"Yeah," she said, chuckling, "I implied I knew what I was doing, so he doesn't realize we're just keeping our heads above water."

Finally, he turned to face her, trying to read her expression. "Regrets already?"

She shrugged. "The odds are finely balanced, but we're still on top of things. Still moving forward."

"Why don't I believe you?" She looked calm, professional, but there was something behind her eyes that told him it was another example of the mask she wore for the world.

She glanced up at him, surprise clear in her expression, and then shrugged. "I guess I'm just used to being the one advising clients on how to deal with PR problems, or implementing solutions, not being the one in the center."

He grinned. It seemed that he wasn't the only one who preferred being in control.

"You know they say doctors make the worst patients," he said gently.

She arched an eyebrow. "What are you saying?"

"Just that it would make sense that you're having trouble adjusting to being on the other side of the clipboard."

She rubbed her eyes and gave him a reluctant smile. "I guess that's true. And on the bright side, I'll probably have a much better understanding of my clients when this is over."

"That's always a bonus in business."

She paused and her expression changed, soured. "He also said that Terence, the guy who threatened to tell the tabloids about us in the first place, had offered assistance with the account if I needed it."

Adam wasn't sure whether to swear or laugh at the man's ridiculous optimism. "Terence obviously has some underhanded scheme in mind. What did you say?"

She tipped up her chin. "That everything was under control."

"Good," he said, wishing there was something he could do about the bottom-dweller who'd threatened Callie. The best he could do was make sure that their plan went off flawlessly so she secured the partnership. Her success would be the best revenge.

The security intercom sounded. Adam pressed a button on the wall, gave instructions to the staff from the delivery truck and let them in. Then he turned back to Callie.

"Come on," he said. "Time to set up your new office."

Five

The next morning, Callie met Jenna and Adam in the living room. After she and Adam had arranged her new office the day before, Callie had stayed there, catching up on emails and phone calls and letting people know she'd moved. At dinner, they'd ordered takeout and she'd eaten hers while still working. So, beyond a quick discussion about what to eat, she'd avoided conversation with her husband ever since he'd shown her around the beach house.

Which was for the best—she'd decided that approach would give her the strongest chance of surviving this craziness. She had a feeling that Adam Hawke sometimes saw right through her, and that made her feel... exposed.

Jenna grinned when she saw her and held up a bag. "I brought breakfast. Pastries and muffins."

Callie took the bag and returned the grin. "You're a goddess. Don't suppose you also brought coffee?"

"I can take care of that," Adam said from the other sofa. "Cappuccino?"

Callie finally allowed herself a glance at him. In the short time of their acquaintance she'd already learned that avoiding looking at him helped a lot in coping with his presence. He had the power to overwhelm her senses if she didn't ease into it.

Though, as she raked her gaze over him now, hungry to simply see him, she had to admit that even easing into it wasn't helping this time. Maybe she should try the opposite strategy—look at him as much as she could and build up a tolerance to him.

Develop immunity to his presence.

He raised an eyebrow and she realized she was supposed to be answering a question. What had it been about? *Coffee. That's right, coffee.*

She'd seen a state-of-the-art coffee machine when she was in the kitchen yesterday, so she jumped at the offer. "An Americano would be great, thanks."

"Jenna?" he asked, turning to his brother's fiancée.

"I'd love a cappuccino."

He nodded and left, and Jenna turned concerned eyes to her. "I was hoping we'd have a moment alone." Her lilting Scandinavian accent seemed to grow stronger as she lowered her voice. "I wanted to check if you're all right."

Callie frowned. "Why wouldn't I be?"

"It's just been a bit of a whirlwind. Many people would find it disorienting."

The situation wasn't as disorienting as Adam him-

self, she wanted to say, but she wasn't prepared to discuss something she didn't fully understand herself yet.

"I'm fine," she said instead. "I'm staying in a multi-million-dollar beach house and Adam set up an office in a guest room for me. I'm *more* than fine."

Jenna patted Callie's knee. "I'm glad. But just remember, you married a Hawke, so you're one of us now."

"We're not—" she began.

"It doesn't matter how long this marriage lasts, or that you're exaggerating your relationship at the moment. You're part of the family. If you need help from any of us, say the word."

Callie's throat thickened. Never in her wildest dreams would she have expected such a warm welcome to the family, especially from a princess who must have spent her life surrounded by people wanting to be close to her.

She swallowed to get her voice to work. "Thank you. I appreciate that more than I can say."

Adam reappeared carrying two coffee mugs, and Callie took the momentary diversion to compose herself. She found a blueberry muffin, then lifted her clipboard holding all her printed-out notes on the Hawke Brothers' Trust. She had all the information on her laptop, but found that in meetings, she was able to forge stronger connections with clients if she had pen and paper in hand. It seemed somehow more personal.

"So I've had some ideas about the trust's PR and I think a couple of them really have legs." She'd stayed up late getting all her thoughts together so she could make a strong proposal.

"Excellent," Adam said. "Before you outline them—

Jenna, have you checked the donations for the trust since our story went public?"

"Actually, I've checked often, including just before I left to come here."

"Any fallout?" Adam asked, and Callie held her breath. The last thing she wanted was to have this blow up in the charity's face. Hopefully they'd had an increase.

"They've gone up. In fact, they've *shot* up. Maybe more in the last twenty-four hours than in all the months since we started the trust."

"Really?" Adam said, and leaned back in his chair, obviously pleased.

"I'm so glad," Callie said. "And relieved."

This would be a great lead-in to their new PR strategy. She couldn't wait to get started, not in the least part because it would give her something to focus on besides her husband sitting across from her.

Jenna nodded. "I've been thinking—I'm sure your ideas are excellent, but perhaps we should be focusing on the wedding? Make *it* the PR campaign?"

Callie's gut clenched tight. It was one thing to do some media interviews to spin a story that protected them from potential damage, but quite another to make it the entire focus. To invite more scrutiny and keep herself in the spotlight. But she'd started this—she'd said yes to Adam's proposal in Vegas, and it was her job that foisted her back into his world, her colleague that had created the problem and her plan to fix it with this wedding. If they decided this direction was in the best interests of the trust, she'd see it through.

Her mind rapidly flicked through the pros and cons,

and landed on the biggest issue of making the wedding itself the PR campaign.

"Where do we stand on the ethics of raising money using a fake wedding?"

"I like that you're concerned about that," Jenna said, and then paused, considering. "Any money that's donated to the trust goes to help homeless children—there's nothing fake or dishonest about that. It's transparent and those children are in genuine need. Also, you and Adam are already married, and you really are going to renew your vows, so that's not a lie, either."

Callie leaned back in her seat. They were good points. "But we're pretending to be in love, so the heart of this campaign wouldn't be authentic."

"It seems to me," Adam said, "that rather than a lie, it's more akin to a PR stunt, which happens all the time. Besides, I don't think we're the only couple in the media who are together for reasons other than love."

"You think the ends justify the means?" Callie asked him. "The benefit to the children?"

Adam nodded. "If we wanted to use that strategy, then yes."

"So," Jenna said. "What do you say?"

Callie felt Adam's gaze on her and lifted her own eyes to meet it. His expression was masked but she knew this wasn't his preferred direction, despite him weighing in on the ethics of the situation. She raised an eyebrow, asking a silent question, and she watched his chest rise and fall once before he gave her an almost imperceptible nod that sealed their course of action.

She turned back to Jenna. "It would make sense to

build on what's already working. Keep things moving along."

"If you both think that's the most effective strategy, I'm on board," Adam said. "Though won't it be a vow renewal?"

"Technically," Callie said. "But in the media we'll mainly refer to it as a wedding—it's more romantic." She flipped to a blank page on her clipboard. "The wedding *is* the campaign."

Jenna smiled. "Sounds fun. What do we do next?"

She mentally switched gears from a woman sitting in a room with a princess and a virtual stranger who was actually her husband, to a public-relations professional who needed to come up with a strategy.

She took a sip of her coffee and set the cup back on the side table as she collected her thoughts. "The main thing will be to keep the trust and our wedding firmly tied together in the public's mind."

Adam rested an ankle on his knee. "We'll mention it in interviews?"

"At bare minimum," Callie said, making notes as the ideas came to her. "But we need to plan specific strategies. Maybe we could sell the wedding photos to one publication, with the money going to the trust."

Jenna sat up straighter. "We could do a professional shoot before that, too, and sell the photos for the trust."

"Like engagement photos," Callie said, "except we're already married so we'll need a different term. Why don't we call them wedding announcement photos?"

"I love that," Jenna said. "If it would help, Bonnie and Meg could be in that shoot."

Adam raised an eyebrow. "You wouldn't feel that was exploiting them?"

Jenna shook her head. "I'd have to check with Liam, but people try to take their photo all the time as it is. This would be something we chose, and it's about family and charity. They're two things that are important in how we're raising the girls."

"If you and Liam are sure," Callie said, "two baby princesses will certainly increase the money we raise from the photos."

Jenna dug into the pastry bag and came out with an éclair as she spoke. "Meg can toddle around, so we could make her a flower girl at the wedding and play that up in these photos."

"Great," Callie said. "Adam, how do you feel about the official wedding announcement photo idea?"

He rubbed a hand across his jaw, contemplating. "The part of this strategy that I like is that the photographer will work for us, so we'll control the shoot and choose which photos we pass to the publication. So I'm okay with it."

There was something in the way he said the words that made her think he'd been as unhappy with the surprise picture of him kneeling at her skirt as she was. She gave him a small smile to show she understood, and his gaze softened in response. That simple change in the way he looked at her set off a domino effect in her body, starting with a tingling in her toes and ending with heat in her cheeks.

She turned back to Jenna and refocused on the task at hand. "We'll implement more strategies to link the trust to the wedding—perhaps make a visit to somewhere the trust assists, with a journalist in tow? But the next thing we should consider is the wedding."

"Do you have thoughts on what you want?" Jenna asked.

Callie nodded. "We have to not think of it in terms of *my* wedding, or *Adam's* wedding. We've agreed this is the PR campaign for the trust, so the details have to be ones that suit the charity."

Adam frowned. "I don't follow. How can a wedding suit a charity for homeless children?"

"Well—" Callie tapped her pen on her notes "—we need to make it stylish, but not over-the-top. If it looks like we've spent a ridiculous amount on a lavish wedding that will only imply that we're out of touch and have too much money. Donations would drop."

"Stylish on a budget," Jenna confirmed. "We can do that."

"Also, we make children a visible part of the wedding. Having Meg as a flower girl is a good start, but perhaps the rehearsal dinner could include one hundred children from a charity the trust supports. No photos that night—we don't want those children to feel exploited or have their identities compromised—we just let the media know that it happened."

"So the hundred children have a fairy-tale night," Adam said, approval warm in his voice, "and we keep the wedding and the trust linked in people's minds."

"Exactly." Callie smiled and tried to ignore how much his approval affected her.

"And we have the Bridal Tulip," Jenna said. "Perhaps sales of the flower in the first week after release—which would be the week of the wedding—could go to the trust."

"I love that idea." Callie made a note. "We could link the advertising to the fact that we'll be using it at a vow renewal and suggest couples who've already married buy a bunch for their spouse to remember their wedding. Adam, is that feasible?"

Adam shrugged. "Sure. From a business perspective, it would mean increased exposure for the flower, which would help future sales. I'd have no problem with that strategy from a sales or charity angle, even without the wedding."

Jenna glanced about the room, and then frowned. "Speaking of flowers, I've just noticed something. I've only been in this house a couple of times before, but I've only realized this time that there are no flowers."

"You live at the flower farm," Adam said pointedly. "Of course your house is full of flowers."

Jenna shook her head. "Yes, but I didn't always live at the farm." She turned to Callie. "I met Liam when I was Dylan's housekeeper—I'd run from my family and my homeland when I found out I was pregnant. I would have never forgiven myself for causing a scandal for my family because I was an unwed mother. I wound up working incognito as Dylan's housekeeper. Dylan lives in a downtown apartment and he has a delivery once a week. When I worked for him, it was the highlight of my week to arrange the fresh flowers."

Callie looked around. Now that Jenna mentioned it, it did seem strange that a man who had made his fortune from flowers didn't have a single one in his house. In fact, besides furniture, the space was practically empty. No personalized...well, anything.

"It would be a waste since I'm at work all day." He waved a dismissive hand.

Intrigued, Callie persisted. "Do you have any on your desk at work?"

"No." He shifted in his seat. "But I do look at photos of flowers several times a day."

Perhaps Adam Hawke needed to slow down and literally smell the roses. He had this great view from the living room, but had admitted he was rarely here. It seemed most of his life was work. But she didn't want to push too hard in front of Jenna.

In front of Jenna? Jenna was his actual family—if anyone was going to press him, she would have more right. Not a virtual stranger who'd been plonked down in the middle of his life.

Uncomfortable with the stark reminder of reality, she changed the subject. "Okay, is there anything else we need to focus on at this stage?"

Jenna glanced from Adam's hands to Callie's. "Do you have rings?"

Callie felt her thumb rub over her naked ring finger of its own volition.

"Not yet," she said to Jenna. "In fact, Anna asked about them at the photo shoot and I said we were getting new ones for our fresh start, but then the whole thing slipped my mind."

"I'll call a jeweler this morning," Adam said. "I'll get them to come to the house with a selection as soon as they can arrange it."

Adam had spoken in a pragmatic tone, yet the idea of looking at rings with him sounded just a little bit magical. Ruthlessly, she pushed the thought away. This was not the time for flights of fancy.

Jenna flicked through her notes and looked up. "What about the bachelor and bachelorette parties?"

Adam cocked his head. "Is that what we'd call them when we're already married?"

Jenna shrugged. "We can call it something else if you prefer. Technically you're not a bachelor, but it's like the vow renewal being called a wedding."

"You know," Callie said, "I think it would be simpler for the sake of the campaign to call them bachelor and bachelorette parties, even if it's not strictly correct. Everyone knows what the term means."

"Suits me." Jenna made a note. "Here's another thought. Since neither of you need a traditional farewell to your single life, how about we do something different with them?"

"How different?" Callie asked.

Jenna smiled. "We could hold them jointly."

"A bachelor-bachelorette double bill?" Adam asked, rubbing his jaw. "Sure, why not?"

Callie's mind kicked into high gear. "That could work. It would be an integral part of the overall strategy, and we'd invite a journalist along to cover the event."

Jenna nodded. "And instead of bachelorette games, we could have some fundraising events during the night."

"That's just the sort of thing that's non-traditional enough to get some traction in the media. I'll start getting some ideas together and send them to you." Callie glanced down and reviewed the notes she'd made. "I think we have enough for now. Adam, if you organize the rings and get things set up for the Bridal Tulip sales to go to the trust in the first week, and, Jenna, if you start setting things up with the charities the trust supports for the children to attend the rehearsal dinner, then I'll get to work on a plan for the rest."

"Done," Adam said.

"Will do," Jenna said. "Faith will be back in town

in a couple of days. Shall we schedule another meeting for then? I know she's keen to do something with the Bridal Tulip on her show, and she'll love the idea of linking it closely to the children. She'll want to be part of the planning."

"That would be great. How about the same time, same place, in two days' time?"

"I'll bring the pastries." Jenna packed her things into her handbag and stood. "Now I'll head home to Bonnie and Meg. As soon as I make it through that throng at your gate."

Callie winced. "That's one aspect of your life I don't envy. They'll fade away for me, but you'll always have the paparazzi following you."

Jenna shrugged one shoulder. "I'm used to it. I grew up with public scrutiny, so I barely notice anymore."

"How do you deal with it?" A princess was probably the perfect person to ask for advice.

Jenna flashed a resigned smile. "You learn to let go of the worry. The media will always want what they can't have."

Callie thought about that for a moment. "So basically, our strategy is going to give them what they want and it will benefit the trust."

"See," Jenna said, walking to the door. "You're smart about dealing with them already. Now you forget about them."

They said their goodbyes and Jenna went out to her car, leaving Adam and Callie standing in the foyer together.

"Forget about them," Adam said wryly.

Callie turned on her heel to face into the house again.

"While we're here in lockdown, we don't have to think about them."

"True, but we might go stir-crazy."

She gave him an assessing look. She hadn't thought about the impact this was having on him besides the inconvenience of having her move in. But it made sense that a type A personality who was used to overseeing a vast company would find this lockdown rather confining.

She wanted to offer to help, but didn't know him well enough to know how.

"Do you want to watch a movie or something?" she offered.

His expression gentled. "Thanks for the offer, but no. I have a lot of work to get done today, including a video call in about ten minutes."

"Right. Of course," she said, feeling stupid for making the offer. "I have a lot to do, too. I'd better, uh, go and do it."

He reached out and grasped her hand. "I really do appreciate the offer. It was sweet."

"Oh, that's me," she said on a dry laugh. "Sweet as pie."

Something that looked like a genuine smile flitted across his face. "I've been thinking about your offer to cook. I should have been the one offering. I can do tacos—refried beans, guacamole, shredded lettuce, tomatoes, cheese, salsa."

He was the one who seemed a little uncomfortable this time, and she smiled indulgently. "Sounds nice."

"All the ingredients are in the fridge, so if you'd like, I can make them for dinner tonight. Say, eight o'clock?"

She froze as she realized that would mean sitting

alone with him, sharing a meal in an intimate setting, all while pretending not to be affected by him—a task that was fast becoming harder than pretending to be in love with him for the cameras.

Then she remembered the new strategy she'd decided on this morning. Spend more time with him, look at him more. Develop immunity.

Dinner would be her Adam Hawke vaccination.

She drew in a breath and nodded. "I can't remember the last time I had a good taco. I'm in."

"Eight o'clock, then."

"Eight o'clock," she said and watched him walk away.

One thing that interested her was that he'd taken a throwaway comment and thought about it. Moreover, he was making an effort to do something.

There was more to Adam Hawke than she'd even suspected.

Adam answered the security buzzer and let the jeweler through the gates out front. Luckily the man had been able to schedule a visit for the same afternoon. Well, either it was luck or enthusiasm over being the provider of rings for a wedding that was getting media coverage. Either way, Adam appreciated that it would be dealt with so quickly. He was no fan of loose ends.

He'd let Callie know the jeweler was on his way and she was waiting in the foyer for him.

"I guess it's showtime again," she said with a half-hearted attempt at a smile.

He dug his hands in his pockets and sought a calm that he didn't currently feel. "We're back to a couple in love."

There was a small change to her stance, a slight stiffening in her spine, but then she relaxed her shoulders and gave him a more believable smile. Still not a real one—he had memories of those burned into his brain from their time in Vegas.

"At least we've had a little practice this time," she said brightly.

"Listen, when he's here, just choose whatever ring you want." He said it casually, just wanting them to be on the same page, but as the words left his mouth he realized how unromantic that had sounded. Sure, they were playing roles and she didn't need romance when no one was looking, but still, didn't all women dream about moments like this? He gave himself a mental slap. He should be sensitive.

"Sorry, that sounded very…"

"Unromantic? Practical?" she queried. He nodded and she chuckled. "Adam, don't worry about my delicate sensibilities. For better or for worse, we're in this together. And if we can't be honest with each other, then who else have we got?"

"Okay, good."

The doorbell chimed and Adam opened it to the jeweler, Daniel Roberts, who was accompanied by a well-built man in a suit carrying a heavy-looking reinforced briefcase.

Adam stuck out his hand to the first man. "Thanks for coming on short notice, Mr. Roberts."

"Good afternoon, Mr. Hawke. Mrs. Hawke. You're very welcome. Thank *you* for choosing us."

Adam slid an arm around Callie's waist as he stepped back to allow the men entry. Interesting how natural it felt to hold her against him. They'd been pretending to be a couple for less than a week, yet already it was beginning to feel like second nature. Like she fit him perfectly.

They all walked into the living room, which now had more people in it in the past twenty-four hours than Adam could remember ever being there before. Once they were settled, the jeweler brought out tray after tray of exquisite rings.

Callie played her part well by oohing and aahing and looking tickled pink as she modeled various rings for Adam, and he, in turn, smiled indulgently.

He also spent the time acting like a man besotted, which generally involved sitting on the armrest of the sofa she'd chosen and touching her.

Even though she'd given him permission to touch her in these situations, he still wanted to respect her boundaries, so he settled on stroking the skin from her shoulder down to her elbow—a fairly innocuous area. It was silky soft beneath his fingers and every stroke made his gut swoop. The scent of her coconut shampoo surrounded him, cocooning him from the rest of the world. Perhaps spending time together in this charade would be more pleasant than he'd anticipated.

Thankfully, Callie took the lead in choosing the rings, finding a plain gold band for him and offering it up to him for an opinion. He didn't care, as long as he could stay like this, touching her skin, surrounded by her scent, pretending to be in love with her. In some ways, this was a perfect way to spend a day. He could spend some time enjoying being near her, with the safeguard of them both knowing the limitations of their arrangement. Callie wouldn't read too much into it, and he wouldn't get carried away. Control would be maintained.

She offered a pretty solitaire diamond for approval and he murmured, "It's perfect," before dropping a kiss on her temple.

A delicate pink flush stole up her throat to bloom on her cheeks. He knew it was probably embarrassment, but in the role of besotted new husband, he chose to interpret it as Callie liking his touch. A thought more appealing than it should have been.

When they'd made love in Vegas, she'd responded to him with no reservation—something that had moved him deeply. Now that they knew each other a little more, would she still be unguarded with him if they made love? Or would that have been lost because of their complicated relationship?

Of course, the point was moot—she was the last person he should be thinking of sleeping with. If they did, how would he be able to walk away from her a second time? It had been hard enough when they had no ties between them besides a piece of paper. Now? Things were so much trickier.

And one thing was certain—walking away once this was over was imperative. He didn't want their fake relationship to become real. At least on that they were in agreement.

He glanced down at Callie as she tried on wedding rings and a thought hit him with the force of a Mack truck—*were* they in agreement?

Callie had wanted to dissolve their marriage, and seemed uncomfortable with their current arrangement…but what if she was secretly hoping this could turn into something more?

"Very fine choices," the jeweler was saying. "I can see you have exquisite taste."

The man began putting the trays back into the special briefcase, and Adam stood, still reeling over the questions in his mind.

"Thank you, you're very kind," Callie said.

"Yes, thank you," Adam echoed. He moved to the side to give Callie room to stand, but this time he didn't stay close to his wife or touch her. He needed to be certain of what she was thinking before he did that again. Why had they never explicitly discussed it?

He walked ahead and opened the front door for the visitors.

The jeweler stuck out his hand. "I'll give you a call the moment the rings are resized and ready to be picked up."

"I appreciate it," Adam said, shaking his hand.

The two men left and Adam was once again alone with Callie. It was the perfect opportunity to have an honest conversation about where Callie saw their relationship heading, yet part of him wanted to put it off. If she was hoping it would evolve into something permanent he'd have to lay his position on the line, which would hurt her. Callie was the last person he'd ever want to hurt.

Then again, if she really did feel that way, the longer he let it go before addressing the issue, the more she'd be hurt. He had to do it now.

She turned. "I'll just head—"

"Can we talk about something first?"

"Sure," she said, turning back and folding her arms under her breasts.

Now that he'd started, he wasn't quite sure how to word it. The topic called for finding a balance between clarity and sensitivity.

He drew in a long breath. "Ah, I just wanted to touch base with you about our situation."

"What do you mean?" she asked, her head cocked to the side.

"We made this plan that day in my office, and since then it seems to have taken on a life of its own."

She chuckled. "It has rather become a bit of a monster, hasn't it?"

"Do you want to call it off?" he asked, watching her reaction carefully.

Without hesitation, she shook her head. "I want the partnership. And from Jenna's figures, it's helping the trust." She unfolded her arms and tucked one hand into her back jeans pocket. "Do you want to call it off?"

"No, I made a commitment and I'll see it through." He shifted his weight, wishing he'd found somewhere more comfortable for this conversation. "I also need to check that you're not hoping for...more."

She frowned. "More?"

"From me," he said simply. Clearly. No misunderstandings. "From the marriage."

She arched one eyebrow. "You think I'll succumb to your charms and beg you to make the marriage real?"

Adam flinched. Said like that, it did sound over-the-top. "Sorry, I didn't mean to offend you. But I have to make sure that we want the same things. That I wasn't leading you on."

"No one could accuse you of leading me on, Adam," she said drily. "As soon as we're not in front of people, you drop the act pretty quickly."

He felt as if he was missing half the conversation. Was she saying that was a problem? She'd just mocked him for suggesting she might want more, so surely she *wanted* him to drop the act as soon as he could?

But before he could find the right question to work out what he was missing, Callie had turned away.

"I'll see you at dinner," she said over her shoulder and walked down the hall.

"Sure," he said to her retreating back, and wondered if he'd ever completely understand her.

Six

Callie pushed her empty plate away and sighed in satisfaction. "You undersold your cooking abilities."

Adam shrugged a broad shoulder. "My repertoire is small. Basically the tacos you just had and scrambled eggs. I have dreams of one day branching out into pizza."

Callie laughed—both at the words and from surprise at his easy self-deprecating humor. Adam Hawke liked to stay buttoned up, but she suspected if he ever let his guard down he could be a whole heap of fun.

No, scratch that. She didn't suspect it—she knew it. Their time in Vegas had been amazing. On the way to the chapel, they'd laughed and run through a fountain, and on the way back, Adam had insisted on carrying her over the threshold of the hotel, much to the amusement of the security team and everyone else in the foyer.

"Penny for your thoughts," he said.

She glanced up. "You really don't want to know."

"I offered money, and I'm always serious when it comes to money," he said, a grin dancing at the corners of his mouth.

Still she hesitated. Should she lie and avoid talking about a time she knew he regretted, or do as he asked? She was never quite sure with Adam. Always second-guessing herself.

He fished a hand into his pocket and threw a quarter onto the table. It rolled and did a few lazy spins in front of her plate before falling flat.

She picked up the coin and flipped it over in her fingers, not meeting his gaze as she spoke. "I was thinking about the people we were in Vegas. Would those people even recognize the man and woman sitting at this table?"

His fingers started tapping on the side of his wineglass, until he looked at them, as if surprised to find them moving without his permission. They abruptly stopped. "You mean me, don't you? You're basically the same, if a little more subdued without the alcohol."

She dared a glance at his eyes. They were the dark green of a deep, stormy ocean, and they made her heart catch in her chest.

"I guess I did, yeah." She took a sip of her wine and then studied him over the rim. "I saw a side of you that you rarely let out to play, didn't I?"

His fingers began to tap again, before they once more abruptly stopped. "Do you want to get out of here? I'm going stir-crazy."

It was the same phrase he'd used earlier when talking about the possible problems of their living arrangement, but now he was admitting to feeling trapped. It seemed quite a strong admission coming from a man who usually kept his innermost feelings and reactions locked down tight, and part of her was glad he'd shared even this small snippet with her. But that didn't mean she was going to leap at his suggestion.

"I know that now that we've changed the plan to the wedding becoming our PR strategy we don't need to be in lockdown anymore. In fact, we'll probably want to be seen together a couple of times before the ceremony— maybe dinner out or something. But I don't think I'm up to being that public just yet."

"There's only one guy out in front now," he said with a dismissive shrug, "and if we go out the back door down to the beach, he won't know."

It seemed too easy after the drama of the past couple of days. "What about other people?"

"It's usually pretty deserted at night, but I have some sweats you can borrow to make sure no one recognizes us."

The idea of escaping the four walls around them without causing a spectacle was too good to pass up.

"Let's go," she said.

As she cleared their plates, Adam left and returned a few minutes later in nondescript gray sweatpants and a matching hoodie. He passed a black set to her.

"You'll have to roll the legs up, but not too much— you're so tall that I think I only have a couple of inches on you. The top will swim on your frame, though, sorry."

She took the clothes and held them against her chest. Even though they were clean, they smelled of him and she had to fight the impulse to breathe in the scent. "Everything I brought is brightly colored, so I'll be much less visible in these." Even if she would be completely surrounded by his scent.

A few minutes later she'd changed and they were heading down the outdoor stairs that separated his yard from the beach. A gentle breeze blew, and the moonlight sparkled on the inky water. They made it through the soft sand to where the edges of the waves played around their bare feet.

"I always forget how much I love the beach," she said, trying to take it all in at once. "I live in LA, but hardly ever take time to enjoy its treasures."

Maybe Adam wasn't the only one who needed to stop and smell the roses. When things returned to normal, she was going to make some changes, starting with regular visits to the beach.

"I know what you mean. I bought the house for its location, but..." His voice trailed off.

"But you're at work most of the time," she said.

He let out a short laugh. "Something like that. Do you want to walk?"

"Sure."

For a couple of minutes, they walked in silence until she broke it by saying, "Look, I'm sorry for what I said back at the house. How you live your life is none of my business."

"If it's anyone's business," he said with humor in his gaze, "it would be my wife's."

She sighed and splashed at the water with her toes. "I guess that's the problem. We've crossed lines back and forth so many times that we're going to wind up making mistakes about where they are now."

Silence descended around them once more, but it

was far from comfortable. There was tension in it be-yond what had been between them the past couple of days, and it was all coming from Adam. There was clearly something on his mind, so she waited, hoping he'd start talking.

"I saw you looking at the family photos along the wall in the dining room while I was fixing dinner," he finally said.

She stole a quick glance at him, unsure if he was annoyed, but he seemed not to have a problem with it. So she nodded. "You have a very photogenic family."

He seemed to ignore the compliment. "Did you see the older man who was in lots of the photos where we were children?"

She had noticed him. Tall, with striking looks and silver hair. "You look a lot like him."

"My grandfather, Adam Hawke." He said the words without inflection. Without emotion. "I was named after him, and people often told me that I was like him."

"Looked like him?" she asked, sensing there was more to this.

"Looks and personality. I was always fairly serious and responsible, which probably isn't too unusual for an oldest sibling, but it was more than that."

"Your grandfather was serious and responsible, too?" she asked gently, unsure how far to push.

"All his life." He folded his arms over his chest as he walked. "Right up until his second marriage." His expression turned bitter.

"I take it you didn't like his new wife."

"She didn't like me, or any children. But my grand-father couldn't see that. We'd always been close—when my parents had two more babies, he was the one who babysat me. He taught me to ride a bike." Adam looked up at the starry sky before letting out a humorless laugh. "He used to tell me all the time that my father would inherit the farm from him, and one day it would all come to me."

She'd known this wasn't going to be a happy story from the start, but a feeling of foreboding was growing in her belly.

"What happened to the farm, Adam?" she asked.

"His wife said she was leaving because she hated being stuck on the farm. So he sold it and spent all the money on her." His voice became flat, hard. "It didn't matter enough that we were all living on that farm, or that my dad was working it. My grandfather sold it anyway."

Her heart squeezed tight. Having met his parents and brothers, she hated thinking of them in that situation. "So that was your family's home and income gone in one swoop?"

"Pretty much. My parents had saved a little so they used that to move to California and start fresh."

"And your grandfather?" she asked warily. The fact that there had been no recent photo of him was telling.

Adam drew in a deep breath and shuddered as he released it. "After the money ran out his wife left anyway. And so he shot himself."

Callie found Adam's hand and intertwined their fingers, wanting to offer as much comfort as he'd allow. After a moment's hesitation, he squeezed her fingers back.

"How old were you when he died?"

"Twelve."

"What an awful thing for a child to go through. Especially when you'd been so close to him." If only she could do something to take away the pain, but realistically, she knew that nothing could, except maybe time.

"I learned something that day," he said, sounding resolute. Determined. "You might feel like you're in control of your life. You might think you're on top of the challenges, the way that my grandfather did before he married. But that control can snap at any time, and you lose *everything*."

A lightbulb went off, and Callie finally had an insight into why Adam was so determined to stay in control all the time, and it only made her want to know more. Though one thing didn't add up.

"Why are you telling me this? You think I'm after your money like your grandfather's wife?" She didn't really believe he thought that way about her, but needed to hear him deny it.

Adam shook his head abruptly. "The story wasn't about her. It was about him. About what happens when someone like him—like me—throws caution to the wind."

And suddenly it all made sense. "You keep yourself locked down not because you're less wild than your brothers, but because you're afraid you're the wildest of the three."

"Everybody always told me I was like him," he repeated as if that explained everything.

"That doesn't mean you are," she pointed out.

"Some people go to Vegas and have a drunken one-night stand. I took it a step further and got married."

Everything kept coming back to that snap decision three months ago. "You weren't the only one," she said ruefully.

He continued without missing a beat. "My family wanted to turn a roadside stall of homegrown flowers into their very own store. I created a national company that's still expanding."

"That's a great outcome." The first time she met him, she'd been almost as impressed by his success as by the man himself. Almost.

"It is." He shrugged, as if dismissing the achievement. "But I have a tendency not to do things by halves. If I'm not careful, I get carried away. The only times that works well for me is if I take a considered, logical approach."

"Our wedding wasn't logical or considered," she conceded, and he laughed.

"No, it wasn't." He blew out a long breath. "I learned something with my very first girlfriend."

"Is this going to be a dirty story?" she teased, hoping to lighten the mood a little.

"I was thirteen. How dirty can it get?" he said with humor in his voice. Until he started talking again. "I was supposed to be watching my brothers after school until my parents picked us up, but I was crazy about a girl and I convinced her to sneak behind the shed and make out. Long story short, Dylan went missing on my watch and when we found him he was covered in cuts and bruises."

"Having met Dylan, I have a feeling he spent much of his childhood getting himself into mischief." And probably his adulthood, too.

"Which was even more of a reason to keep a close eye on him," Adam said, clearly disgusted with himself. "But I was carried away and let my guard down."

She tried to imagine a thirteen-year-old Adam, already serious, but flush with first love. "You were only a kid yourself."

"Maybe, but it was exactly the same thing that happened with my grandfather. Obsessed with a girl and forgot my responsibility to my family."

Her eyes stung, but she blinked any sympathy away before he noticed. He wouldn't welcome it.

How hard had he been on himself back then? She'd bet more than the quarter he'd given her that he'd been harder on himself than anything his parents had dished out.

"I'm guessing you broke up with that girl."

"The next day. I had to."

The jigsaw pieces fell into place. "And anytime you felt yourself getting close to a woman since then, you break things off?"

He didn't need to answer—the way he rolled his shoulders back and glanced over to the horizon told her. They might not be emotionally close, but they were married. His internal alarm must be deafening.

"You're warning me off, aren't you, Adam?"

"No, I'm filling you in. We have a false sense of intimacy around us because of our situation and I don't want you to come to hope that I could give you more than I'm capable of giving."

"I'm not asking for more."

"I know that."

"And I—" She stopped walking and dropped his hand as his earlier words replayed in her head.

The story wasn't about her. It was about him. About what happens when someone like him—like me—throws caution to the wind.

It hardly seemed possible that someone with as much

self-control as Adam Hawke could be worried about his reaction to a woman. To her.

"I get to you, don't I?" she said, hearing the wonder in her own voice.

He didn't bother denying it. "I think our twenty-four-hour marriage already proved that you're a potential trigger for me." He stopped walking again and glanced around. "I think this is far enough. We should start back."

Everything inside her seemed to be unsettled. Agitated. Thrilled. He'd wanted her when they hooked up in Vegas at the three conferences, but he'd played it so cool afterward each time that she'd assumed his attraction to her was nothing particularly strong. Nothing especially urgent. Nothing near how much she had wanted him. Still wanted him.

Wordlessly, she followed his lead. Since the day in his office, when she'd told him about her coworker's threat and they'd embarked on this plan, she'd been feeling at a disadvantage. She'd understood that she had a stronger attraction for him than he had for her.

She'd been wrong.

He was just better at hiding it. More practiced at denying himself.

The newfound power was exhilarating, setting her pulse fluttering.

"You still want me," she said, though she didn't need the confirmation.

"Of course I do." He stopped and faced her. Framed by the star-studded sky, his skin luminescent in the moonlight, he seemed different from both her Vegas groom and her housemate who kept his emotions tightly leashed. His eyes held a potent mix of surprise and open desire.

"You didn't know?" he whispered.

She swallowed. "You're very good at playing your cards close to your chest."

"That was for my own benefit." He winced, clearly uncomfortable with the confession. "More denial than secrecy."

"I thought I was in this hell alone." Despite his own admission, as soon as the words left her mouth, she wished them back. He may still feel desire for her, but he clearly didn't want to let things develop between them.

She looked over his shoulder at the surf pounding behind him, trying to find her equilibrium. In Vegas, even after they'd sobered up, she'd been infatuated with him. In all honesty, she had been since the first conference where they'd met and she'd spent the night in his bed. By the third conference, when he'd suggested saying vows, she'd been halfway in love with him. His quick backtracking the next morning had taken those fledgling feelings and stomped all over them. Not quite broken her heart, since she hadn't handed that to him, but close.

Her gaze found his again, and she felt the connection like an electric jolt.

If she let herself develop feelings for him now— and that would be such a simple thing to do, given the way he was looking at her, his expression open and troubled—it wouldn't be as easy to shrug off the hurt when he turned away again. In fact, she had a suspicion it would be harder than anything she'd ever had to overcome before. And yet, she couldn't look away.

Couldn't make herself start walking again. Couldn't stop wanting…

"You're not alone," he said, his fingers brushing her hair back behind her ears.

As he touched her cheek, her breath caught and his gaze dropped to her mouth. The sound of the ocean receded and all she could see was him. Adam. His lips were slightly parted, his chest was rising and falling in rhythm with hers.

If she had felt this way about any other man, any other time, she would have leaned in and kissed him, but this was Adam who had just trusted her with his deepest fears about losing control. She had to wait for him to decide. That was if she survived the time it took for his decision. Every moment of hesitation felt like a lifetime.

Her tongue darted out to moisten her lips, and he watched the motion. Her skin grew warmer, and still she waited.

Finally, with a groan, he reached out and wrapped his arms around her, pulling her to him. His mouth landed on hers, all heat and need and heaven, and it felt as if they'd never been apart. As if this was where she always wanted to be.

She leaned into him, feeling the strength of his frame as he drew her closer. His tongue stroked along hers, causing a sinfully glorious sensation. The touches they'd shared during their charade were like a candle flame compared to this bonfire. Lost to the magic of his kiss, she reached her hands to thread through his hair.

"Adam," she murmured. In response, he eased back.

For long seconds all she could hear was their loud breaths before the rest of the world began to intrude.

His expression was stunned, which pretty much summed up how she felt. Their chemistry was as explosive as ever.

"Maybe we should keep walking," he said, and she nodded. For some reason a public beach felt more intimate right now than a house with only the two of them.

They headed for home, walking close, but not touching.

"I'm thinking it might have been better if we hadn't had this conversation tonight," she said once her breathing was even.

"The conversation or the kiss?" His tone was lower, rougher than before.

"Both, but I meant the conversation. We're pretending to be head over heels for each other when the cameras are on. Keeping the line between fantasy and reality would be an issue for anyone in a similar situation, but we've just blurred the line a little."

"You think keeping it firmly in place was easy these past few days?" As they walked, he stroked a hand down her back, sending shivers across her skin. "Shutting down my response to you when other people left the room? Hauling myself back when the camera was packed away?"

"There's no alternative—we got ourselves into this situation." Except there was another option, one she'd been refusing to consider. But perhaps now was the time...? "Okay, what if there was? An alternative."

Dark eyebrows swooped down in a frown. "Stage a breakup?"

"No, the plan is still working for the trust and my career. But we're stuck together, alone, letting the world think our marriage is real." Her heart skipped a beat as she contemplated saying this aloud. "Why not take advantage of the perks of the situation instead of fighting them?"

"Isn't that dangerous considering what we just discussed? This can't go anywhere." His words weren't enthusiastic, but he didn't move away from her side as they walked; his expression didn't close off.

It was a good point to have in the back of their minds, but it didn't have to stop them. "We've already slept together. More than once. And this time we're going in with our eyes open."

They reached the stairs that led to his house, and he turned to her.

"Are you saying you want to have a fling with me, Callie?" His voice was low and as dark as night.

A fling? It sounded so deliciously decadent. Her heart fluttered, and she had a moment's doubt—could she be involved with Adam Hawke again, share his bed, and not start to hope for more? She looked away, then back to her husband. Of course she could. If he could keep his heart guarded, then she could, as well.

"If we're not expecting it to develop into more, what could it hurt?"

He took a step closer. "Are you sure?"

"If you're willing to try it, then I'm in." She crossed her fingers behind her back for luck, hoping she knew what she was doing.

His gaze dropped to her lips and lingered a moment before returning to her eyes. "Then I have a proposal."

"You've been there and done that. I have the marriage certificate to prove it."

The corners of his mouth twitched. "A proposal of a different kind."

"I'm listening." In fact, he had every last scrap of her attention.

"We go inside now and give ourselves tonight." He traced a warm palm down her arm. "One night to share a bed, and we reassess in the morning."

Her body had gone into meltdown at the mention of sharing a bed, but she forced herself to think through what he was offering. "What do you think will be different tomorrow?"

"We make sure we're both happy with the arrangement. Neither one of us feels…emotionally compromised."

"Emotionally compromised? You say the sweetest things." She drew in a breath. "And if neither of us does?"

A slow smile spread across his face. "Then we consider turning this into a fling for the duration of our sham marriage."

Every nerve ending in her body lit up and buzzed. She had trouble finding her voice, until finally she whispered, "Deal."

Seven

Adam led Callie by the hand through the house to his bedroom, resisting the urge to haul her against him the entire way. If he did that, they wouldn't make it to his room, and it was of burning importance to make love to her in his bed.

The other times they'd slept together, the situation hadn't quite felt real. It wasn't just that they'd been drinking, it was also because they'd been at a conference in Vegas, away from their everyday lives. For three years running, they'd carved a slice of time together that didn't have to mesh with their reality.

Tonight things would be different.

Tonight, it was real.

As they reached the threshold to his room, he paused and glanced at Callie. Perhaps because it would be more real than anything that had come before, he needed to make extra sure she was fully on board with the step they were about to take. Nothing would be the same after this.

Her gaze steady on his, she leaned against him and cupped the sides of his face in her palms. Then she stood on tiptoes and kissed him. Everything inside him burst to life, as if he was hyperaware of each cell in his body. And each cell wanted one thing—to be closer to Callie.

With her mouth moving over his, he gripped her hips, digging his fingers into the flesh there, anchoring him to the world. To have her pressed along the length of him, kissing him, was almost too much sensation at once, but he wanted more.

He tore his mouth away and tugged her toward his bed. Still fully clothed, he half laid, half fell onto the mattress, bringing her with him, and then resumed the kiss. Her mouth was hot and sensuous, and part of him felt as if this was the same kiss from three months ago, that it had been merely interrupted.

He pulled his sweatshirt over his head and then also stripped off the sweatshirt he'd given her. The feel of her skin against his chest was heavenly and a groan of satisfaction rumbled deep inside him.

"I've missed touching you," he said, his voice barely a rasp.

She found his hands and brought them to her breasts, holding them over the cups of her bra for a long moment. "Then by all means, touch me some more."

The note of teasing while her eyes were practically glazed with need was pure Callie. He rolled onto his back, taking her with him so that she was above him, straddling his hips, her torso bare except for the white lace bra, and he took her up on the invitation to touch her some more.

His fingertips stroked down her sides, across her slightly rounded abdomen, back up to her collarbone. Her skin was smooth and silken and he might never get enough. Then he found her breasts once more and brushed across their peaks with his thumbs. Callie's thighs tightened around his hips and her breath picked up speed. He repeated the motion, this time paying more attention to her reactions. A slow smile spread across his face—she liked it when he did this.

He should already know her likes and dislikes, but the alcohol had distorted his memories. Reaching behind her, he unhooked her bra and tossed it to the side of the bed. He was going to need more freedom to discover everything he wanted to know.

He lifted himself to a seated position on the covers with Callie still straddling his lap, his hands on a journey of investigation. And everything he learned was like a secret as old as time, a secret he was privileged to be granted.

She tried to wriggle back and make room for her own hands.

"Oh, no," he said, staying her hands. "I've been dreaming of this moment. I need a chance to explore."

She smiled and rested her hands on her thighs, allowing him this.

"Thank you," he said, punctuating it with a kiss on her collarbone, then another. When he reached her shoulder, he scraped his teeth across the skin, tasting as he went. She was faintly salty, with a trace of soap... and something extra—something that was hers alone.

He laid her down on the cover and pulled the track

pants from her legs, taking her underwear with them. The sight of her naked was one thing he had retained complete memory of from their twenty-four-hour marriage and the times they'd come together before that, and yet…she still amazed him.

"Callie."

Her gaze softened. "Nobody's ever looked at me the way you do."

He prowled over her on all fours, leaning in to whisper, "Then they were blind," before taking her earlobe into his mouth, glorying in her gasp.

He kissed a path down her body, until he reached the juncture of her thighs. She deserved to be worshipped, and he set about doing just that. Every whimper that escaped her lips urged him on, every time she writhed under his mouth made him want to push her further. When she reached her peak and shouted his name to the ceiling, a surge of satisfaction filled his chest.

He pulled himself up the bed, holding her as she floated back to earth, feeling more content than he could remember. Finally, her eyes fluttered open and he wanted to do it all again, to make her call his name, so he raised himself on one elbow and trailed a hand over her stomach.

She gently pushed him back against the pillows.

"It's my turn to explore," she said, her eyes sparking.

His pulse spiked. He reached up and gripped the headboard and then nodded. "That's fair."

Her fingers lightly caressed his chest, sending goose bumps racing across his skin, and, as she moved down lower, his abdomen clenched tight at her touch. Then her tongue began to follow the same path, her teeth nipping every few heartbeats. He was on fire. The things she did to him with mere touches... It was craziness.

She moved farther south, and her mouth found him hard and ready. Her tongue licked up one side then down the other, and he gripped the headboard so forcefully he was surprised it didn't break. Her hand joined her mouth, and he groaned out her name, trying to restrain his body from thrashing against the sheets, knowing he couldn't stay completely still, but not wanting to break the contact with her mouth.

She moved higher, to his stomach again, then higher still, until her pelvis was over his groin, pressing down with luscious pressure. She kissed him, and he released his grip of the headboard to wrap his arms around her, finally touching her again.

Holding Callie in his arms was everything. The friction of skin on skin as they moved was bliss, almost more than he could stand. Not breaking their kiss, he rolled them over until they were side by side, and hooked a knee over her legs, wanting to touch her everywhere at once. His heart thundered in his chest, his mind swam. This was more than making love, but what did that make it?

Her hands began a journey down his sides, over his thighs and back to grip his length. He rested his hands on hers to hold them still. He needed to find protection before things went too far and he lost capacity for thought altogether—a place he was already dangerously close to. The only problem was, where would he find any? He didn't normally like people in his personal space, so even when he was seeing a woman, he rarely brought her here. He squeezed his eyes shut as he forced his brain to reengage. Bathroom. There was a box in his private bathroom.

"Hold that thought," he said and came close to breaking the land-speed record on the way to retrieve a condom.

When he made it back to Callie's side, she put her hand out. "May I?"

He handed it over without hesitation. He'd be crazy to say no anytime she wanted to lay a hand on him. As she opened the foil packet, and then held him in one palm and started rolling the condom down his length, he let out a low groan. The torment of her touch, of it never being enough, was going to kill him.

He eased down to lie along the length of her, pulling her close, needing to feel as much of her body against his skin as he could. As he kissed her, she threaded her arms around him, lightly trailing her fingernails down his back and digging into his buttocks in a delicious nip of sensation.

The kiss became more passionate, his body's demands more insistent, and when Callie began to writhe against him, clearly needing more, he rolled her beneath him and settled himself in the cradle of her thighs. Her hands still gripped his rear end, encouraging him, so he reached down and positioned himself, and then found her silver-blue gaze. How could he have forgotten how exquisite it was to have this woman in his bed? Never again—he'd remember every second of tonight for the rest of his life.

With deliberate slowness, he stroked into her and then held still, savoring the sensation of Callie holding him inside her. But too soon, the insistent beat in his body demanded he move, so he lifted his hips before plunging back again.

She lifted her legs and wrapped them around his waist, changing the angle, and he clenched his jaw as he fought for self-control. He wouldn't let this be over too soon. They'd only agreed on one night, and, though he would definitely vote for many more, he was acutely aware this might be the last time he made love to her. He wanted to make the most of it.

Once his—admittedly tenuous—grip on control was back in place, he began to move again, and she moved with him, finding their rhythm, moving together in a ragged harmony. His body urged him to rush headlong to the goal, his mind wanted him to slow down and take in each detail. The result was somewhere in the middle.

His eyelids grew heavy, but he fought to keep them open, gaze fixed on her face. In that moment, she was the most beautiful woman in the world, her skin glowing, her eyes hungry. For him. It made him burn for her even more.

Each stroke seemed to spark every nerve ending in his body, made his pulse race faster.

She was close, he could see it in the tension in her muscles, in the way her breath was coming in short pants. He reached between them, to the place they were joined, and stroked, and she froze, clenching around him and calling his name, until he couldn't hold on any longer and followed her over the edge. Everything inside him, around him, dissolved into bright light and all there was in the universe was Callie. *Callie*.

Callie.

Callie woke curled around Adam. He lay on his back, one arm above his head on the pillow, the other holding her firmly against him. His breathing was even in sleep, and she carefully inched up on an elbow to look at him in the early-morning light streaming through the window.

His dark hair with its hints of deep mahogany was striking against the white pillow. Her gaze traveled languidly from there, past defined cheekbones to a jaw covered in day-old stubble. He was a picture of masculine beauty, and something moved in her chest as she watched him.

"Regrets already?" he asked without opening his eyes. His voice was gravelly with sleep, and it seemed to reverberate through to her soul.

She eased back down and snuggled into his warmth. "Just looking at what I've got myself into."

His chest rumbled under her ear with a lazy chuckle. "And do I pass muster first thing in the morning?"

"You'll do," she said, her voice teasing.

His eyes blinked open and focused on her. "You'll more than do. Early morning in my bed suits you."

The comment triggered a contented warmth, which spread through her body. In fact, this could easily become her favorite place to wake up, but she didn't want to scare him, so she didn't reply. Instead, she stretched against his luxurious sheets and glanced around the room.

She hadn't paid much attention to the master suite when they'd come in last night, but it deserved a good look. It was huge, done in the same white-on-white color scheme as the rest of the house, with indigo-blue blinds and comforter. A deep navy blue sofa sat beside a bank of white doors to closets that must hold all his clothes and personal items.

"You like plain decorating," she said.

"I like simplicity."

She turned back to face him. "Is this another facet of what you were talking about last night?"

"About only being able to cook tacos and eggs?" The corners of his mouth twitched.

He was being deliberately obtuse, and it delighted her to see him so relaxed. She lightly punched him on the arm and said, "Strangely enough, I wasn't thinking of cooking. I meant about you keeping your wild side under control. You deliberately keep things simple and plain. Not a lot of color, no flowers in the house, nothing to rouse the passions."

"There's you," he said and reached for her.

She went into his arms because it was still a novelty to have him unreservedly want her there, and because he was Adam. It was possible she would never deny him anything.

"In all seriousness," he said once he'd tucked her against him again, her face comfortably nestled under his chin, "we said we'd talk about this—about us—this morning. How are you feeling about moving our relationship in this direction?"

"You mean us starting a fling?" It had been his word, and she wanted it on the table, no confusion.

He nodded. "What are you thinking today about us having a fling while you're staying here? I've probably got another quarter around here somewhere if these thoughts cost as much as last time."

"These thoughts are free." She rubbed a hand over his chest as she spoke. "Having to keep my guard up around you, quite frankly, was exhausting. If we continue, besides the obvious advantage of more nights like last night, I'll have a place I can be relaxed."

"I want you to be able to relax while you're staying in this house," he said, his voice gentle. "That would mean a lot to me."

The unexpected moment of tenderness moved her, and she reached up to place a kiss on his lips that was full of appreciation, though it quickly escalated into something much more. More beguiling. More intimate. More spine-tingling. Just more.

Long moments later, she broke away and lay back against the pillows to catch her breath. His darkened gaze followed her, his chest rising and falling in a similar heavy rhythm to hers.

"What about you?" She laid a hand along the side of his face, the day-old stubble exquisitely abrasive against the flesh of her palm. "How are you feeling about us?"

"Now that I have you back in my bed, I'm reluctant to let you leave again, so I'm all for this plan. In fact," he said, trailing fingers down her side, "I think we should explore the finer points of the plan this morning."

"I'm open to exploring that option," she said, and kissed him again. Whether or not she survived this fling with her heart intact, she had a feeling she was in for the time of her life.

It had been two days since she and Adam had agreed to have a fling, and they'd spent a good portion of that time in his bed. Even when they'd been doing something else, her mind had been filled with memories of making love with him, or plans to maneuver him back to his bedroom.

Today, though, they were having their official wedding announcement photos taken. They'd booked their own photographer to come out to Liam and Jenna's flower farm, and Callie had asked her friend Anna, the journalist, to come along, as well. They'd already brokered a sale of the photos to another magazine with the money raised going to charity, but Anna was covering the rehearsal dinner next week and wanted to attend the shoot as part of the lead-in to the piece she'd write.

There had been a stipulation—which she'd expected—that at least one photo would include the princess, Meg, and the princess-to-be, baby Bonnie. Callie and Jenna had decided to also include Liam, Dylan, Faith and Adam's parents in the photos.

Callie's own family had been invited, as well, but had declined. Her parents and Summer were private people, and Callie had understood their decision and supported it.

So all eight adults and two babies of the Hawke clan found themselves standing among rows of flowers in their Sunday best, laughing and ribbing each other. The photographer called out various instructions, many of which were ignored as the boisterous conversation flowed.

Callie's professional side was watching the scene even as she posed. Some photographers would have insisted that the subjects fall into line, but this one was savvy enough to want to capture the energy and love in the group. And there was a lot of love.

Suddenly, everything in Callie's chest pulled tight and she felt very alone. The occasion might have been about her wedding, but she was the only one in the group of ten people who didn't belong. The others all loved each other; even Faith, the newest addition, had clearly been welcome with open arms, and was now integral—Liam joked with her, Bonnie went smiling into

her arms and Dylan looked at her as if his world began
and ended in her eyes.

Callie knew she had no right to feel bad about it—
she had her own family at home, including a sister who
was her best friend. But something deep inside yearned
to be part of Adam's family, too. To have that casual
ease of familiarity with other people who loved him.

Her body went rigid. *Other* people who loved him?
No, she did *not* love Adam. She'd promised herself
she wouldn't let that happen, and she couldn't afford
to break that promise. Stuffing any remnants of the
thought into a far recess of her brain, she forced herself to smile.

"You okay?" Adam whispered near her ear.

"Couldn't be better," she said brightly.

He moved closer, his lips resting on her ear, voice
low. "You probably haven't had enough sleep lately.
Completely my fault. As soon as this is over, you'll go
straight to my bed."

A surprised laugh burst out before she could stop it.
The last thing she'd expected him to joke about when
they were surrounded by his family was making love.
His eyes danced as he leaned and brushed a chaste kiss
over her mouth.

As they pulled away, she was aware that the group
was quiet. She glanced around and found them all
watching her, their expressions ranging from Adam's
mother's glee, to misty-eyed happy sighs from Jenna,
to a knowing grin from Dylan.

A blush crept up her throat to her cheeks and, despite knowing it would only encourage them, she hid
her face in Adam's jacket while she composed herself.
The whole family cheered.

"Okay," the photographer called out. "I think I have enough. How about we move over to the roses? Just the bride-and-groom-to-be for these."

The group dispersed and, as they made their way, her friend Anna caught up to her.

"Thanks for inviting me out," she said, glancing at Adam, who was deep in conversation with the photographer a few steps away.

Callie smiled. "Thank you for coming out. The more coverage the photo shoot gets, the better for the trust."

"You know," Anna said, "when you first told me about this, I wondered if it was an elaborate PR stunt."

Callie's heart skipped a beat. "You did?"

"Well, you have to admit it was a big coincidence that you landed the trust's account and suddenly you're marrying the CEO of Hawke's Blooms."

"We were already married," Callie pointed out carefully.

"Which would be enough to disprove it if we were talking about regular people, but you and Summer are very good at your jobs—this isn't too complicated for you to pull off. Somehow. With smoke and mirrors. And maybe a time machine."

Callie's lungs constricted until she could barely draw in enough breath. Had Anna guessed the truth? Was she warning Callie that she was about to expose her? Or maybe she was only fishing.

"What do you think now?" She worked to keep her voice even.

"The day I did that interview with you, you and Adam were awkward together at times, but I could see that was probably because you were nervous about the story, and it was your first time being photographed to-gether. But today…" Her voice trailed off.

"Today," Callie prompted.

Anna smiled. "I think that no one who saw you and Adam Hawke together could doubt you're in love."

Relief at fooling a journalist warred with unease about her friend's supposed insight. They were play-ing roles, sure, but Anna had picked up their awkward-ness at the first interview, so she was perceptive. And Anna thought they were in love.

Was Callie coming to feel too much for Adam Hawke? Or was she becoming a better actress?

Adam fell into step beside her and slid an arm around her waist. Without thinking, she leaned in to him, want-ing his strength and support as she grappled with the questions her friend had raised.

"See," Anna said, her voice a little smug. "You can't fake that."

Adam looked down at her. "Can't fake what?" His voice was casual but she knew the wariness behind it.

Callie found a short laugh, as if the idea was crazy. "Anna wondered when we first announced our relation-ship if it was a PR stunt."

She knew from experience that he was good at lock-ing down his emotions so it was no surprise when he merely raised an eyebrow. "It's a fairly complicated and personal plan to be a stunt."

Anna shrugged. "But not beyond Callie's abilities. However I was just telling Callie that no one who sees you two together—how sweet and attentive you are to each other when no one else is looking—could doubt how much you love each other."

Adam pulled her tighter against his side. "I have no

reason to hide what she means to me. My life changed the moment I met her."

Callie suppressed a grin. She had to hand it to him—he'd given the journalist what she wanted, and what they needed her to believe, but he hadn't lied.

Anna had her notebook and pen already in hand. "Can I quote you on that?"

"Absolutely," he said.

"Any reply?" she asked Callie.

Callie thought for a moment. It seemed right to say something just as truthful. "There's no one like Adam Hawke. He makes every day brighter and inspires me."

"How does he inspire you?" Anna asked, her hand scribbling as they walked.

"He's brave. He sees what he wants and goes after it, no concerns about the risk of failure. It's one of the reasons Hawke's Blooms is such a huge success." She found his ocean-green gaze and smiled. "To have all that enthusiasm and energy and determination beside me every day couldn't fail to inspire me."

They'd reached the roses, and Anna backed away, still making notes as the photographer positioned Callie and Adam in front of a shrub bursting with white blooms.

Once everyone else was out of earshot, Adam ran a finger under her chin, drawing her gaze up.

"Did you mean that?" he murmured.

"About you being inspiring?"

He nodded. "I can't always tell when you're saying things for effect, or exaggerating so people believe the story."

"I meant every word." She cupped the side of his face in her palm, wanting him to understand that among their exaggerations, she was completely serious about this. "You might think it's a failing that you get *carried away* by things, but I think it's one of your strengths. Who else would have committed to this crazy plan and then seen it through?"

He leaned in and kissed her forehead, then met her gaze again. "As it turned out, going along with this scheme has been one of my better ideas."

Careful not to ruin her makeup for the photos, or to leave a trace of lipstick on him, she reached up and placed a delicate kiss on his lips.

"Ready?" he whispered.

Taking a deep breath, she nodded and turned to the photographer. "We're ready. How do you want us to pose?"

"No need," the photographer said cheerily. "I got everything I need."

She looked from him to a grinning Anna and back again. "When?"

"While you were talking." He shrugged, as if that was obvious. "They're sweet photos. They should come out well."

"Right then," Adam said, straightening. "What next?"

The photographer picked up his equipment. "We'll just take a few close-ups of the rings, maybe in the house so I have more control of the light, and we'll be done."

Anna and the photographer headed back to the house, and Adam laced his fingers through Callie's, a rueful smile dancing around his mouth. "It seems this is getting easier with practice."

"Seems so," she said, but her earlier unease about their relationship returned. Was it easier to pretend to be in love because it was becoming closer to the truth?

Pushing the thought aside for now, she changed the subject. "Do you mind if we stay a bit longer after these last photos? Since Jenna and Faith are both here, we were thinking it would be a good time to do some more planning for the wedding, as well as the rehearsal dinner and the bachelor-bachelorette party."

"Sure," he said. "There are a few business things I'd like to discuss with Liam and Dylan anyway, so it's good timing."

She leaned in to whisper in his ear. "And after that I'll take you up on that offer to go straight to your bed."

"I'll make my meetings quick," he said, deadpan, and she laughed.

But as they drew closer to the house, she sobered. She was about to plan her wedding to this man, but once that happened, it would be the beginning of the end. As soon as their vows were spoken, they would start planning their separation.

And every day spent in Adam Hawke's company, in his bed, made the prospect of that separation more devastating.

Eight

By the time they left Liam's house, Callie was restless with wanting Adam. After the photographer and Anna had left, they were just with Adam's family, who all believed she and Adam were putting on an act for the camera. And, of course, they had been.

But then, to keep things simple, they'd pretended for his family not to be involved at all, which was also a lie.

The truth was in some messy place in between, and couldn't really be explained to anyone, so they'd spent the afternoon acting more like business associates than two people who were desperate for a chance to be alone together.

Once in the car, they were silent, but the air vibrated with the tension of all the subterfuge.

At the first red light, Adam glanced over. The heat in his green eyes was unmistakable, making her skin

flush. She swallowed. The light changed, and he accelerated, but no words had been exchanged.

At the next light, again he glanced over, and this time
she reached and out laid a hand on his thigh. A tremor
ran through his body.

"San Juan Capistrano back to LA is not a quick trip,"
he said through a tight jaw. "We're not going to make
it if your hand continues on that path."

"Are you suggesting we stop somewhere along the
way?" The idea of Mr. Cool and Controlled being so
overtaken by his passions fascinated her.

He grimaced. "I'd rather make it back to my place."

Grinning, she retracted her hand. "Will that help?"

"It's a start." He blew out a breath. "But we should
talk. Tell me about something that's not dangerous."

Something not dangerous? The only topics she could
dredge up were all dangerous. She tucked her hair behind her ears and tried again. "What do you want to
know?"

"How about when you were growing up? I know the
basic details, but tell me what it was like."

She settled back into her seat and thought over her
childhood. Then she began to talk. She told him about
the school swimming meet where she'd come third in
the two-hundred-meter freestyle event, and the year she
and Summer had dressed up as dalmatians at Hallow-
een. About the time she'd gotten so addicted to solitaire
that she fell behind on her schoolwork, and when her
family had traveled to New Mexico for summer break.

Adam asked questions and laughed in the right
places, and some of the tension in the car relaxed. It was
nice spending time with just him, where they weren't

pretending to either be in love or not involved at all. Just being.

However, when they pulled in to his garage and stepped out of the car, the mood changed. Or rather, it adjusted. For the most part, they'd been ignoring the simmering heat between them on the drive home, but now that they'd arrived…

He took her hand as they walked through the front door and an electric tingle raced from her fingers up her arm to her spine. She'd been waiting for this moment all day.

As he opened the door, they both stopped. There was a trail of rose petals on the floor, leading from the entryway to the hall to his room.

"When did you do this?" she asked. He'd been with her since they left this morning, so it wouldn't have been easy.

"It wasn't me," he said grimly. He glanced around, and found a note propped up on a side table. As he scanned it, he said, "Dylan. He called my housekeeper on her vacation and got her to set it up. It's a surprise from all the staff at Hawke's Blooms. Apparently they all wanted to do something for us, and they said it with flowers."

She scooped up some of the delicate petals and rubbed them between her fingers. "It's very sweet of them."

He cut her a glance. "It is sweet of them, but we've just spent half a day with my brother and he failed to mention it. That part is less sweet."

She held the petals to her nose. "They smell divine. Let's see where they lead."

"I think we can guess," he said wryly.

No one had ever done anything like this for her before, and whether they were suffering under a misapprehension or not when they organized it, it was still lovely, and she intended to allow herself to appreciate the indulgence.

"Let's follow the trail anyway," she said and set off down the hall. Sure enough, the petals led straight to Adam's bedroom, and his comforter was liberally strewn with them, mainly in reds, pinks and whites. There were huge bunches of roses in the same colors in vases around the room and the air was heavy with their rich scent.

Adam came to stand behind her, and she could feel the heat emanating from his body. She leaned back into him.

"It's beautiful," she whispered.

He stroked a hand down her hair. "No, you're beautiful." He kissed the top of her head. "I need a shower. Liam had us standing out in the sun for most of the meeting, going through the rows of his upcoming flowers."

Despite knowing his shower would be quick, and he wouldn't be far away in the attached bathroom, impatience pulled at her. "I'll be here. Waiting."

"Or…" he said, turning her in his arms.

"Or?" she asked, blinking up at him.

"Or you could join me." He tugged on her hand, drawing her into the bathroom with a smile that promised much.

"That could work, too." She allowed herself to be led, and when they reached the shower, allowed herself to be undressed. Adam quickly shucked down his own clothes and turned on the water, testing the temperature with a hand. Then he pulled her beneath the spray.

The warm water was sensual as it poured over her body, but the feel of his slickened skin sliding against hers as he adjusted the water and reached for the soap was better.

"I can't imagine why I've been showering alone since I moved in."

He squirted liquid soap into his hands and began to lather. "You're always welcome in my shower." With hands on her shoulders, he turned her and rubbed the lathered soap over her back. "In fact, I encourage it."

Strong hands stroked over her shoulders and down her back, curving over her buttocks before starting at the top again. She let out a contented sigh. "Will those be full service like this one?"

Her earlobe was sucked into the warmth of his mouth, and a shudder raced down her spine. Then his lips were at the shell of her ear. "You haven't seen full service yet."

He turned her again so that she was facing him and squirted more soap into his hands. Then, slowly, ever so slowly, he washed every square inch of her, paying special attention to her breasts.

"I've heard these can need more washing than elbows and legs," he murmured as he soaped up the peaks of her breasts.

Her blood pumped insistently through her veins. "Your attention to detail does you credit."

"I'm glad you think so," he said, sliding his hands lower, "because I've heard a rumor that there's another part that often needs even more washing."

An ache between her legs throbbed, begging for his touch. "I think it's your duty to investigate."

He stepped behind her and pulled her against him with an arm beneath her breasts, while the other hand continued its descent. "Oh, I plan to."

When his fingers hit their target, her knees wobbled, but he held her firm. The slow, slick movements were designed to drive her out of her mind, and they were working. She moaned his name, and felt him hardening against her buttocks, but his hand didn't falter.

The warm water gently beating down on her skin, Adam at her back, his soaped hand circling and rocking her: it was too much all at once and her release came upon her in a roar of sensation, overtaking her completely then ebbing away, leaving her limp in his arms.

He held her for long moments, kissing her face, before letting her stand on her own once she was ready. The quick, practical movements of his own cleansing routine were in sharp contrast to the lush strokes he'd used on her, but she still admired the process.

The water stopped and he patted her down with a thick towel.

"I could get used to this way of showering," she said on a happy sigh.

He waggled his eyebrows. "That's my nefarious plan. Then you'll be naked in my shower each morning."

Once he was dry, as well, he interlaced their fingers for the few steps back into the bedroom. The curtains were drawn, hiding the magnificent ocean view, but it gave them privacy, which she preferred in that moment. Adam flicked a switch and downlights came on around the edges of the room, creating a magical atmosphere. The rose petals that covered the bed practically sparkled in the light.

She dropped Adam's hand and crawled onto the bed, luxuriating in the rich, creamy texture of the petals against her shower-sensitized skin. Eyes closed, she stretched just to feel their caress.

The mattress dipped, and Adam's arms came around her. "If that's your reaction, I'll make sure this bed is covered in rose petals every night."

"You know, I've always thought it sounded romantic, but it *feels* divine, too." With every movement, the flowers' scent was released until it surrounded them. "Try it."

Adam lay flat on his back, moving his arms above his head as if making a snow angel. "You know what? You're right."

She gathered a handful of petals and sprinkled them over him. "You've never done this before? You're the head of one of the biggest flower companies in the country and you've never lain on a carpet of rose petals?"

One corner of his mouth quirked up. "My brothers were always more hands-on with the flowers. Liam with growing them, and Dylan selling them."

"Even when you were young? Before you ran the company?"

He nodded, his gaze on her hand as she let another handful of petals fall over his chest. "My mother and Dylan were the mainstays of the roadside stall, where we started selling the flowers—I don't know if you noticed, but Dylan can sell anything to anyone. And Liam started helping Dad from a very young age. He was more interested in science and getting the technical details right in growing the best plants."

"And you?" she asked softly, feeling as if she was prying, but dying to know what went on in his mind.

"Me?" He shrugged and pulled her closer. "I had a vision. Right from the start I could see that we had all the ingredients to make it work. Dad could grow anything and Liam could produce new and unusual flowers. Mom had a keen eye for what the customer wanted and Dylan could charm anyone into parting with their money. They just needed someone to dream big for them and turn it into a business plan."

She could imagine Adam when he was young, already driven and focused. "You certainly came through on that."

"They all came through on their parts, too," he said, his voice filled with respect and affection.

She wondered if he had any idea of what he'd really contributed. There were lots of groups and families who had "all the ingredients to make it work," but that didn't mean much without someone with business savvy. Someone who could conceptualize an idea then turn it into reality. From the sound of it, Adam had done that partly through sheer force of will.

One question tugged at her—he'd made it his mission to look after his entire family but who was looking after him?

"You're an amazing man, Adam Hawke," she said, and then reached up to kiss his jawline.

"Oh, you think so, do you?" In the space of seconds, his tone had changed from serious and reflective to something altogether more wicked. It sent her pulse racing.

He rolled them over, pinning her beneath him, his gaze mischievous. "How amazing?"

"Quite," she teased back.

One corner of his mouth quirked. "That's it?"

She pretended to think about it, which was difficult, given that her breathing had become uneven. "Yes, I think that's about it. Quite."

"What if I do this?" He scooted down and took the tip of her breast into his mouth, tugging gently and swiping with his tongue. The action seemed to tug at the very core of her being, setting every nerve ending alight.

"That's good," she said, though her voice was higher than normal.

"Good, huh?" He reached over to the box he now kept in his bedside drawer and withdrew a packet. In seconds, he was sheathed and poised above her. "It seems that I've gone backward from quite amazing to good."

All she could see was him above her as he rested his weight on one forearm. Then she felt his hand come between them, his thumb moving expertly, making her forget any trace of conversation.

"Still only good?" he asked as first one finger then a second slid inside her, his thumb still the center of her world.

"Um," she said. Her skin was hot, so hot. *What was he talking about?* "Yes?"

"You were telling me whether I was merely good, or quite amazing, or maybe something more." He sounded maddeningly patient, but she could feel the evidence of his arousal pressing against her thigh and knew that his nonchalance had to be costing him.

"More. You're more than amazing." She couldn't think of any words that meant more than amazing in the moment, so she hoped the intent would be enough to satisfy him.

His hand disappeared but before she could miss it, he'd parted her thighs wider and was resting his weight on his knees between them. "I think you're pretty amazing, too," he said, his ragged voice finally showing how affected he was. Then he slid inside her.

She arched up to meet him, feeling the perfection of him filling her, stretching her, but still needing more, needing movement.

"Adam." It was more of a moan, a plea, than anything, and he seemed to understand, because he began to move, to find the rhythm that suited them both, and she rose to meet each thrust, an ebb and flow that they'd practiced enough now to create naturally.

Their movements released more fragrance from the rose petals beneath her, and the sound of Adam's rough breathing near her ear made her heart beat faster. Pressure was building inside her, around her, propelling her higher, the momentum driving her further.

He moved his pelvis somehow, and the friction was suddenly different, better, harder, and everything coiled tight then exploded in waves of glorious sensation from her toes to the top of her head and beyond, as if she was too big for her body.

As she came down, the motion continued, with Adam keeping the rhythm going before his entire body stiffened and he shouted his release into the curve of her neck. As he slumped, she wrapped her arms around him, wanting more than anything to be the one who held him. The one who would always catch him. The one who would be there for him.

And for this sweet moment, she was.

* * *

"Another glass?" Adam asked two hours later, holding up the bottle of red.

"Just a little one." Callie held her glass out as he poured the wine, and then settled back into the deck chair on his balcony and breathed in the view. The sun would be setting soon over the Pacific Ocean and the colors were vibrant.

"I'm going to miss this house once this is all over," she said on a sigh. "You have to promise me you'll take advantage of it more, even when you're back to working long hours."

Adam was silent for a moment, so she glanced over. He was deep in thought, his gaze on the far horizon over the water.

"I don't have a quarter on me," she said, "but I'll offer the last piece of brie for your thoughts."

The corners of his mouth quirked and he took a sip of his wine before reaching for her hand.

"I was thinking about what you just said. About after this is all over." The weight of his gaze landed on her. "What if it doesn't have to end?"

Callie's heart picked up speed, racing double-time. "I'm not sure what you're asking."

He let out a long breath. "I'm not sure, either. All I know is I'm not ready for this to end."

She remembered him saying that whenever he grew too emotionally close to a woman, he backed away. If he was willing to continue things, that meant he didn't have feelings for her.

The realization hurt more than she would have expected. She didn't know quite what she felt for him, but whatever it was, it clearly wasn't reciprocated.

She carefully placed her glass on the small table between their deck chairs and crossed the few steps to the railing. She'd known this was a plan with a time limit, and Adam had been completely up-front about not being able to offer more than they'd agreed to, but clearly some naive part of her had been holding on to a shred of hope…

She felt him come to stand beside her. "Callie?"

"I don't know," she admitted with a small shrug.

He was silent for a beat, and when he spoke, his voice was low and tender. "What, specifically, don't you know?"

"Anything." She let out a humorless laugh. "Everything." Finding his gaze, she bit down on her bottom lip. "Except that I'm not ready for this to end yet, either."

His eyes softened, and then heated. "Well, let's not let it."

Her hands trembled. That sounded so easy, and yet…

"If we continue, there's a good chance one of us—" namely her "—would become emotionally compromised."

"If you're worried about hurting me, Callie, don't be. You know I've become good at guarding my heart over the years. And if you're worried about you falling in love with me, there are things we can do about that."

Curiosity piqued, she grinned. "So how do you plan to stop me falling in love with you?"

"We'll start with a visit to my brothers," he said with a poker face. "They'll be eager to fill you in on all my failings. No fledgling love could withstand the way they'll gleefully delve into my faults. And it will all be true."

She crossed her arms under her breasts, smothering a laugh. "And if it's not enough?"

"I'll be sure to stomp around the house and be cranky for an hour each night." He rubbed a hand over his lightly stubbled jaw. "Maybe buy some unattractive underwear."

She let her chuckle loose, but as it faded, she turned to face the ocean. If he thought those few things would stop her falling the rest of the way in love with him, he was sadly deluded about the effect he had on her.

"In all seriousness," he said, pulling her closer, "surely we'd have fallen in love by now if it was going to happen? We've been pretending for the world, and spending all our time together, not to mention burning up the sheets on my bed. If we've held out this long, I think we can make it a bit longer safely."

The skin on the back of her neck prickled, and she rubbed a hand under her hair, trying to ease the sensation. "So you think we should continue our fling indefinitely?"

"We'll already be married. All I'm saying is that we could hold off on the divorce as long as the arrangement is still working for us. As soon as one of us wants to call it quits, the divorce is put in motion, no questions asked."

It sounded so clinical. The opposite of how their marriage had begun, all passion and excitement and spontaneity. Now their divorce would be denied the same energy, of ending in a bang of emotion. Instead, their marriage would slowly peter out until nothing was left, and one of them wanted to move on.

"Let me think about it," she said with an attempt at a smile. "My mind is so full of next weekend's rehearsal dinner, and the bachelor-bachelorette party, there isn't much room to think clearly."

It was an excuse and she saw in his eyes that he recognized it as such, but he didn't call her on it, and for that she was grateful.

"Take all the time you need," he said and fetched their wineglasses. "Now tell me the latest on the rehearsal dinner and our combined bachelor-bachelorette party."

Back on safer ground, she took a sip of her wine and filled him in on all the arrangements she, Jenna and Faith had made in the past couple of days. But even as she spoke, a small part of her mind kept drifting to his suggestion. To the idea of extending her time with him. In his bed. Married to him.

And she wondered—when the time came and he called it quits, would she be able to walk away from Adam Hawke?

Nine

Adam tugged at the collar of his tuxedo and cast another glance around the assembled guests on the four-hundred-foot super yacht. He was looking for Callie, which was pointless, because he'd positioned himself next to the entrance so he wouldn't miss her and she definitely hadn't boarded yet.

Many of the guests for the joint bachelor and bachelorette party had already arrived, and were milling about drinking the champagne the waitstaff was distributing. Several people had stopped to congratulate him. He'd been polite, but had ensured he could still see new guests over their shoulder.

A hand clapped him on the back, and Dylan's voice came from beside him. "Adam, my favorite brother."

"Hey," Liam said, coming from behind.

"Best to let him think that," Dylan said in a stage whisper to Liam. "It's his night, after all."

Adam snagged another glass of champagne from a passing waiter's tray and tried to ignore his younger brothers. They always found the most inconvenient times to get in his face.

"I haven't seen Callie yet," Liam said, frowning as he looked into the crowd.

"She's not here." Adam adjusted his position so he could see past Liam in case Callie was arriving as they spoke. "She didn't have anything formal enough at my house, so she went to her place a few hours ago to get ready."

"She and Summer are holding back to make a grand entrance?" Dylan asked.

Adam snorted out a laugh. "Nope." That was so not Callie's style.

"Okay, listen. Since this is essentially your bachelor party, I have a few ideas. How about—"

"No," Adam said, swinging his gaze to Dylan. "Nothing. Not one thing, I'm warning you."

The youngest Hawke brother held up his hands. "Okay, okay. I wasn't serious."

Liam chuckled. "I told you he wouldn't be in the mood for jokes."

Adam heard the comments as if from a distance, because he'd just spotted Callie. The world stopped spinning and all he could see was her. She was in a figure-hugging bloodred gown, with lips and nails painted to match. Her caramel-brown hair, glossy under the lights, was swept back from her face and trailed down past her shoulders. Her beauty shone so brightly it held him captive. The need to touch her, to have simple skin-on-skin contact, was overwhelming.

As she drew closer, she caught sight of him and their

gazes locked. He noticed the slight falter in her step, and his chest swelled.

When she reached them, he held out a hand for her, and she came into his arms as if she truly belonged there. For a moment, as he felt her against him, he let himself imagine it was true—that he'd found someone he could love, the way Liam loved Jenna, and Dylan loved Faith.

But it was dangerous to think that way. He was different from his brothers. He didn't have the same luxury of falling in love.

No matter how breathtaking Callie was in that dress, or how she made his heart sing.

She eased back, and he murmured hello and kissed her cheek, careful not to ruin her makeup. Then she was claimed by Dylan and Liam, who had already greeted Summer, and were now congratulating Callie on the success of the rehearsal dinner two nights earlier.

The dinner had been a resounding success. The adults had all dressed as characters such as fairy godmothers and princes, and the looks on the children's faces when they saw them and the room decorations had melted the hearts of everyone there. Jenna was already considering making a dinner for children aided by the trust an annual event.

Callie modestly protested. "Your fiancées and Summer did most of the work."

Liam shook his head. "That's not the way Jenna tells it. And the next day when Anna Wilson's article about it hit the web, the trust had another boost to its donations, which looks like it will have a long tail."

While Liam spoke to Callie, Adam pulled Summer into a brotherly hug.

"Good to see you again," he said, meaning it. He was coming to see Summer as a sister, much like Jenna and Faith.

It was a funny thing—he'd spent most of his life in a family that was dominated by men, with his father, two brothers and himself, and only his mother holding the flag for women. Now he had a wife, three sisters-in-law and two nieces. The gender balance had definitely tipped in the other direction. He liked it.

"You, too," Summer said. Then she laid a hand on his forearm and pulled him back a step, where they couldn't be overheard. "I've finished writing the vows for the wedding. I have a copy in my purse, or would you rather I email them to you so you can check them over?"

Vows. One more detail that he was glad he didn't need to take care of himself for this wedding. "No, I trust you. With your PR experience, you'll be much better at this kind of thing than I would. Whatever you've done is fine."

Callie finished with his brothers and came to stand beside him again, lacing her fingers through his. Summer discreetly slipped away, following his brothers back to mingle with the crowd—something he and Callie should do, as well, but he wanted a little time alone with her first.

"I missed you," he said, close to her ear.

She shot him a teasing look. "Did you think that before or after you saw this dress?"

He chuckled. "Before. After I saw it my thoughts went in another direction entirely."

The teasing light faded from her silver-blue eyes and her expression became serious. "I missed you, too."

Everything inside him seemed to settle into place.

That was a good omen for their continuing the fling after their wedding. Surely, if she missed him, she wouldn't be keen on running off straight away. But he wouldn't ask. He'd told her she could have as much time to think about it as she needed and he'd meant it.

"Regardless of what you said to my brothers, I know you did most of the work organizing the rehearsal dinner and this party tonight. And it's very good work. Both events have come off flawlessly."

She smiled and seemed to stand taller. "Thank you. Your standards are high, so I appreciate that feedback."

"In fact, I've been thinking that your work is so good, that perhaps you should be working for Hawke's Blooms." In truth, the thought had only just occurred to him, but it made complete sense. She was good at her job and their company could use someone with her skill set.

She dropped her voice. "How do you think that would go once we divorce?"

It was good she was looking at the issue from all sides—it was one of the things he liked about her—but he couldn't imagine ever having a strained relationship with Callie. They got on too well.

"That won't be a problem for us," he said, shrugging a shoulder. "Unlike most divorces, ours will be a well-planned and friendly parting."

"You don't think it will be—" her teeth worried at her bottom lip as she searched for the word she wanted "—awkward to see each other at work once we're no longer involved? No longer sleeping together?"

He rubbed a thumb over the inside of her hand, trying to soothe away her concerns. "If we're no longer involved, it means that what we've had will have run its course. When I look into the future, I see us still being friends."

She blinked. She obviously had a different vision of their future, but that didn't mean his was wrong.

"The offer is on the table," he whispered just as an older couple approached them. Callie introduced them and she and Adam spent the next hour mingling with their guests, sometimes together and sometimes individually.

"Adam," Callie said a little later, laying a hand on his arm.

He turned to find her standing behind him. She was radiant.

"There you are," he said and kissed her cheek. "Ten minutes is entirely too long to be away from me."

She gave him a quick smile, and then stepped away to reveal two men standing with her. "Adam, I want you to meet two of the partners at my firm, John Evans and Ted Parker."

Adam shook the men's hands, resting one arm securely around Callie's shoulders.

John, the taller of the men, planted his hands on his hips. "Good to meet you, Mr. Hawke." Then he turned back to Callie. "I have some news you might be interested in about Terence Gibson."

Adam felt Callie tense beside him. It was the name of the coworker who'd tried to blackmail her into giving him the trust's account.

"Oh?" she asked politely.

John nodded. "He seemed unnaturally interested in your work on the Hawke Brothers Trust account, so I pressed him for a reason, and he told us what a bad choice you'd be for partner."

Callie's face paled, but Adam saw red. After all her work, would they really believe that guy's trash talking? He cleared his throat. "The opinion of one co-worker hardly seems to be enough to base an important decision on."

John's expression gave nothing away. "I'm afraid he had quite a detailed list of the disadvantages to us of promoting you. Coincidentally, he also had reasons we couldn't promote Michael, Angela or Diane."

Callie's eyes widened. She obviously hadn't realized how broad an agenda her coworker had. "They're great workers, especially Diane—"

Her boss held up a hand. "We agree. And after we started asking the right questions, we realized Terence had been undermining his coworkers for some time, which is not the way we like our team to operate. So we fired him."

"You fired him," Callie repeated.

John's mouth pulled into a tight smile, but it was far from warm. "Just thought you might like to know. Anyway, I'm going to find one of those waiters and grab another glass of that very fine champagne you're serving. Congratulations again to you both."

And suddenly the partners were both gone.

"Are you okay?" Adam whispered near her ear.

Callie only had time for a quick nod when Summer made a beeline for them through the crowd. Her cheeks were a little flushed, possibly from the champagne, but her eyes said she was focused.

"How do you think it's going?" Adam asked her when she reached them.

"Definitely a success," she said with barely contained delight. "Hey, since we're creating new traditions all over the place by having the bachelor and bachelorette parties combined, how about another new tradition?"

"Should I be worried?" Adam asked.

Summer grinned. "Just a dance between the happy couple. Do you two have a special song?"

"No—" Callie said, just as Adam blurted out, "'The Lady in Red.'"

Summer glanced down at Callie's bloodred dress and grinned. "Good choice. I'll tell the DJ."

After she left, Callie smiled at him. "That was quick thinking."

"Actually, it's a coincidence that your dress tonight is red," he said, still considering how much to say. Almost by unspoken agreement, they'd never talked about the night they'd met. The time they'd spent together over the three conferences hadn't involved much talking at all, and ever since she'd hurtled back into his life they'd barely mentioned their time in Vegas. But for some reason tonight felt like another first and had him thinking back to that time.

He lowered his voice. "Do you remember the first night we met?"

"At the conference a couple of years ago?" she asked, tilting her head to the side.

He nodded. "We were sitting at the bar the first night."

She'd been a few places down the bar and he'd been watching her, mesmerized. She'd turned away a couple of guys who'd tried to hit on her, so he'd wondered if she just wanted to be left alone. Then their gazes had snagged as she took a glance around, and he'd felt a connection, and knew he had to try his luck, even if she might shoot him down.

"You asked me if you could buy me a drink," she said, her voice nostalgic and hypnotic.

"Not very original of me, I know." In fact, he'd been tongue-tied for the first time in his life. Possibly his first clue that maintaining self-control around this woman was going to be difficult.

"It worked." She moistened her lips. "I'd been trying to think of a line to introduce myself to you."

"Really?" He'd had no idea, and it changed the way he thought about that night. Made it even more special, because it meant she'd felt it right from the start, just as he had.

"If you hadn't come over—" she arched an eyebrow and looked as majestic as she had that night "—you probably had about four minutes before I found a line and came to your bar stool."

"Now part of me wishes I'd waited, just to hear your line." He grinned and was rewarded with a laugh. Her eyes, already impossibly large with the dark makeup, shone from within, and he wondered if he'd ever be able to look away.

"It would probably have been worse than yours," she said, shaking her head.

He waited for their amusement to subside, before he said, "And do you remember what song was playing in the bar?"

She frowned. "No." Then her eyes widened. "'The Lady in Red'? Seriously?"

He nodded, inordinately pleased with himself. "You weren't wearing red that night, but it was definitely playing."

"And you remembered," she said, a touch of awe in her voice.

Keeping her gaze, he placed a kiss on the back of her hand. "That moment is indelibly etched in my memory."

There was an announcement that dancing was about to start, and then the strains of "The Lady in Red" came through the sound system.

Adam put out his hand. "Would you like to dance?"

Callie took Adam's hand and walked with him out to the dance floor, but it felt as if they were doing more. Taking a step into their future.

The old-fashioned ballad was designed for swaying so many other couples joined them on the dance floor. And it was also a thinly disguised chance to be in each other's arms and sneak a kiss or two.

"Are you enjoying yourself?" he murmured near her ear. "You wouldn't have rather had a stripper, or a toilet-paper wedding-dress game?"

"A bachelorette party like that would have been awkward with a journalist along." She nodded in the direction of where Anna was collecting quotes from their friends and family to go with the article she'd write about tonight. "And what about you? An opportunity for drinking and strippers has passed you by."

He caressed her back slowly. "I'm sure I'll cope with the disappointment."

His hand was warm through the fabric of her dress. She could stay like this for hours, just being close to him.

"I made a decision tonight," she said, her voice dreamy even to her own ears.

"Just tell me it's not about sleeping somewhere other than my bed tonight. I have plans for the removal of this dress."

She smoothed her hands over his shoulders as they danced, loving the shape of him, and especially the freedom to touch him whenever she pleased.

"It's about the future removal of dresses."

He leaned back and looked at her with a hopeful gaze. "The fling?"

"It's working for us, so it seems silly to stop at an arbitrary date like the wedding. I agree that we should continue while it still works for us."

He lifted her off her feet and spun around. People made way for them and gave them indulgent looks, which was the advantage of displays of affection at your own prewedding party.

"I can't tell you how happy I am about this," he said as he settled her down again.

The song ended. The next one was modern with a faster beat, and she didn't feel like dancing to it in the heels she'd worn, so she suggested they get a drink. As they went their separate ways in the crowd and fell into conversation with their guests, she found that they were looking for each other across the room, and when she would find him, his gaze would heat and she could feel the answering burn across her skin.

Continuing to sleep with him even after they no longer needed to pretend felt right. In fact, maybe it could turn into something more. Everything inside her lifted, glowed at the thought.

Obviously Adam would be resistant to the idea at first, but that was merely his fear. It shouldn't take long for him to realize they enjoyed each other's company, respected each other, had a passion unlike any she'd had before. They had shared intimate stories with each other about their backgrounds. When they'd first married, they'd practically been strangers, but this time…

This time it seemed to be a recipe for a happy marriage.

The idea was so bright and shiny that for a moment she forgot to breathe. Adam shot her a quizzical look from the other side of the room and she realized she probably had a goofy grin on her face. The older woman she was talking to patted her hand and mumbled something about brides and newlyweds then left, but Callie was still stuck on the sparkling possibility that she might have a real future with Adam.

She smoothed down her dress and found her composure, but inside she was still buzzing.

Could it work…?

Ten

Feeling as content as she could remember, Callie sat in the backseat of the limousine, Adam's arm around her shoulders, as they arrived back at his place from the marina.

The night had gone off without a hitch, and she felt closer to Adam than ever. Everything was wholly perfect.

"You awake?" he said softly when the limo pulled up.

She arched her neck back to look at him. "I am. Just thinking over the night."

"My favorite part was our dance," he murmured.

It was one of her favorite parts, too, but there was something that had underpinned the night, something she couldn't quite put her finger on, that made the entire experience magical.

The driver opened her door and Adam released her with a quick kiss to her forehead before she stepped out.

They went through the routine of walking through the house and getting ready for bed, with minimal conversation but sleepy smiles, and within ten minutes, they were under the covers together.

"We didn't get to talk much about your decision tonight," Adam said, smoothing the hair back from her face. "But I have to tell you how happy I am about it."

Callie snaked an arm over his waist and snuggled in. "I am, too. It feels right."

A few minutes earlier, she'd been feeling exhausted, but now that she was alone with him, talking, touching, suddenly she wasn't as tired anymore.

She started to trace a pattern over his torso. "Would you like me to show you how right it feels?"

His fingers traced a mirror image on her back of the pattern her hand was making. "Oh, I think I could be talked into that."

She stretched to reach his mouth and kissed him. His breath was minty, his lips ready for her and hungry. Heat filled her body, and she moved farther over him, the abrasion of the light dusting of hair on his chest a delicious friction.

"Callie," he groaned and pulled her tighter. "What you do to me…"

His skin was hot to touch, and she couldn't get enough. She slid her palms over every square inch she could reach. The need to be close was the driving force, one she couldn't resist. Didn't want to resist. The man she loved was…

Wait…

Everything stopped, even the breath in her lungs.

The man she loved?

Was that her mind playing a trick with words, or was

it true? Stomach churning, she flicked through memories, feelings, any information she could dredge up until the pieces of the jigsaw started to fit into place—she'd been so incandescently happy tonight on the yacht as they talked about a future together. She felt herself light up from inside whenever she saw him. And it was his touch, and his touch alone, that she craved like a drug.

She flinched. Oh, yeah. She was in love with him.

What a stupid, stupid thing to let happen. This plan had never been about love—it was a straightforward arrangement to convince everyone else they were in love.

Had she fallen into her own trap? Believed the lies she and Adam had been spinning for other people? Perhaps pretending to be in love with Adam Hawke had seeped into her subconscious somehow and become tangled with her real feelings until now they were inseparable.

Whatever the cause, there was no doubt that it had happened. And now, instead of happy, it just made her feel emotionally vulnerable.

"Something's changed," he said. "Are you okay?"

She didn't want to explain, not yet. Not until she'd had time to think it through properly. So instead, she hid her face against his chest and placed a kiss against the warm skin beneath her lips. "I'm fine."

His abdominal muscles clenched as he lifted himself into a half-sitting position, trying to see her face. "Would you rather we stopped?"

She needed him now more than ever—needed the mindless moments and the release before she had to face the situation she'd created. She rolled onto her back and pulled him with her, until he was above her. "No, I don't want to stop. I want you to stay close, as close as we can be. I want you touching me."

His eyes softened, and he leaned down to claim her mouth in a scorching kiss before whispering against her lips, "Then stay with me."

There was no mistaking what he meant—she must have zoned out for a few seconds after her realization, and her actions would have seemed more like an automaton's. But staying emotionally engaged with him while making love now, while she was raw from the discovery, was like ripping out her still-beating heart and handing it to him. The only way to survive was to try to hold a little of herself back. At least until she had things clear in her head.

She kissed him again, taking his mind off his request, and moved beneath him in the way she knew would drive him wild. A shudder ripped through his body, and he kissed a path down the side of her throat, nipping at the sensitive skin, making her writhe. And then his hand was between them, working its magic until her hips bucked with wanting him.

And yet, a small part of her, detached and clinical, seemed to be watching them from above. Keeping her heart safe.

"Give me a second," he said, and reached for the bedside table. He sheathed himself quickly and then was back by her side, making her feel beautiful and desired.

He lifted her knees and wrapped them around his hips, and she nudged him with her heels, impatient. Wanting. Always wanting with Adam.

As he entered her, she discovered that holding part of herself back hadn't been enough. The intensity was too much. She squeezed her eyes shut, unwilling to risk him seeing everything she was feeling, but he wouldn't let her keep him out.

"Open your eyes, Callie," he said, and when she didn't, he kissed each eyelid in turn. "Please don't hide from me. Let me see you."

The comment about hiding from him hit home, but it was the "please" that did it. Her eyelids fluttered open and she was confronted with Adam's deep green gaze. It was unwavering, inviting her to fall away with him, and she did.

He moved within her and the pressure built, taking her higher, higher than she'd ever been, the intimacy of being joined with the man she loved overwhelming. His hands moved over her even as he stroked into her, and he whispered her name in her ear, roughly, as if he was as lost as she. Higher, she flew higher, until she hit the peak, crying out that she loved him, and then crested the wave, feeling him follow her, before slumping, spent, to her side.

For several minutes she floated on a blissful cloud, not moving, not thinking. But slowly, the nagging memory of what she'd said crept into her mind.

She'd called out that she loved him.

Had he heard her? She tried to remember if he'd reacted, but those moments were hazy at best. Was it possible that he'd flinched when she'd said it, or was that her imagination?

The worst part was, despite saying it without thinking it was true.

As she lay in his arms, she made herself face reality. She was in love with Adam. Head-over-heels, lost-her-mind-crazy in love.

And there were consequences of falling in love with Adam Hawke...

She couldn't have a fling with the man she loved. Couldn't stay married and share his bed until he grew tired of her. She'd end up with a heart torn to pieces.

And she couldn't walk away—she'd made commitments to the trust, and to her bosses. And even after they were over, would she be able to walk away from him? Leave Adam when he still wanted her? She couldn't imagine having that level of internal strength.

And that fact meant she needed another way forward. A new plan.

Adam curled into her, letting out a contented sigh, and she squeezed her eyes shut. She'd give herself this one night to enjoy him and then work out that new plan tomorrow.

Callie woke slowly the next morning, and before she was even fully aware, the memory of the night before came crashing back. She was in love with Adam. She'd told him—screamed it to him, actually.

Her stomach swam. She opened one eye, then the other, and found his side of the bed empty. She gave thanks for small mercies. She needed a few minutes on her own. More than a few, but she'd manage with what she could get.

She dragged herself into the shower and threw on some clothes, the whole time thinking through possible solutions. Several ideas occurred to her, but no one plan that would work for everyone. Keeping her feelings a secret was no longer an option thanks to her chattiness.

Unless...

What if Adam had changed his feelings, too, and was just as worried about bringing it up with her?

If he'd had a change of heart, or was at least open to exploring that possibility, then they could try a relationship for real. Sure, there would be a lot of pressure since they were already married, but nothing they couldn't overcome with a little dedication.

She owed it to herself, to their relationship, to at least try.

She smiled. It was funny that only last night on the yacht she'd been having similar thoughts—that perhaps they could try to make things work. But then she'd realized she loved him, and that she couldn't have a fling with a man she loved, waiting for him to become bored. And here she was now, full circle, wondering if there was a chance he would return her feelings, hoping…

Searching through the house, she found him on the balcony with a coffee in one hand, scrolling through online newspapers on his laptop.

"Good morning, beautiful," he said when he saw her.

"Morning," she said, not knowing how to start the conversation now that she was here.

"There's more coffee in the pot, if you want some."

Coffee would definitely help, and going to get it would give her a little more time to organize her thoughts. She headed into the kitchen.

When she ventured back to the balcony, steaming mug of coffee in hand, Adam closed his laptop and put it on a side table.

"How did you sleep?" he asked, and then watched her over the rim of his mug as he took a sip.

She tucked her feet up under her on the deck chair. "Pretty heavily, I think."

She was surprised she'd slept at all, given that her mind was worrying over what her heart had been busy doing, but the exhaustion must have caught up with her.

"Me, too," he said, and she knew from the look in his eye that he was crediting their presleep lovemaking.

The lovemaking that had brought her face-to-face with reality. She took a breath. It was time. If she didn't address this now, it would only drag out.

"Adam, there's something I want to talk to you about." She took a sip of coffee for courage and he waited. "About us."

"If you're embarrassed about what you said, don't be." He shrugged, as if it was nothing more than telling him the coffeepot was empty. "People get carried away in the heat of passion."

She blinked. That answered the first question about how he'd taken it last night. If she wanted the coward's way out, all she had to do was nod, agree and change the subject. Everything could go back to how it was before she'd blurted out the truth during her release.

Despite part of her wanting that easy route, she knew it wouldn't solve anything. She couldn't live with their current plan of continuing their fling after the wedding, until Adam wanted to move on. It would be Adam moving on, not her. She was in love and here for the long haul. And waiting around for the ax to fall? Purgatory.

The only way forward that gave her a chance to keep her sanity intact was to tell him the truth and give him the chance to rise to the occasion.

"So this might seem crazy," she said, noting the waver in her voice but being unable to doing anything about it, "but what if I wasn't just 'carried away'? What if love has crept into the equation for us?"

He was suddenly alert. Every muscle in his body seemed to tense, his gaze sharpened. "You know that was never part of the deal."

Carefully, she put her mug down on the little table between the chairs and found his gaze. "Well, it seems there's some bad news coming for you. Because I love you."

He looked dumbstruck. "No, you don't."

Annoyance wriggled in her belly. "You don't get to tell me how I feel."

"You're right. I'm sorry, I was just caught off guard." He rubbed a hand over his eyes. "Okay, thinking on my feet—maybe this will work well for our marriage."

His solution hit her with the force of a brick in the center of the chest. He thought she would stay in a one-sided marriage? It took her long moments to even find her voice again.

"Adam," she said slowly and carefully, "I don't want a sham of a marriage for the rest of my life. I don't even need a big wedding, second or otherwise. All I need is a man I love, who loves me back."

His face went white. "I've been up-front with you. You know that can never be me."

And there it was. The death knell to her hopes and dreams of a future with him. She was vaguely surprised she was able to sit straight in her chair, unemotional. If she'd been considering options earlier, she might have thought she'd dissolve into tears, but part of her felt detached—the part that was keeping her safe. Whatever it was, it was helping her dignity in this moment, so she was grateful. There would be time for grieving later.

Adam still looked at her, pale-faced and dismayed, and she realized she needed to release him. He hadn't done anything wrong. In fact, he'd stuck to what they'd agree on.

"It's okay, I know." She even tried to smile for him, but couldn't quite pull it off. "I know. I guess I just hoped…"

He pushed out of his chair and crouched down in front of hers, finding her hands and squeezing them. "I'm so sorry, Callie. I really am. But I can only offer you the plan we agreed on. I wish it was different."

The moment he took her hands, any illusion of detachment or control over her emotions evaporated. The full force of her life falling apart hit her and she started trembling, deep inside. She gulped in air, trying to keep herself balanced. Adam frowned even more than he had been and stroked her forehead; but pity was not what she wanted from him, so she shakily removed his hand. He didn't release her other hand, however, or move from crouching in front of her chair.

She swallowed, moistened her lips, took a breath and said a prayer that her voice would be steady. "Then we need to start talking about a new plan."

His eyes widened. "Don't abandon this one. Your partnership—"

She held up a hand in denial. "If I don't get the partnership, then so be it."

He sat back on his haunches, his face closing off. "Then what do you want?"

She almost laughed. Almost. What she wanted was not even close to being an option. But then she had nothing to lose, so why not give it to him straight?

She lifted her chin and met his eyes, despite hers burning with unshed tears. "Honestly? I want you. I want you to be by my side. But fully here, not with the mask you wear for the rest of the world. That mask you've put back in place in the last thirty seconds. You, open and willing to enter into a true partnership with me."

His shoulders slumped, as if in defeat. "I can't offer you that. All I can offer is myself as I am."

She'd known that would be his answer before she'd laid it all out for him, yet it still felt as if she was being torn in two. The tears she'd been holding in check started to escape, but she didn't let them have free rein. She still had to pack her things and drive away. She'd need clarity for both those tasks.

Swiping at her face, she stood. "I have to go."

"Don't leave over this," he said, his voice edging on alarm as he came to stand beside her. "We can work past this. I don't want to lose you."

She paused, blinked hard and looked out over the Pacific Ocean. It was impossible to look at Adam while she was refusing him. "It's too late for that."

And it was. She could never be in a relationship with a man she loved but who couldn't give her his love back. The only remaining question was whether she could go through with the wedding for the sake of the charity...

He cleared his throat. "What about the wedding? We've made it the heart of the trust's PR campaign."

It was no surprise their thoughts had been along the same lines—this wedding had been dominating their lives since the day she'd arrived in his office. After all that work—hers, Adam's, Jenna's, Faith's—*could* she walk away?

The weight, the complexity of what she was contemplating pushed down on her.

She glanced up at him, and he held her gaze. It hurt

deep inside, down to her soul, to even look at him. And then she realized that even if she wanted to, she'd never be able to pull off pretending to be happy on her wedding day. The guests, the media, everyone would see through her.

She'd damage their work more by staying than leaving.

She swallowed hard and found her voice. "I'll write up a statement from both of us, saying we deeply regret that we're separating and asking for understanding."

It wouldn't be the first time the public heard about a split just before a wedding, and she sent up a little prayer that the trust's stream of donations would survive any scandal.

He took a shuddering breath, then another. "Are you going back to your place?"

She chanced a look at him and found anguish almost strong enough to rival her own in his features. Her first instinct was to soothe him, take away his pain, but she had to stay strong or she'd give in and stay in a one-sided marriage with him forever.

She wrapped her arms around herself, trying to hold herself together through sheer force of will. "I'm not sure yet. I just need to disappear for a few days. I'll be back and I'll be back to work with Jenna on a new campaign for the trust, but not yet."

It would be torture still being a part of his world after their personal life had detonated, but she wouldn't walk away from a commitment—she'd been handed the trust's account and she'd see it through. Given Jenna was the head of the trust, she might be able to avoid Adam until his presence no longer tormented her. If that day ever came.

He opened his mouth to say something, and from his expression, she knew it was another attempt to get her to stay, so she jumped in before he could say it. "Please, Adam. Please just let me disappear until I have my head together."

It seemed as if there was a war being fought inside him in the moments that followed until finally, his jaw tight and his eyes unnaturally bright, he gave a sharp nod and stood back.

Her heart breaking, Callie set off to pack her things and leave before she could change her mind.

Eleven

Callie threw the suitcase she'd taken to Adam's place onto her own bed, unzipped it and blindly stared at the contents. Tears made everything in front of her blur, but she needed to check that she had everything she needed before she left again, so she swiped the tears away. Having no idea where she was headed didn't help the packing situation in the least. All she knew was she needed to be far, far away for a few days.

The apartment's front door opened and closed, and then her sister appeared in her bedroom doorway.

"Hey," Summer said, "I didn't know you were coming over today. Picking up more clothes?"

Callie didn't reply or look up. Couldn't. It was all she could do to keep it together at the moment so she could keep packing.

Summer came around the other side of the bed and plopped down. "Hey, are you okay?" Then she must have seen the tears because she jumped up and pulled her into a hug. "Oh, sweetheart, what's happened?"

The sympathy was too much to take, and Callie burst into sobs against her sister's shoulder. She'd been holding back, not letting herself cry since she'd spoken to Adam, knowing that once she started she might not stop. The priority had been getting her things together and driving home.

"It's okay," Summer said, stroking her hair. "Whatever it is, I promise we'll fix it together, just like we've always done."

"You can't." Callie's voice was high and she was hiccupping, but she and Summer had been interpreting each other's crying voices since they were kids.

"Is it Adam?"

Callie nodded wordlessly.

Summer swore. "I'll kill him. Where is he now?"

Miraculously, one of her sobs turned into a stuttering laugh, and she pulled away to wipe her eyes with her sleeve. "It's not his fault."

"Tell me what happened and I'll be the judge of whether it's his fault or not." Summer's voice held a little humor, but there was an edge to it, as well.

Callie sank down onto the side of the bed, and her sister sat beside her with an arm around her shoulders, waiting.

She took a couple of steadying breaths, hoping her voice would work properly. "Nothing more than me wanting to have my cake and eat it, too."

Summer sighed. "You fell in love with him, and wanted the fake marriage to be real."

"Yeah," she said, dropping her head into her hands. Somehow it felt worse to have it said aloud, not to mention being so obvious that her sister had guessed it on her first try.

"Knowing you," Summer said in a soft voice, "and watching you from the beginning, I have to say I've been expecting this. You started off acting, but it changed. And then you weren't acting anymore."

Callie risked looking up, worried about finding judgment or pity in her sister's expression, but all she found was loving acceptance, and that gave her the confidence to open up a little more. "For a while I was kidding myself that the acting was getting easier with practice, but you're right. It wasn't acting."

"I knew for sure the night on the yacht." Summer lay back on the bed and pulled Callie with her so they could look at the ceiling as they talked. "I had my fingers and toes crossed that it worked out between you two. He was making you so happy."

"He did," she said with a nostalgic smile. "He really did, for a while."

"Did you tell him?" Summer turned on her side and propped her head on her hand.

Callie swallowed hard and tried not to let the tears take over again, but as she remembered the scene—and the outcome—she almost lost the battle.

Finally, she was able to nod, and whispered, "About an hour ago."

"And…?"

"And—" she looked back up at the ceiling, wanting to say the words as if she was merely reading a menu "—while he's happy for us to sleep together during our fake marriage, he can't offer me any more than that."

"I'll kill him," Summer said again, shaking her head.

"So, you told me what happened and now I get to tell you whether it's his fault or not. It is."

"You can't blame him. I'm the one who wants more than we agreed to. I guess I just got greedy." She bit down on her trembling lip and looked away.

There was silence for a few beats before Summer said, "You want to know what surprises me the most about all of this?"

"That I was stupid enough to fall for my own spin?" She rubbed her hands over her face, trying to refresh herself.

"Nope," Summer said, her tone brooking no disagreement. "That he said no to you wanting more when he's in love with you."

"See, this is the problem, though." Callie sat up, scooting up to lean against the headboard. "He's not in love with me."

Summer shot her a meaningful look. "Oh, he's in love with you. Believe me, it was as plain in his eyes as your love was in yours. He's just refusing to admit it for some reason."

Callie had a sneaking suspicion that her sister might be right, which was why she'd given Adam the chance to confirm or deny it. He'd done neither, and that had told her more than anything.

She shrugged to cover any evidence of the trembling that was coming from deep inside. "Even if you were right, isn't it all the same, though? He doesn't love me enough to overcome his fears and create a future with me. Either way, there's nothing there for me."

Summer looked as if she wanted to say more but held her tongue, and when she steered the topic to a side issue, Callie was appreciative.

"What about the wedding and the PR plan for the trust?" Summer asked.

The wedding. That had been a wrenching decision. Many people had put work into that plan, and she was tossing all of that away. She felt sick about doing that to them, but it would tear her in two to go through with the charade now, and seeming happy on the day was way beyond her acting skills. People would see through her in minutes and realize the entire plan had been a fake from the beginning.

"I'm calling the wedding off," she admitted, her voice shaky. "I just can't do it. The trust has already had a solid increase in donations, and I'll work harder than ever on a new campaign. I'll make sure the charities don't suffer because I've made a mess of things."

Summer glanced at the half-packed suitcase. "Where are you going?"

"I don't know. Somewhere away from here for a few days." She'd thought she'd figure that out as she went along. All her carefully laid plans were ruined, so perhaps it was time to try a different way.

Summer's face suddenly lit up. "My boss has that place at Long Beach we use for clients, and I know it's vacant this week because I was making the arrangements today for the next person. I'm sure I can swing the use of it if you want."

A house that was already set up and a short drive sounded perfect. "If you're sure, that would be great."

Summer reached out and grabbed her hand. "Do you want me to come with you?"

She'd been wondering the same thing. Company to distract her was wildly appealing, but in some ways, she didn't *want* to be distracted. Deep inside, something was telling her she needed the time to release and to heal.

"You know what?" She spoke gently, so it didn't sound like a rejection of her sister's sweet offer. "I think I need some alone time. Besides, I need to start making cancellations for—"

"Don't give that a second thought," Summer said over the top of her. "I'll call Jenna and Faith, and between the three of us we'll sort that all out. You just have some time for you."

"You're the best. I'll write a statement that you can release and email it to you." Overcome with gratitude, she hugged her sister tightly. When she released her and sat back, her thoughts returned to Adam. "One thing— just in case Adam calls, don't tell him where I am, no matter what he says. I know he can be persuasive."

"Oh, believe me, your location is not what I want to tell him—"

She took her sister's hands in her own. "Please don't. If you're right and he does love me, then this will be hard enough on him already."

"Okay, I promise," Summer said grudgingly. "But only to give you peace of mind on this, not because I think it's the right thing."

Callie smiled through the remnants of her tears. She knew full well she'd lucked out in the sister department. As soon as she felt human again, she was going to repay her for all the support over the years. However, how she would do that was a question for another day. Today was for allowing herself to grieve for what she'd lost.

A small voice at the back of her mind piped up, pointing out that she couldn't lose what she'd never had. And that was true. She sighed, scooped a top off the bed and added it to the things already in the suitcase. It sure felt as if she'd lost a lot. Though, if she was ruthlessly honest, she'd also gained.

"You know what?" she said, turning to Summer. "Something has come out of this. I've changed. I'm a different person than I was before I met him."

Summer paused in trying on a long-sleeved top she'd fished out of the suitcase. "In what way?"

"I've changed my mind about what's important in life." She thought back over who she'd been and who she was now, trying to pinpoint the difference. "I think I've been clinging to superficial things. Being with Adam, planning this society wedding, the media coverage—all of it has put things in perspective."

Summer arched an eyebrow. "You mean *we've* been clinging to superficial things?"

"Maybe," she said with an indulgent smile. "Once I come back I think we need to have another look at our life plan. It could do with some refining. Maybe we should start our own business sooner rather than later, and focus more on what we actually want, not what we thought in college we'd want by now."

"Sure." Summer took off the top and returned it to the suitcase. "I'd be up for that. In the meantime, you keep packing, and I'll make some phone calls about the place at Long Beach."

Callie watched her sister leave the room and then turned back to her suitcase. Long Beach didn't seem far enough away to give her psychological distance from Adam, but then, she wouldn't have that even if she traveled to Australia.

As her eyes filled with the never-ending supply of

tears, she grabbed a tissue and pressed it against her face. Would she ever get over Adam Hawke?

On the night Adam was supposed to be marrying Callie, one week after he'd last seen her, he was instead sitting at his desk at work, searching Callie's social media profiles for a clue as to where she'd gone. A noise caught his attention, and he looked up to find his brothers standing in the doorway. He swore under his breath. This was the last thing he needed. He was strung so tightly he was practically vibrating, and his brothers had a habit of pushing his buttons.

He stretched his arms over his head and rubbed his eyes. Since it was a Sunday night and he was the only one in the office, he was surprised he hadn't heard them walking along the corridor, but then he'd been pretty engrossed in his search. Unfortunately, Callie still hadn't posted anything on any of her social media pages.

At first after she'd left he'd comforted himself with the age-old method of denial. That had lasted less than twenty-four hours before reality had sunk in.

He loved her.

And if he was honest, he'd probably known for a while. Known it when she'd asked for a future with him, but couldn't admit it because it scared him more than anything in his life. His love for Callie made him feel vulnerable, stripped all his defenses away. How could he keep the world a safe place for his family, for himself, for the woman he loved, when he felt so out of control? He'd learned early that bad things happened when he let down his guard. People had gotten hurt. It wasn't something he could risk, so when he'd felt it slipping with Callie, he locked his heart down even more tightly than ever before.

He'd been stupid. So determined not to let down his guard, not to fall into the same trap as his grandfather and make himself vulnerable to a woman, or to *anyone* besides his parents and brothers. But it had happened nonetheless. He'd give her the sun, the moon and every star in the sky if she asked.

The thing about Callie, though, was that she wasn't wired to be able to ask him for something that would hurt him. He knew with as much confidence as he knew anything that Callie would give that sun, moon and stars right back to him if he asked it of her.

His grandfather's feelings had never been the problem. It was the person he'd chosen to give his heart to. And by choosing Callie, Adam hadn't even come close to making the same mistake as his grandfather.

Of course, now that he'd realized this, it was too late. Callie was gone, leaving a huge gaping hole in his life. He'd tried everything he could think of and, true to her word, she'd disappeared.

Liam cleared his throat. "Are we interrupting?"

Resigned, he glanced over at his brothers. "What can I do for you two?"

Liam stepped forward into the room. "We're here to offer you some advice."

Adam sighed and tapped his pen on his desk. This was new. And unwelcome. "If you're worried about the trust—"

Frowning, Liam shook his head. "We've already told you that we have faith that when Callie says she'll create a new campaign, she'll pull it off. She's good. The trust will be fine."

Adam called on his last shred of patience. "Then advice about what?"

"Callie," Dylan said. "Between us, we have some expertise in the matter of being left by the women we love."

"Lord help me," Adam mumbled and pinched the bridge of his nose. "You need to leave. Now."

Instead of leaving, his brothers both took a seat across from him. Adam pressed the security button under his desk. He had no time for this—he had to find Callie. Then he went back to his web search.

"You can ignore us," Liam said, "but you need to hear this."

Adam scowled at his screen. "No, I really don't. And you should go."

The sound of running footsteps came from the corridor, getting louder, until his six-foot-four head of security appeared in the doorway, ready for action. Jonah liked to rotate through all the positions in his team to keep his hand in and stay abreast of the situations, so tonight must have been his turn as a night guard.

Liam looked from the guard back to him. "Seriously? You called security on us?"

"I'm busy. I asked you to leave and you declined." He turned to his guard. "Jonah, will you please see my brothers out?"

"Certainly, Mr. Hawke." The guard took a step into the room, and Liam and Dylan both held up their hands in surrender.

Adam had met Jonah back when they'd opened their first store and Jonah had been a homeless teen sleeping on the front door stoop. After Adam offered him a job and supported his career, Jonah's loyalty to him was beyond question.

"Adam," Liam growled, and Adam felt like smiling for the first time in days. Maybe his brothers' arrival had been good for him after all—seeing them thrown out of the building should help his mood considerably.

"Hang on," Dylan said. "Jonah, you work for Hawke's Blooms, and the three of us are joint owners. That means all three of us are your boss. Any two of us can overrule a decision made by the third." He turned to Liam. "Motion to overrule the cranky one behind the desk?"

"Seconded," Liam said. "Motion is passed. You can stand down, Jonah."

Jonah swung around to Adam, his raised eyebrow asking how he should proceed. Adam swore again. It wasn't fair to put an employee between them in a family fight.

"You can return to your desk, Jonah." He offered an apologetic smile. "Sorry to involve you."

The guard looked unconvinced. "Are you sure, Mr. Hawke? I can stay in the corner here and keep an eye on things if you'd like."

Adam sighed, resigned to his fate. "No, I'll be fine."

With one last look at Liam and Dylan, Jonah left.

"You know," Dylan said, frowning, "after that stunt, I don't think we should offer our help."

"Good. That's settled." Adam turned back to his computer. "I'll see you later."

Liam's chair creaked as he sat forward. "No, he's annoying, but he helped both of us when we were in the same situation. We owe him."

"No, you don't," Adam said in exasperation. "You can go."

Ignoring him, Dylan crossed an ankle over his knee. "Do you know what time it is?"

"Late," he said dismissively.

"It's two o'clock in the morning."

Adam shrugged. Even if he'd been at home, he wouldn't be able to sleep. His bed reminded him of Callie, and when he lay in it, he could almost feel her body pressed to his, hear her soft breathing, smell her floral shampoo on his pillow. He gave himself ten minutes a day to lie there, holding her pillow, missing her, but to get any sleep he used the sofa.

"You're in bad shape." Dylan tried to appear sad, but couldn't quite hide an undercurrent of amusement at his brother's misfortune. "As I was saying before we were interrupted by someone *calling security on us*, Liam and I have some expertise in being left. Though I should point out that the woman I love only went across state lines, whereas his woman left the country."

"Hey," Liam said. "She comes from another country. She was going home."

Dylan waved a hand in the air. "Whatever. What we need to do now is make Adam realize he's making a big mistake so that he goes after her."

Adam glanced at the ceiling and prayed for patience. "You two always were slow. I've been looking for her for a week. She's not at her place and she's not answering her cell. She's disappeared without a trace."

Liam sat back, all comfort and ease. "You couldn't have been looking too hard. Jenna and Faith had lunch with her yesterday."

Adam went still and then rounded on them. "Where is she?"

Dylan shook his head. "They won't tell us. Faith said something about the three of them needing to talk about how stupid the Hawke men can be. Which is crazy, because I—"

Adam held up a hand. "Get Faith on the phone. Or Jenna."

Dylan shrugged. "Neither one of them will break. Those two are better than the CIA with secrets. You might have better luck with Callie's sister."

Adam shook his head as he blew out a breath. "Summer said she didn't know where Callie went."

Summer had been his first phone call as soon as he'd realized what a humungous mistake he'd made. She'd taken a message and promised to pass it on as soon as she heard from Callie, but had said she couldn't make any promises about when that would be since Callie was incommunicado. Adam hadn't been willing to wait, so he'd kept looking.

A self-satisfied smile danced around Liam's mouth. "She was at lunch with the others yesterday."

Adam swore again. "So they've closed ranks."

Part of him was pleased that Callie had people who supported her enough to create a shield around her, but dammit, how was he supposed to find her if none of them would talk?

"You look like you could use some advice after all." Dylan was far too smug for Adam's tenuous grasp on control. His brother was clearly unaware just how tightly Adam was currently gripping the armrests of his chair.

"The only thing I need," Adam said through a tight jaw, "is information about Callie's whereabouts. You've both admitted you have no idea where she is, and are unable or unwilling to talk your fiancées into sharing the information."

"What have you tried?" Liam asked.

"Everything. I've left about a billion messages on her cell, checked in with her sister, her parents, the friends I've met and her work, trawled through her social media pages, called random hotels at places where she likes to take vacations."

Liam frowned, suddenly serious. "Have you considered she doesn't want to be found?"

"Says the man who followed a woman to another country after she ran away from him."

"True," Liam said, his eyes full of sympathy, "but Jenna's family helped me speak to her. And she helped Dylan find Faith. If Jenna and Faith won't help this time, and Callie's family won't help when they know where she is, perhaps it means you should let her go."

Let her go? Simply give up? The emptiness inside him screamed in rebellion. Besides, she might not want to be found now, but that was because he'd said crazy things to her, before he'd realized what she meant to him. That she meant everything to him.

At the very least he owed her the truth. He just hoped with every fiber of his being that she let him give her a whole heap more than that.

He straightened his spine and stared down his brother. "There's something I need to say to her. If I say it, and she still wants to be left alone, I'll do it." His heart would break in two, but he'd honor her wishes.

Dylan rubbed his stubbled jaw, apparently considering Adam's words, and then nodded. "Well, if she won't listen to you, perhaps it's time you do something she can't ignore."

Hysterical laughter bubbled in Adam's chest before dying in his throat. "Like what?" Did they realize he'd tried everything he could think of already? Why else would he be in his office at two in the morning, chasing flimsy leads?

Dylan turned to Liam. "Seriously, I can't believe we voted to make him the boss of the company." Then he faced Adam again. "I don't know. You're the ideas man, and you're the one who knows Callie. But it had better be something she won't expect, so she knows you're serious, or it's not worth doing at all."

Adam started to frown, but then an idea struck him, one so simple yet so perfect that his heart leaped to life again. He could do this. He'd explain everything and show her he was serious. He reached for the phone and started leafing through papers, looking for Callie's friend Anna's number.

"You do remember it's after two in the morning, right?" Liam said.

Swearing, Adam dropped the phone and speared his fingers through his hair. Now that he had a plan, every second it was delayed was agony, but his brother was right. He'd have to wait a few more hours.

He stood and reached for his suit jacket. "Time you two went home," he said and herded them out his office door. "Actually, why are you here at this time of night, anyway, and not at home with those fiancées you worked so hard to win over?"

His brothers shared a look before Liam said, "Jonah."

"The security guard who was going to throw you out was the one who called you?" Adam huffed out a laugh. "He's always taken his job of looking out for the staff seriously. I'll have to give him a bonus."

"Right after you find Callie, right?" Dylan said from beside him.

"Oh, yeah." Adam closed his office door behind him, feeling a sliver of optimism starting to glow in his chest. "Nothing's happening before I do that."

Twelve

When her cell rang, Callie was reading a book in a deck chair on the veranda overlooking the beach. She checked the caller ID, an action that had become second nature in the past week.

Since the announcement of her split from Adam had gone public, her phone, email and social media had gone crazy. The only calls she'd been taking were from her parents, Summer, Jenna and Faith. She'd had a few from random friends, but unable to face the world just yet—or the world's questions—she'd decided to return the calls when her impromptu vacation was over.

Although there was one person she'd made herself call on the first day—John Evans, her boss. She'd explained the hiccup with the Hawke Brothers Trust account, and promised that she was working on a new campaign. He hadn't been impressed, but was prepared to give her a chance. She had a meeting scheduled with him next week to look over her new ideas, which meant she needed to start having those ideas soon...

This time the call was Anna Wilson, and Callie debated whether to answer or not. Anna was a friend, but she was also a journalist, and she was probably hoping for a scoop on the breakup. Admittedly, Anna hadn't been part of the flurry of online stories and gossip pieces that had broken out since she'd left Adam. Many of those articles had claimed a secret source who had all sorts of completely untrue morsels of information, and who was likely Terence Gibson. Anna had stayed silent so far, but perhaps she now wanted to wade into the water.

Callie sighed. Her vacation was coming to an end and she was going to have to start facing the real world soon, and Anna was probably a good place to start, so she thumbed the answer button.

"Hi, Anna," she said as brightly as she could manage. "How are you?"

"Hey, Callie. I'm good, thanks." There was a short pause on the line. "I was just wondering... Have you seen my column today?"

Yesterday, when she'd seen the headline, "Anon Source Claims Hawke Wedding a Scam," she'd sworn off the web. There was nothing she could do about Terence having a field day at her expense, but she didn't have to put herself through reading it. "Sorry," she said, tucking her legs up underneath her. "I haven't had a chance."

"You should have a look."

"I'm actually in the middle of something. I'll grab a

few minutes later this afternoon." Or perhaps tomorrow. Or even the next day.

"Now, Callie. It's Adam."

A chill raced down her spine. "What do you mean, it's Adam? Is something wrong?"

"He has a message for you and it's running in my column today."

Callie leaned back in her chair, the sudden rigidity in her muscles dissipating. There was no way Adam would have done something so public about something that was private. He must have given an interview about the trust, or about the company, and mentioned her name when questioned. His words might even have been written for him by Jenna, to keep it on the track they'd decided to take.

Callie ran her free hand through her hair. "Okay, thanks. I'll check it out."

"Really, Callie. You need to see this." Anna's voice was insistent, which was strange. "Promise me."

Her stomach clenched. It was clear that there was more to this. "I promise. I'll look at it now."

They ended the call, and Callie retrieved her laptop from her suitcase where she'd put it yesterday after the sham headline. In the time it took her to boot up her computer, her cell practically exploded with messages. She checked a few and they were all saying the same thing. Adam had left her a video online. Adrenaline spiked through her system. He couldn't have actually addressed something to her, could he...?

When the laptop displayed its welcome screen, she opened her browser and found Anna's column. Before she'd braced herself, Adam's face appeared on her screen, as dear and beautiful as she'd remembered. A harsh pressure pushed against her chest, making it hard to draw breath.

And yet, it was Adam like she'd never seen him before. She'd seen him disheveled from lovemaking. She'd seen him after he'd had too much to drink in Vegas. She'd seen him windswept on the beach. But this? This Adam had eyes that were wild and untamed. He seemed to be exerting no control over himself to keep his guard up. He wasn't trying to keep part of himself hidden.

And he was doing it in front of the world.

His words finally registered—she'd been too busy looking at him, desperate for his face, that she'd paid no attention to what he was saying. Clicking on the play button, she dragged it back to the beginning and listened.

"Callie, I've tried every method to find you that I can think of, and a few more. I was stupid, I know that, and I'm begging you to overlook that fact. Hoping and praying that I haven't destroyed your feelings for me. If that's happened, I understand, and all I can say is I'm sorry. For everything."

Hot tears built until the image on the screen blurred and she blinked them away, unwilling to miss a second of Adam's message. She still couldn't believe this was public, that he was saying these things, knowing that anyone could see.

"If there's a chance you could ever feel the same for me again, then all I want to say is, I love you." He paused and swallowed. "I love you so much I've been going crazy without you. Not knowing where you are."

A stab of guilt pierced her chest at causing him pain. When she'd left, she'd only been thinking of her own emotional survival, and had no expectation that her leaving would cause him this much sadness.

"I'm sorry, Adam," she whispered at the screen, but his recorded message continued on regardless.

"I guess you could say I'm emotionally compromised after all," he said and offered a sad smile.

She let out a surprised laugh through her tears.

"One last thing, Callie. If you do still feel the same, if it's possible that you still want me, I'll be waiting at the place it all started. This week—same day and time, at the place I first proposed."

The video ended, but she was lost in the memory of walking past a small Vegas chapel and his saying, "Hey, I have a crazy idea. Let's get married." And fueled by alcohol and infatuation, she'd pretty much squealed a *yes* then jumped up and hugged him,

It had been a Tuesday, about eleven o'clock at night. She double-checked her computer's calendar—it was Monday. He wanted to meet her tomorrow night at 11:00 p.m. in Vegas.

Everything inside her wanted to go, to meet him and feel his arms around her again. She'd been lying awake every night since she'd left him, dreaming of a chance to be held by him again. But something even stronger was gnawing at her belly, holding her back.

There was no question he was being genuine on that tape. He'd exposed himself in a way she'd never thought he was capable of. But what if he regretted it now?

He'd made declarations to her before, made vows, and then changed his mind the next morning. Would he even be waiting in that chapel, or was the tape some-thing he'd made in the middle of the night and already regretted? Was he working with his lawyers right this minute to get the video taken down?

And even if he made it to the chapel tomorrow night, would he change his mind in a day, a week, a month or a year?

The sad truth was, she wasn't sure if she could trust him with her heart. Was a potential future with Adam Hawke worth the risk?

Callie huddled closer to her sister under the bright yellow umbrella as they trudged down the wet Las Vegas street. Her thoughts were all crammed together in her head so hard, all jumbled, and none of them clear enough to even consider properly.

"Stop it," Summer said.

Callie flinched and then frowned at her sister. "What?"

"I can hear you second-guessing yourself from here."

"Actually, I haven't first-guessed yet, so there's nothing to second-guess." She'd been too busy replaying Adam's message in her mind to do much more than walk in a straight line.

"Oh, come on," Summer said, rolling her eyes. "You're here. That's a decision."

Callie placed a hand over her chest, as if she could brace her heart, and then admitted the awful truth. "It might not even be an issue. I don't think he'll come."

"Of course he'll be here." Her sister waved her concerns away with a flick of her wrist. "No one who saw that video—which is everyone in the country—could doubt that he's head over heels about you. Plus, you're a trending topic on social media and the consensus is definitely that you'll both turn up. The people have spoken and they're demanding a happy ending."

"That's lovely of the people," Callie said, trying not to cringe at being the topic of so many conversations, "but I don't think the weight of public opinion is going to affect Adam's decisions."

"Well, *I'm* sure he'll come." Summer gave her a smug smile. "I hate to say this, but you knew I would at some point… I told you he loves you."

A seething mass of confusion churned in her gut. How easy it would be to simply believe what he'd said. It would be a dream come true. But life was rarely that simple.

She glanced over at her sister and tried to explain. "Adam changes his mind quickly. Last time, it was less than twenty-four hours after promising me the world that he asked for a divorce."

"You two barely knew each other back then," she pointed out.

"Which is why I was blindsided." In some ways, the pain of that time was still fresh. It was sitting on the sidelines, warning her, trying to keep her safe from being hurt in the same way again. "Now I know him and I understand how much he hates being…emotionally compromised."

"But you're here, you're going to meet him, so what's the plan?"

Callie stopped and looked out over the light but steady rain that hit the pavement and the palm trees, and was bouncing off the umbrellas of people around them.

"I'm waiting to hear what he says and I need to see him in person for that, not a video message. I'll know by his eyes." She had to see how deeply he was affected.

In the meantime, the agony of having no idea if this was real or not was killing her.

As they rounded a corner, Adam came into view. He stood alone, a large, black umbrella shielding him from the rain. A few feet behind him, his brothers and their fiancées stood huddled together in an alcove in front of the chapel.

At the sight of him, her body froze, as if it had gone into internal meltdown. She couldn't take another step, couldn't even feel—her emotions had become numb, as well.

He wore dark trousers and a coffee-hued shirt, his hair clearly damp, his shoulders tight. Tension flowed off him in waves as he scanned the area around them. She'd never seen a man more magnificent.

As soon as he saw them, his shoulders relaxed a fraction and he strode over. Summer squeezed her hand and nodded her greeting to Adam. Adam returned it and edged his umbrella over Callie. As soon as she was covered, Summer scurried off to stand in the alcove with Adam's family.

Adam's gaze was dark and intense. "I wasn't sure you'd come."

"I wasn't sure you'd be here, either." She was still cushioned by the emotional numbness, or she would never have been able to get those words out as evenly.

"Didn't you see the video?" he asked, his voice rough. "I told you I'd be here."

"You forget, I've been through this with you before and you changed your mind once you had time to think it through." She'd tried to say the words gently—this was about having the truth on the table, not about accusations, but still she saw him flinch.

"That was different, and so long ago. Everything has changed."

She glanced at the chapel with its flashing neon lights, and then over at their siblings and partners, all gathered and pretending not to be watching them, and her emotional numbness dissolved. The emotions of the past few weeks came crashing in on her in a tidal wave, and it was all she could do to stay upright.

She rubbed a hand over her eyes and then looked at him. "Adam, what are we doing here?"

"You tell me. I'm here to marry the woman I love. What about you?" His eyes were unwavering, challenging.

She shrugged one shoulder, determined to keep her distance until she was ready. "I'm still thinking about that one."

"If it helps your decision, I've done a lot of thinking, and I've let go of the comparisons to my grandfather. I'm more like my brothers than I ever was like him, and Liam and Dylan are stronger men, better men, with Jenna and Faith in their lives. I want that. I'm ready for that. With you."

That did help, but there was more, and she hardly dared ask…

There was no moving forward until she heard his answer, so she straightened her spine and asked outright. "What about your self-control? Letting your guard down?"

"Not an issue. When we were together, I was letting my guard down without even realizing it." His Adam's apple bobbed up and down. "I thought control was the most important thing in my life, but it's not. You are."

He reached into his pocket and drew out a velvet box.

She recognized the logo of the jeweler who'd custom-ized the rings they'd chosen.

Her bottom lip trembled, so she bit down on it to keep it still. "You really want to get married here, and not at a fancy place with all your friends?"

"You were right. The fancy version we were plan-ning was about everybody else—the trust, the media, your job. That suited our purposes at the time, but what I want now is something stripped back. Something that's just you and me and the promises we want to make to each other. Although," he said with the trace of a smile, "I can't promise my words will be as pretty as the ones Summer wrote for me."

A huge lump lodged itself in her throat, and she had to swallow twice before she could get her voice to work. "I'd rather plain, stumbling words that were heartfelt and yours alone than all the pretty words in the world."

Adam's eyes misted over, and she knew in that mo-ment, beyond any doubt, that he felt this as deeply as she did, and he was making a commitment to her for life, not until he changed his mind. The sight was beau-tiful and it filled her with joy.

He leaned in and kissed her. It was like stepping off a ledge, flying in free fall, without having to worry about the landing, because this man would always be there for her, she knew that now. Just as she'd always be there for him.

At a certain point, she'd wondered who was there for him, and had desperately wanted to be that person. And now she was. It was almost too much to contem-plate all at once.

Dylan's voice rang out. "Are we having a wedding or what?"

Adam raised an eyebrow in question, his gaze steady on her. "Callie? It's your call. You know what I want."

Her heart felt as if it was hitting her rib cage on every beat. "If you're proposing again—"

"I am."

"—then yes. A thousand times yes."

Adam dropped the umbrella, gathered her up in his arms and kissed her again. A cheer went up from the combined family group and she smiled against his mouth, but didn't break the kiss. The light rain was soaking her dress and dripping down his face, but she didn't care. Nothing mattered but being in his arms again.

When they finally broke apart, he lowered her to her feet. "Come and marry me, Callie."

Heart overflowing, she picked up the discarded umbrella and took his proffered hand. While they walked with him into the chapel, she was unable to look away from the man at her side. At the door, they were met with hugs and well-wishes.

Liam said, "Should I tell the celebrant we're ready?"

"Yes," Adam and Callie said together, smiling at each other as they left Liam to organize the details.

Faith carefully reached into a large handbag she had in the crook of her elbow and came out with a small bouquet of the Bridal Tulip, interspersed with tiny blue flowers.

She slid off a clear plastic cone that had been protecting the flowers and handed the bouquet to Callie. "I had it ready, just in case."

"It's perfect. Thank you," Callie said, touched.

Faith again reached into her bag and came out with a single snowy white tulip and pinned it to Adam's lapel.

Then she stood back and grinned. "You might be having a simple wedding, but we couldn't have a Hawke brother getting married without *any* flowers."

"Or something borrowed," Jenna said from beside her. She had a glittering tiara in her hands. "This also counts as something old, since it's been in my family for several generations."

Callie took the tiara, her heart in her mouth. If this had been in Jenna's *royal* family for generations, then it was quite possibly priceless. "These diamonds are real?" she asked, hardly daring to consider the possibility.

"Shhh," Jenna said with a sparkle in her eye. "I'm not really supposed to bring it out without a bodyguard. But I don't think Adam is going to take his eyes off you tonight, so it should be safe."

Adam took the tiara from her fingers. "It's beautiful, thank you, Jenna." He slid it onto Callie's head and smiled. "A princess for a night, but queen of my heart forever. I love you so much, Callie Mitchell. I love you with everything inside me."

The tears she'd been holding back finally started to slide down her cheeks. Since her face was already damp from the rain, she didn't need to wipe them away. Everything just blended together.

As Jenna stood back, Callie could see Faith was pinning single tulip buttonholes to Liam and Dylan's jackets and then she handed Summer a bouquet consisting of a single tulip and tiny blue flowers.

Dylan stepped forward. "Faith said you have something blue in the flowers and that Jenna brought something borrowed and old. So you just need something new." He pulled out a long silver necklace with a locket.

"I had this made for your original wedding—wait, no, that would have been your second wedding. Man, you guys need to stop getting married!"

Callie laughed and kissed Dylan's cheek. "Thanks."

"Open it," he said, and she did. It was a tiny picture from the official wedding announcement photos, which was strange, because he'd thought their wedding was a sham when he would have had this made.

Before she could ask, he said, "I wanted you to know that even after your official wedding ended, you'd always be a part of this family. No matter what was going on with Adam and you, the rest of us would always be there for you. Of course, now you're making it all official and real, so this doesn't have the same meaning—"

His words cut out when she threw her arms around his neck. "Thank you, this means a lot."

The celebrant appeared and called them in, so the group moved into the chapel, but Callie hesitated, tucking her damp hair behind her ear.

"What is it?" Adam asked.

"What about our parents? Neither set is here." This wasn't the wedding with the complete guest list that they'd been planning, but she was sure all four parents would hate to miss the event.

"My parents are babysitting Meg and Bonnie so Liam and Jenna could come, but Dylan has them on a video call, so they can watch." He nodded to where they could see Dylan through the arched door, talking into a phone cradled in his palm.

Surprised, she swung her gaze back to her groom. "You told your parents about tonight before you knew whether I'd come or not?" He was always so guarded and unwilling to share information that would make him emotionally vulnerable that this didn't make sense.

"I have nothing to hide. I want you, and I'm happy for the world to know it." He kissed her forehead, then the tip of her nose and each cheek. "Also Liam said he asked Summer for your parents' contact details a few minutes ago, and they're calling your parents now." On the other side of the short aisle, Summer was talking to someone on a tablet screen, then she handed it to Jenna and moved to the front of the pews, beside a waiting Liam and the celebrant.

Callie shook her head in amazement. "Considering this wasn't planned, everything seems to be falling into place."

Adam grinned at her. "I have no idea what we were doing, spending all that time planning the other wedding. This one took hardly any effort at all."

"Just a video message," she said and then placed a hand over his heart. She could feel its steady thump through his shirt and jacket. "Adam, I understand how difficult it would have been for you to make that message. It means a lot."

"It resulted in you coming here tonight, so it was nothing." He leaned in and kissed her lightly on the lips in the sweetest of kisses.

Prerecorded organ music started playing, and Adam eased back and held out his arm. "Ready?"

"Wait!" Summer called to the room and then whispered something to the celebrant, who flicked a switch on a panel to his side and the music stopped. Summer pulled an MP3 player from her pocket and connected it to the panel with a cord the celebrant handed her, then thumbed a button on the player. The room was flooded with the introductory notes of "The Lady in Red."

Adam chuckled. "I think that's become our song."

"It's perfect," Callie said, and walked down the aisle on the arm of the man she was going to spend the rest of her life with.

Ten minutes later, they were married. Again. Each of their five guests threw streamers and popped party poppers. Then they all headed back to a suite Liam had booked for a low-key reception, filled with champagne, room-service food and as much love as one room could hold.

After only an hour or so, Callie met Adam's gaze from across the room. Within seconds, he was at her side. "Ready to get out of here?"

Callie smiled. "Absolutely."

Adam cleared his throat and raised his voice. "Thank you for everything you all did tonight. It's time for us to go."

"You have to throw the bouquet first," Jenna called from the sofa.

They all looked around the room. Everyone was paired off except Summer, who said, "I'm fine. Don't throw it just for me."

Faith gently turned Callie by the shoulders. "It won't be just for you, Summer. Jenna and I aren't married yet, and we don't know which wedding will come first. We'll all play."

Callie picked up her bouquet, turned her back to the women and threw it over her head. When she turned around, Summer was holding the tulips with a look of resigned humor.

Then Adam slid his arms around Callie from behind,

and she forgot all about everyone else. All she wanted was to be alone with her new husband.

Sliding her hand into his and interlacing their fingers, she tugged a smiling Adam toward the door. Toward the rest of their lives.

* * * * *

If you loved this story
pick up these other HAWKE BROTHERS
books from Rachel Bailey

THE NANNY PROPOSITION
BIDDING ON HER BOSS